Shadows
of the
White City

Center Point
Large Print

Also by Jocelyn Green and available from
Center Point Large Print:

The Mark of the King
A Refuge Assured
Between Two Shores
Veiled in Smoke

**This Large Print Book carries the
Seal of Approval of N.A.V.H.**

Shadows of the White City

The Windy City Saga - 2

JOCELYN GREEN

CENTER POINT LARGE PRINT
THORNDIKE, MAINE

This Center Point Large Print edition is published in the year 2021 by arrangement with Bethany House Publishers, a division of Baker Publishing Group.

Map of the 1893 World's Fair by Rob Green Design.

Epigraph Scripture taken from the HOLY BIBLE, NEW INTERNATIONAL VERSION®. Copyright © 1973, 1978, 1984 Biblica. Used by permission of Zondervan. All other Scripture quotations are from the King James Version of the Bible.

This is a work of historical reconstruction; the appearances of certain historical figures are therefore inevitable. All other characters, however, are products of the author's imagination, and any resemblance to actual persons, living or dead, is coincidental.

The text of this Large Print edition is unabridged. In other aspects, this book may vary from the original edition. Printed in the United States of America on permanent paper. Set in 16-point Times New Roman type.

ISBN: 978-1-64358-902-2

The Library of Congress has cataloged this record under Library of Congress Control Number: 2021930324

To Bettina,
Who loves fiercely,
Who holds on, and lets go,
Even when it hurts.

I cannot fix on the hour, or the spot, or the look, or the words, which laid the foundation. It is too long ago. I was in the middle before I knew that I had begun.
—Jane Austen, *Pride and Prejudice*

How great is the love the Father has lavished on us, that we should be called children of God!
—1 John 3:1

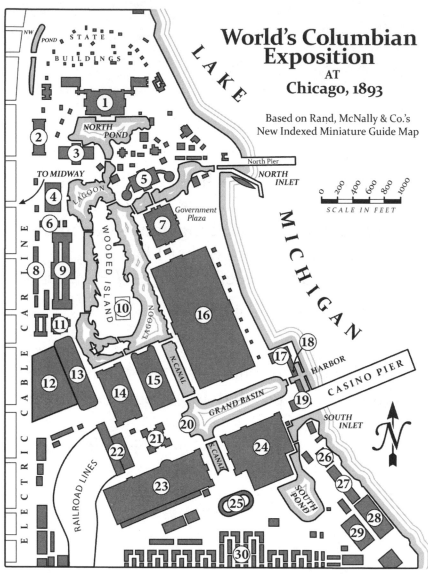

World's Columbian Exposition
AT
Chicago, 1893

Based on Rand, McNally & Co.'s
New Indexed Miniature Guide Map

SCALE IN FEET

1. Palace of Fine Arts
2. California Bldg.
3. Illinois Bldg.
4. Woman's Bldg.
5. Fisheries Bldg.
6. Children's Bldg.
7. Government Bldg.
8. Greenhouse
9. Horticulture Bldg.
10. Rose Garden
11. Festival Hall
12. Transport. Annex
13. Transport. Bldg.
14. Mines Bldg.
15. Electricity Bldg.
16. Manuf. & Lib. Arts
17. Music Hall
18. Peristyle
19. Casino
20. Columbian Fountain
21. Administration Bldg.
22. Railroad Terminal
23. Machinery Bldg.
24. Agriculture Bldg.
25. Stock Pavillion
26. Krupps Bldg.
27. Leather Exhibit
28. Forestry Bldg.
29. Anthropology Bldg.
30. Stockyards

PROLOGUE

Chicago
December 1880

"Look at them," Sylvie Townsend whispered to her sister. "I wish we could do more." The cold seeped through her cloak and into her boots.

They shivered in the alley outside the orphanage. Meg, surrounded by her own three children, looked through the grimy window. "We've done what we can. For now, at least."

It felt like precious little.

On behalf of the Chicago Women's Club, Meg and Sylvie had delivered donations from local grocers for the Christmas holiday and were then quickly ushered out. Before they left, Sylvie couldn't help peering into the dining hall at the children she longed to help.

Her eyes burned as she watched the orphans and half-orphans—those who had one parent living. There were so many of them packed onto the benches, hunched over bowls of thin soup. This building wasn't a home. It was a warehouse for unwanted goods.

"So much children!" Five-year-old Hazel stood on her tiptoes to see, her nose red with cold. "Do all their mommies and daddies live here, too?"

"Hush, Hazel." Walter, older by two years, stuffed his hands into the pockets of his wool coat. "You don't know anything."

Meg picked up her four-year-old, Louise, and held her close, though the child was getting too big for that. "Those children's parents can't take care of them anymore."

Frowning, Louise clasped mittened hands around her mother's neck. Two braids the color of Meg's blond curls trailed down her back. "Will you ever stop taking care of us?"

"Never ever. Your father and I will always take care of you." Meg gave Louise a squeeze before setting her down again. A raw wind cut through the alley, bringing with it the stench from the privies behind the orphanage. "Walter, take your sisters to the carriage while I talk to Aunt Sylvie for a moment."

Bending, Sylvie kissed three cold cheeks, then watched the carriage driver bundle them into the landau. The difference between those bright-eyed children and the wan souls inside the orphanage was so stark it stung. "Oh, Meg. It isn't enough to bring extra food a few times a year. How far will that nourishment go when they need the nourishment of loving parents far more? I wish there was more I could do."

Meg tucked her hands into her muff. "I know how you feel."

Sylvie doubted it. Meg had a houseful of her

own children and a husband who adored her. Sylvie had none of that. She was thirty years old, the sole caregiver for their aging father, Stephen. She owned a bookstore across from Court House Square and managed two rental apartments above her own, since they'd added a fourth floor to their building after the Great Fire. Though there was no husband on the horizon, Sylvie had plenty of space for a child in her home and heart. But the orphanage wouldn't let her adopt one as a single woman.

The waiting horses swished their tails, their breath small puffs of white. Meg turned her back to them. "Sylvie, I worry you're taking on too much."

Sylvie laughed, and tiny crystals formed inside her muffler. "You're the one who encouraged me to join the Women's Club to begin with. You said I needed something else to do, something else to think and care about aside from Father and the store. And you were absolutely right. My world had become far too small."

"I fear you'll wear yourself out, between your volunteering activities and taking care of Father and the store and your tenants' needs. I don't see anyone taking care of *you*."

"What exactly are you saying?" Not that Sylvie couldn't guess.

"There's still time." A lock of hair whipped about Meg's collar, and she tucked it back under

11

her hat. "You could still find someone to love you."

"You love me, and so do your children. Nate is like a brother to me. Father loves me, as do Karl and Anna Hoffman."

"You know what I mean."

Sylvie folded her arms. "And you know where I stand on the subject of matrimony." She didn't need a husband in order to be fulfilled. Furthermore, she had no time for one. The fact that she'd had her heart smashed to bits by her first love years ago didn't need to be mentioned. Since then, there'd been a couple of suitors, but she had only entertained the idea of courtship to please her father, who claimed he wanted to see her settled. Ironically, however, he'd declared neither suitor could pass muster. She'd agreed.

"All right." Meg rolled her lips between her teeth, hesitating. "I just don't like to think of how lonely you'll be after—well, Father isn't getting any better."

Sylvie dipped her chin into the folds of her muffler. As much as she wanted to, she couldn't deny it. Her father's health had been broken by his time in the Andersonville prison camp during the Civil War, and it only grew worse with each passing year. There was a reason he'd recently transferred ownership of the bookstore to her.

She took her sister's hands, Meg's scar tissue a reminder of all they'd been through together, including and after the Great Fire that ravaged Chicago nine years ago. "I'll adjust. And I'll always have my sister."

Meg replied with a fierce embrace, then joined her children in the carriage and wheeled away. Sylvie would return home by streetcar.

Picking her way between islands of slush, Sylvie emerged from the alley's shadows onto the street the orphanage faced. The sun was bright in the powder-blue sky but held little warmth. While she paused at the front doors, a brawny man approached with a little girl who clutched an adult-sized peacock-blue shawl at her neck.

"Excuse me." The man tipped his cap to her with fingers chapped red at the knuckles. He carried the raw smell of keeping company with animals, living and dead. "The orphanage is open, yes?"

Dread for the child tightened her chest. "It—it is," she stuttered. "I hope you have no need of it." It wasn't her business. But if this child was to join the orphans in this facility, then she would become her concern in an instant.

The man frowned. "I heard they take in children whose parents can't provide for them well enough." His voice was as gruff as his beard, his words thickly accented. Broken blood vessels spread tiny red webs across his nose and cheeks. "I heard they offer clothing, food, and shelter. They keep them safe. Is it not so?"

The little girl tugged the hem of his unraveling sleeve and said something in a different language.

He placed his hand on her uncovered head. "Not now, Rozalia." He said the name with such tenderness, it sounded like a poem: *Rosa Leah*. He looked up. "My name is Nikolai Dabrowski. This is my daughter. My wife didn't survive the journey from Poland. I cannot care for the girl on my own."

Rozalia brought his hand to her cheek and watched Sylvie from behind a tangle of dirty blond hair.

"She's lucky to have one parent living," Sylvie said after introducing herself. "She needs a father's love. Besides, the conditions inside this orphanage are deplorable. There's not enough food or soap or tender care."

"I work fourteen hours a day at the stock-yards," Mr. Dabrowski said. "She stays in our shack alone, or plays in the street with other children. This isn't safe or right. Believe me, Miss Townsend, I bring her here because I love her, not because I don't."

But Sylvie could tell he wavered. "No one in that building loves her," she told him. "They will not ask her what she likes to eat or sing her songs to soothe her." She listed her complaints and described the orphans who had reverted to sucking their thumbs and wetting the bed. She told him of children wasting away and becoming mute with neglect and despair. "Do you really think she'd be better off there than with you, or perhaps a relative of yours who could care for her during the day?"

His broad shoulders sagged. "We have no other kin here. The neighbor women have their own worries. They work at factories, or they do piecework at home with barely enough attention left to keep their own babies from falling into the fire. Rozalia is in danger almost every hour as it is."

Sylvie looked at the girl, a lump forming in her throat. "I'm sure that's not—"

"True? And how do you know what is true and what is not in the place where I live?"

Heat flashed through Sylvie. He was right. They shared a city but lived worlds apart.

Mr. Dabrowski's hand cupped Rozalia's chin. "She is already a beauty, no? And not yet five years old."

Despite the lack of hygiene, she was an uncommonly beautiful child, with delicate features and eyes an enviable cobalt blue.

"People have noticed. Vile people."

Goose bumps lifted Sylvie's skin. "What do you mean?"

"I mean that wicked men have tried to buy her from me, and next time they'll make no offer before they take her to be raised in a brothel, trained for a life of sin. Now tell me, Miss

Townsend, do you still believe my daughter is better off with me than she would be behind those doors?"

On an impulse founded on years of thought and striving, Sylvie decided right then that she might not be able to change the system, but she could change the life of this one precious girl.

"I can take her." Her heart hammered as she heard the words, but nothing had ever sounded or felt more natural. "For as long as you need, Rozalia can live with me and my father." She described their home and the bookshop below it on the corner of Randolph and LaSalle Streets. She offered to show him their property for his approval. "I'll bring her to see you any time you wish, and you're always welcome to visit us, too." She took his rough hand in hers. "Make no mistake. She is your daughter. I'll only care for her until the two of you can be together again."

Grooves furrowed his brow. "I cannot pay you. But she can work for her keep, if that suits. You can dust, Rozalia, can't you? Wash dishes? Tend the fire?"

She nodded.

Sylvie wasn't after domestic help but had the sense to recognize a man's pride when she saw it. She knelt, the cold creeping through her skirts to her knees. "That's all fine, dear. But I will also want you to play. I have a very old cat named

Oliver Twist, and he would love to have a little girl to keep him company. *I* would love to have a little girl to keep me company, and so would my father, I'm sure. Shall we try it and see what happens?"

Rozalia loosened her grip on her father and gave another tentative nod.

Mr. Dabrowski cleared his throat. "She isn't so good with English now. The people in our neighborhood don't speak it. But with you, she will learn English very good, yes? This is what I want for her. She's an American now."

Sylvie unwound the muffler from about her neck and wrapped it around Rozalia. "I'm sure she'll learn quickly." She stood to address one more concern. She knew few Protestant Polish and wondered if her religion would pose a problem. "Mr. Dabrowski, I feel I ought to make you aware that I'm neither Jewish nor Catholic."

"Neither am I, miss." He sniffed and rubbed his nose. "It's been a long time since I've believed in anything. If you have faith of any kind, it will be more than the girl gets from me." To Rozalia, he spoke in Polish. The girl protested. He replied with a stronger voice. To Sylvie, he said, "It is settled."

For a few weeks? A few months? A year? There was no way to know how long this arrangement would last. To Sylvie, it didn't matter.

17

Too overcome for words, she held out her hand. Rozalia took it.

"Keep her safe for me, Miss Townsend."

"I promise. For as long as you need."

CHAPTER ONE

Chicago
Friday, August 4, 1893

Sylvie hadn't always leapt to the worst possible conclusion. But being a parent seemed to enlarge her imagination as much as it did her heart.

Tightening her grip on her parasol, she paced the broad sidewalk parallel to the many-columned Peristyle—one column for each state of the Union—that stretched between Music Hall and the Casino. She squinted against the blinding white buildings, straining to find her seventeen-year-old daughter among the thousands of other visitors here at the World's Fair.

"You worry too much," Beth Wright called to her from the shade of the Peristyle's central arch, one hand planted on her hip. At forty-three years of age, the same as Sylvie, she'd already been a widow for five years but had no children. Sylvie didn't expect her to understand the niggling dread Sylvie felt. "So what if she's a few minutes late? What's so urgent, anyway?"

Sylvie returned to her friend, ducking into the shade. "Her violin lesson with Kristof was supposed to start at two o'clock. Right there."

She pointed to Music Hall. It was the off-season for the Chicago Symphony Orchestra right now, so Kristof and Gregor Bartok, her third-floor tenants, were both performing in the Exposition Orchestra at the Fair. Rose met Kristof between their two daily performances for her weekly lesson. He wasn't her first violin teacher, but he was the best.

Beth fanned herself with her hat. Coils of cinnamon-colored hair swayed at her neck, the only soft aspect of her otherwise wiry frame. "When we were children, the idea of a woman playing the violin was scandalous. The times are changing indeed, and I'm glad of it. But don't tell me you go with her to her lessons."

Sylvie peered up at her friend, who had three inches on her. "I don't. I just finished my tour early at the Manufactures Building." The massive structure was adjacent to Music Hall.

Most World's Fair tour guides were men, but a select band of female guides, including Sylvie and Beth, were hired to lead groups of women. Two or three days a week, Sylvie conducted tours based on each group's interests. On Friday afternoons, many of those tours overlapped with Rose's lesson time.

Brassy notes marched through the air, courtesy of the Iowa State Band. "Good group today?" Beth asked.

"Very. Seventeen young ladies from New

Orleans, with three nuns as chaperones. We visited the model of St. Peter's Basilica on the Midway, Queen Isabella's relics in the Woman's Building, the Louisiana State Building, and the Catholic School Exhibit in Manufactures, among other things." Tours were paid for per person, per hour, which made today's work a valuable supplement to her rental and bookstore income. "The nuns work with blind children too, so I took them to see the inventor of the braille type-writer and his machine. While we were there, a girl who was both blind and deaf came forward—Helen, I think, was her name—and when she was introduced to the inventor, she gave him a hug and a kiss. It was so moving, watching them meet." It was easily the highlight of Sylvie's week.

Beth gave a low whistle. "Lucky. My five ladies from Minnesota wanted to stay at the Stock Pavilion for two hours before they let me show them around the Agriculture and Dairy Buildings. I'll have to wash my hair twice to get the smell out." She brushed a piece of hay from her sleeve. "Anyway, don't worry about Rose running behind today. It happens." Her brown eyes were soft, but her opinions remained as plain as the tip of her nose.

Sylvie prayed her friend was right, even as she scolded herself for being ill at ease. Still, she looked for Rose's figure and golden hair.

Lake Michigan lapped against the back of the Peristyle. Before her lay the marble-edged Grand Basin, surrounded by the principal exhibit buildings that bordered the Court of Honor: Manufactures and Liberal Arts, Electricity, Mines and Mining, Machinery, and Agriculture. The gold dome of the Administration Building reflected the sun at the opposite end of the Basin. Each of the colossal, classically styled buildings was designed to dazzle, all of them resembling white marble.

But not everything at the Fair was what it seemed. Just as nearly every structure here was made of a temporary substance easily deconstructed, every well-dressed man was not necessarily as well-behaved as he appeared.

"Come on," she said, nudging Beth. "Let's rest our feet while we wait."

Repinning her hat in place, Beth followed Sylvie down the steps and into the glaring sun. They sat on a bench beside the Basin where they could see the Roman Corinthian–style Music Hall and the matching Casino, which hosted no gambling or gaming, but only a restaurant, cloakrooms, toilet facilities, and other public comforts. From its roof, American flags snapped in the wind. People passing by in their Sunday best were dwarfed by both buildings, and they weren't even the largest on the grounds.

"Honestly, what's the worst that could

happen?" Beth asked. "There are twelve hundred Columbian Guards stationed at the Fair."

Sylvie didn't want to think about the worst that could happen, let alone list the possibilities aloud. There had been a fatal accident at the Ice Railway last month, and a deadly fire at the Cold Storage Building. People stepped in front of speeding cable cars. Girls disappeared. *Not my girl, Lord. Please not mine.*

Mastering her imagination, Sylvie limited her reply to Beth's comment. "The Fair covers six hundred acres, and that doesn't even include the Midway. That's only two guards per acre, for pity's sake." She didn't spot any of them now.

"Do you want me to wait with you?" But Beth was already standing.

"No need." Sylvie waved a fly away. "I don't want to keep you."

"Come to the suffrage meeting with me. It'll do you good to set your mind on more important things. Wherever Rose is, she knows how to get home."

"Next time," Sylvie said.

Beth shook her head and took her leave.

Rising, Sylvie walked around the edge of the Basin, weaving a path between other visitors. The Statue of the Republic reared up out of the Basin on its pedestal, nearly blinding in its gold-leaf brilliance. Passing under a massive arch, she entered Music Hall and closed her parasol.

Rose had probably slipped inside unnoticed, and Sylvie had worried for nothing.

Forgoing the grand auditorium, her heels tapped briskly up the stairs and down the hall toward the practice rooms, following the sound of strings to an open door.

The small space was alive with music. Kristof's tuxedo jacket was folded over the back of a chair and his shirtsleeves rolled up to his elbows, revealing forearms finely honed from a lifetime of playing the violin. A black bow tie flared at his collar. He exuded precision, control, command.

"She hasn't been here," Sylvie said.

Kristof's bow lifted as he faced her. The last note bounced off the wall and fell. "Not yet. If she doesn't come soon, we'll have to reschedule the lesson." A hint of impatience threaded his tone. He wasn't really angry, Sylvie knew. He was punctual and expected everyone else to be the same.

"If she doesn't come soon, the lesson will be the least of my worries." Sylvie snapped open a paper fan painted with the Court of Honor.

Brows lowering, his expression shifted from a violinist strung tight to that of a compassionate friend, which was what the confirmed bachelor had become to her over the last two years. Reserved, yes, and somewhat preoccupied, but he was reliable and metronome-steady. He was safe.

"Please, sit." He laid down his instrument, then pulled out the piano bench for her. "What's going on?"

She remained standing.

Sunlight shone on his dark brown hair, glinting on grey threads at his temples. "Is she on her own?"

"She was meeting Hazel and some of Hazel's friends—all responsible and a little older than Rose. It's likely they lost track of time." Yet she could not keep the concern from her voice.

Kristof walked to the window facing Lake Michigan. Sylvie joined him. Endless blue water extended to the horizon. Boats and watercraft of all kinds dotted the lake. Benches bolted onto a Movable Sidewalk carried fairgoers out along the Casino Pier nearly half a mile into the lake before bringing them back again. Rose had far too much energy to sit for a ride that moved so slowly.

After rolling down his sleeves, Kristof buttoned the cuffs. "She could have misjudged the amount of time it takes to get from one part of the Fair to another."

Before she could reply, hurried footfalls sounded in the hallway. Sylvie stepped outside the practice room to find Rose heading toward her, violin case swinging from her hand. Relief surged, then ebbed away. A snap of irritation followed.

"Where have you been?"

Rose brushed past her and into the practice room. She smelled of a man's cologne.

Sylvie stared after her, unable to reconcile this. "Rozalia. Why—"

"I'm sorry I'm late," she said breathlessly. "Mr. Bartok, do you have time to listen to my pieces, or must you go down to the stage?"

Kristof looked from Rose to Sylvie. "Sylvie would like a brief explanation first. I can step outside if you like, and then yes, I have a few minutes to spare, but not many."

"No need for you to leave. It's simple." After removing her gloves, Rose opened her violin case, tightened her bow, and began rubbing a block of rosin along the horsehairs. "I went to a lecture at the Palace of Fine Arts. They're inaugurating the Polish art section today, and I couldn't have left early without being rude. Since the Art Palace is clear at the northern end of the fairgrounds, I thought I'd take the electric elevated train to get here—and I did—but I just missed the one I wanted and had to wait for the next. Then there was a huge line at the cloakroom in the Casino where I'd checked my violin. I couldn't very well come here without it, could I?" She set the violin to her shoulder. "I told you it was simple. I'm sorry you didn't trust me."

"It's not that I don't trust *you* . . ." Sylvie said.

Rose cut her off, sawing away on her D string,

twisting a tuning knob until the tone rang true. "You don't trust anyone."

Sylvie made no response, nor did she register Kristof's reply, other than that it was in her defense. She couldn't stop staring at a thumb-sized bruise on the inside of Rose's left wrist.

It hadn't been there this morning.

The performance was over. The applause had faded from Music Hall, and the audience trickled toward the exits. Kristof Bartok and the rest of the Exposition Orchestra should have been free to pack up their instruments and have the rest of the day to themselves.

Instead, Maestro Theodore Thomas gripped both ends of his conductor's baton and told them to wait where they were. This had been their eighty-third performance together since May 2, but it was the first time he just stood there, bushy mustache drooping, while the hall emptied. Behind him in an enormous horseshoe, a dozen mammoth Corinthian pillars soared from balcony to ceiling, each wrapped with laurel garlands to match those draping between them. Laurel wreaths topped and anchored each pillar.

Papers shuffled on stands as one hundred and fifty orchestra members gathered their music into leather folders. Beside Kristof, his younger brother shrugged and stashed his violin beneath his chair, displaying the same lackadaisical attitude that pervaded every corner of his life. Kristof had earned the position of concertmaster and first chair violin, but only because Gregor— who had more natural talent by far—had no discipline. If only he cared enough to practice, if he cared about his potential half as much as their father had, he would be the star of the orchestra, and Kristof would literally be playing second fiddle to him.

Even if the maestro didn't know that, surely Gregor did.

Kristof dabbed a folded handkerchief to his brow, then rested his instrument across his lap and waited for whatever Maestro had to tell them.

Gregor made a show of yawning, then shoved a thatch of oak-brown hair off his brow.

"Out too late last night?" Kristof asked, *sotto voce*, though he already knew the answer. Gregor was so loud coming home that surely Sylvie and Rose could hear him tramping above them. Just as he had heard one of the Hoffmans stirring upstairs after Gregor slammed the door to their apartment.

Gregor rubbed his hand over his face. "No later than usual."

True. And that was the problem. There was always something to do, see, experience that was more alluring than home. Before Kristof could reply, however, Maestro Thomas rapped his baton on his stand.

"I have an announcement," he began. "You've all played well here at the World's Columbian Exposition. Two concerts daily, plus rehearsals, for the last three months has been a grueling schedule. I have been proud to stand at the helm of this body as you've offered the public a more cultured, sophisticated music experience than they get anywhere else in the city."

Gregor leaned over and whispered, "This can't be good."

As much as he wanted to disagree, Kristof sensed the same. Thomas's demeanor was too sober for mere praise.

"But as you've noticed, our afternoon concerts have suffered shamefully low attendance." Thomas's eyebrows knit together.

"Pardon me, sir," Gregor inserted, "but I'm not surprised. The public can attend our free concerts in the morning, plus hear bands throughout the fairgrounds, all included with a fifty-cent ticket to the Fair. Why, then, would they pay another dollar to attend the afternoon concert?"

He had a point. The Exposition Orchestra's morning concerts of popular music averaged thirty-five hundred patrons. The afternoon concerts: one hundred.

"Why indeed?" Maestro echoed. "As the musical director for the Fair, my aim has always been to use music to both amuse the crowds and to elevate the more discerning European visitor.

But I'm forced to concede that music as art and education has been an utter failure. Music as amusement is all the people want, and they won't pay extra for it."

Kristof shifted in his chair, making a mental note to change the programming. As concert-master, he would suggest more Wagner, Brahms, Dvořák, Tchaikovsky. Fewer of the longer pieces they'd played this afternoon from Beethoven and Liszt. He tugged his damp collar away from his skin. The ninety-six-degree heat lately hadn't made the stuffy afternoon concerts more popular either.

"As free music doesn't pay the bills," Thomas continued, "I'm resigning my position as musical director and disbanding the Exposition Orchestra."

"What about the contract?" Kristof asked quietly. It was a six-month agreement, and they were months shy of completing it.

"We're breaking the contract," Thomas replied. "Cutting our losses, so to speak. The Fair officials agree that, in this case, the only way forward is to find the way out."

Kristof was out of a job. They all were, until the Chicago Symphony Orchestra season began the day after Thanksgiving. But it was only the start of August. The end of November loomed far away.

Surprise rippled through the orchestra sections,

but none louder than that from Gregor. "This can't be happening." He stood. "What about our salaries?"

"The last concert I'll conduct will be August 11, and that will be in support of the chorus at Festival Hall. After that, I assume none of us will be paid. I certainly won't ask for money I didn't earn. Will you?"

"This is outrageous. You can't do this to us. I was counting on that money. That is, we were all planning to be fully employed for the duration of the contract. Did you think of that—think of us—before you resigned?"

Kristof kicked his brother's shoe to silence him. "Sit," he hissed. Nothing could be gained by attacking the maestro.

"I regret any financial hardships this may cause you," Thomas boomed. "But if you've been wise, you have saved some of that generous salary you've been paid all summer."

Kristof had. One hundred fifty dollars a week was more money than he could possibly spend. Apparently his brother had found a way to do it.

Gregor sank back into his chair and held his head. "This wasn't supposed to happen," he whispered. Sweat beaded his upper lip.

At thirty-five years old, Gregor ought to be able to take care of himself. But when Kristof looked at him, he saw the younger brother always getting into scrapes, always reaching to Kristof for rescue. He set his jaw, already frustrated without even knowing why. But he knew Gregor. That was enough.

As soon as Thomas adjourned the meeting, Kristof swiveled in his chair to face his brother and braced for confrontation.

"Did you know about any of this?" Gregor asked.

"Why should I?"

"He relies on you. If you had any idea, and you didn't tell me . . . If I had only had some idea my funds would dry up—"

Kristof leaned forward. "I'm a concertmaster, not a consultant. I mark the bowings on the sheet music, help with programming, and perform the violin solos. I am not the maestro's confidant."

"If only I'd known, I would have—I wouldn't have—" Cutting short his confession, Gregor shoved his fingers through his hair.

"Tell me." Kristoff kept his tone low. "What have you done?"

And what must I do to fix it?

CHAPTER TWO

Corner Books & More was empty when Sylvie and Rose returned to it late that afternoon—aside from Tessa Garibaldi, the twenty-one-year-old woman Sylvie employed, and Tiny Tim, the little black cat with white belly and paws who had adopted Rose the minute he'd seen her.

The walls were deep purple, which might have made the space too dark if the store's corner position didn't double the amount of natural light. Orange velvet drapes framed the windows, and copper ceiling tiles stamped with medallions reflected gaslight chandeliers. Above the bookshelves hung portraits Meg had painted of literary characters, from Fanny Price to Frankenstein's monster, from Jane Eyre to Jean Valjean.

"Welcome back." Tessa hooked a lock of brown-black hair behind her ear. She bore a strong resemblance to her older brothers, Lorenzo and Louis, whom Sylvie had known for more than twenty years. "You didn't miss much, other than a few sales of the World's Fair guidebooks."

Sylvie was afraid of that, but not surprised. "All right. Thank you."

"One lady came who didn't buy anything," Tessa added, "but she asked for you. A Polish lady, maybe in her late forties, beautiful and charming. Jozefa Zakowski? Zapinski, maybe . . ."

"Zielinksi?" Sylvie guessed.

"That's it! Chatty lady, asked several questions. She was disappointed not to meet you both."

Rose looked at Sylvie. "You know her?"

"We've corresponded." As a member of the Chicago Women's Club, Sylvie had served on a committee that recruited several international guests to the Fair. "She's an actress from partitioned Poland and is forward-thinking about women's issues. I invited her to come lecture at the Woman's Building, and she expressed an interest in touring the rest of Chicago, as well. She was particularly interested in Hull House when I told her about it."

Most people were interested in Hull House if they had any concern for the plight of the urban poor, which happened to be mostly immigrants. Founded by Jane Addams and Ellen Gates Starr just four years ago, the settlement house on Halsted Street was a beacon of hope and education in a rough section of town. Sylvie had volunteered with their Reading Club almost since Hull House opened.

"Since Miss Zielinksi is an actress, do you suppose she might visit during the Hull House Players' practice?" Rose asked.

"I've already invited her," Sylvie said. "I forgot she was arriving in town this week. She's scheduled to speak on Tuesday, and I'm to be her personal tour guide. I'll see her then, if not before." She smiled at Rose, gratified that she seemed to approve.

"Did you have fun with your cousin today?" Tessa asked Rose, one inky eyebrow arching.

"I had a grand time with Hazel and her friends, yes." Rose removed the pin holding her straw hat in place and set it on the counter. "But she isn't really my cousin, you know."

Sylvie bit her tongue before she could disagree aloud.

Tessa checked the clock and filled in her time card. "She might as well be, though, right?"

Rose shrugged. "It isn't the same. It's not like you and your family."

"My family has more cousins than we can fit in one house." Tessa laughed. "Don't forget, I moved out as soon as I could. I love them, and I don't mind helping them when I can. But I have a new family, of sorts, with the Jane Club."

"That's right," Sylvie couldn't resist remarking. "Some families we're born into, and some are of our own choosing. Just like I chose you, Rose. We chose each other, didn't we? Isn't that a bond at least as strong as blood?"

Rose gave Sylvie a warm smile. "Yes, Mimi. I love you, too." She kissed her on the cheek.

Mimi. The endearment never failed to reassure Sylvie. It was the name Rose had decided to call her when she was a child and Sylvie became her legal guardian. Sylvie would have preferred to hear *Mama* or *Mother* instead, but those names had been locked away for Rose when her biological mother, Magdalena, had died on the ship that carried them to America. Sylvie understood.

Still chatting about the Jane Club, Rose and Tessa took the armchairs flanking the fireplace near the back of the store, Tiny Tim curled on Rose's lap.

Sylvie loved this bookshop. After the hubbub and flurry of the Fair, she relished the quiet of this book-filled oasis that smelled of pages and the pastries the Hoffmans sold at her counter. Karl and Anna were now seventy and sixty-seven years old, and had given up their bakery and become her fourth-floor tenants a few years ago. Before that, they'd been her neighbors for as long as she could remember, and they had become dear friends. Now they baked for the bookshop and for themselves.

Sylvie had arranged a few bistro tables and chairs in the back of the store, where customers could enjoy their pastries and begin reading their new books right away. Before her father had died, the space had been his book-repair workshop. But since she'd never learned the skill of binding books, she'd transformed the area into something new.

She was good at that—at adjusting and

36

renewing. All of Chicago was. It had grown to one million souls, and that wasn't counting all the visitors in town for the Fair.

Taking off her hat, Sylvie moved to the front window, the view from which was dominated by the eleven-story courthouse across the street. The columned and porticoed granite building, together with city hall, took up the entire block bordered by Randolph, LaSalle, North Clark, and Washington Streets.

Nothing on the display table needed straightening. Copies of *Rand, McNally & Co.'s Handy Guide to Chicago and the World's Columbian Exposition* were expertly arranged, along with a fanned-out stack of *Chicago by Day and Night: The Pleasure Seeker's Guide to the Paris of America*. A model of Mr. Ferris's wheel, one of the most recognizable landmarks of the Fair, towered over the books, its cars holding pocket-sized maps and *The Time-Saver* guidebook.

A smile lifted the corner of her mouth. She was proud of her city. Just twenty-two years ago, the Great Fire had devastated the business district and rendered one-third of its population homeless, including Sylvie's family. But Chicago had rebuilt itself in record time and was now hosting the world.

Sylvie had reconstructed herself, too, after that harrowing chapter in her life.

"Mimi, listen to this!" Rose called.

Gladly, Sylvie joined the young women, seating herself in a bistro chair, her dark skirt blotting out the cream tiles that distinguished this area from the rest of the bookshop. "Yes?"

"This Jane Club sounds amazing. You already know all about it, I suppose?"

Sylvie did, in fact, know quite a bit about the Jane Club, but Rose looked ready to burst. "Tell me."

"It's named for Jane Addams, of course," Rose began. "I'm sure you knew that. And it's a group of single women working in Chicago who share apartments. They cook for each other, share the housework, all of that."

"I told you," Tessa said. "It's like a family. Not that we always get along, but we're there for each other. If one of us loses a job suddenly, she doesn't also lose her room and board. The others can cover it until she finds a new situation. That's the idea, anyway. We're no longer dependent on our fathers, but we're not 'girls adrift' either. Independent, making our own way, but not alone. You see?"

"It truly is a lovely arrangement," Sylvie agreed.

"And Tessa's roommate is cooking tonight. She's Polish, Mimi, and she's going to make pierogis. I'd like to join them. Tessa invited me." Rose clasped Sylvie's hand. "Please. I want to learn how to make them, and you know I won't learn it from you."

The Jane Club was wonderful, but it was an apartment building in a seedy section of town. And there were so many strangers in Chicago to visit the Fair—or to prey upon those who did. "Who would bring you back home when you're done?"

"I'm sure I could find someone."

But it didn't feel right, especially after Rose had shown up to her violin lesson with bruises and smelling of cologne.

"Another time," Sylvie said gently. "We'll make arrangements to be sure you have a proper escort home afterwards, all right?" She could go with Rose herself this evening, if only to see her safely home afterward. She could stay at the coffeehouse around the corner from the Jane Club until it was time to pick Rose up and head home. But she was spent. All she wanted was a quiet evening.

To Tessa, Sylvie said, "Thank you so much for the offer. Rain check?"

"Of course, Miss Townsend. Now, if you'll excuse me, I ought to be going."

Sylvie bade her good-bye and waited for the door to close behind her.

"I'm sorry you're disappointed," she told Rose. She glanced at the bruise again, and Rose hid it behind her back. "I saw that." The words slipped out before she could think to frame them better.

"Saw what?"

"The bruise. How did you come by it?"

"It's nothing." Rose looked at it. "I didn't even notice it before now."

"It looks like someone held you too firmly. What happened, dear?"

Rose shrugged. "I rode the Ice Railway this afternoon."

"You what?" Sylvie had expressly forbidden her to board that rickety contraption.

"Hazel and her friends were all doing it. Walter was there, too. He said he'd ride with me to keep me safe and assured me you wouldn't mind if you knew that."

Sylvie had a soft spot for Meg's oldest child, but she did mind being dismissed.

"We picked up a lot of speed, and on a curve I started to—well, I leaned out of the car unintentionally. Walter grabbed my wrist and yanked me back in. See? Nothing to worry about."

Sylvie didn't understand why the Ice Railway was still in operation after the accident two months ago that had killed a man and injured five others. But at least it explained the marks and why Rose had carried a hint of Walter's cologne. Still, Sylvie couldn't resist pointing out that this was exactly why she'd told Rose not to ride it in the first place.

Rose stood, fire sparking behind her eyes. "You have so many rules for me, Mimi."

"Because I love you."

"No, because you don't trust me to make any decisions on my own, even though I finished school. My best friend got married this summer, my other friend left for Cornell University, and you're still telling me what not to do. That doesn't feel like love to me, it feels like a cage. But, in the words of Jane Eyre, 'I am no bird; and no net ensnares me; I am a free human being with an independent will . . .' "

Sylvie finished the quote in her mind: *which I now exert to leave you.*

"You misunderstand. There's no need for—" She stopped herself before she would make things worse, pushing Rose away even further. She needed time to think things through. It was true that Rose had completed her schooling this past spring, but she was the youngest in her class. Too young to know yet what she wanted for her future.

Sylvie fiddled with the buttons on her cuffs. "I'd like to check the ledger before closing up here. Then I'll come up and start working on dinner. We'll talk more then."

"Don't bother." Rose scooped up Tiny Tim and held him to her chest. "Suddenly I'm not hungry."

Whatever fear Kristof had glimpsed in Gregor in Music Hall seemed to vanish once they began walking through the Midway Plaisance. Gregor had always been easily distracted, and nowhere on earth was there more to catch the eye than right here.

Violin cases in hand, they walked west, putting behind them the Fair's manicured lawns, sculptured fountains, and neoclassical buildings of monumental scale. The World's Columbian Exposition was a stately affair designed to awe, educate, and inspire. The Midway, a mile-long strip of park stretching inland from one of the Fair's west entrances, was a rambunctious assault on the senses. By the looks of the crowd, they didn't mind.

"We could catch the Houdini brothers if we hurry," Gregor said. "Did you know they were born in Budapest?"

"Who?"

"They do this trick called Metamorphosis where Harry gets trussed up, tied in a sack, and locked in a trunk. A curtain is drawn and pulled back again, and quick as a wink, Harry is free and it's his brother in the trunk!"

Mildly intrigued, Kristof mused that he would have given anything to trade places with his brother while they were growing up. "We're not here for a magic show," he said instead. They'd agreed to find dinner among the many options on the Midway on the condition that Gregor would tell him the truth behind his reaction to Maestro's announcement. "German Village?" he suggested. A forest of half-timbered buildings reminiscent of Bavaria rose up on their right behind a gate.

Gregor waved a hand in dismissal. "How about something a little more exotic?" He pushed ahead in the crowd until smells of sauerkraut and beer gave way to pungent aromas of cooking meats, unusual spices—and camel and donkey dung. Cairo Street was up ahead, a towering minaret spiking the cloudless sky.

A line of people waited for a uniformed young man to shred their tickets in the turnstile and allow them past the eight-foot-high wall encasing the village of imported Egyptians. Fortune-telling, dancing, and donkey and camel rides were only a few of the attractions available. If they went inside, Kristof wouldn't stand a chance of commanding Gregor's attention.

"Not today." Kristof steered Gregor around a hawker standing on two chairs outside the Persian concession, past the Eiffel Tower model, and into the shadow of Mr. Ferris's wheel, the spectacular engineering feat that dwarfed the pride of Paris. Screams crescendoed and decrescendoed from thrill seekers riding the Ice Railway on the left. "We need somewhere we can talk."

"We're talking now."

"Not nearly enough."

Within three more blocks, they had passed the East India Bazaar, Austrian Village, Chinese

Village and Theater, Dahomey Village, and more. "Here we are."

Gregor squinted at the unassuming building at the end of the Midway, just beyond the Lapland Village. "Of all places. You can't be serious, Kristof."

"Aren't I always?"

"Quite. Serious enough for the both of us."

"One of us ought to be." Kristof chuckled. "After you. No place like home, eh?"

He extended his hand for Gregor to enter the Hungarian Orpheum and Café. In truth, though they'd been born and raised in Budapest, it had been more than twenty years since he had called Hungary home. After studying music in Vienna and then in Naples, Italy, they'd played with symphonies across Europe before moving to New York and then to Chicago.

Inside the Orpheum, a large café was arranged in front of a concert stage. A young lady in a bright national folk costume approached them. A scarlet vest trimmed with gold braid covered her white shirtwaist. She spread her embroidered, ruffled apron in a curtsy and flashed a dimpled grin. Gregor charmed her with small talk in Hungarian as she seated them at a table near an open window.

"Suddenly you don't seem to mind the venue," Kristof pointed out as soon as she'd poured their water and left them to their menus. He stowed his violin case beneath his chair while Gregor did the same.

Gregor's gaze roved over the dozens of girls serving tables, all of whom seemed to be formed from a similar mold: young, blond, and curvy. "The ambience is more inviting than I expected."

"The ambience?" Kristof raised an eyebrow. A breeze fluttered the window's red-and-white-checked curtain and ruffled his hair. "Keep in mind that these young ladies are other men's daughters, and they ought to be treated as such. With respect."

"Other men's daughters, eh?" Gregor laughed. "I'd expect such a comment from someone old enough to be their father."

Unfazed, Kristof smiled. "You're right behind me, brother."

A waitress arrived at their table, this one wearing an emerald-green vest and an apron embroidered with blue flowers. After introducing herself as Margit, she took their order and whisked away. A Gypsy band from Budapest struck up their next piece from the stage, stomping their tall black boots to the music.

Kristof took a drink, then focused on Gregor. "No more stalling," he said. "What's going on with you? Don't tell me you've already spent your earnings."

A muscle twitched next to Gregor's eye. He plucked a petunia from the window's flower box and rolled it between his fingers. "Fine. Then I won't tell you." He tossed the crushed petals out the window.

Kristof bit down on his frustration. "Then I'll assume that since you've brought nothing new into our apartment this summer, you haven't spent the money so much as lost it. Gambling."

The water glasses on the table began sweating. Gregor shifted to watch the musicians play. He clapped his hands to the beat, effectively shutting off the conversation. But the façade of mirth was pastry thin, and he turned back to Kristof when the song concluded. "All right. I did lose it. I lost pretty big, as it happens. I lost more than I had at the time. I owe a guy."

Applause filled the café as the band members took a bow. Neither Bartok brother joined in.

Gregor wiped the condensation from his glass. "If I don't get the money to pay him off in the next ten days, I don't know what will happen to me." When he looked up, his eyes were slick pools of blue. "How was I to know Thomas would break our contract? How could I have predicted the loss of work?"

Margit returned, setting before Gregor a plate of *lángos*, deep-fried bread topped with sour cream and cheese. In front of Kristof, she placed a bowl of *meggyleves*, a sour cherry soup served cold, perfect for an August day. With a final flourish, she served an order of *hortobágyi palacsinta*, which they would share. Savory aromas rose from the crepes filled with meat, onions, and spices, served with a paprika sour cream sauce.

"Anything else I can get you?" Margit asked, her cheeks flushed from the heat.

"No." Kristof didn't mean to sound short with her, but his curt tone sent her quickly away. In a manner just as businesslike, he said a brief prayer to bless the food before addressing his brother. "Gregor, you know my views on gambling. Are you able to stop, or is this a sickness, an addiction as strong as liquor?"

"If it is, this experience has cured me of it. I swear." Gregor tore off a piece of the fried bread, folded it in half, and stuffed it in his mouth. After wiping a red linen napkin over his lips, he said, "I just need a little help to pay off my debt, and then that's it. It's over."

A sigh swelled in Kristof's chest. He had heard such a speech before. "How do I know you're serious this time?" With the side of his fork, he cut off a piece of the *palacsinta* and swirled it in the cream sauce before eating it.

"The man I owe is no joke. You'll have him to thank for scaring me straight. If he doesn't get the money on time, he'll come after me. I don't want to get hurt, and I don't think you do either. If, by chance, you should happen to be home and get in the way."

Anger licked through Kristof. "If I'm in

danger because of your mistakes, it won't stop there. We have neighbors, Gregor. We all live in the same building. Think of that! Sylvie and Rose, Karl and Anna Hoffman. Women and old people! Even Tessa Garibaldi, the girl who works at the bookshop, could be at risk. Because of you."

Gregor blanched. "I never intended to involve you in any of this, let alone all of them. I never thought—"

"No, you didn't. You never thought. It seems I'm still doing all the thinking for you." The rescuing, too. For what choice did Kristof have but to bail him out? He forced himself to take a spoonful of his cherry soup, then another, waiting for more of Gregor's excuses. He was already calculating how far his own savings would go to cover rent and food for both of them for the next few months.

"Losing my job—our jobs—wasn't my fault," Gregor said. "I could have handled this if it weren't for that." He cut and stabbed a bite of the crepe. "I don't want to need you right now, but I do. Please. Just do this one thing for me, and I'll never gamble again."

Several beats passed while Kristof studied him, allowing his brother to squirm. Gregor was far too old to behave with the recklessness of an adolescent. Yet he couldn't bring himself to deny a lifeline to a drowning man, no matter that

Gregor had sabotaged his own well-being with foolishness. Besides, this wasn't just any man. Gregor was family. The only family Kristof had left.

At last, he spoke. "How much?"

Gregor named the sum.

Kristof leaned back in his chair, stared at the open timber beams of the ceiling, and prayed for patience while he mastered his composure. Gregor ought to feel the consequences of his poor decisions. But this time he wouldn't be the only one paying.

"All right," Kristof said. "I'll cover it, but now the man you owe is me."

A smile pushed brackets into Gregor's cheeks. He reached out and grasped Kristof's shoulder. "Fine, yes, thank you. At least you won't break my legs if I need more time to pay you back, yes?"

"I'd settle for breaking your bad habit."

Gregor laughed at that, then made quick work of finishing his meal. "I think I'll celebrate."

The color returning to his face, he pulled out his violin case and freed his instrument. Before Kristof could persuade him otherwise, he bounded up on stage and improvised a harmony to the Gypsy violinist, making the man's solo a duet.

Kristof watched in genuine awe as the Gypsy eventually bowed out of the spotlight with good humor, allowing Gregor to command center stage. And command it he did. The thrum of the café died away as everyone fell under his spell. Diners forgot their food and clapped in time to the magic coming from Gregor's strings.

However Gregor played, in music and in life, Kristof returned to the same refrain: they were brothers. And Kristof wouldn't give up on family.

CHAPTER THREE

Monday, August 7, 1893

Sylvie tried not to breathe deeply. Halsted Street, especially in August, had that effect on people. This southern portion of the road, a few blocks west of the Chicago River's south branch, bordered immigrant colonies the city didn't often service. Trash built up in people's front yards while privies crowded the backs. After the weekend's heavy rain, some of the pine blocks that paved the street had broken loose and floated around, leaving gaping holes in the road. The sewage-contaminated rainwater made puddles that smelled so horrid they made Sylvie's eyes water.

Rose didn't complain, but her footsteps quickened on the slimy wooden sidewalk. In an effort not to stand out too much, the pale pink shirtwaist she wore was one of her simplest, the sleeves slim. Sylvie kept pace with her as they passed shops lining the street. A red-and-white-striped pole marked a barbershop, and a large glass globe filled with colored water indicated the drugstore. A brightly painted wooden Indian stood outside the cigar shop. Behind all of these establishments were overcrowded tenements, none of which were graced by a single tree or blade of grass.

At half past seven in the evening, peddlers still called out over children playing in the street.

Shiny red apples, come out and see!

Any rags, any bottles, any junk today?

Ripe bananas, five cents a dozen!

Just before reaching Hull House at 800 Halsted Street, Sylvie and Rose turned onto Polk Street and entered the Hull House coffeehouse, where the theater group met.

With the windows closed against the summer stench, the air inside was even more humid than it was outside. But most of the Hull House Players were used to it.

"Sylvie! Rose!" Beth Wright waved them over to where she shared a long wooden table with another woman of middling years. "I'd like to introduce you to someone before practice begins."

The rich smell of coffee flavored the air. The woman with Beth held herself with excellent posture. Her ash-blond hair was in a perfect chignon.

"This is Jozefa Zielinski, the actress from partitioned Poland," Beth said.

"Of course!" Sylvie greeted Miss Zielinski, feeling rather plain in her sensible brown dress compared to this European fashion plate. "So lovely to meet you at last. I'm Sylvia Townsend, but call me Sylvie. And this is my daughter, Rose."

Miss Zielinski bestowed a warm smile on both of them. "And you must call me Jozefa." Her English was excellent, her accent charming.

Rose offered her hand, as well. "Pleasure to meet you. And I'm not really her daughter. That's just something she likes to say. She calls me Rose, and I don't mind it, really, but my real name is Rozalia, and I'm Polish, just like you."

Sylvie felt the color drain from her face.

"Who's thirsty?" Beth cut in, her voice a little too bright. "Coffee? Water? Tea?"

As soon as she bustled away with an order, Jozefa leaned closer. "So, the two of you are not family?"

"Of course we are," Sylvie insisted. Rose was the only child she would ever have.

With both Jozefa and Rose staring at her, Sylvie swallowed.

"It's true she's Polish." Briefly, she explained the circumstances that led to Rose becoming part of her life.

"So, you just took her from her father?" Jozefa asked.

Sylvie studied the actress, trying to register the question. "Against his will? I would never do that. Before he died, he asked me to promise I'd raise her as my own, and it has been my greatest joy to do so." She had promised to keep Rose safe. All these years later, she was still trying to keep that promise.

Beth whisked back and set a tray on the table, handing a water to Rose and coffees to Sylvie and Jozefa. The glazed earthenware mugs were the color of new buds in spring. Beth excused herself again, and Sylvie slipped her fingers through the handle and drank. A hot beverage on a hot day was far from refreshing, but she hoped it would bring clarity of mind.

Rose ran a fingertip around the rim of her water glass. "In Chicago, even small children could have gone to work in the factories or lived on the streets if they weren't in a family or an orphanage," she explained. "So I went with her, where she let me do light housework. I don't remember what I did to earn my keep. I wasn't afraid of replacing my parents when I moved in because she wasn't married. It was just her and her father."

This story wasn't the way Sylvie remembered it. "That's not all you did," she said. "You learned to read, you went to school. You helped me in the bookshop. You were never just a servant to me. Never. We cherished you." She thought she'd made that clear. She had treated Rose like her own daughter for more than a decade. With Meg's family, Rose also had an aunt, uncle, and three cousins who adored her. Before Sylvie's father died, he was as much a grandfather to Rose as he'd ever been to Meg's children. "I may have saved you from a life of poverty, but you saved me from a poverty of soul. I have always loved you with a mother's love."

"How would you know?" Rose bit her lip.

Sylvie stilled. "I'm going to forget you said that."

More young people from the neighborhood poured into the coffeehouse, swapping greetings in Italian, Dutch, Bohemian, Russian, and English. Their voices dimmed in Sylvie's ears.

Rose frowned. "It's just that I'm not a Townsend, I'm—"

"A Dabrowski," Jozefa said. "Rozalia Dabrowski. Yes?"

"That's right." Rose locked her gaze with Jozefa's.

Sylvie pushed her mug away. "I'm sorry, how do you know her last name?"

"She didn't tell you?" Jozefa clucked her tongue.

"I was going to." Rose slid Sylvie a guilty glance. "I wrote a notice and gave it to the special information bureau and the general headquarters for World's Fair visitors from Poland. An advertisement, really, for them to put in their bulletins. It says my name and my parents' names, our birth dates, and when my family came to Chicago. I asked for anyone who had any information about my relatives to write me

55

at our address. I may never hear anything, but I had to try. It seems the whole world is coming to Chicago. It could be the best chance I'll ever have of finding a real connection."

Sylvie marveled at Rose's resourcefulness even as she tried to deny the sting it brought her. "So you saw this notice," she said to Jozefa.

"I never forget a name."

Rose took a drink of her water and dabbed her mouth with a napkin. "You understand, though, don't you, Mimi? I'm almost eighteen years old. I'd like to find my real family before it's time to make one of my own."

Sylvie nodded. On an intellectual level, she did understand. But on a deeper level, all she could think was that their little family of two had been real to her. And now it was falling apart.

"It's time for practice to begin." Rose stood, smoothing her skirt away from her belted waist. "Jozefa, I hope you've come to advise us."

"I am at your service, my dear."

Sylvie watched as the Hull House Players finished clearing some long tables out of the way, then acted out a scene from Shakespeare's *As You Like It*. About a dozen actors practiced tonight, aged from fifteen to twenty-two years old. Beth stepped aside as theater director and allowed Jozefa freedom to coach. Following every piece of advice offered, Rose bloomed under the attention. Beth scribbled notes in the margins of her playbook, copper curls bouncing beside her jaw.

The coffee was tepid by the time Sylvie thought to try drinking it again. She pulled from her bag a well-worn copy of *A Tale of Two Cities* by Charles Dickens, the current selection for the Hull House Readers Club. Their meetings were also on Monday evenings, after the Hull House Players' practice, to allow those who wanted, like Rose, to participate in both. Rose was the only player who didn't live in the neighborhood. But since she'd been coming here for so long with Sylvie, they let her act with them.

Before Sylvie opened her book, a familiar face caught her eye. Twenty-five-year-old Ivan Mazurek leaned against the wall, his folded arms brawny from laboring at the stockyards. Sylvie had known his family for years. She watched him, ready to wave should he look her way.

He didn't. His walnut-brown hair was combed to one side, and a fresh nick on his cheek betrayed that he'd recently shaved. Frankly, Sylvie was surprised to see him here. If he was still as frugal as he'd always been, he'd never spend money at the coffeeshop, and she'd never known him to be interested in Shakespeare. He attended Readers Club but didn't comment on the text.

Curious, she followed Ivan's line of sight to

Rose, who seemed completely oblivious to him. All the better.

Sylvie laced her fingers around her mug. Was this man a potential suitor for her daughter? He was Polish, but that alone did not make a match. In fact, Sylvie wasn't convinced Rose needed a match at all. One's happiness and fulfillment didn't depend on it, at any rate. A truth Sylvie's own life proved.

Giving it no further thought, she opened her novel and immersed herself in the story.

She was deep into Revolutionary Paris via Charles Dickens by the time practice ended and Rose returned to the table, glowing. Jozefa and Beth came right behind her.

"Will you come again, Jozefa?" Rose asked, and Beth echoed the invitation.

"Perhaps I will." Jozefa smoothed her hair and brushed at a wrinkle in her skirt. "And perhaps next week I'll come properly pressed, as well."

"Where are you staying, Jozefa?" Sylvie tucked her book into her bag and stood. "Are the valet services inadequate?"

"My reservation is with the Palmer House, on the European plan."

Sylvie's brows lifted in surprise before she could hide her reaction. Then again, not all rooms at the hotel were as expensive as others, and the European plan meant Jozefa would find her own meals rather than eating each one at the hotel on the American plan. Still, she hadn't realized the actress had the means to stay at the Palmer for an extended period of time. Perhaps Bertha Palmer, wife of the hotel owner and the director of the Fair's Board of Lady Managers, had arranged a special rate for speakers at the Woman's Building. It was the sort of thing she would do.

"But there's been a mistake with the dates of my lodging," Jozefa went on. "They weren't expecting me until next Monday."

Beth's face screwed tight. "So where have you been sleeping, the broom closet?" She snorted when she laughed.

A hint of a smile tilted Jozefa's lips. "Not quite. The Palmer staff referred me to the Sherman House while I wait for my room to open at the Palmer, but the Sherman is full up, too. Still, they've given me a cot and a corner of the lobby, among several other cot-sleepers. In Chicago during the World's Fair, it seems there is literally no room at the inn."

"Oh no." Sylvie felt her cheeks flush at the thought of an international guest being treated this way.

Rose gasped. "That's terrible! The Sherman House is just down the block from us." She clutched Sylvie's arm. "She can stay with us, instead, can't she, Mimi?"

Before Sylvie could reply, Jozefa broke in. "I couldn't impose."

"Nonsense." Rose turned back to Sylvie, pleading. "She can have my bed. I'll sleep on the sofa. I don't mind at all, and I'll help with all the cooking, I promise."

Beth lowered her voice. "If you don't mind, Sylvie, it really would be a step up from a cot. I'd take her in myself if I had any room to spare."

"Of course," Sylvie said, and she meant it. After all, she had been the one to invite Jozefa to come at her own expense, which was no small sum. "It's the least I can do, and we really are neighbors to the Sherman House. What we have isn't fancy, but it's home, and you're welcome to it."

Rose hugged Sylvie with a spontaneity that called to mind years past, when affections between them were freely bestowed and received. Heart in her throat, Sylvie held her daughter, then let her go.

Thursday, August 10, 1893

If Sylvie's pulse skittered with excitement, she could only imagine how Rose felt as they sat with Kristof at a table near the restaurant's entrance. She could scarcely believe it had worked. But here they were, waiting for a man who had answered Rose's notice searching for her Polish roots. Wiktor Janik hailed from the Dabrowskis' hometown of Wloclawek, Poland.

Beyond the second-floor windows of the Casino, Lake Michigan sparkled beneath the midday sun. Inside, waiters glided between tables. Swags of red, white, and blue festooned the Corinthian pillars designed to match those in Music Hall, the building's twin on the other end of the Peristyle that connected them. Chatter hummed in the open, airy restaurant.

"I'm so nervous," Rose murmured. "How well did he say he knew my parents, again?"

"He was their neighbor for several years," Kristof said. "It sounds like they might have been friends. We'll find out soon enough, won't we?" He had been the one to translate the note sent in Polish and pen the reply on Rose's behalf.

Sylvie thanked him again for meeting for lunch between his concerts so he could interpret for them. She'd known he was multilingual from growing up and studying in Europe, but she hadn't realized until he met and spoke with Jozefa that his languages included Polish. The actress had offered to come and translate today but then recalled she had a lunch date with other women speakers. It was just as well. For such a momentous occasion, it was more fitting for Kristof to be here than a woman they'd met less than a week ago.

"Oh, I'm so nervous," Rose said again, her knee bouncing beneath the table. "I don't know why, but I am."

Sylvie could practically feel Rose's anxiety radiating from her. She looked younger than her seventeen years just now, and yet it seemed a lifetime since she'd been parted from her father. Sylvie prayed she would learn something meaningful today, something she could hang on to.

"Are you sure you want me to be here for this?" Sylvie asked. She wanted to stay, but she would understand if Rose wanted to receive Mr. Janik privately. As long as Kristof was there to translate and chaperone, she had no qualms about it.

"Of course, Mimi. You deserve to know about my family as much as I do. And if this man was my family's friend, I'm sure he'd want to meet the woman who raised me."

Sylvie exhaled. "I'm eager to meet him, too."

Across the expanse of white linen, Kristof smiled at her over the centerpiece of pink and lime-green hydrangeas. As usual, his tuxedo appeared crisp and spotless, even after his morning concert.

She nudged the salt and pepper shakers out of alignment on the table and waited. Two seconds later, Kristof's long, lean fingers moved them back into perfect place. This was what he did.

She teased him about his need for order, but in all honesty, it was comforting that he took what was crooked and made it straight again. He fixed things.

She arched an eyebrow at him. He shrugged and smiled, that particular smile she'd noticed was only for her. The one that said, *I know what you're doing. I know you.* He did. In her mind, they were older versions of Jo March and Laurie from *Little Women*, the way they understood each other. Friends, yes. Lovers, never.

His smile turned wistful, and the smallest question mark unfurled somewhere in her middle. She drank her water to drown it.

Movement caught her eye. An older gentleman approached the entrance to the restaurant, scanning the diners.

"That's him," Kristof said. "See his lapel pin, the white eagle with a golden crown? That's a Polish emblem. Be at ease, Rose. He wants to meet you as much as you want to meet him." After this reassurance, he went to Mr. Janik with a warm greeting and an outstretched hand.

When the men returned to the table, Sylvie and Rose stood for the introductions. Mr. Janik held Rose's hand between both of his, wonder in his expression. After he spoke, Kristof translated. "I can't believe it. I see your mother in you, Rozalia."

"Really?" The tip of Rose's nose turned pink.

Mr. Janik doffed his derby hat, revealing white hair that matched his neatly trimmed beard. He touched his hair, pointed to his eyes, then at Rose.

"Your hair, your eyes," Kristof said for him, "are Magdalena's. She was beautiful. I'm so sorry you lost both your parents at such a tender age. They were good people. And so are you." Mr. Janik pressed Sylvie's hand. "You took in the only child of my friends. My thanks are not enough."

They took their seats, and Sylvie's heart swelled to see Rose drinking in every word Mr. Janik offered. She was so thirsty for information, and now, finally, she was getting it.

Plates of pork chops and buttered sweet potatoes appeared but were largely ignored while questions and stories flew through Kristof, the conduit.

Rose's tears dampened her folded and refolded handkerchief. "What else can you tell me?" she asked again and again. Surely each recollection furnished the bare room in her mind that held memories of her parents.

The Dabrowskis had lived in a large house a few blocks from the white sandy beaches of the Vistula River. Nikolai had been a tombstone carver, an honorable occupation that paid well.

"And my mother?" Rose kept her gaze on Mr. Janik while Kristof's low voice kept up with both sides of the conversation. "How did she spend her time?"

"In the usual ways. Cooking, cleaning, mending, gardening. She loved taking you for strolls on the cement walk along the river. People promenaded there every afternoon while an orchestra played. Small tables and chairs were scattered about so people could buy tea and small cakes. Your parents did that with you. Magdalena, especially, enjoyed the music. She played the violin at home."

Rose gasped. "So do I!"

Mr. Janik brightened. "Do you?"

"Yes! Mr. Bartok is my teacher! He's first chair with the Chicago Symphony Orchestra, and with the Exposition Orchestra, too."

"Well." Mr. Janik finally availed himself of the pumpkin pie. "Now you know where your talent comes from. Magdalena learned from her father."

So Rose had been carrying on a family tradition without even knowing it. Blinking back the heat in her eyes, Sylvie laughed with Rose at this unexpected revelation. It was a gift.

Around the table, coffee cooled, and ice cream pooled around each wedge of pie. Eventually, Rose asked why Nikolai came to America. In lower tones, Mr. Janik shared that Nikolai hated the Russians who had taken over their section of partitioned Poland.

"We were made to light candles in our windows

for the birthdays of members of the royal family. It was no great hardship for us, personally, but many families spent their last *kopecks* on candles when they ought to have spent it on bread for their children instead. Russian soldiers were sent to private homes to billet. These things, Nikolai would endure. But when all men of a certain age were made to serve in the Russian military—"

Kristof paused, waiting for Mr. Janik to regain his composure.

Rose remained riveted, handkerchief bunched in one fist.

The older gentleman shook his head, his face creased in a frown. "This, your father could not abide. He would not fight for the Russians who oppressed Poland. He would not join the Russian army and let other Russian soldiers live in his house with his wife and daughter. It was too much. When he left for Chicago, Magdalena took you to live with your grandmother, God rest her, until he sent word for you to join him. After you left the neighborhood, we lost touch."

Rose's chin dimpled. Nodding, she drew herself up straight, as though she'd just remembered that she was grown up now and resolved to act like it. But she was neither woman nor child, caught in that in-between place that could feel like either.

Sylvie ached for the loss of Rose's parents. She ached to think of the lovely home Nikolai and Magdalena had given up, and for the disappointment that met them after they left it. She could barely stomach that they had decided to emigrate so they could stay together, and had ended up dying alone.

"Seeing you again brings them back, Rozalia. They both would be so proud of you. Never forget that. You are a credit to them, and to the woman who raised you in their stead." Mr. Janik bowed his head to Sylvie before focusing again on Rose. "You are exactly where your parents wanted you to be. You are free, in ways that we in Poland still are not. One day, God willing, Poland will be sovereign again, rid of our oppressors. Pray for that day, sweet Rose, but never forget that you are right where you're supposed to be—here, in America. Your parents gave their lives for this."

Chapter Four

Saturday, August 12, 1893

The floor beneath Kristof's feet trembled as the elevator rose to the top of the tallest building at the Fair. Packed into the small space with Gregor and several others, he held his violin case upright against his chest until the motion stopped. Wooden bars on all four sides caged them in.

"Watch your step." The mustached operator opened the collapsible doors and stretched out his arm, inviting their exit onto the roof of the Manufactures and Liberal Arts Building.

"Relax," Gregor said as they stepped out onto the wide expanse. "We're plenty early."

But Kristof found it difficult to relax when his violin case held not just his instrument, but more cash than he'd ever carried. The price of his brother's gambling habit. "The man you owe, Johnny Friendly—how will we find him?"

Gregor smirked. "He'll find us, I'm sure." He tapped his own violin case. "We're easy to spot. See any other musicians up here?"

After the day they'd had, the rest of the orchestra was most likely ready to turn in for the night. This afternoon they'd performed to an audience of eight thousand in Festival Hall under the direction of the famous Czech composer Antonín Dvořák, in honor of Bohemian Day at the Fair. The concert had included his Symphony No. 4 in G major and selections from his *Slavonic Dances*. The applause for Dvořák had lasted an entire two minutes. As far as Kristof knew, the orchestra's former maestro, Theodore Thomas, hadn't even come to watch.

A gust of wind off Lake Michigan cooled the sweat on Kristof's brow. He made his way to the waist-high chain link fence that served as the only barrier between the roof and the ground and lagoons two hundred feet below. The searchlight in the corner flashed on and beamed a thick stripe of light across the sky. White electric lights bordering every building in sight made the Fair appear to be a city made of tiny stars. Those gathered on the rooftop behind Kristof gave a collective murmur of delight, but the dazzle was lost on him.

Gregor came and stood beside him. "It's a white city, even at night," he mused, but his tone sounded vacant. Growing serious, he turned his back on the view and leaned his elbows on the fence. "This won't happen again, Kristof. I mean it."

Bending, Kristof picked up an empty paper cup. He crushed it and tossed it in a nearby wastebin. "Actually, it will. This is only most of what you owe. We'll pay the rest after our next paycheck."

"That shouldn't be a problem. He said I had ten days to pay. It's only been eight. He's lucky to be getting this much now."

"Lucky?" The unfamiliar voice, a distinctive tenor, came from a wiry gentleman sauntering toward them with movements as smooth as a cat's, his fedora cocked slightly. "I don't call it luck to get what's mine. I call that fitting. You lost. I won. That's that."

"Johnny." Gregor nodded. "This is my brother, Kristof. You brought some friends, too, I see."

"You could say that. Say hello, fellas." He introduced the man with thin lips and a notch taken out of his ear as Tiny O'Bannon. He stood more than six feet tall, and his hands were the size of mutton chops. The shorter man of stocky build with wide-set, thick-lidded eyes was called Smokes Quinn. Cloying smoke lifted from the cigar in his mouth.

Neither said a word.

"Can we get the party started, then?" Gregor asked with a lightness Kristof didn't feel.

A red silk handkerchief gleamed in the breast pocket of Johnny's suit. "You're the ones keeping it locked up."

This wasn't the place Kristof would have chosen for such an exchange. There were no tables or chairs on the rooftop, and the wind was strong at this height. Taking a knee, he set his violin case on the platform on which the searchlight was mounted, opened it, and withdrew a paper bag of cash.

Gregor handed it to Johnny, who opened the bag and counted the bills. "You're light."

Quicker than thought, Quinn slammed his fist into Gregor's nose, the sickening sound of bone crunching cartilage stunning Kristof.

"What do you think you're—"

O'Bannon grabbed both Kristof's hands in his and squeezed so tightly that Kristof thought he might hear his own bones snapping. Pain stabbed up his arms. The pressure was building, crushing. Though every instinct told him to break free and fight back, reason told him the reward for that would only be escalating injury.

"You said ten days, Johnny!" Gregor leaned forward, blood dripping from his face. "This is our first installment, and the lion's share of the debt. We'll get you the rest on time, you have my word. You think breaking his hands will get you the money faster?"

At the flick of Johnny's wrist, O'Bannon released Kristof, who shook out his hands. He'd never felt more powerless.

A couple promenading the perimeter slowed as they approached. "I say! Are you quite all right?" The woman covered her mouth.

Gregor grimaced. "Quite." With a flourish, he whipped a handkerchief out of his pocket and held it to his nose.

The couple passed by, followed by others far more interested in what was going on below. Two pairs of young people paused at the railing to watch Venetian gondolas strung with lights carry passengers across the lagoon, then finally lost interest and moved on. Moths fluttered in the searchlight's beam and pinged against the lens.

Hands still pulsing with pain, Kristof bridled his anger. Lashing out at these men would only bring more harm. Swallowing his pride, he handed Johnny two narrow sheets of paper and a pen. "Receipts, so we have a record of having paid you tonight. Sign both and keep one for yourself."

Johnny's eyelids flared. He jerked his chin toward his so-called friends. "Tiny? Smokes?"

Smiling for the first time since their arrival, the men each took one receipt from Kristof, ripped it to shreds, and sent them swirling on a breeze.

Kristof's temper smoldered. Gregor had gotten himself mixed up with bona fide thugs. "Just the same, Mr. Friendly, we know how much we've paid and how much we need to bring in a few days' time."

Johnny stepped closer. "Your debt is paid when I say it's paid. Got it? We've no call for your records. But you won't mind if I help myself to a little insurance. Just to make sure we get the rest."

His complexion waxen in the unnatural light, Gregor balled his soiled handkerchief in his fist. "You have all the cash we could put together. We have nothing else to offer right now."

"I disagree." Johnny snapped his fingers and pointed to Kristof's violin.

Before Kristof could react, Quinn yanked the instrument from its velvet nest. "This looks valuable." He smirked around the cigar.

"Not a smart move," Kristof said. The humidity in the night air mixed with the sweat filming his skin. "That's my livelihood you're holding." It was also worth far more money than these goons could possibly guess.

"Then you'll be sure to bring the rest of the cash in exchange for its safe return, won't you? And if you don't, I'll get what I can for your fiddle." Johnny tugged the brim of his fedora.

"Don't be daft." Kristof flexed his hands at his sides. "How am I supposed to earn more money without my violin?"

"No imagination. That's your problem, not mine." But with an almost imperceptible twitch, Johnny signaled Quinn to hand the instrument back to Kristof. "Then I'll take out a different insurance policy on you boys. And this time, I'll get creative."

"What's that supposed to mean?" Gregor asked, his pitch rising.

Johnny only smiled, and Kristof went cold.

These were the wrong men to cross. The sooner they cut ties with them, the better.

From the shadows, the elevator operator called for passengers.

"Going down?" Johnny asked.

"We'll take the next," Kristof replied.

Quinn and O'Bannon made clumsy pivots as Johnny turned, and all three walked away. The elevator gate slammed shut.

"Charming friends you have," Kristof grumbled as he strapped his violin back into the case and fastened the clasps.

"You think I like them any more than you do?" Gregor refolded his handkerchief and brought it to his nose once more. "A few more days, and we'll have the rest of the money to pay them off. I wouldn't mind if I never see them again."

In that, at least, they were agreed.

"We should get going." They'd been hired to play on the Wooded Island tonight to provide ambience in the Rose Garden before the fireworks display stole the show.

Kristof curled and stretched his fingers. His knuckles stung, but he had full range of motion. Once he started playing, he was confident he'd forget about the pain.

It took them fifteen minutes to reach ground level and walk past the North Canal and the Electricity Building to reach the nearest boat landing, which was perfumed by honeysuckle and summer sweet. As they crossed the lagoon in a silent electric launch, Kristof spotted a snowy egret standing near the island's shore.

The Wooded Island was a fascinating study of man's attempt to perfectly orchestrate nature. The landscape architect, Frederick Law Olmsted, had carefully curated plants for their color, foliage, height, scent, and bloom time. On the banks, milkweed, ferns, cattails, and bulrush provided a graceful screen from the rest of the Exposition. Wildlife had been imported to add a sense of motion to the island. Kristof wondered how much it bothered Olmsted when plants outgrew the desired perimeter, or worse, died without permission. He'd heard the architect was irritated to learn the island would be divided into plots for nations to exhibit their finest flowers, with no consideration for the aesthetics of the whole.

What a challenge it must be, working with living things like that—plants and people, both. At least with music, Kristof mused, the violin always obeyed his fingers. Then again, any mistakes were his to own in full.

Once on shore, Kristof could hear a band's program wrapping up in the center of the teardrop-shaped island. It wasn't all he heard. He looked over his shoulder and saw nothing but the movement of wind through silver maple and willow branches.

"Forget something?" The glow of the lanterns highlighted Gregor's swollen nose.

Kristof shook his head. The fact that he'd heard footsteps wasn't unusual on the island. But snapping twigs and crunching leaves meant someone wasn't keeping to the path—despite the many signs instructing visitors to do so.

They passed German exhibits of tea roses and dahlias, and beds of azaleas and rhododendron from New York. Before they reached their destination, Kristof smelled the roses, their scents sharpened in the night's dew-laden air. Roses, and something else.

The unmistakable smell of cigars.

CHAPTER FIVE

Chicago had grown too big, too fast. But here on the Wooded Island, Sylvie could almost forget the crowded city's problems. Scents of exotic flowers and of rich earth damp with dew were a heady combination. Fireflies twinkled golden in the purpling shades of night, more winsome and whimsical than even the Chinese lanterns bordering the paths and gardens. A younger version of herself would have fully embraced the enchanted evening, imagining that she'd stepped into a fairy tale.

The older, wiser Sylvie looked beyond the surface of things. Before the landscape architect had begun his work, this so-called island had been a peninsula of sand dunes and mosquito-laden ponds. Then they'd dredged out lagoons and canals to create the island, and used the dug-up land to form the gently rolling hills. All this beauty had been built on twenty acres of wasteland.

"Just think, Meg." She looped her arm through her sister's. "None of this was here two years ago, and in a few months more, the spell will be broken. All the more reason to enjoy it while it lasts." Ahead of them on the paved path broad enough to fit ten abreast, Meg's husband, Nate

Pierce, walked with their twenty-year-old son, and Hazel chatted with Rose and Jozefa. Seven-year-old Olive flitted between the men and the women like a puppy in search of attention. "I'm so glad you all came tonight."

"So am I." Meg's picnic basket, long since emptied of the dinner it held, dangled from her left hand beside the lavender skirt that matched her belted jacket. Wind whispered through the cottonwood trees along the western bank and set a row of sunflowers gently nodding. "Nate has been working so much lately, and so have Walter and Hazel, which has left poor Olive alone with me for most of the summer. This is the first time we've been out as a family together in far too long. Speaking of family . . ." She raised an eyebrow. "How are things in your home these days? Rose seems to be getting along splendidly with your houseguest."

"So you noticed." Sylvie laughed. "Jozefa moves to the Palmer House Monday, and I'm sure Rose will miss her. Those two have a con-nection—a Polish one—that I can't participate in."

"Rose has been with Polish people before this. We see them every week at Hull House. What's the difference?"

A break in the trees showed the lagoon reflecting the electric lights trimming the glass-domed Horticulture Building. Italian gondoliers in fourteenth-century costume steered couples beneath the stars.

"Jozefa brings more glamour, I suppose, being an actress," Sylvie said. "Rose attended her lecture at the Woman's Building this week and then joined our tour of the Fair afterwards, going to buildings and exhibits she's seen with me before."

"Does Jozefa seem to mind the attention?"

"Not at all." Sylvie swallowed, still tasting the tea she'd sampled at the Japanese temple on the north end of the island. "In fact, she's been nothing but kind to Rose, and I'm so grateful. Rose has been more interested in her ethnic heritage lately, and Jozefa has been answering questions that I can't. They even made pierogis together."

"Oh, really? Were they delicious?"

Laughter bubbled to the surface. "Let's just say I think Jozefa has spent more time on stage than at a stove. Still, they had a marvelous time trying."

Meg chuckled.

They strolled in companionable quiet, veering off the perimeter path and onto the interior walkway. With the longest strides, Nate and Walter were the farthest ahead, while the young ladies kept their pace manageable for Jozefa.

Hazel hurried back to Meg. "Our friends from church are just over there," she said. "Walter and I will walk with them and meet you at the Rose

Garden for the fireworks, all right?" She said it all at once, without leaving space for anything to follow save a nod of agreement from Meg. "Do you want to come, Rose?"

When Rose declined, her two cousins crossed a Rialto bridge and disappeared into the shadows.

"Finally!" Olive cried, claiming her father's hand. The ribbon in her dark auburn hair matched the white sailor's collar on her dress. "I have you all to myself at last."

"Is that so?" Nate looked over his shoulder at Meg. Paper lanterns hanging from the tree branches highlighted the silver threads in his chestnut hair. At the age of fifty-two, the *Tribune* editor's steel-blue eyes still sparked with energy. "What about your mother?"

"She has Aunt Sylvie, of course!" Olive threw out her arm in a broad gesture toward where Meg walked with Sylvie.

"That she does." He offered Olive the crook of his arm and escorted her around the bend. A Columbian Guard stood at attention at the edge of the path. The black pompon topping his cap matched the five horizontal braids crossing his blue jacket.

Jozefa turned to Meg. "You have a lovely family, dear. It's a pleasure to watch you enjoy each other."

"Thank you." Meg smiled. "I'm quite smitten with them, myself."

Rose pointed to a stone bench framed by spears of iris foliage. Behind it was a bed of English phlox in stunning mixed colors. "Would you like to rest for a spell? I'm sure we have plenty of time before the fireworks begin." She glanced at Sylvie. "Meet you there? At the clematis bed."

With a grateful sigh, Jozefa limped off the path and lowered herself to the seat. "I'm not old, mind you." Indeed, she was only a few years beyond Sylvie. "It's these shoes. Not made for a walk in the woods, however smooth the trail. But you go on, ladies. We'll find you in the garden before it's time."

Sylvie agreed.

The path circled toward the center of the island, past a variety of wildflowers in muted yellows, oranges, and purples. In a small stream nearby, she heard the splash of a turtle falling off a log. Frogs twanged.

"Do you mind at all?" Meg asked.

"Mind what?" But Sylvie knew exactly what her sister meant. "I admit I'm a little surprised at how quickly they've forged their friendship. But I understand."

"We predicted this might happen. Her searching for her roots, for her family. What a miracle that Mr. Janik came forward and answered some questions for her."

Sylvie took the empty picnic basket from Meg and looped it over her elbow. "I agree. I'm so glad for her. But she told me she wishes a long-lost relative would come forward. I should have just told her that would be wonderful, since the odds of that happening are so small. Instead, I replied that a claim like that would be difficult to prove."

"She didn't like that?" Meg's glance swept over plantings of coreopsis and goldenrod.

Sylvie sent her sister a wry smile. "She said *I* was the one being difficult. So of course I felt compelled to point out that a man could approach her claiming to be kin, ask to take her out for a soda or ice cream, and never bring her home again. At least Jozefa agreed with me. Girls go missing in Chicago all the time, even more so at the Fair."

"It's terrible. You're right to be careful, even if Rose doesn't see it that way."

Their steps took them around the pavilion where the John Philip Sousa Band had been playing an hour ago. In the open space surrounding it, paper cups, napkins, apple cores, and popcorn littered the grass.

"Do you feel, in any way . . . ."—Meg waited until she had Sylvie's full attention—"rejected?"

"I don't mind her wanting to find her family history," Sylvie replied.

"Then, what troubles you?"

Sylvie caught a firefly in her palm, closing her fingers over the pulsing yellow glow. "Rose is practically lunging to launch herself out of the safe little nest I've worked so hard to provide. I'm doing my best to prepare for when she leaves for good." She released the firefly and watched it fly away. "You know how it is. They grow up so fast."

"Yes." Her sister's voice was suddenly thick. "If we're lucky, they do grow up."

"Oh, Meg," Sylvie murmured. "I'm sorry. With all the activity with Jozefa and the Fair, I forgot that we're approaching the anniversary of Louise's death. Forgive me."

"I can't imagine forgetting." Her tone was flat and held no judgment or accusation. Her steps slowed, and a couple passed them on the walkway. "Louise would be close to Rose's age, had she lived."

Sylvie knew. She ought to have been more mindful of that before confessing her dread over the day Rose would leave home. Rose was only doing the right and natural thing, exerting her independence. When she left, it would only be a change of address. There was simply no comparing that to when Meg lost Louise to typhoid.

Meg, who had been large with child in the waning summer of 1885, had been with Nate and eight-year-old Louise in the child's room. Sylvie had stayed with Walter, Hazel, and Rose elsewhere in the house. Nate's sister, Edith, had been there, too, and so had Father, bless him.

Stephen had paced a path on the parlor rug until she thought he'd wear a track into it, a prayer for his youngest grandchild ever on his lips. *"Take me instead, God. Spare the child and call me home."*

Then came the scream. Everything stopped in the house except for Meg's keening. Frightened, wide-eyed children looked to Edith and Sylvie, and Father's footsteps finally ceased in front of the mantel, where he stopped the clock from ticking, then sank to his knees.

No one knew then that he would follow Louise to heaven two weeks later.

Olive was born two days after Louise died. She came early, as if rushing to fill her grieving mother's arms. Meg was so distraught over Louise, and the birth was so difficult, that she'd barely had strength for the labor.

Meg never spoke of Louise's final hours or what it had been like to bring new life in the wake of death. Perhaps it was too sacred, or too awful. Perhaps both.

"Are—are you painting much these days?" Over the years, Sylvie had been able to gauge Meg's frame of mind by the answer to this question. Her art shows drew a crowd whenever she held them. Even more important than the income it provided, it served as a creative outlet that both soothed and filled her spirit. Meg needed to paint as much as Sylvie needed books.

"It's been a few weeks."

Sylvie tried to hide her concern. "Then, I take it, it's been hard for you this year." The anniversary of Louise's death, she meant, but didn't say again.

"It's hard for me every year, Sylvie." Meg stretched her fingers away from her palms, a practice she'd maintained to combat the relentless pull of scar tissue after her hands had been burned during the Great Fire. Surely the scars on her heart contracted no less. "One does not simply get over the death of one's child."

"That's not what I meant."

Crickets chirped. An electric lamppost illuminated the palette of plants and trees behind it. Pine trees released their spicy scent into the air.

"I know." Meg sighed. "Thank goodness for Olive Louise. God granted me another daughter when I needed her most. The Lord takes away, and He gives."

"Yes, Olive is a gift, indeed."

Music floated toward her as they approached the entrance to the Rose Garden. "Have you been here yet?" Sylvie asked.

Meg's smile, though forced, showed a valiant effort. "I haven't. Please, Miss Tour Guide, tell me all about it."

Sylvie squeezed her arm in understanding. If her brave sister was willing to find relief—or at least distraction—in roses, Sylvie was happy to share. As she led her sister beneath a gigantic burr oak tree and through the north gate into the garden, she told her that this one-acre rectangle held two thousand varieties of roses on fifty thousand bushes, but that wasn't all. Bordering the entire space were pink and yellow hollyhocks, blue larkspur, and purple-speckled foxgloves.

A violin duet accompanied their stroll between beds of flowers from California, Germany, the Netherlands, Pennsylvania, Kentucky, and Chicago. Sylvie pointed out favorite varieties she thought would catch her sister's beauty-loving fancy, from the light yellow tea rose Perle des Jardins to a creamy pink one called Grace Darling.

Smiling, Meg bent to smell each one, lingering over a bright pink hybrid perpetual called American Beauty. "How charming," she said. "This color is incredibly rich."

Sylvie watched her study the petals without touching them, though she could tell Meg itched to do so. "Why don't you try capturing that color on canvas?"

"I'm not a botanical artist." Meg straightened. "I paint people. Life."

"Then paint life. You're surrounded by it, you know." Sylvie extended her arm, palm raised. People of all walks of life, ages, and ethnicities had gathered in a rose garden for the promise of fireworks on a summer night.

"Real life," Meg said. "Not artificially orchestrated displays."

She'd made a name for herself in the Chicago art world with her first art show twenty-two years ago, depicting scenes from the aftermath of the Great Fire. The next show displayed the Great Rebuilding of the city. Ever since then, she'd been painting humanity in all its beauty and frailty. Her series on the Hull House neighborhoods was hanging in the Woman's Building right now. Meg painted what she cared about, and in turn, the painting cared for her, too.

Which was why Sylvie wouldn't back down. "The setting may be artificial. The people here are not."

Meg pressed her lips flat, and Sylvie gently guided her toward the four beds of clematis in the center of the garden.

"There you are." Threading their way between other fairgoers, Nate and Olive joined them. "You look thoughtful, Meg. What did I miss?"

Sylvie prayed she'd just found an ally. "I was just telling Meg she ought to bring her paints to the Fair and capture some of the scenes here. What do you think?"

Nate raised his eyebrows. "There would be no end to the possibilities here, that's certain."

"And can you imagine how popular your paintings will be?" Sylvie pressed. "Photographers need to pay for a special license to take pictures, but there's no restriction on painting."

"Let's be practical, Sylvie," Meg replied. "Not all of us have a season pass like you and Rose do. Outside the White City, times are hard."

Nate slipped his arm around his wife's shoulders. "Times are not so hard as that. We can pay your entrance fees if this is what you want to do. With Walter, Hazel, and me working all day, it would do you good."

Sylvie heartily agreed.

Olive touched her mother's elbow, dismay written in her expression. "Do I have to come and watch you paint?"

Sylvie jumped in before Meg could use Olive as an excuse. "Just come on the days I'm here, and I'll make sure you have fun, Olive. I know all the best places to see. Have you ever heard of a knight on horseback—made solely of prunes? I can show that to you in the California building. What about a castle made of soap? That's in Manufactures. In the Agriculture building, you can find a building made from corn, a chocolate statue of Christopher Columbus, and a map of the United States made entirely of pickles!"

Nate laughed. "And here I thought you might show her something educational. Not that a map doesn't have value."

Olive wrinkled her nose. "But it's summer!"

Sylvie bent. "It's all right, honey. Tell me what you learned about this year."

"George Washington."

"Perfect. The Virginia Building is an exact replica of his home, Mount Vernon. What else?"

"Well, Christopher Columbus, of course."

Of course. Sylvie expected all schoolchildren in Chicago had studied the explorer in honor of the World's Columbian Exposition. "We could see a replica of the *Santa Maria*. It sailed across the Atlantic to get here from Spain."

Olive raised a delicate eyebrow. "We also learned about the six days of creation and the animal kingdom."

"The birds of the air, the fish of the sea? We can visit the Ostrich Farm and Hagenback's Animal Show on the Midway, and the Fisheries Building has all kinds of fish, plus a shark and octopus and electric eels. Perhaps a camel ride would be in order, too?"

Green eyes rounding, Olive spun toward Meg. A tendril of hair blew across her face and she tucked it behind her ear. "Can we? The World's Fair in our own city *is* a once-in-a-lifetime opportunity, after all. For both of us!" She grinned.

"Well! When you put it that way, how could I resist?" Meg said. To Sylvie, she whispered, "Are you sure you have time to entertain Olive?"

"I have no tours scheduled for Monday, and the store is always closed that day. Why don't we plan for then?"

The violin music stopped, which meant the

fireworks would be starting soon. White moths fluttered near the evenly spaced lanterns, and fireflies blinked above the blooms.

"Over here!" Olive waved, and Sylvie followed her line of sight, smiling when she spotted Rose and Jozefa making their way toward them. Olive sprang forward and clasped Rose's hand. "My mother and I are coming back to the Fair soon. While she paints, Aunt Sylvie is going to show me a castle made of soap and a map of pickles."

"She is?" Rose straightened the bow on Olive's collar. "That sounds like a lot more fun than the tours I've been on with her."

"Do you want to come?" Olive asked. "My father says I have to see something educational, too, but we might also ride the camels, so it would be worth it. You can come with us if you want."

"Only if I can ride a camel, too. Would you make room for me on yours if I asked you nicely?" Rose waggled her eyebrows, eliciting laughing agreement from Olive.

"If you come with us, sweetheart, we'll even ride Mr. Ferris's wheel," Sylvie promised.

Rose drew herself up tall, propping one hand on her hip. "Deal! It's high time, after all." She grinned at her own play on words, then squeezed Olive's hand. "You won't be scared, will you, Olive?"

This was the Rose Sylvie was accustomed to. Warm, engaging, ready for adventure but still looking out for others. Taking a cue from the young woman, Sylvie approached Jozefa, who was admiring a waterfall of mauve clematis blooms tumbling over a trellis. "How are your feet holding up?"

"They're protesting." Jozefa chuckled. "But I'm ignoring them. This garden alone is worth any discomfort. I've never seen anything like it."

Sylvie supposed no one had. "I'm so glad you're enjoying it. I know Rose has especially enjoyed your company this last week." She added, "I appreciate it, too. I've done my best with her, but—"

Jozefa raised her hand, lantern light catching on a garnet ring that matched the jewels in her ears. The burgundy jacket she wore shimmered over a white shirtwaist ruffled at the neck. "You've done your best, period. That's all anyone can do. She's lucky to have you, and no matter how it may seem, she knows it."

Sylvie smiled her heartfelt thanks.

A boom cracked through the night, commanding everyone's attention. Applause accompanied the starburst of red embers. Inhaling the overwhelming sweetness of this place, Sylvie watched her family take it in. Nate held Meg close, his spectacles reflecting the light. Heedless of getting her skirt dirty, Rose knelt beside an awestruck Olive, her puffed sleeve pressed into her cousin's shoulder as she pointed up.

But not everyone was looking skyward. One man was riveted by—Rose. When his gaze met Sylvie's, he looked away with such sharpness that she wondered at it. There was something about him that registered. *Ivan?*

Sylvie stepped around Nate and Meg to get a better view of him. He was walking away from her now, ignoring the second burst of fireworks in the sky.

She heard Nate hailing Walter and Hazel, then guiding Meg and Olive toward them. She didn't follow. Instead, she maneuvered between clusters of people, moving tentatively after the man who had been watching Rose.

CHAPTER SIX

Fireworks blasted the sky, the sound reverberating on the buildings bordering the lagoon. His violin once again secure in its case, Kristof looked over his shoulder for Quinn, the stocky Irishman with wide-set eyes, quick fists, and a penchant for strong cigars.

"Ready to go?" Kristof asked his brother.

"Are you kidding me? There's nothing waiting for me back at the apartment that trumps a fireworks show. Relax."

Relax. With a nose that might have been broken by that gambling goon a few hours ago, this was the best advice Gregor had. Did he really fail to understand they were likely under surveillance even now?

"Find me if you change your mind. I need to stretch my legs." Kristof also needed to see if he could draw Quinn out—if, in fact, he truly was spying. Kristof couldn't imagine the motive, unless they suspected the Bartoks had more cash and were hiding it.

Smoke drifted down from the explosions in the sky. It was easy to weave through the crowd, since they were almost all standing still or sitting on folding wooden chairs that had been set out for the show.

When fireworks boomed, he watched for anyone who appeared uninterested, and wondered what he would do if he did confront Quinn again. If it came to a fight, Kristof would lose. He had no delusions about that. But perhaps, surrounded by so many witnesses, he could simply question Quinn without coming to blows. He'd assure the skittish bully that he hid nothing and would pay in due course, just as he'd said he would.

Another boom from above shed eerie green light over all the upturned faces.

And there he was, at the other end of a smoking cigar. It was almost as though he wanted to be found, the way he stood staring at Kristof. A small orange glow flared and faded, marking his presence.

Right, then. No use pretending they hadn't seen each other. Setting his jaw, Kristof headed toward him, crunching caramel-coated popcorn beneath his shoes. Quinn made no sign of slinking away.

Before Kristof could reach him, however, a woman to his right gasped quietly. He looked again.

Sylvie Townsend looked back. "Oh! Kristof. I wondered if that was you and Gregor playing." She nodded to the violin case he held, but she was visibly shaken.

"Sylvie? Are you unwell?" He offered his arm should she need steadying.

She took it. "I thought I saw someone. Someone

who didn't want to be seen. I may be mistaken." She was ghostly pale.

Kristof peered into the shadows but no longer spied Quinn anywhere. Just as well. "Are you . . . is there anything I can do for you?"

She said there wasn't. Still, he guided her to an alcove made of climbing roses, which he hoped would make her feel more secure, less exposed.

"Please tell me you're not alone." He wished he could read her face. All he could see was a pair of fine eyes shining like obsidian and the contours of her cheekbones and chin.

"My entire family is here. You can see Rose, just over there. She's standing between my two nieces. You remember Olive and Hazel?"

Of course he did. Rose's blond hair and light-colored dress made her stand out in the crowd. She bent like a willow branch to hear Olive, then straightened, spoke to Hazel, and laughed with her. "They're having a wonderful time, I'd say." He paused. "And you're not with them."

"I should be. I just—like I said, thought I saw someone. But I was mistaken, so it doesn't matter."

Her voice had always affected him like music. The more he heard of it, the more he wanted to hear.

"I've been meaning to ask you," she said. "I heard that Theodore Thomas resigned from directing the Exposition Orchestra. Is that true?"

"That and more." An explosion of blue and orange fireworks lit the sky.

Sylvie beckoned him to join her beneath the rose-laden arbor. He sat on the bench beside her and briefly explained what had happened while assuring her she could expect to receive her rent as usual. If Quinn was still listening, he'd learn only the truth about their financial situation. He had nothing to hide.

"I'm not worried about the rent, Kristof," she replied. "And I'm not surprised about this development, given that the Fair still hasn't earned back what it has spent. But did you know about this on Thursday, when you treated me, Rose, and Mr. Janik to your concert after lunch?" When he hesitated, she pulled on his arm. "You did! Oh, why didn't you tell me?"

"And spoil the afternoon?" He clapped a hand over hers. "Honestly, I wasn't keeping secrets from you. I just didn't want to ruin the joyous mood."

"But what will you do? You were counting on that income until the symphony season begins, weren't you?"

"There are a few more concerts scheduled that must go on as planned, most of them accompaniments to the Festival Choir. I also managed to secure some odd jobs around the Fair and Midway for Gregor and myself. Please don't worry, Sylvie. If things are tight for my brother and me, that's our problem. I won't let it be yours." She discounted their rent in exchange for Rose's lessons. Kristof wouldn't repay that with unpaid debt.

"I know." A smile flickered. She reached up and tugged his bow tie askew, and he straightened it back into place, fully aware she was teasing him. Fully charmed that her little game, which she had started a year ago, still amused her.

"Speaking of things we meant to say," she went on, "I'm sorry for Rose's tardiness at last week's lesson, and for the scene we treated you to. I wish I could promise it won't happen again, but—" She stopped herself, shoulders sloping slightly. "I wish a lot of things. I wish I was better at this. Parenting, that is."

"You're better at parenting than you think you are," he told her. "Don't—how do you say it? Don't call yourself short."

The corner of her lips lifted. "You mean, don't sell yourself short."

Mild embarrassment flared beneath his collar, but he'd long ago asked her to correct his speech when necessary. His mother had been English, and he'd studied languages at the university— a requirement for any musician aspiring to international success—but American idioms had never been part of the curriculum. "Yes. Don't *sell* yourself short. Your love for her is evident, and that's more than countless children experience." It was more than he had growing up, by far.

"Thank you."

"You're welcome."

Kristof rose, and so did she. He saw in her a longing for family and belonging he recognized in himself. It was an ache so deep he habitually denied it was there at all, just so he could survive it. He glanced toward Meg's family and Rose. Not one of them looked around for Sylvie. He wished, for her sake, one would.

They emerged from the perfumed alcove together, and he scanned for Quinn. Though he could no longer smell his cigar, Kristof remained wary. Had he said anything he'd regret Quinn overhearing? For a few moments with Sylvie, he'd forgotten about Gregor and the gambling debt and the Irishmen they owed. Now it came rushing back to him.

"Sylvie." He touched her back to make sure she heard him amid the applause. "Unless you're going somewhere after this, Gregor and I will accompany you and Rose home. Naturally," he added.

She returned his smile. "Naturally."

By the time Kristof finally retired to bed two hours later, he was exhausted to the bone. He turned out the light and closed his eyes, only to see pieces of the day dance across his eyelids. To the tune of a Slavonic national folk song, images of Antonín Dvořák mingled with visions of the White City by day and night, Gregor and his bloody nose, gondolas on the lagoons, flowers and fireflies. He saw Sylvie and Rose. And three Irish thugs.

Not exactly the images he preferred as he fell asleep. Rolling onto his side, he swept his mind clean and tried to focus instead on the heavy-laden breeze wafting through the open window.

No good.

Kristof sat up, swinging his legs over the edge of the bed, his fingers digging into the mattress. As he replayed the events of the evening, he grew even warmer than the summer air on his skin.

Cicadas thrummed. Rising, he moved to the window and looked for the glowing orange tip of a cigar. Didn't see it. But maybe Quinn just wasn't smoking right now, or O'Bannon had taken a shift. Kristof exhaled slowly and ran his hand through his hair. Once followed, always suspicious, he supposed. With reason.

He'd been as careful as he knew how to be when he and Gregor escorted the ladies home. They'd changed course a couple of times, Kristof blaming the crowd for the redirection. He'd made use of passing streetcars and omnibuses to obscure their path. They'd even stopped at a diner for a late-night snack until he and Gregor could be sure they weren't being followed.

But what if he had still inadvertently put everyone in this building in danger by leading Quinn here? He might have put Sylvie in danger as soon as he paused and spoke to her. There'd been no choice about it, for ignoring her was impossible. Ignoring his true feelings for her, however—that, he'd learned, could be done.

Had he led a wolf to her door tonight?

Until the Irishmen had been paid off, Kristof ought to sleep with one eye and one ear open.

From the Hoffmans' apartment above him, he heard shuffling feet and water running through pipes in the wall. Nothing out of the ordinary there, since neither Karl nor Anna slept straight through the night. From Sylvie's apartment below, he could hear stirring. It was probably the cat playing while she stayed up reading *A Tale of Two Cities*.

Not a bad idea. He slid his own copy from the small table beside his bed and reached for the lamp. But when a snore sounded from the other side of the wall, Kristof decided to pay a visit.

In Gregor's room, Kristof turned on the lamp in the corner and cast a disgusted gaze on the dirty laundry strewn about the room. An apple core on the windowsill would be covered in fruit flies by morning. But he hadn't come here to clean.

He shook his brother's shoulder and sat on a wooden trunk opposite the bed. "Out of all the people in this building, why should you be the only one enjoying an untroubled sleep? Especially after what happened tonight."

Gregor groaned. "You call this *untroubled?*" He put a pillow over his head. "Go away."

"We need to talk about Johnny Friendly and his henchmen."

"Lovely people once you get to know them," came the muffled reply.

It was almost funny. In two strides, Kristof was at the bed. He pulled the pillow off Gregor and used it as a cushion on the trunk. "Much better."

"Not from here." But Gregor sat up and squinted at Kristof. "So talk, if there's anything else to say. We paid what we could, they know we'll pay more by the deadline. End of story."

"Not end of story. End of chapter. Now turn the page. What happens when we meet again to pay the rest of our debt, and Johnny says we owe more?"

"What makes you think we won't be in the clear by next week?"

Typical Gregor. All his life, his attitude toward the law of cause and effect was nonchalant at best. He'd been scolded before, slapped on the wrist, but never suffered lasting consequences. This was different.

Kristof flexed the hands Tiny O'Bannon had nearly crushed. "A man who shreds receipts is not concerned with an accurate reckoning. Didn't you hear what he said to me? He said our debt would be paid when *he* called it paid."

"Sorry, I must have been too busy trying not to drip blood on my tuxedo."

"Another red flag, perhaps?"

Gregor wiggled his nose. "Good as new. You thought he busted it, didn't you? Guess I'm stronger than you think. Or luckier."

Luck again. There was no such thing. "You're a fool, Gregor."

His brother chuckled. "But I'm *your* fool. Good night." Grinning, he slipped back under his sheet and faced the wall. In a moment, he was snoring again.

Beneath Gregor's carefree façade, a more thoughtful, selfless version of the man resided. If only he didn't make that side of himself so hard to find.

A framed photo on the bedside table showed the two brothers when they were seven and sixteen years old, both holding violins sized to match the scale of their arms. One of them was smiling.

It wasn't Kristof.

He still remembered why.

That morning, the two brothers had played their recital pieces for their parents in the parlor. The recital was still several weeks away, and Kristof had been struggling to master a piece Gregor played with his eyes closed and only half trying. Humiliated by his mistakes, Kristof had stumbled through the piece beneath the cold weight of his father's disapproval.

When Gregor got up to play, he astonished everyone by making mistakes, as well. It was likely as difficult for Gregor to play the wrong notes as it had been for Kristof to find the right ones. At the age of seven, Gregor had adored his older brother. This was his way of trying to protect him from their father. He had sabotaged his own piece in order not to outshine Kristof, who had been playing for years longer.

Even so, Gregor's performance was better. Anyone could tell the misplaced fingers had been deliberate. At the end of it, Father had berated Gregor for not playing to his potential, striking the boy's palm so hard, so repeatedly, that Kristof's hands had stung in sympathy. *"When he was your age, Mozart played for Marie-Antoinette. Who do you think you could play for with these sloppy hands?"* he had railed.

By the time Father stopped, Mother was weeping, but Gregor hadn't made a sound, though his face was mottled pink. *"He'll need to hide his hand behind his back for the photograph now,"* she'd told Father. *"We don't want a bandage in the image."*

Father remained unmoved. *"Maybe we do. May it serve as a reminder of what happens when he does not perform his best."*

Kristof picked up the photo and peered at the

image of his little brother smiling despite the pain. Perhaps he had even smiled because of it, in defiance. This image had captured far more than Father had intended. *"Why did you do it?"* Kristof asked him later.

"I thought it might help Father love you," Gregor had replied, *"if he wasn't so busy loving me."*

It was a warm memory of Gregor's selfless act, and a terrible memory of his own deficiencies. His little brother was already better than him, loved more than him. And Gregor knew it. They both did.

Quietly, Kristof set the frame back on the table, watched Gregor roll onto his back, and wondered if his nose might be broken after all.

CHAPTER SEVEN

Monday, August 14, 1893

Sylvie couldn't remember the last time she had laughed this hard.

It had started as a giggle behind her gloved hand, Meg smiling beside her as they watched their girls climb onto a kneeling camel in Cairo Street on the Midway Plaisance. If ever there were a time to wear the bloomers the dress reformers were pushing, this would have been it. As it was, Olive and Rose sat sideways on the blanketed beast, in a saddle that offered little security.

"Come on, Mama," Olive called to Meg. "There's another camel for you and Aunt Sylvie!" Smoke billowed out from under an awning, carrying the aroma of strong, exotic spices.

Rose laughed. "I'm not sure Aunt Sylvie is quite adventurous enough for this."

"No matter," Meg replied as she sketched. "We much prefer the view from right here."

Dancers in bright flowing robes threaded through the crowded street, clicking castanets as they went. Musicians strolled behind them, playing some kind of horn, stringed instruments, and a drum so loud the rhythm reverberated through Sylvie's chest.

Wearing a long white gown with a dirty, threadbare hem, the camel driver prodded the animal with a stick to stand. It repaid him with a warbling shriek the likes of which Sylvie had never heard. It was so loud that it drowned out all but raised voices, and it didn't let up. After the initial shock of the sound faded from Rose's and Olive's faces, they shook with laughter. Even Meg had paused her drawing to wonder at the camel's screech.

At last the beast made to stand, but it started with its back legs first, pitching the girls forward, Rose leaning on Olive, and Olive nearly leaning on the camel's neck while gripping the metal ring on the saddle with all her might. They yelped in surprise, then with unbridled hilarity as the camel delayed the rest of his job. If the girls were to let go, they would dive headfirst into the street, or at least somersault off the camel's curving neck.

Once Sylvie was confident they wouldn't let go, she laughed so hard her sides hurt, and tears streamed down her face. "Oh, Meg!" she gasped. "Please, please paint this scene, I beg of you."

Laughter broke free from Meg, too, her shoulders bouncing while their daughters and the camel shrieked.

"Up up up!" The camel driver tugged on the crimson tasseled rope tied around the animal's muzzle, and it finally complied. The girls tipped toward the rear this time before settling back in place.

Wiping her eyes, Sylvie followed them over the rough pavement, Meg trailing behind, scribbling along the way. Her notebook was filling up with studies of the narrow roadway, a turbaned snake charmer with his serpent coiled in a basket, and balconied houses.

Sylvie slowed her pace so as to walk nearer to Meg, sharing the shade of her parasol. "This is the most authentic concession on the Midway," she told her. "Do you see the lattice-like woodwork that makes up the balconies on the houses? It's called *mashrabiya*, and those aren't reproductions. They were purchased from homeowners in Cairo whose houses were slated for demolition, then shipped here, along with three hundred and fifty Cairo residents, their camels, donkeys, monkeys, and a variety of other materials."

"That's fascinating." Meg's gaze darted to the camel carrying Olive and Rose, then up to the laundry flapping on a clothesline strung between the upper stories of two houses. Behind that, obelisks soared heavenward, marking the entrance to the recreated Luxor Temple. Chanting filled the air as a procession of costumed Isis priests of ancient Egypt paraded by. "It's all fascinating. I'll need to come back a few more times to get it right."

An Arab child ran by, stick in hand, chasing a donkey past booths in a bazaar. Sunshine glinted on jewelry for sale. "I was hoping you would," Sylvie told her. "And this is just the beginning. Keep bringing Olive, won't you? We'll have lots of time to learn things in the exhibition buildings later, but the weather today is perfect for outdoor activities."

"Like standing in line for Mr. Ferris's wheel?"

Sylvie grinned. "I did promise them. Besides, we're practically right next to it already. You'll ride it with us, won't you?" The camel driver began leading the girls back.

Meg hesitated. "I've already spent fifty cents for Olive and me to enter Cairo Street, and another fifty cents on the camel ride. Two tickets for the wheel will cost another dollar. Really, I ought to remain on terra firma and save fifty cents. I'll stay busy sketching. You go with the girls."

Of the two sisters, Sylvie had always been the one to count the costs, reckon accounts, and calculate risks. But it didn't surprise her to hear Meg pay strict attention to budgeting now, too. Since June, almost five hundred banks across the country had suspended operations, including a couple of large ones in Chicago. The Erie and Reading Railroad companies had both gone bankrupt, and millions were out of work nationwide. The depressed economy had flattened everyone's pocketbooks.

When the girls returned, Sylvie explained the plan to them as she handed back their parasols.

Olive latched on to Meg's elbow. "Please, Mama! I want you to come with me. You can't imagine what you'll see from up there! Won't you want to paint that, too?"

Meg's resolve was clearly cracking, so Sylvie pressed. "We'll save money elsewhere. Lunches at restaurants cost between fifty cents and a dollar, for the most part, but we can get Vienna Sausages at a snack counter for ten cents. And when we come back to the Fair on other days, we'll bring our own food."

Rose discreetly nodded her approval, but Sylvie was sure it was Olive's silent pleading that ultimately closed the case.

Meg bent and kissed her daughter's cheek. "You win."

"Do you know something?" Rose said to Olive. "When you smile like that, you look just like your mama."

Olive's grin broadened. She looked from Rose to Sylvie, then back at Rose. "Why don't you look like yours?"

"Actually, I do," Rose said. "But my mother died, remember? I don't resemble your aunt because we're not related."

"Biologically," Sylvie told Olive. "But we're still family. Just like your dad and his stepsiblings are still a family, even after their parents died.

Families are born, but they can also be chosen. I chose—I choose—to love Rose as my own. She *is* my own."

Olive tilted her head toward Rose. "And you chose Aunt Sylvie."

"I was younger than you when my father handed me over," Rose answered. "I wasn't given a choice."

Sylvie's cheeks burned. Since their meeting with Mr. Janik, Rose had swung between grateful and pensive, still wishing for a blood relative to materialize. Sylvie ought to say something right now to unravel the sudden tension between them, but it coiled so tightly that she wasn't sure how. What Rose had said was true, and Sylvie sympathized. But the fact that she'd said it aloud, while saying nothing of their mutual affection, smarted.

Meg wrapped an arm around Rose's slim shoulders. "We all love you, dear. More than you could possibly know."

Simple words, gently spoken. Comforting and perfect. Meg was gifted in nuance and sensitivity. Sylvie wasn't. She was bristly where Meg was soft, cool when Meg was warm. Would Rose love her more if she could shape herself into her sister's likeness?

Nonsense. Rose had been glum this morning after Jozefa moved out of the apartment and into the Palmer. Her discontent had less to do with

Sylvie specifically, and everything to do with sorting out who she was and who she wanted to be.

By the time they'd finished lunch and were next in line at the bottom of the wheel, however, Rose's angst had receded before the towering adventure before them. It was impossible not to be thrilled by its colossal size. The wheel was taller than any building in the United States, save for a handful in Chicago and New York. Thirty passenger cars, as big as streetcars, each held up to sixty people. Encasing the wheel was a structure with wide stairways to platforms at staggered elevations, so that several cars could be loaded and unloaded at once.

"Get ready, Olive, here comes our car!" Rose took the little girl's hand in hers while Olive bounced in excitement.

The wheel slowed, then halted as a car hovered at their level. At platforms up and down the wheel, doors opened and passengers streamed out. Blue-uniformed conductors stood at the thresholds of their cars. "All aboard!"

Olive claimed Meg's hand, too, and the three of them climbed into the car. Sylvie followed.

"Step right up, ladies and gentlemen, for the ride of your life! My name is Marvin Lindstrom, and I'll be your conductor, your tour guide, your doorman, and your security guard for the duration of the twenty-minute ride."

111

"Twenty minutes?" echoed a woman beside Sylvie.

"That's right, ma'am, you get two—I said *two*—full revolutions for your maximum enjoyment of this wonder of the world. It takes twenty minutes, and you'll wish it were longer."

"Over here!" Olive waved to Sylvie. "I saved you a seat."

Sylvie sat beside her in a rotating metal chair attached to the floor and waited while the car filled. The quiet was charged with anticipation, if not flat-out awe.

"That'll do!" Marvin boomed as he closed the door and locked it. "As you can see, ladies and gentlemen, you need not fear claustrophobia here. The ceilings are a generous nine feet high. You are free to move about the car and enjoy the views as you wish. The wire over the windows is for your comfort and protection. There is no danger of falling out, no chance of a madman jumping out, and no way a bird can fly in."

With the smallest lurch, the wheel began rotating. Sylvie held on to her seat at the completely foreign sensation of being suspended above ground.

Olive grasped Sylvie's hand as they climbed higher and higher into the sky. Then all at once, the little girl leapt up and ran to the window where Meg stood. "We're so high!"

More people grew brave enough to stand and

move about the car, Rose among them. Commanding her queasy stomach to still, Sylvie joined her at a window that faced west. A light sheen of sweat broke out over her skin. The ride was smooth enough, but there was so much air, so much nothing between their car and the ground.

She put her back to the window. Perhaps she wasn't quite as daring as she'd thought.

"Having fun, Mimi?" Rose grinned.

Sylvie placed a hand on her waist and defied the turbulence within. "Rose, Meg was right when she said that we all love you. I love you more than I can say. Do you know that?"

"I do."

That was something. Feeling bolstered, Sylvie faced the window again. While Marvin droned on about the 825-foot circumference of the wheel, the people on the Midway grew slowly smaller.

She frowned. "Rose." She pointed at a man watching the wheel, his hands stuffed in his pockets. "Isn't that Ivan Mazurek?"

Rose squinted. "I think it is. He lost his job at the stockyards recently. I wouldn't be surprised if he were after a little cheer, or at least a distraction."

Strange. The Midway Plaisance didn't have an entrance fee like the Fair did, but with all the concessions and dining, it was still an expensive place to be for a young man fresh out of work.

"He's looking right at our car," said Sylvie.

"Did he know you would be on the Midway today?"

"I don't see how he could have. We certainly didn't make arrangements for a rendezvous." She brushed a wrinkle from her skirt.

"Do you suppose he comes to the Hull House Players' practices just to watch you? Have you considered he may come to Readers Club just for you, too? He never contributes to the discussion. If he is enamored with you, dear, you must be careful not to lead him on."

"Enamored? You think he's enamored with me?" The slightest blush crept up Rose's neck and into her cheeks. "If he is, I had no idea." Her hand fluttered to her collar.

"I get the feeling he's following you, and I don't like it. Have you done anything to encourage him?"

Rose folded her arms across her pleated bodice. "You know my every move. I'm rarely out of your sight, so you tell me. Couldn't he just happen to be on the Midway along with thousands of others? Why wouldn't he see this wheel? It's the biggest attraction at the Fair, even if he can't afford a ticket."

They were nearing the apex of the ride. Dizziness buffeted Sylvie, and she held on to the rail to steady herself. As they descended toward the east, she could see miles of blue Lake Michigan.

She didn't care. Squeezing her eyes shut, she leaned against the rail with her jaw locked until they were lower.

"You sound so paranoid," Rose said. "Your father was this way, too, wasn't he? So maybe it runs in the family, but there is no reason to be so suspicious."

The remarks stung. Her father had only wanted to protect his daughters, a desire that sharpened and strengthened after the war. She understood that now more than ever. If Ivan was gone by the time the wheel started to ascend again, she'd drop the matter.

Two slow minutes later, Sylvie peered out through the wires meant to keep them safe. Ivan wasn't where he'd been standing earlier. He was half hidden behind a soda-water stand but still watching. She waved at him. He didn't return it. Brow folded beneath the brim of his cap, he looked sullen. Why?

Sylvie's imagination exploded with possibilities. Truly, she had no desire to be overly suspicious, but as a parent, wasn't that part of her job, to be aware of hidden dangers?

Rose shaded her eyes with her hand, her lace-trimmed cuff sliding on her wrist. The bruise Sylvie had spotted more than a week ago was gone. Sylvie's questions weren't.

"I need to ask you something." The car swayed gently, and Sylvie widened her stance. "Are you sure the mark on your wrist was from Walter trying to keep you inside the Ice Railway car?"

Eyebrows plunging, Rose faced her. "What are you asking, exactly?"

"I'm asking if it could have been Ivan—or anyone else—who laid a hand on you." And if she ought to be more worried than ever.

"You're asking if I lied to you. If you don't believe me, that's your problem, not mine." Spine stiff, Rose stepped around Sylvie to join Olive, and her demeanor immediately changed. "What do you think, honey? Ready to go around once more?"

Sinking into a chair, Sylvie pressed a hand to her temple. Metal squeaked as Meg sat beside her and rotated toward her, notebook on her lap. The folds of her jade-green skirt brushed Sylvie's knees. Her pencil poked out from above her ear, a habit she'd picked up from Nate. "What's wrong?" she whispered.

What wasn't wrong? Sylvie glanced at the girls, who had moved to the other side of the car. Men and women shuffled around them. "Oh, I've irritated Rose again."

"It'll blow over. Girls this age seem to be on an emotional pendulum. Hazel was the same way and sometimes still is. She'll come back to you."

"She called me suspicious. Like Father was."

Meg's eyes softened. "Are you?"

"I begin to wonder. Ivan Mazurek is down

116

there, watching Rose. I thought I saw him in the Rose Garden during the fireworks, too."

The ride was ending soon. Meg slid her notebook and pencil into her bag and slung the strap over her shoulder. "You know what to do. Examine your fears, and if they're baseless, discard them."

She made it sound so simple.

Sylvie was still considering this when the wheel stopped at the bottom and everyone left the car.

Persian sword dancers demonstrated their skills in the street while Meg, Sylvie, and Rose popped their parasols open again. Olive spun in a circle. "What's next?"

Rose checked the timepiece pinned to her shirtwaist. "I'm afraid I must be going if I'm to get to my violin lesson on time."

"On a Monday, dear?" Meg asked.

"Mr. Bartok had rehearsals all day last Friday for the Dvořák concert, so we rescheduled it for today. I checked my violin at the Casino before we met you this morning." She turned to Sylvie. "I'll see you at home later this afternoon. Or, if I'm not there when you get back, I'll be at the Jane Club for dinner with Tessa, and I'll meet you at Readers Club." Her hard stare held a challenge.

"I understand," Sylvie said calmly, willing herself not to scan the crowd for Ivan again. "I'm so glad you could spend so much of the day with us, Rose. I'll see you later."

Rose stepped back, only by a foot, but Sylvie felt a new distance fall between them. "One more thing, if you please. My name is Rozalia. It's time we call each other by our real names, don't you think?"

"If that's what you want, of course. Rozalia."

"Thank you, Sylvie, it is."

Rose walked away, leaving Sylvie, speechless, behind.

CHAPTER EIGHT

Sylvie could hardly wait for the Hull House Readers Club to be over. Rose had never come. But Ivan had.

After an hour of halting discussion about *A Tale of Two Cities*, she dismissed the group and then signaled for him to stay. The seams of his shirt strained at his shoulders, and he looked miserably out of place against the grey-and-yellow floral wallpaper behind him. Framed works of art hung from the picture rail circling the room.

"Yes, Miss Townsend?" Sweat dotted his brow. It was suffocatingly hot in the upstairs room of the Butler Gallery, the building adjacent to Hull House on Halsted Street.

"I thought I saw you on the Midway today." Her voice lifted as though in question.

The young man twisted his hat in his broad hands. "I was there. But I didn't do anything wrong."

Sylvie fingered the frayed corner of her novel's cover. She hadn't meant to put him on the defensive. Maybe he really was just a harmless, lovesick fellow who was even worse with conversation than she was. She could understand that. Maybe he even appreciated literature but simply wasn't confident enough to comment.

"Actually, I'm glad you were there," she tried again. She needed him to feel at ease if he were to share anything helpful with her. "I wonder if you saw Rose after our ride on Mr. Ferris's wheel."

He shifted on the chair. The patched newsboy cap in his grip had already lost its lining. Now he was battering it to a pulp.

"I hope you did," she rushed on. "I was expecting Rose to be here this evening. The last I saw of her was on the Midway." Sylvie had stopped at the Jane Club apartment building already, but Tessa had told her Rose had never come.

He stilled. "You mean she's missing?"

So far Sylvie had managed to keep that word at bay. "She could be at home even now," she admitted. "I just thought I'd ask if you happened to see her after I did."

A pleat formed between his eyes. "I saw her go to the Fair, but I didn't go in."

"So you did see her get in through the gates, at least?"

He seemed hesitant but finally nodded. "It wasn't right, Rozalia going alone like that. I wanted to go in and keep an eye on her myself, but I—I didn't have the money with me. For a ticket. Did you really send her in there alone? Was her cousin waiting to meet her, or Miss Wright?"

Sweat trickled from the nape of Sylvie's neck

to her collar. "I'm sure she's home right now. Perhaps she felt ill."

She rose, clutching her book. Part of her wanted to ask him what he'd been doing, watching them like that without coming to say hello. The rest of her cared about one thing only: getting home and assuring herself that Rose was fine.

So with a brief thank-you and farewell, she descended the stairs, hand gliding over the black walnut rail, and rushed out onto Halsted Street. The usual odors pinched her nose, but she was so distracted she didn't even bother with her lemon-verbena-scented handkerchief as she waited for the streetcar at the corner. Flies buzzed over mounds of rotting garbage in the gutters. In an upper-story tenement, a couple quarreled, glass broke, a child screamed. Babies cried weakly for milk. In front of a saloon, a cluster of men argued in languages Sylvie couldn't understand.

Her pounding pulse made all of it sound very far away.

Kristof didn't need to eat another bite. But when Anna Hoffman offered her famous homemade Berliners, resisting was futile.

"Come, dear." Anna set a plate of the pastries in front of him. Plaited silver-gold hair crowned her head. "I made these just for you, a small reward for all those lovely concerts you give us. You'll only hurt my feelings if you don't eat them."

"Woman!" Karl Hoffman dropped his fist on the kitchen table in mock dismay. "You'll hurt *my* feelings if you give those all away! What do you say, Kristof? We can share these, ja?"

Kristof patted his belly, imagining how it would strain his belt if he ate everything Anna offered. "I wouldn't have it any other way."

Gregor was missing out, wherever he was. The Hoffmans were rare and giving souls, as eager to hear whatever Kristof would share as he was to hear any stories they wanted to recount. Often they spoke German together, the official language of the Austro-Hungarian Empire, which Kristof had left for America.

Knocking cut through the conversation. "Anna? It's me, Sylvie."

Something was wrong. Kristof heard it in the urgency of her tone. He swallowed and wiped his mouth while Anna answered the door.

"Hello, Anna, I'm actually looking for Kristof." Sylvie's voice sounded sunken and distant. "Is he here?"

He was already on his feet, smoothing a hand down his shirtfront to dispel any crumbs. Anna led Sylvie inside. She clutched her hat in front of her waist, bending the brim.

"What is it?" Kristof moved toward her. "What can I do?"

She was even paler than she'd been that night on the Wooded Island, her pressed lips a colorless portent. "Did Rose come to her lesson this afternoon?"

The question alone was not alarming. But paired with her agitation, it dropped a stone in his gut.

"Yes," he told her. He did not say she'd been distracted and played poorly.

"Did she say anything about where she was going after that?"

"She did not." Kristof held her red-rimmed gaze.

Karl exchanged a startled glance with Anna. "You'd better sit down, ja?" He leaned over and shoved out a chair for her. The blue braided chair pad peeked out from under the yellow cloth that covered the table.

Sylvie wouldn't sit. She paced from the kitchen into the parlor, cinching her grip on a hat that would never be the same. Kristof had seen her do this once before, when Rose was ill and not responding to the doctor's treatment.

Anna followed her. "I take it you haven't been able to ask her yourself."

"She's not home. She didn't come to Readers Club like she said she would, and she didn't have dinner with the Jane Club, which she also told me she planned to do." She crossed to the window and stared out.

From where Kristof stood, he could easily see what she saw. The granite courthouse building, wrapped in columns and topped with porticoes, filled the view. The structure grew ever darker with the setting sun. Soon homeless men would begin trickling over streets striped with cable car rails to find their spot of floor space in City Hall's corridors, in which they'd spend the night.

"It's dark. And I don't know where she is." Sylvie spun around. "I'm afraid. Tell me not to be if there is no reason for it, but right now, I am terrified. Am I wrong to feel this way?"

She wasn't wrong. But Kristof didn't want to say so.

Anna gathered one of Sylvie's hands in both of hers. "Could she have gone to your sister's?"

Sylvie shook her head. "If she had, Meg would have sent word."

With a grunt, Karl pushed himself out of his chair. "The police, then. We've got to file a report." He passed a hand over his pate, combing his thinning hair from right to left.

"Karl, wait." Kristof stayed him. "The police won't file a report unless someone has been missing for at least forty-eight hours. I saw Rose at three o'clock today, so we have to wait another forty-two and a half hours before they will listen to us."

Karl muttered in German as he stiffly retook his seat. Sylvie looked outside again.

A pigeon landed on the windowsill. Streetlamps shone, marking the official beginning of night.

Anna turned on a lamp to chase the shadows away, then lowered herself onto a sofa. Lines etched her face.

Kristof wouldn't sit until Sylvie did. "Something was clearly bothering Rose during her lesson, but it didn't seem the right time to inquire, rushed as we were." If anything, he had urged her to set the circumstances of her day aside and focus on the music like a professional.

"I know what was bothering her." Sylvie's posture flagged for the first time since entering the apartment. Dropping the mangled hat to the rug, she sank onto a cushion beside Anna. "Me."

Straightening a pillow on the armchair, Kristof sat across from the women, burdened with the knowledge that it was he who had last seen Rose, as far as they knew. The cuckoo clock clicked on the wall behind him.

He should have made sure Rose had a chaperone waiting for her after the lesson. He should have seen her to safety himself. Those Columbian Guards had become a joke on the fairgrounds, after all, incompetent at even clearing a restaurant at closing time. No one was laughing now.

"This is my fault. Could this be my fault?" Sylvie rested her head in her hands.

"Now, now," Anna crooned, spreading her hand over Sylvie's back. "I doubt that."

"I said the wrong thing. Again. She told Olive

that her real mother died, and I was so hung up on convincing her that *I* love her that I didn't acknowledge her grief for her own parents, at least in words. I know better than that!" She marshalled her composure. "I lost my own mother and father. I understand that grief."

Kristof leaned forward. "Telling Rose you love her is never a mistake."

"But my timing came across as dismissive. I'm so sorry she lost both her parents. That's what I should have told her. But I'm not sorry that raising her fell to me." She looked at Kristof, guilt lining her brow. "She's right about me, after all. I'm not like a real mother. Mothers are not this selfish. No wonder she stopped calling me Mimi today."

"What's this?" Anna's surprise reflected Kristof's.

"She asked me to call her Rozalia, and then she called me—Sylvie." She spoke her own name like a plucked string, untuned.

Kristof longed to comfort her, to snap the pieces of her world back in place. Instead, he left her to Anna's motherly ministrations while he made a study of his hands, from the indentations on his finger pads from violin strings to the nails he'd just trimmed.

Oh no. Johnny Friendly. O'Bannon. Quinn. They'd tried to confiscate his violin as collateral for the rest of the debt Gregor owed them, then realized the folly of that plan. *"Then I'll take out a different insurance policy on you boys. And this time, I'll get creative."* Had Quinn heard Kristof talk to Sylvie on the Wooded Island? Had he seen them pointing out Rose, or even followed them home despite their precautions?

Sweat sprang beneath his collar. This wasn't Sylvie's fault, it was his—or at least that was a possibility too strong to be ignored. They would know the police wouldn't search for a missing girl for at least two days. Their next meeting to pay the rest of the debt was exactly two days from now, after the Midway Ball. Kristof wasn't sure which was harder to believe: that all of this was a coincidence, or that it wasn't.

"All I want is for Rose to be safe," Sylvie went on. "Then she can call me a skunk cabbage, for all I care. But this not knowing where she is or if she's all right . . . I don't know how I'll endure the uncertainty until the police will accept a report, let alone after that. I do know I can't just stay here."

From the kitchen, Karl cocked his head, brows sinking. "What do you intend?"

Sylvie looked from him to Kristof with as much doubt as determination in her expression. "I'm going to look for her myself at the Fair. Many of the exhibitors know us from my having given so many tours. I'll ask if they've seen her. She's hard to miss. Either Tessa can mind the store on her own, or I'll close it. Either way, I'm searching first thing in the morning."

Madness, Kristof thought. Not including the exhibitors and staff, the visitor attendance was between fifty and seventy thousand every day.

But he said, "I'll go with you." There was no way he would let her take this on alone.

Karl's chin bobbed. "Quite right."

Anna exhaled, visibly relieved.

Sylvie's eyebrows arched. "You will?"

Of course he would. "This is what friends do, Sylvie." Or had he misunderstood their relationship entirely? He didn't expect love, but he had supposed there was a measure of loyalty between them. "Besides, not everyone you'll want to question speaks English. Would it not be helpful to have an ally who speaks Hungarian, German, Polish, Czech?"

Her shoulders relaxed. "It would be. I hadn't thought of that. Thank you."

She wasn't used to needing help, he realized. Given all she'd accomplished on her own, she was even less accustomed to asking for it.

"Do you have time?" she asked him.

"More than ever. My next performance isn't until Wednesday night. By then, either Rose will be back, or you'll be able to get the police involved."

Anna absently traced the crocheted lines of a doily with her finger. "Sylvie, dear, did you check her bureau? Are any of her clothes missing?"

"I would feel better if they were. But no, her room is just how she left it this morning. Wherever she is, she has her parasol, her violin, but no changes of clothing or nightdress."

"She could still come back tonight, then, couldn't she?" Karl lumbered from the kitchen, the arthritis in his joints slowing his pace. "She is young. Hasn't she been late before?"

"Not like this," Sylvie whispered.

Anna closed her eyes, the lines smoothing on her face, and placed one hand on Sylvie's knee. Karl pulled Kristof into the little knot of neighbors until they were all entwined, Karl touching his wife's shoulder, Kristof resting his hand on Sylvie's. Sylvie bowed her head, fingers digging into her hair.

"Gracious Father," Anna prayed, "Good Shepherd, one of your lambs has gone astray. Keep her safe, make her strong. Lead her back to where she belongs, and make her paths straight. Show us what to do while we wait. Give Sylvie peace. Help us trust you and entrust Rose to your care."

Kristof added his amen to the chorus that followed.

"Thank you." Sylvie embraced Anna, then rose and hugged Karl, too. "I needed that." When she turned to Kristof, he steadied her trembling hands in his. "And thank you, Kristof. Meet me in the store tomorrow morning when you're ready to go?"

He nodded, aware he still held her hands in a way he never had before. Her eyes and touch told of a woman barely staying above a rising panic, a woman who had lost her moorings and fought for faith in the dark. That he could be to blame for that in any way made him sick. He had to make this right.

"You're not alone, Sylvie," he told her.

She withdrew, and he watched her go, presumably to her empty apartment, just as he would return to his.

Chapter Nine

Tuesday, August 15, 1893

Morning had not come soon enough.

Rose's absence took up space in the apartment, siphoning air from the atmosphere. Every tick of the clock had marked a new worry. Was Rose trying to get home in the dark? Was she happy to be gone? Was she hungry? Afraid? Unanswered questions had crawled beneath Sylvie's skin, merciless and unreachable, stealing any chance of slumber.

Each moment was burdened, laden with the necessity of hope and a terrible imagining of the worst.

When Rose had first come into Sylvie's care, the little girl had proven her love for exploring. While Sylvie worked in the bookshop, leaving Rose with her father in the apartment, Rose had wandered off, just as she'd done in the Polish neighborhood when Nikolai was at the stock-yards. That first time, she'd found her way to the Hoffmans, who had fed her pastries and returned her to Sylvie before she even knew the little girl was gone. It had been a shock, but there'd been no time for fear.

At least, not that time.

A year later, Rose had gotten all the way outside the building and across a busy street. A policeman found her on Court House Square and brought her back, but not before Sylvie noticed she was gone. She still cringed when she recalled shouting at Stephen out of the deepest fears she owned, and his tearful, anguished response. He'd dozed off in his chair for a few minutes, he'd said. He hadn't slept much the night before. But a few minutes was all it took.

Sylvie had known terror before, running from a wall of fire destroying the city. Losing a five-year-old child in Chicago rivaled that. When the policeman escorted Rose home, a lollipop in her hand, Sylvie had been so overcome that she'd collapsed to her knees, unable to speak while she clasped Rose to her.

"Don't cry," Rose had said, wiping the tears from Sylvie's cheeks with sticky, sweet fingers. *"I only wanted to see. I was coming back for you."* Then she'd demanded that the policeman give Sylvie a lollipop, too. *"She's been through a lot,"* Rose told him, echoing what she'd no doubt overheard Sylvie saying about Rose.

Everything that could have happened to Rose had haunted Sylvie. Was it Stephen's fault for not watching more closely? Was it Rose's fault for wandering away again, after being told not to? Possibly. But Sylvie was to blame for trusting either of them. For not managing Rose's safety herself.

This morning, by the time Tessa had arrived and agreed to mind the store on her own for the day, Sylvie had already dusted, straightened, reckoned accounts, refreshed the window display, collected and arranged the Hoffmans' baked goods on glass-domed pedestals by the cash register, and placed an order for more inventory. When Kristof appeared, she whisked him out the door.

Eight miles later, they stepped off a crowded cable car and entered the Midway beneath a sky bunched with clouds.

Kristof drew Sylvie's hand through the crook of his elbow. "I suppose you've prepared a list of folks you want to talk to." His long strides had no trouble keeping up with her brisk pace.

"I have. The first one is Meg. I need to tell her what's going on. She mentioned she was coming back to paint Mr. Ferris's wheel this morning, before the crowds get too thick." They walked past the Hungarian Orpheum and Lapland Village on their right, and the American Indian Village on the left. "She may be there already."

"Good. I'm sure she'll want to help."

"She'll want to. But she has responsibilities with her own family, too." As they passed the Austrian Village, golden-crowned fräuleins in laced-up dirndls trickled through the entrance on their way to work. "In a way, I envy you and Gregor. You have so much in common, and you've forged a life together you're content with. I remember when Meg and I imagined we'd remain spinster sisters living above the bookshop to the end of our days. We wanted to be like Jane Austen and her sister Cassandra. Their mother once said they were 'wedded to each other.' "

He chuckled, the sound almost too low to hear. "Interesting choice of words. Gregor is the only family I have left, but there are days when I am reminded that when God said it wasn't good for man to live alone, He didn't give Adam a brother."

Any other day, Sylvie would have laughed out loud. Today, she barely smiled. "Don't tell me Gregor is not your perfect helpmate."

"Not by a long way."

"You mean, a long shot."

He winced at his mistake. "Ah, yes. A very long shot, indeed."

Sylvie patted his arm consolingly. Her stomach soured on the smell of coffee coming from the Vienna Cafe. She'd had too much of the stuff this morning, with no food to support it.

"Do you see her?" Kristof peered through the men and women gathering around the wheel's ticket office.

"There." Sylvie's middle clenched. "She brought Olive. I thought she was leaving her with her aunt Edith today." Her voice trailed away beneath the bawling of an uncooperative donkey near the Cairo Street entrance.

"Why don't I stop at the Fire and Guard Station, give them a description of Rose, and see if they know anything?" Kristof suggested.

Sylvie agreed. "Show them this." She opened the chatelaine bag hanging from a silver clip hooked to her belt and withdrew a small framed photograph of a smiling Rose. "It was taken on her birthday this year."

He took it.

Sunshine broke through the clouds, casting long geometric shadows from the giant metal wheel. Walking through them, Sylvie reached Meg and Olive.

"Aunt Sylvie!" Olive lunged to give her a hug. Her hair smelled like lavender soap, her pleated dress like starch.

Paintbrush in hand, Meg spun to greet her. "Well, this is fortuitous! Edith came down with the flu and couldn't take Olive this morning. I know you weren't expecting to, but do you have time to watch her for a bit? My work bores her to tears, and I can't paint and keep an eye on her simultaneously."

"I want to see the giant map made of pickles today!" Olive spread her arms as though to reach from sea to sea. "Will you take me?"

Sylvie swallowed. "I wish I could. But, Meg—" She hated what she had to say next.

Meg lowered her paintbrush. "Sylvie?"

That was all it took for everything to grow blurry. "Rose didn't come home last night."

"What?" Meg set the brush on the easel's ledge and came closer.

"What do you mean?" asked Olive. "Where did she go instead?"

"Well, sweetheart, that's what I'm here to find out. Mr. Bartok is here to help me." She didn't want to say much more for fear of upsetting Olive. "I'd like to talk to Walter and Hazel, too."

"They're both working today." Meg's voice held restrained alarm. "Come for dinner tonight, and you can have as much time with them as you need." She glanced up as Kristof approached. "Both of you would be most welcome."

"I still don't understand," said Olive. "Where is Rose? Can she at least come tonight for dinner?"

Sylvie forced herself to answer her. "I—she—it is my dearest hope that she can."

Meg pulled out a notebook and began sketching a portrait of Rose from memory. The emerging likeness was remarkable. "I'll canvas the Midway with this. See you tonight."

Gratitude washed over Sylvie. After embracing her sister, she kissed Olive on the cheek, told her to stick close to her mother, and left the Midway in Meg's capable hands.

"You're not going to talk to anyone else here?"

136

Kristof asked as she hurried east on the main thoroughfare.

"For now, Meg will do it. At least all the ticket takers speak English. This gives us more time on the fairgrounds, since that's where Rose was last seen. What did you learn at the Fire and Guard Station?"

"Nothing yet." He handed the framed picture back to Sylvie. "I showed them the photograph, gave them Rose's physical description and where we saw her last. If any guard has any information, they'll telegraph it to all the stations around the fair. We can check back later at any one of them."

It was a start.

Sylvie hooked her arm through Kristof's and remained quiet as they passed various concessions. Everything felt monumental. The Midway and the Fair. Her feelings. The stakes.

After a while, Kristof spoke. "I wish I could snap my fingers and magically hand you all the answers you need. Waiting is more trying than searching."

An understatement. "I've waited for things before," she reminded him. "When my father was in the prison camp and then later the asylum, we waited for him to be restored to us." She'd shared these chapters of her life with him eighteen months ago—sparingly at first, even haltingly, gauging his reaction.

Then she'd shown him her father's published memoir, which Nate had edited and filled in with facts and explanations. Kristof had purchased it on the spot and stayed up late into the night to finish it. The next morning, he'd said, *"I wish I'd known him. Stephen loved his family imperfectly but absolutely. He never stopped trying to be a better man. And you were his biggest ally in that, ever since the Great Fire."* Sylvie had scoffed a little, saying he couldn't have read that in the book. But he'd held her gaze, insisting it was there. *"I saw you behind the lines."* If what he'd meant to say was "between the lines," she hadn't corrected him. For the last fourteen years of her father's life, she *was* behind the lines in the sense that she battled for his welfare, the recovery of his wounded spirit.

Sylvie looked at Kristof now and saw the same earnestness he'd worn then.

"Those were painful seasons of uncertainty, but at least we knew where my father was," she went on. "This situation with Rose is completely different."

"I know it is."

As they neared the Fair entrance, children in crimson uniforms cried out above the din of the crowd, selling overpriced World's Fair guidebooks.

"I assume we'll go to the Casino and see if she

checked her violin back in to the cloakroom," Kristof said.

"We will, but that's clear on the other side of the grounds, by the lake. We'll stop in the Woman's Building first, as it's just past the Viaduct. If you want to split up, you could head toward—"

His brown eyes sparked with golden flecks. "Sylvie, I am not leaving you, do you understand me? I am here as much for you as I am for Rose." There was an authority to his voice he hadn't used with her before. "We don't know what happened to her. God forbid anything should happen to you, as well." His hand covered hers in a gesture that pushed at the edge of friendship toward something else.

Only when they approached the ticket gate did they separate and show their individual season passes. While Sylvie waited to be admitted, Kristof stood just on the other side, watching her intently. Though he wasn't in concert attire, his posture was no less commanding.

Heat rippled over her, but when she reached his side, she was ready to take his arm once more. Had he ever looked at her in quite this way before? Her stomach flip-flopped as it had when she rode the wheel yesterday, lifting off solid ground.

She should have eaten breakfast.

From the gate between the Midway and the Fair, it was a short walk east to the Woman's

Building. Already, ladies could be seen on both the ground floor loggia and upper-level balcony, which wrapped around the building for a view of the White City. A red silk shawl marked Susan B. Anthony, surrounded by admirers, as usual. The seventy-three-year-old suffrage heroine had come to speak in May and decided to stay all summer.

Passing into the shade as they neared the door, Sylvie led Kristof inside and made a sharp left into the salesroom before they reached the rotunda. They weaved between tables displaying souvenir spoons, plates, and bookmarks—all of which bore likenesses of either the Woman's Building or of Bertha Palmer—past racks of postcards and books, and finally to the back corner, where they took their place in line behind women waiting to check their parasols or request a guide.

Five minutes later, they reached the counter.

"Hi, Dorothy," Sylvie greeted her colleague, then gave her a nickel for that day's issue of *The Daily Columbian*. The paper held all the news of the Fair, from schedules of music concerts and lectures to any special events. "Do you have any copies from yesterday?"

Dorothy ducked behind the counter and came up with an issue creased through the middle. Tortoiseshell combs shone in black hair just a shade darker than her skin. "Here's one. Most of

the events listed in it are in today's issue, too."
She wheezed, a reaction, she'd said, to the twenty
thousand plants beautifying the Fair.

"I'd still like to have it, if that's all right. Is
there a charge for it?" Sylvie was pretty sure it
was garbage to anyone else, but it might hold a
clue as to where Rose had gone.

Dorothy slid her spectacles up the bridge of her
nose. "Help yourself." She sneezed.

"Sylvie?" Beth Wright poked her head
around the corner from inside the check room,
brightening when she saw her, then clouding
when she saw Kristof standing so close. "Excuse
me, Dot." Budging past Dorothy, Beth swung
open the half door to step into the salesroom.

Quickly, Sylvie told her their mission.

"Missing?" Beth repeated, her complexion
paling a little. A mop of russet curls completely
obscured her forehead. "Oh dear. Of course we'll
keep a lookout and tell the rest of the staff."

"I need to speak to Jozefa," Sylvie added. "I see
she's on today's schedule to give another lecture
in the Assembly Room upstairs, but do you know
if she's here early?"

Dorothy called from behind Beth. "Jozefa
Zielinski? She told me she was headed to one of
the sitting rooms before her lecture."

"Perfect. Thank you." To Kristof, Sylvie
whispered "shortcut" and led him through the
salesroom, into the adjoining one, and out to

the stairway, completely bypassing the exhibit-packed rotunda.

On the gallery level, they found themselves on a balcony corridor, overlooking the exhibits below. Ignoring those, they passed the Assembly Hall, then took the corridor that led to various reception rooms.

Kristof looked behind him as they entered the Japanese Parlor. Light glinted on painted silk screens and hangings. The walls were covered in depictions of white-capped waves, cherry blossom trees, snowy egrets, and misty mountains. Three Japanese visitors spoke in their own language, while an older fair-skinned woman was pushed about in a wicker rolling chair. Jozefa wasn't there.

"Next." Sylvie brought Kristof into the next reception room, this one named for California. Polished California redwood gleamed from the paneling on the walls, the ceiling beams, and the parquet floors. Flanked by cactus plants in terracotta pots, a giant mirror doubled the space.

"There." Sylvie found Jozefa, who sat in a corner in a brown-and-burgundy gown, conversing with another lady in Polish. Sun poured through the floor-to-ceiling window behind them, casting their silhouettes upon the floor, along with the shapes of cacti etched into the glass panes.

Stepping around a huge bearskin rug, Sylvie

approached them while Kristof stood back and kept an eye on the door.

"Jozefa?" Sylvie wiped her palms on her skirt. "I'm sorry to interrupt you."

The actress smiled and folded her hands. The lace trim on her high collar brushed her jawline. "Sylvie. So good to see you. The Palmer is a fine establishment, indeed, but I've missed the company at yours." The other woman politely took her leave.

Grasping for what to say next, Sylvie lowered herself to the armchair near Jozefa's. A handful of stiffly starched ladies strolled into the room, guidebooks in hand, then left again almost as quickly. "I wonder," she began, "could you tell me, has Rose—Rozalia—come to see you?"

"She's welcome to any time, of course, but I haven't seen her since I left your apartment yesterday morning."

Sylvie broke from her probing gaze. She glanced to the painting of Lake Tahoe on the wall across from her, then to Kristof. He nodded to her, and she continued. "I would never ask you to break Rozalia's confidences if it weren't important. But she didn't come home last night. Has she said anything to you that might help us know where she is?"

"She didn't come home," Jozefa repeated. Her expression hardened with judgment, not for a wayward adolescent, but for the woman who had pretended to be her mother.

Or perhaps Sylvie only saw a reflection of what she felt about herself. If she had handled Rose differently, if she had said or not said certain things, she was sure she wouldn't be here right now, telling a near stranger she'd lost her daughter and feeling crushed by guilt and fear.

When Jozefa spoke at last, her voice was soft with compassion, not condemnation. "Your daughter has said many things to me, Sylvie, but none of them led me to suspect something like this. Has she done anything like this before, to get attention?"

Sylvie held back a laugh. "No. If anything, she'd say she gets too much attention as it is. But I don't believe she would do this just to prove she can make it on her own. She took no clothes with her, no money that I know of."

After Sylvie explained what had been done to find Rose and what would be done soon, Jozefa raised her chin and straightened her shoulders. "If she contacts me, or if I learn anything, I'll send word to you right away. Likewise, would you do the same for me?"

"Of course."

Jozefa kissed her cheek, and Sylvie took her leave.

"Let's go." She took Kristof's offered arm. "She doesn't know anything."

They reached the stairwell and met a tide of people coming up. Kristof angled his body, pushing through them, allowing her to follow in his wake.

At the ground level, Sylvie told him to head for the south exit, and he forged their path through the Gallery of Honor, around statues, past wood carvings and paintings in oil and watercolor. Passing through an arch, they wound between displays of women's work from all over the world and finally stepped outside.

She squinted, and he took her parasol, opening it and holding it above her.

Panic swirled and eddied about her, causing a dip in her knees. She steadied herself on Kristof's arm, then headed east, toward the main path along the lagoon. "Next stop, Administration Building. I want to put a notice in the bulletin for fairground tour guides."

"Certainly." He made no comment on the tremor in her voice, and she was grateful. She was scared. He knew it. There was no reason to point it out.

Kristof cleared his throat. "I heard that a young lady architect designed the Woman's Building. Is that right?"

She confirmed that it was.

When he asked about the exhibit they'd passed featuring a woman missionary to Siberia, and then inquired about the woman who invented an automatic dishwasher on display, she narrowed her eyes. "Are you trying to distract me from the fact that we're here because Rose is missing? Or are you really interested in these women?"

His eyebrow twitched up. "I'm interested in some women more than others." He patted her hand.

She managed to summon a small smile for her friend.

CHAPTER TEN

Balancing a glass of iced tea on his knee, Kristof caught Olive's eye as she peeked around the corner. The little girl had been banished from Meg and Nate's parlor while the grown-ups spoke after dinner, but she clung to the edge of it. He smiled to signal he'd seen her.

"I just can't believe Rose would do this on her own," Hazel was saying. She'd just arrived home from working at Marshall Field's department store and still wore her black skirt and white shirtwaist with faux-pearl buttons and puffed shoulders. "She left no note, sent no word?"

"Nothing," Sylvie replied. "All we know is that she didn't check her violin at the Casino after her lesson. Wherever she is, she has it with her—or she did, at least for a while. When we arrived back at the bookshop this afternoon, Tessa had no news for us."

Frowning, Meg stretched her hands before resting them on her lap. "I talked to every ticket taker on the Midway this morning. None of them recalled seeing Rose after she left the Midway around two o'clock." She draped an arm behind her younger sister. "Rose was short with you at the Fair yesterday, Sylvie, but nothing you said to her could have possibly driven her to do such a thing."

"Which leaves us with far worse options to consider." Nate removed his spectacles and rubbed the bridge of his nose.

"Should we expect someone to demand a ransom?" Hazel offered. She twirled a long brown lock around her finger.

"I'd gladly give it." Sylvie adjusted her skirt over her knees. "I'm short on cash, like everyone else, but I could cut my inventory. I'd sell the store itself if I had to."

Kristof squinted in thought, ran the pad of his thumb over the condensation on his glass. He leaned forward, elbows on his knees. "We're missing some pieces to this puzzle."

Olive sat quietly on the other side of the doorframe. With a curled finger, Nate beckoned her to him and kissed her cheek. "Olive, sweetheart, go play in your room until one of us comes to get you. And close the door. No eavesdropping."

Her lower lip fluted. "I already know something happened to Rose. Maybe I can help! I have good ideas."

"Olive Louise," Meg said quietly. "No arguing. Go."

With a puff of frustration, she did.

"We don't have time for this," Sylvie blurted as soon as Olive's footsteps faded. "Someone has taken Rose, and I have no idea what they plan to do to her or when."

If she truly had no idea, that was a mercy. The Columbian Guards he'd spoken to this morning had minced no words with their own speculations. Girls disappeared from Chicago all the time. From the streets. From train stations. From the Fair. Cab drivers were paid to deliver unsuspecting girls to an empty apartment where they would be "broken in" and then delivered to the brothels to perform the only kind of work they'd ever be good for again.

Kristof was sick at the idea. For any girl, let alone his own violin student and Sylvie's daughter.

A hair ribbon, possibly Olive's, lay discarded on the floral rug at his feet. He picked it up, spooled it around his index finger, and set it on the table beside him. "There's another alternative we haven't considered," he began. "Love. Or the illusion of it." He turned to Hazel. "To your knowledge, could Rose have fallen in love with someone and run off with him?"

While Hazel pondered this, Sylvie shook her head. "I seriously doubt it. I raised her better than that."

"You raised Rose better than to fall in love?" A hint of laughter rode Hazel's words.

"Better than to hide things from me, for one. And yes, I had hoped I'd raised her with a realistic view of romance, love, and marriage. It isn't always as fine as novels make it out to be."

And there it was again. Any time Kristof imagined their friendship deepening, Sylvie found a way to emphasize that romantic love wasn't necessary for a fulfilling life, a stance she likely assumed he shared.

He used to.

Lips pressing thin, he looked away from her. Meg sent him a gentle smile.

"You're right," Meg said to her sister. She took Nate's hand. "Sometimes, if you're very fortunate, it's better."

Kristof believed her.

"Walter." Ignoring Meg's comment, Sylvie faced her nephew. A few curls of caramel-brown hair coiled at the nape of her slender neck. "Almost two weeks ago, I noticed a bruise inside Rose's wrist. This was the day she went around the Fair with you and Hazel. When I asked her about it, she told me you'd ridden the Ice Railway together and that you grasped her wrist to pull her back inside when the car flew around a corner. Is that true?"

Walter shoved his fingers through his straw-colored hair. "It is, Aunt Sylvie, and I gripped her pretty hard. But I'm not the only one who grabbed her wrist that day."

The color drained from Sylvie's face. "Go on."

Meg speared her son with a gaze particular to

mothers, then cast the same upon Hazel. "Tell us everything."

Hazel dipped her chin and slid him a sideways glance. "We didn't think much of it at the time. Someone outside the Hungarian Orpheum complimented Rose and asked her if she would be a waitress. She said no."

Kristof set his jaw. He didn't like where this was going. "And then?"

"He caught her wrist and tried to pull her closer to him. She gasped, like he was hurting her."

"I was right there, though," Walter rushed to add. "I put an end to that, and we moved along. That was that."

"Not exactly." Hazel scratched a spot behind her ear. "Rose turns men's heads without even trying. I suppose her coloring made her a favorite of the Germans, as well, because another man tried recruiting her to work in a beer garden. He didn't touch her, though. It happened so quickly, I'm not surprised Walter didn't notice."

Sylvie's complexion burned a deep red. "What are we supposed to do? Keep our daughters locked in a tower like Rapunzel?"

"Sylvie," Meg said softly. "This isn't your fault."

The setting sun washed the parlor with blushing, watery light. Kristof drained the last of his drink and set his glass on a newspaper on the tea table. "I have an idea." It wasn't much, but it was worth a try. "Gregor and I are playing at the Midway Ball tomorrow night. People from every village, settlement, theater, bazaar, and café on the Midway have been invited to attend. It's the perfect opportunity to talk to them all in one place, in the course of an evening, without needing to pay to enter their concessions for access to them. I'll be there anyway, so I can question them about Rose. How do you say it? Two birds with one stone?"

Sylvie sat taller. "Is it by invitation only?"

"No," Kristof replied. "Anyone can purchase a ticket, but—"

"I'm going." Her tone brooked no argument, despite the fact that her limited language skills would put her at a disadvantage with the Midway crowd.

But that was where he came in.

"We'll go together," he said.

CHAPTER ELEVEN

Wednesday, August 16, 1893

Beth Wright blustered into the bookshop just as Sylvie was closing up at five. A whirlwind unto herself, she released a gusty sigh while flapping her straw hat at her face. "Please say you have news of Rose."

Batting a mosquito away, Sylvie locked the door before returning to the counter. "Not yet."

Beth's brow compressed as she followed her. "Oh no. I can't believe this! She can't have vanished into thin air," she sputtered. "Did you tell the police?"

"I did."

"They better put their best detective on the case. A young girl like Rose, why—I shudder to think what might have happened." Her heat-flushed complexion paled. "But they'll find her. Or we will."

Sylvie had to believe that was true. She told Beth about yesterday's efforts on the Midway and at the Fair, and the possibilities they'd discussed at Meg's house. "I'm going to the Midway Ball with the Bartoks this evening to see if I can find out anything from those in attendance. Kristof will translate."

Beth leaned against the counter while Sylvie hurried to finish her bookkeeping. "Ooh. That's a good idea." She paused. "Be careful how much you rely on him. You say the two of you are only friends, but I'm not sure he's on the same sheet of music on that score anymore, if you know what I mean. I saw the way he looked at you Monday."

"And how was that?"

"As though you're a damsel in distress and he the knight in shining armor. But we're a little too old and wise for that now, aren't we?"

"For which part?" Sylvie fought to keep the irritation from edging her voice. "Too old to need help? Too old to accept it?"

Beth cocked her head, mouth screwing into a button. "Too mature to rely on a man for rescue. We've always agreed on this."

They had. Before she had been widowed, Beth's marriage had slowly siphoned the vigor from her. Her husband never laid a hand on her in anger, but neither had he touched her in love. As a girl and young woman, Beth had dreamed of escaping an overbearing father by marrying out of his household. In her rush to leave, she'd unwittingly wed a man who had only been interested in the property that became his with the match. He'd tolerated her opinions during their courtship, but ridiculed, then silenced her after they'd wed. Beth had always insisted she didn't mind being barren, but Sylvie had wondered if there was a different reason, too private and humiliating, behind her childlessness. She could think of few things worse for a woman than to be trapped in a loveless marriage.

"Just watch out," Beth said. "Pretty soon he'll decide friendship isn't good enough and propose to you, and if you marry him—or any man— everything you own becomes his. The book-store, the apartment building, your money. Your time. Your very self. All of it suddenly transfers ownership, and you're left begging for crumbs."

Sylvie could understand where Beth was coming from. She also saw that her friend's experience colored her view of every man. "Beth," she said gently, "no one is thinking of marriage."

"I should hope not. I should think a suffragette would know better than to yoke herself to one of *them.*"

The naked disdain demanded response. "I don't need to think less of men to believe that women deserve the right to vote, do I? Many men share our views on suffrage. Remember Buffalo Bill?"

It had been the talk of the Fair. Earlier that summer, Buffalo Bill Cody had sent box-seat tickets to Susan B. Anthony for his Wild West Show, held just outside the official fairgrounds. With the packed stands watching, he'd entered the ring on horseback, galloped up to her box, and halted. In a cloud of dust, he'd removed his white hat from his grey head and bowed to her so low that his nose almost touched the saddle horn. She had stood and returned the bow, then waved her handkerchief with unbridled glee. Sylvie wished she'd been there to see it.

"I can be faithful to our cause without dis-respecting men," she continued. "I don't require a husband to be a complete person, but neither will I tread on men in order to elevate myself."

Beth gave her a look that implied she would do enough treading for both of them.

"But to your point," Sylvie said, "Rose needs help, and I'll take any kind I can get."

"All right, if you say so. I'm just worried about Rose, and now I'm worried about you, too." She reseated her wilting hat.

"And you said *I* worried too much."

"I was wrong. It was the right amount, or not enough. I've got to run now, dear. The Hull House Players have an extra practice tonight. We're trying out a replacement for Rose. While I'm there, I'll ask if any of them know anything that could point to where she is. Good luck tonight!" She bussed Sylvie's cheek and whisked away.

After locking the front door again, Sylvie pulled the shades and called to the cat, who scrambled up the stairs before her.

The quiet in the apartment pulsed in her ears. Sylvie was exhausted, not having been able to sleep more than an hour together since Monday.

More than that, she was frustrated that after two days, there had been zero progress in the search for Rose. Was she hungry? Was she in pain? Was she afraid? Did she wonder why Sylvie hadn't come to save her? The same questions beat their path through Sylvie's worn-out brain. If she let herself, she could surrender to panic and be utterly swept away by it.

Gathering her courage, she refused. She would be no good to Rose that way.

Mechanically, Sylvie set out food for Tiny Tim. The sound of his eating tickled the silence as she drifted into Rose's bedchamber, hunting for the hundredth time for anything that might be useful.

The room was neat as a pin, only because Sylvie had already combed through everything and set it all to rights. Any wrinkles on the quilted counterpane were the result of Sylvie sitting on the bed, thinking, looking, praying. Orange-red paisley curtains swayed in the breeze, and the sun that filtered through them cast a fiery glow reminiscent of Rose's personality. She was warm, her feelings close to the surface and quick to kindle into stronger flames of love or anger. She had been this way since she was a child, especially after her father passed away. The hotter Rose had flared, the cooler Sylvie made herself, to compensate. There had to be balance, or they'd both burn up in Rose's passions.

"Calm down, Rose." Sylvie's own words came

back to her. How often had she said it? *"You make too much of this."*

Had her passions finally, literally, carried her away?

A rhythmic scratching drew Sylvie's attention to Tiny Tim, who was stuffing his paw beneath Rose's bureau, trying to pull something out. Hoping it wasn't a mouse, she knelt beside the little cat and felt until her fingers found the edge of a book. Pinching the cover, she pulled it out.

Only it was not a book. It was a diary.

Any twinge of guilt Sylvie felt for invading this private space quickly dissolved. Rose was missing, and this book might hold some clues.

Shifting to sit cross-legged on the floor, Sylvie opened it to the most recent entry. It was dated August 12, the night of the fireworks on the Wooded Island. She began reading:

> I hope Jozefa felt welcome here. I know what it's like not to belong. Even Mrs. Górecki is getting tired of me.

Rose had never mentioned a Mrs. Górecki before. Were their visits another secret?

> The contrast between her neighborhood and ours is overwhelming. But that's where my father lived, or in a neighbor-

hood just like it. I've always wondered if I was dishonoring him by being grateful I didn't grow up there. I feel guilty for all my privileges when so many Polish people are barely scraping by.

Jozefa says I shouldn't worry about that, that my parents would be proud of me, just the way I am. Mimi has said the same thing to me many times, but some-how, hearing it from Jozefa was a relief. She has no reason to lie to me. She has no reason to be kind to me either, but she has been. Between her and what Mr. Janik said, I feel a little closer to my mother, even though all I remember of her is the feel of her shawl on my face when she held me, and the song she used to sing to me. I wish I had a photograph of her. At least I have the shawl.

Sylvie edged closer to the bed and leaned back against it, stretching her legs out in front of her. The shawl, she understood, was as important to Rose as Sylvie's copy of *Little Women* was to her, since it had been cherished by her own mother, Ruth. The folded shawl draped the foot of Rose's bed now, its bright blue and dove-grey wool fringe brushing Sylvie's neck. Rose would never have left it behind if she'd known she wasn't coming back.

A headache pressed behind Sylvie's temples. Tiny Tim crawled into her lap, and she welcomed the purring ball of fur.

> I can't tell if it bothers Mimi when I talk about my parents, which is why I've done it so much with Jozefa instead. It doesn't hurt her feelings like it might hurt Mimi's when I say I miss my own family. When I was little, Mimi was actually wonderful about it. She told me she was sorry, so sorry, when my father died, and I believed her. She let me cry, and she cried with me.

Sylvie's throat burned. The words grew blurry as she skimmed further down the page.

> I feel like she tries to control me now, but is she trying to protect me, or only herself? I want to be loved for who I am, but sometimes I wonder if she needs me to feel better about who she is.

Enough.

Tears rolled down Sylvie's cheeks as she closed the diary, nudged the cat from her lap, and stood. Rose had misinterpreted everything Sylvie had tried to do for her. She'd gotten it all wrong.

Hadn't she?

• • •

Sylvie felt like an imposter arriving at the ball on Kristof's arm, an old maid pretending to be Cinderella. He and Gregor were distinguished in their concert tuxedos, but as she had no fairy godmother, she wore only the most formal dress she already owned. While other ladies shimmered in off-the-shoulder ball gowns and bejeweled ostrich feather fans, Sylvie made the best of a deep crimson dinner gown with matching gloves that went up past her elbows. It felt too snug across her middle, another sign her body was relaxing with age.

She felt anything but relaxed tonight.

"Enjoy the ball. Or at least enjoy the music, won't you?" Gregor winked, then parted from their little trio to join the chamber ensemble at one end of the room.

Kristof lingered, even when Sylvie released his arm. "Are you going to be all right?" he asked.

"Why wouldn't I be?"

"You hate crowds, unless you're guiding a small group that hangs on your every word. And the room will be twice as full within the hour. The Midway guests will arrive shortly after nine."

He was right. She enjoyed giving tours but could do without masses of people in general. Last year, one of Meg's art shows had drawn so many admirers that Sylvie had felt like she might suffocate. Kristof had noticed, ushering

161

her into the courtyard for some cool evening air.

The knot between her shoulders loosened a bit, just from being known. "The hope of gaining some insight makes it bearable. I'd do far more than this if it meant finding Rose."

Kristof nodded. "I'll do what I can, but right now I need to join the ensemble and relieve the pianist of his set." Mozart piano music floated over the room. Near the piano, a cellist and violist were settling into their places while Gregor rubbed a block of rosin on his bow-strings. An oboist adjusted the reed in his instrument.

She patted his arm. "I plan to sit on the edge of the room until the Midway folks arrive, sipping punch and wishing I'd brought a book."

"Planning to shun the poor fellows who ask you to dance?" His mouth twisted into a wry grin. "All the better. Less chance for you to be whisked out of my sight."

"I'm not here to dance."

"Your secret is safe with me," he said. He joined the other musicians while Sylvie receded to the periphery and sat in a row of chairs lining the wall.

Red and yellow bunting hung from the ceiling of the Midway's Natatorium Building. Galleries overlooked the ballroom, their railings draped with silk triangles embroidered with gold arabesques that reflected the light of incandescent bulbs. It was one of the most opulent atmospheres Sylvie had ever experienced.

Rose would have loved it.

Crossing her ankles, Sylvie watched the musicians tune their instruments and tried not to think about the money she'd spent to be here. Her funds were thinning. Coming to this ball had been a gamble with her resources, and she could only hope it would pay off.

Though impatient to continue her investigation, she feigned a casual air and adjusted her mother's pearls at her throat. If a ransom needed to be paid, they would be among the first valuables she would sell. But if someone were after a ransom, wouldn't he have demanded it by now?

The music began, instantly drawing her attention to Kristof. He led the chamber ensemble into a lively piece that was the perfect background to the evening's gaiety. Gregor barely seemed to notice Kristof's wordless direction. While Kristof was sharp and precise, Gregor was devil-may-care and yet still made no mistakes.

Only during the last, lingering note of the piece did Kristof seek her out with his gaze. The intensity in his eyes brought a flush to her cheeks, and she was glad he wouldn't notice from this distance.

Even so, she looked at her hands, lest her expression betray her. Just as she had when she'd made that comment in Meg's parlor about romance and love not living up to fictional renderings. Even to her own ears, it had seemed a false note, when for so long it had been her resounding refrain. *"You might change your tune on that,"* Meg had whispered to her later that evening. But it wasn't that simple. Beyond Beth's objections, she had her own. Sylvie loved the life she'd built for herself, the freedom and independence. And she had Rose to think of.

Especially now. She was the only reason Sylvie was here.

As the music moved into a waltz, couples took to the floor. Sylvie scanned the entrances, hoping to see the Midway guests, and spotted a man in Hungarian folk dress lingering just inside one of the arched doorways. He might be waiting for the right cue for his entrance, but Sylvie would do no such thing.

Faster than thought, she was on her feet and marching toward him, reticule looped over her wrist. "Excuse me," she said when she neared. "You speak English, yes?"

His eyebrows spiked, almost disappearing beneath the brim of his green felt hat. The feather in its band quivered as he appraised her with a grin. "A little English. Yes."

"Good. You work at the Orpheum on the Midway, don't you? I'd like to talk to you for a few minutes."

"Yes, I do." He introduced himself as László

Varga. She guessed he was older than she was, but not by much. His shoulders were broad beneath his white shirt and embroidered vest. Tall leather boots covered black trousers that widened from knee to waist. "I'll talk to you, of course. But only while we're dancing."

A wave of heat splashed over her. "That won't be necessary. We can chat right here."

He cupped a hand behind an ear. "I can't hear you. Too close to the music. It's better if we dance."

She couldn't interpret the smile flashing in his olive complexion. He might simply be friendly and eager for the ball. Then again, he was a stranger who hadn't yet earned her trust.

She pulled the photo from her reticule. "Have you seen this girl? Blond hair, blue eyes."

Mr. Varga barely looked. "I told you, I can't hear you." Strong fingers wrapped around her elbow, tugging. Sylvie quickly stuffed the photo back into her bag so it wouldn't slip from her grasp and be trampled as he pulled her onto the dance floor.

She'd been a fool to approach him alone. But now that his attention was completely hers, there was no getting out of it. "Someone from the Orpheum asked my daughter to be a serving girl there," she tried.

"Oh?" He turned his head so she could speak more directly into his ear.

"The girl in the picture I showed you, Rozalia Dabrowski. Have you seen her there?"

"I have seen many girls like her," he said. "But their names do not interest me. I would not keep them straight even if I tried. They come, they go."

"Do you mean they disappear?"

"What? Disappear?" A frown twitched his mouth. "No. I just don't see the same girls from one week to another. Unlike the Egyptians, we did not bring enough countrymen with us to fill a village. Some of them we hire from your city. There are many Hungarians already living in Chicago, isn't it so?"

"Yes, but my daughter is not one of them. Are girls forced to work for you, even if they'd rather not?"

"And how would we do that? You think we are all gypsies, that we would kidnap blond girls and keep them for ourselves?"

"That's not what I meant."

"What?"

She repeated herself, louder this time, yet still he drew her nearer. Truly, the noise level didn't warrant this.

"Ah, but you are thinking it is good you are brunette, otherwise who knows what I would do with you," Mr. Varga said. "Is that it?"

Suddenly mute, she tried to twist away from him.

His fingers dug into her back as he pulled her closer to his broad chest, asserting his control.

With just one glance, Kristof read the alarm on Sylvie's face. To the ensemble, he said, "Skip the coda, end the piece," and brought the waltz to an early conclusion.

Couples broke apart.

"What was that about?" Gregor muttered, and the flutist echoed the question.

Kristof set down his instrument. "Change of plans. Gregor, take the lead. Charles, play louder," he told the young violinist near Gregor.

Straightening his bow tie, he wove between couples until he reached Sylvie and a fellow he'd seen at the Hungarian Orpheum. Her complexion was mottled white and pink.

"What did you say to her?" he asked in Hungarian.

"I didn't say anything. She practically asked me to dance."

"What's he saying?" Sylvie whispered. "I thought I could question him about Rose, but he insisted on dancing, and I didn't learn a thing."

"Did she tell you she didn't want to dance?" Kristof asked him.

When the man shrugged, Kristof pulled him aside. Keeping his voice low, his temper barely in check, he filleted him for forcing himself on

Sylvie when she clearly hadn't wanted that type of attention.

The Hungarian trudged away.

Sylvie's pearl choker dipped into the hollow of her throat. "I didn't mean to interrupt your playing."

"I thought you weren't going to dance. You ought to have waited for me to speak to him in the first place." He gentled his tone. "Are you all right?"

She didn't look all right. "My imagination got the better of me, I'm afraid. He was probably harmless. But I think I offended him somehow. Then he wouldn't let me go, and I couldn't help but wonder if Rose had felt a similar powerlessness, and if she felt it even now, wherever she is." She trailed off. "There are so many loose ends surrounding Rose's disappearance that I feel like I'm unravelling."

Kristof wanted nothing more than to hold her together.

A minuet started up. He opened his arms, and Sylvie placed herself in his hold, her gloved fingers cool on his shoulder and in his hand.

"The last time I danced was at Meg and Nate's wedding," she told him. "I'm terribly out of practice, so don't be surprised if I trip us both."

"I'll take care of you."

A smile tipped her mouth as he led her into the dance. With the slightest guidance, Sylvie responded to his leading as if she were an extension of his will, his body. As one unit, they swirled together through a room that blurred into unimportance around them.

Then the music changed.

The violin broke away from the rest of the ensemble in an attention-grabbing solo. It was no longer a minuet. Dancing slowed and halted all over the ballroom, since couples could no longer fit their steps to the tune. All eyes turned to the violinist who had transformed the performance into a stage from which to flash his own talent, deliberately leaving others behind.

"Gregor." Kristof seethed. The room had been overly warm before. Now he felt as if he'd been wrapped in steaming flannel.

Sylvie had dropped away from him, and his hands, now empty, curled into fists at his sides. If Gregor didn't stop showing off soon, he would jeopardize not only their payment for tonight but their chances of being hired again for future events. No one wanted to pay musicians who didn't follow directions. Didn't he know what was at stake?

"That's amazing," Kristof heard a woman say. "I've never heard anything like it."

Sylvie seemed to be gauging Kristof's response. He knew he looked angry. He was. He just hoped she didn't think he was jealous, for what he felt went far deeper than that.

"He's done this before, hasn't he?" she asked.

"Whenever he feels underappreciated." He massaged the back of his neck. While Gregor played on, sweat trickling down the sides of his face, Kristof told Sylvie that when they were younger, they had competed in chamber music contests. "This type of surprise solo performance from Gregor threw everyone off and lost us the competitions. He said he thought his improvisation would win it for us, so he took a risk, and it always failed."

Those awards meant nothing to Gregor, but Kristof had worked three times as hard, hoping for validation, yearning for approval from their father. When they lost, their father hardly knew who to blame more. Gregor for not playing by the rules, Kristof for not being able to improvise right along with him, or the judges for not recognizing great talent when it was ringing in their ears.

"He's a grown man now, there are no judges here, and neither is your father," Sylvie said. "So who is he trying to impress?"

Gregor stomped his foot, smashing all traces of the minuet while charging forth in a whirling Gypsy rhythm, though he had not one drop of Gypsy blood in his veins. Eyes squeezed shut, his slender fingers flew and his bow danced on the strings. Perspiration streaked his face.

"It's obvious, isn't it?" she whispered. "He's

trying to impress himself. Why else would he go to such lengths, if not to make himself feel better about his own worth?"

"He loves praise," Kristof suggested. In his mind, it had always been as simple as that. "He feeds on it, even if it means others get less."

Gregor's last note stretched, the vibrato strong to the end, and the room burst into applause. He bowed, neglecting to invite the rest of the ensemble to bow with him. Shameful. The way he used music to separate himself from others cheapened his talent.

When the clapping died down, a man in a long-tailed tuxedo took the stage to introduce, at long last, the parade of Midway employees waiting to enter. A man known as Citizen Train, wearing a white suit with a red belt and red Turkish fez, led the procession, carrying an armful of blooming sweet pea down a grand staircase and into the ballroom.

Sylvie leaned into Kristof and nodded at Citizen Train. "Did you know that man, George Francis Train, was the model for Phileas Fogg, the main character of Jules Verne's *Around the World in Eighty Days*?"

Kristof chuckled. "I can see it. But Phileas Fogg was no hero. Any man who wagers half his fortune on a dare is too reckless to be admired."

On Citizen Train's arm was a Mexican ballerina who could be no more than twelve years old, and behind him were scores of men and women, many barefoot, wearing clothing native to their culture.

Into a world of black-and-white tuxedos and pastel silk ball gowns entered a riot of color in skin and fabric. There were Indians, Amazonians, and Africans, wearing skirts resembling small American flags if their normal custom was to wear none at all. There were Japanese in red silk, Romanians in red, blue, and yellow. Sioux Chief Rain-in-the-Face wore green face paint that was already melting, streaming toward his chin in the heat. A Laplander wore fur, and Eskimo women wore shirts of walrus skin. Belly dancers wore robes and turbans.

Kristof didn't know how any of them could bear the stifling heat.

Sylvie discreetly dabbed a lemon-scented hand-kerchief to her neck before snapping it back into her reticule. "All right, partner. At least one of these people is going to help us find Rose. I know it. Where shall we begin?"

"I'm supposed to be playing right now, but those women over there sound like they're from the Irish Village. Why don't you question them without me?"

She turned toward them, her dark hair gleaming in the light. "Perfect."

Thirty minutes later, the ensemble finished its set of music, and the pianist returned to his bench to take over. While Gregor headed straight for a belly dancer near the punch bowl, Kristof rolled his head from one shoulder to the other, stretching his muscles while scanning for Sylvie. He'd watched her move among the Irish women, showing the photograph of Rose, before finding a couple of Sioux Indians who spoke English and were willing to talk to her. Now that he was free, they could question many more.

Before he could reach her, however, a voice snagged his notice. The Hungarian fellow Sylvie had danced with earlier stood far too close to a blond woman, his arm wrapped around her waist to keep her there. She looked familiar. She looked young.

Rose's age.

Over her white shirtwaist, the girl wore an emerald-green vest, her ruffled apron embroidered with blue flowers. It was Margit, the waitress who had served Kristof and Gregor at the Orpheum. Was she in trouble?

Catching Sylvie's eye, Kristof cocked his head toward the Hungarians, indicating his intention to approach them. A pair of Romanians blocked his path, followed by a Laplander carrying two drinks, mittens dangling from his sleeves. By the time Kristof reached Margit, however, the Hungarian man was nowhere in sight.

"Good evening, Margit," he said to her in their native language. He reminded her they'd met before and introduced himself. "The man who was just with you—was he bothering you?"

"Who, Mr. Varga? Why do you say that?"

Sylvie joined them. "What did I miss?"

Margit's eyes narrowed. "Who's she?"

As quietly as he could, while still being heard above the crowd, Kristof explained they wanted information about a missing girl. "She's about your height, blue eyes, blond hair."

Sylvie produced the photograph.

Margit looked at it. "I see a lot of people." She tucked a strand of hair beneath the wreath of flowers crowning her head.

"We heard she was offered a job at the Orpheum, and that when she said no, the man recruiting her grabbed her before her cousin intervened. Have you seen her? Do you have any idea what could have happened to her?"

Margit scanned the image one more time. "I honestly haven't seen her, Mr. Bartok. But if I were to guess, I would say it was Mr. Varga who talked to her. He's deaf in one ear, hard of hearing in the other. If he can't understand us, he pulls us closer without even thinking how rude it seems."

Sylvie clutched Kristof's arm, obviously impatient for the translation. He obliged.

Her eyebrows plunged when he mentioned Varga being hard of hearing. "He did tell me he couldn't hear well. That doesn't make him innocent. He would have had to squeeze Rose pretty hard to make those bruises. Walter said she gasped in pain."

The piano music stopped, and the Dahomey Africans formed a circle in the middle of the ballroom, treating the guests to a performance with drums and other native instruments they'd brought with them.

"I don't know where this girl is, and I doubt Mr. Varga does either," Margit said above the pulsing beat. "He seems rough, but he's harmless. He certainly isn't stuffing girls in closets or dumping them in the river—or worse, if that's what you're wondering."

Sylvie's lips pinched as Kristof filled her in. "Just ask if she knows if any other girls have gone missing. From the Orpheum or anywhere else on the Midway."

He did.

According to Margit, three weeks ago, a waitress named Laura, hired locally, had been suddenly dismissed, reportedly because she didn't speak Hungarian well enough and customers complained. Last week, the same thing happened to another server named Danielle, also from somewhere in Chicago.

"Odd, isn't it?" Kristof muttered to Sylvie after sharing what Margit had said.

She agreed. "If non-Hungarian girls had already been fired, why would anyone recruit Rose to join the staff? Unless they planned to use her only to fill water glasses or bus tables." She slipped Rose's photograph back into the reticule and snapped it shut.

"I'm confused about the language requirement," Kristof said to Margit. "Customers could just point to the menu item to order if there was a language barrier."

"Most of the time, yes," Margit replied. A purple petal dropped from her wreath, catching on her shoulder before she brushed it off. "But we get many Hungarians who come expecting an authentic Hungarian experience. They want to chat with the waitresses, and if the girls can't converse in Hungarian, or at least in German, they get frustrated. If they give a special order about how the food is to be cooked and the waitress doesn't get it right, it's even worse."

"So is a language test part of the interview process to be hired?" Kristof covered Sylvie's hand on his arm to let her know he hadn't forgotten her, even though he wasn't including her just now.

Margit shrugged. "I wouldn't know. I was hired in Budapest to come with my brother, who's in the Gypsy band, and I learned just enough English to get by. *Welcome. How is the food? Can I get you anything else?* That's all I know, Mr. Bartok. I hope you find who you're looking for."

"So do I."

CHAPTER TWELVE

Thursday, August 17, 1893

Sylvie didn't like the person she was becoming.

She suspected everyone she met at the ball of some hidden darkness that would lead him or her to abduct a young lady like Rose. Even those who had no obvious motivation were not safe from her paranoia. Her thoughts contorted to connect crimes and people that ought to have remained far apart. She found herself far too much like her father, God rest him, when he'd been consumed with protecting her.

The ball ended at half past four in the morning. Riding home in a cab, wedged between Kristof and Gregor, she wondered if she might genuinely lose her mind to fear. She wondered if it ran in the family, just as Rose had said.

"We'll keep looking," Kristof murmured.

That was what people said when they didn't have answers.

"Someone had to have seen her," Sylvie insisted. "Someone has to know something." She couldn't accept that out of all the people they'd spoken with, only Margit had offered any information, and that had only prompted more questions.

"To be fair, Sylvie," Gregor began, "the Midway folks see tens of thousands of people every day. Many of them beautiful young women with blond hair and blue eyes, just like Rose. It's not likely they'd remember her in particular."

"László Varga ought to have remembered her, if Margit's hunch is correct," she countered. "Whoever tried to recruit her for the German Village would, as well. And she was carrying her violin when she was taken, which would have set her apart from the crowd."

Kristof shifted beside her. "We spoke to every Hungarian, German, and Austrian at the ball. Only the beer garden worker remembered the incident Hazel told us about, and his story matched hers," he reminded Sylvie. "Rose said no to the offer and left."

Sylvie closed her eyes. Fatigue weighted her as the carriage wheels clattered beneath her seat, jostling her between the two brothers. She was tired, not just from lack of sleep but also from the exhausting tasks of waiting, dreading, hoping.

The cab clunked into and out of a pothole, jarring Sylvie to wakefulness. Outside the window, insects clouded about the streetlamps. The night air chilled the sweat on her skin.

One of her conversations came back to her. "I spoke with a woman named Colleen from Irish Industries. She said one of her girls, a wild and unruly sort, ran away earlier this summer and joined a brothel and has no intention of leaving it. The girl says she's pampered now and will live like a queen long past the end of the Fair."

"Rose would never do that," Kristof said.

"I agree." Sylvie's stomach churned. "But she said not all the girls in the brothels begin willingly."

"White slavery," Gregor said. "It's common knowledge, unfortunately, and becoming more common in practice. You don't suppose . . ."

Sylvie thought she might be sick. Despite Margit calling László Varga harmless, all she could think was that if he had tried to recruit a girl who spoke no Hungarian, it was for a role in which she would have no voice. "I have to find her. If I have to go inside every brothel in the Levee district, I'll do it."

"What?" The whites of Kristof's eyes gleamed. "Sylvie, no. I share your concern, but you can't go there."

"Why not?"

"You're a woman."

"Little Cheyenne is full of women, and not just those employed by madams. Evangelists and reformers traffic those streets on a regular basis. I'll go during daylight hours, when 'customers' aren't calling." She paused, imagining herself walking up to houses of ill repute, saloons with brothels in the rear, and massage parlors. "I can do this with Beth. I don't want you to come with me, Kristof." She couldn't abide the idea of dragging him through a place where women brazenly advertised their bodies in the windows.

"That district is known as the wickedest place in America," said Kristof, "and you want to walk right into it, unprotected? Even with Beth, this is a terrible idea. I can't let you do it. We'll find another way, one that doesn't involve you endangering yourself."

"Like what?" Sylvie angled to face him, even though shadows veiled them both. Every frustration she'd felt over the last three days filled her voice. He meant well, but he had no authority over her. "I can't tell you how much I appreciate all your help so far. But I'm going regardless of your opinion, and I'm going without you."

Beth would be proud of her for being so decisive. But somehow Sylvie felt smaller. She'd sounded shrill, even to herself, when all she wanted was to be strong. She needed Kristof's friendship now more than ever, but she felt a cold wind blow between them, for she had pushed him away. And she'd done it in front of his brother.

Kristof said nothing for several long moments, the quiet broken only by hoofbeats. At last, he said, "I did not speak from a wish to rule over you, Sylvie. All I desire is to protect you."

She could form no response to this.

The cab slowed to a halt in the alley behind

her building. Gregor cleared his throat. "Here we are."

Kristof climbed out first and handed Sylvie down. The streetlamp on the corner illuminated half his face. "Don't lose heart," he said.

But she was in danger of losing far more than that. He escorted her as she unlocked the rear door of the building with leaden limbs, then climbed the stairs with her to the second floor. She let herself into her apartment, then stopped.

On the floor just inside her door was an unstamped envelope, addressed with one word: *Mimi.*

Sylvie scooped it up and spun toward Kristof. "It's Rose," she breathed. "She wrote me." With trembling hands, she pinched the fingertips of her gloves and pulled them off, clutched them both in one hand, and tore the envelope open while Kristof turned on the light in the hall sconce.

Dear Mimi, she read. *I am fine and safe.*

Sylvie gasped with the force of her relief, the pressure releasing tears that traced hot paths down her cheeks. Her strength draining, she braced herself against the doorway and covered her face as her shoulders shook with silent sobbing. There was more to the note, but she couldn't possibly read it through her tears.

"What is it? What can I do?" Kristof's hands came gently around her arms.

"She's all right," Sylvie told him. "Thank God,

she's all right." She wiped her face with the heel of her hand and lifted the note again.

I'm sorry I couldn't get word to you until now. I'm sure you've been worried. Don't be. Do not come looking for me. I have everything I need now.

Your loving Rose

"You're sure this is her handwriting?" Kristof asked after she'd handed it to him to read.

"I'm sure." Sylvie looked up at him through lashes still wet. The relief that had flooded through her began to dry up, leaving only more confusion behind. "Do you think she ran away?"

He gave back the note. "If she did, she'll come around."

She studied Rose's message again. "I'm still afraid for her, Kristof," she admitted. "Even if she did leave of her own accord. And if you tell me to simply have courage, I'm afraid I'll disappoint you."

"No." He lifted her chin so she looked him in the eye. "The opposite of fear is not courage. The opposite of fear is faith. You can't take care of her, but we can still believe that God can, and will, and is doing so right now. *Faith,* Sylvie."

"Faith," she repeated in a whispered prayer for more.

He swept a tear from her cheek with the pad of

his thumb, swallowing hard. "Get some rest." He bade her good night.

Somehow she managed a suitable reply, watched him go, and locked the door behind him.

Everything I need. Rose's words leapt off the page as Sylvie reread it. But that couldn't possibly be right. She'd left her mother's shawl behind, her most treasured link to her family.

Dropping her gloves on a hall table, Sylvie rushed into Rose's room and turned on the lamp on the bureau.

The shawl was gone.

Whoever had delivered the note had been here tonight.

Was it Rose? Or had Rose lent her key to someone else?

Pressure mounted in her head. With hands that were suddenly freezing, she threw open the doors of the armoire. Empty. Then the drawers in her bureau, one by one.

Empty, empty, empty.

Her clothes, undergarments, and shoes were gone. Her silver-plated brush and hand mirror, her hair combs and ribbons, all gone. All that was left of Rose in this room was her bedding, the vanilla-scented sachets, and an old photograph of her with Sylvie, on the day she'd been baptized, with Meg and Nate, her godparents, standing proudly with them.

Sylvie sank to the floor.

Empty.

Kristof hated that he had no comfort to offer Sylvie other than the hope that Rose would return on her own. Relationships had never been his forte, and he had no insights based on his own upbringing. His father, a frustrated composer, had been more interested in raising a prodigy than a son and had made no secret of his disappointment with every wrong note Kristof played. Gregor was the miracle child, not only for being born nine years after Kristof, but for his innate talent. There had been a time when Kristof had considered running away and joining a Gypsy caravan, but he could never bring himself to part from his brother.

He didn't like thinking about that time in his life. Instead of escaping, he had multiplied his devotion to his music studies. There was a logic to music that appealed to him, a mathematical equation in every measure. The notes and rests in each bar added up to a whole, and all his practice added up to progress that approached perfection. Finally. There was an angst inside his young soul that could be calmed by nothing else. It calmed his father, too, when he got it right.

Kristof carried his violin case and Gregor's up to their apartment and conducted his thoughts back to the note from Rose. It proved she was still alive, but she could have been forced to write it. He hadn't wanted to say that, but he could read in Sylvie's eyes that she'd already drawn the same conclusion. So he'd left her with a feeble good night when what he wanted was to gather her into his arms, to hold her up when she might be breaking down.

After locking his apartment again, he descended the stairs, exited the building, and inhaled the cool, damp air of early morning. Climbing back into the cab with Gregor, he thought of Sylvie in her empty apartment. The idea of her crying alone wrenched his gut. Someone ought to be with her at a time like this. Perhaps she would take his suggestion to confide in Anna Hoffman, who was no doubt already awake and baking. Or perhaps Sylvie would sleep, at last.

But Kristof wouldn't, or at least not yet. He looked out the cab window for the telltale glow of a cigar. He knew their building had been watched ever since their first meeting with the three Irish thugs on the roof of the Manufactures Building. "There's Quinn," he muttered to Gregor.

"Shall we offer him a ride?" Gregor yawned. "Then again, that would mean one of us would have to sit on another's lap." He shuddered, then leaned out the window and waved. "Sorry, ol' chap! You'll have to meet us there!"

Gregor's laughter grated on Kristof's nerves. "You're in a good mood."

"Why not?" His brother leaned back. "We played, we got paid, and we're about to pay off our debt."

"*Your* debt," Kristof corrected him. Although it had become his problem, too, so technically his brother was right. "And you had me worried tonight when you went off the program to pull your Gypsy stunt."

"Stunt?"

"You're risking our reputation as reliable musicians. Word travels fast. If one patron is dissatisfied, others will know it before we have time to apply for another event."

Snoring answered Kristof's rebuke.

Fifteen minutes later, they arrived at O'Donnell's, a South Side Irish pub on Wabash Avenue, tucked into the ground-floor unit of a narrow, eight-story brick building. Milky moonbeams fell across the warping sidewalk leading up to its front door.

Kristof roused his brother and paid the driver, including extra to have him wait.

Gregor knocked. "Here for Johnny Friendly," he called.

The door unlocked and opened. A balding man in a bar apron and sleeves rolled to his elbows waved them inside. "Back table. Floor's wet, by the way." His lower eyelids drooped like a bloodhound's.

Stools sat upside down on the bar, and upended

186

chairs topped the tables, their legs spiking toward a water-stained ceiling. The recently mopped floor sent the sharp smell of ammonia into an atmosphere that reeked of smoke and liquor. Framed photographs hung on paneled walls.

Kristof and Gregor passed through the forest of bristling tables toward the lone candle burning in the rear. Flickering from inside a red glass hurricane, it cast an eerie glow on the white linen-clad table, and upon the men sitting behind it.

Johnny Friendly and Tiny O'Bannon watched the Bartoks approach. It was half past five in the morning by now, and Kristof couldn't tell if they were up very late or very early.

Gregor took an envelope from his pocket and laid it on the table. It was their evening's pay, plus the income they'd received since their last meeting. Little had been held back to pay the rent. "It's all there." He stood back.

O'Bannon picked it up and opened it to count the bills. Apparently satisfied, he slid it to Johnny and resumed rolling a small glass jar of red pepper flakes between his massive hands.

"That's it, then," Kristof said. "The debt is paid. You can have Quinn stop following us now. And you can let Rozalia Dabrowski go." It was only a guess, but he had nothing to lose by trying.

Gregor stared at him. Johnny and O'Bannon said nothing. A knock on the door drew the bartender to it. Smokes Quinn entered the pub, shuffled to the rear, and sat beside O'Bannon.

"I'm confused." Johnny looked to Quinn, then O'Bannon. "You know a Rozalia Dabrowski in connection with these two?" Outside, a block east of the pub, a train roared by, hissing and chugging as it clambered toward the Illinois Central Railroad station.

"Yeah." O'Bannon rubbed a meaty hand over his face. "Blond girl, very pretty. Very shapely, very nice, you know what I mean. Pure as the driven snow. Sweet girl."

"You followed her," Kristof guessed.

He shrugged. "She was much nicer to look at than the two of you."

"And you took her?" Gregor's pitch climbed half an octave. "Your creative insurance policy, in case we didn't pay."

Johnny turned a scowl on O'Bannon. "Did you pick off a girl without my say-so?"

O'Bannon held up his palms. "No! I don't have her and I didn't touch her."

"Then what happened to her?" Kristof willed his pulse to a steady tempo. "Monday afternoon she had a violin lesson with me at Music Hall. Did you see her after that?"

"I might have. What's it worth to you?"

Kristof sat across from him. "A seventeen-year-old girl is missing. If you have information that may help us find her, it would be worth a lot to me."

Twenty feet away, the bartender wiped tumblers dry and stacked them on a shelf, each knock of glass on wood thumping against Kristof's nerves.

Exhaling, Gregor pulled out a chair and sank into it. "You have all our cash. Just tell us what you know."

"Something for nothing?" Johnny smiled. "Since when did the world work that way?"

Gregor paled in the red-tinged half-light. He pulled his timepiece from his waistcoat and pushed it across the table. Their father's watch, and his father's before that. A family heirloom left to Gregor. "That's gold." He tapped the casing. "And those are diamonds in the face, at twelve and six."

With a snow-white handkerchief, Johnny picked it up and rubbed it clean before touching it with his own skin. As he held it to his ear, Kristof could hear every tick as loudly as if it had been held to his own.

Eyebrow arching, Johnny glanced at Kristof. "This is genuine?"

"It is."

"Because if I take this to my guy and he comes back and says otherwise, I'll be more than a little concerned that you two are disrespecting me."

"I said it's genuine."

Johnny's mouth curled in an upside-down smile. "Good. If it isn't, I'll find you. I know where you live." To O'Bannon, he simply nodded.

O'Bannon popped his knuckles, one by one. "Yeah, I saw her leave Music Hall with her violin. She was walking in the shade of the Peristyle toward the Casino when someone stopped her, and they talked for a good ten minutes."

"Who?" Kristof asked. "Who was she talking to?" If only he had walked Rose out, if only he'd served as her chaperone until she was safely home, he could have prevented all of this.

"Relax. I didn't get a good look. Whoever it was stood in the shadows. Then they both headed to the Casino Pier and boarded the steamship *Arthur Orr* for an excursion into the lake. I didn't bother getting on with them, since I knew they'd be back an hour later. And so they were."

O'Bannon wasn't talking fast enough. "And?" Kristof prodded.

"She was easy to spot, still swinging that violin case. No one was with her except for the crowd. She walked through the Court of Honor and into the train station. That's where I lost her."

"You *lost* her?" Gregor leaned forward. "Isn't that your job, to follow her?"

"Hey. A minute ago you weren't so pleased I was following her. Now you're not so pleased I let her go. Which is it?"

It was something. She got as far as the train station. It was more information than they'd had all week. "If you can't think of anything else to

190

share, then our business here is through." Kristof rose.

O'Bannon's grin pushed back his corpulent cheeks. "If I think of something else, you'll have to make it worth my time to tell you."

Shaking his head, Gregor stood. "If I get enough money together, I'm going to buy that timepiece back from you."

"Sure," Johnny crooned. "You get enough money, come see me."

Outside the pub, night rolled away from the dawn. Tugboats on the river puffed dense columns of smoke into a sky already layered with low, grey clouds.

"That's it," Kristof muttered to Gregor. "No more dealings with those three."

Gregor's hooded gaze climbed the building from which they'd just emerged. Like all the other structures in this district, its face was stained with soot from coal-burning tugboats and trains. "I agree. As soon as I buy Father's time-piece back."

"With what money?" Kristof pulled his empty pockets inside out. "Forget it, Gregor. We did what we had to do. That heirloom is gone for good. But if the information it bought us gets us one step closer to Rose, it will be a price well paid."

Chapter Thirteen

A few minutes after ten on Thursday morning, the bell tinkled over the door of Corner Books & More. Sylvie pasted a smile in place before stepping out from between two bookshelves to greet her customer.

As soon as she saw Meg and Olive, she allowed her mask of composure to fall. Her face twisted with all the emotions she'd bottled up.

"Sylvie." Meg rushed to her, reaching out.

Sylvie shaped her hands around her sister's scarred ones. "She wrote to me."

"Thank God. Come, sit, and tell me all about it. We'll jump up the moment a customer comes in."

The coffee was nearly done percolating on the refreshments table, and Sylvie poured two mugs, adding cream to both, plus sugar for Meg. "Help yourself." She lifted the glass dome from the pedestal holding a mound of Anna Hoffman's Berliners. "We'll never sell all these in one day, and they won't be as good tomorrow."

"Divine," said Meg. "Thank you. Olive, dear, why don't you run upstairs and visit Mr. and Mrs. Hoffman while Aunt Sylvie and I chat?"

Berliner in hand, Olive scampered to the rear of the store. Meg and Sylvie took their pastries and drinks to one of the bistro tables opposite the empty fireplace. Ferns spread their arms over the hearth, claiming it as their summer home.

Sylvie took Rose's note from her skirt pocket and slid it across the table for Meg to read.

Her sister's brow crimped as she scanned the lines. She flipped the page, then read it again. "Was there a return address?"

"No. It wasn't even stamped. Whoever delivered it also cleared out Rose's things. Her clothes and toiletries, her mother's shawl, all gone."

"What?"

"That's not all." Unable to eat, Sylvie sipped her coffee, willing the caffeine to clear the cobwebs from her sleep-deprived mind. "Tiny Tim is gone, too. Or else he's hiding better and longer than he ever has before. I haven't seen him since before the ball. He hasn't even come out to eat." She missed him more than she'd admit, for he'd been a special comfort to her. Now that, too, was taken away.

"Do you suppose he escaped when whoever it was came in?"

A muscle cramped in Sylvie's neck. She rubbed at it. "It's possible. But far more likely than running away is that he would have stayed and demanded attention from the visitor. I think—" A lump swelled in her throat. "I wonder if he's with Rose." She tapped the note. "She says she has everything she needs, and she loved that cat. She doesn't have anything to come back for now."

Meg swallowed a bite and wiped her mouth with a napkin. "But she calls you *Mimi*. She signs her name *Rose*. Yet the last thing she said to you, if I recall correctly, was that she wanted to start using the names Sylvie and Rozalia. Surely this means something."

Sylvie had noticed that, too. "But taken together with everything else—the cleaned-out bureau and armoire, the missing cat—it seems more like a concession. A way to take the sting out of what she's decided to do."

After refolding her napkin in her lap, Meg propped her chin in one hand. "If you take this note to the police, it will no longer be a missing person case. Just the case of a young woman who has willingly left home."

Sylvie sat back in her chair and looked out the window. Blousy petunias in flower boxes rippled in the breeze. Beyond them, ladies strolled the sidewalk with shopping bags on their arms and gentlemen at their sides. A few maids darted by on their errands.

"Maybe that's all this is, Meg. I pushed Rose so far that she's afraid to tell me where she is for fear I'll come after her. She says she's fine but orders me to leave her be."

Meg took a drink of coffee. "It doesn't add up. Has she kept such secrets from you before?"

"If she had, would I know it?" Her voice was serrated with exhaustion, her eyelids like sandpaper. She'd fallen asleep on the floor in Rose's room last night, but only for an hour or so.

The front door jingled open, and Sylvie winced at the thought of playacting like nothing was wrong.

"I've got this," Meg said, rising. "I might not be on your payroll, but I still know my way around this store." With a wink, she swept away to help the customers.

Assured they were in good hands, Sylvie rested her eyes. Visions of Rose on Mr. Ferris's wheel revolved through her mind. It was only three days ago. It felt like a hundred.

"Aunt Sylvie? Are you sleeping?" Olive's whisper was loud enough for the stage.

Sylvie opened one eye and smiled in reply.

"Mr. and Mrs. Hoffman say you are invited to dinner with them at six o'clock tonight."

Sweet Anna and Karl. What would Sylvie do without them?

"Did you know my birthday is coming up?" Olive went on. "I'm going to be eight years old. I don't think Mama will like that much." She arranged her auburn braids over her shoulders, then retied the yellow ribbons around the ends.

Sylvie frowned. "Why not?"

Olive kicked her toe against the chair leg. "That's how old my sister Louise was when she died. I don't think I will have a party this year. Mama seems too sad about it."

Pushing her chair back from the table, Sylvie opened both arms wide, and her niece flung herself into them. "Losing Louise was very, very sad," she said. "But you, my dear, are worth celebrating every single year. You are God's gift to your family, the one who brought smiles to all of us at a time when we had too many tears."

Olive wiggled out of the embrace and nodded solemnly. "I'm the replacement. That's why Louise is my middle name."

"Well, no." Sylvie hesitated. "That's not— You're important for exactly who you are, not just because you were born right after Louise died."

"But Mama needs me to make her happy again. Just like you need Rose, or else you'll be too lonely."

Sylvie sucked in a breath. The way Olive phrased that made it sound like it was the child's responsibility to fill in what was missing in the parent. But that was too much pressure for any child, and backwards. It was the parent's job to provide what the child needed, not the other way around.

"Who told you that?" she asked Olive, then reached for her mug again.

"I already knew it about myself. But Rose told me that you needed her, too. Because you never married and so you couldn't have your own children, you wanted her to keep you company. She said that having her made you feel important."

Sylvie nearly spit out her coffee. Recovering, she asked, "She said that to you? What else did she tell you?"

"Lots." Olive climbed into the chair her mother had vacated and nibbled at the Berliner still on the plate. "She has always hated small men."

Sylvie searched her memory, grasping for context for such a statement. "Do you mean the novel *Little Men*?" She had read that to Rose after reading her *Little Women*. Those quiet times together ranked among her most cherished recollections. She'd never thought to ask if Rose had enjoyed those stories, too.

"Yes. She hates that book." She tipped forward Meg's coffee mug, then set it back down, nose wrinkling.

"Did she tell you why?"

"No. Why?" Olive looked at her as though she were being quizzed and Sylvie already held the answer.

She didn't. It was one more blank in a growing list of things Sylvie didn't know.

Kristof was stuffed, again. Laying one hand on his stomach, he held up the other to ward off the oncoming bowl of potato salad. "I couldn't eat another bite, Anna, truly."

197

She beamed as though he'd just paid her the highest compliment.

"I don't know where Gregor is dining this evening, but I'm certain he couldn't have eaten better than I have."

Sylvie murmured her agreement.

Karl downed the last bite of Wiener schnitzel and let his fork clatter to his plate. "Your brother isn't home much, is he?" He wiped a smudge of jam from the corner of his mouth.

"Not more than he can help," Kristof admitted. "From his perspective, there are far more exciting things to see than the inside of our apartment." He only hoped that didn't include a gaming table. Gregor had promised he was through gambling, but he'd broken promises before.

"What is the latest on the orchestra, son?" Karl asked. "Must you wait until November for steady work?"

Kristof pressed his fingertips together. They were sore from the hours of practice he had put in today, a soreness he wouldn't feel if he'd been playing regularly. He'd been rusty in some sections, too, which unnerved him. He was first violin, after all. The standard was perfection. Anything less, and he wasn't worthy of his position.

"A lawyer has taken up our case with the Exposition officials, since they broke our contract," he said. "We should hear on Monday what the decision is."

"You played at the Midway Ball last night, didn't you?" Anna asked. "How was that?"

Kristof caught Sylvie's eye. "Stranger than you can imagine."

After a brief description of the ball and those who attended, Sylvie rose and began clearing dishes. "Stay, Anna. I'll take care of it," she said when Anna stirred as though to help.

Kristof watched her. Purple crescents hung beneath her eyes, and she had barely touched her food. They hadn't spoken about Rose during the meal, since no one wanted to broach distressing topics while eating. But once dinner was over and Sylvie had poured coffee for the four of them, it could no longer be avoided.

When Sylvie resumed her seat, Anna laid her blue-veined hand atop Sylvie's thin shoulder. "Any news on our Rose?"

Sylvie unfolded a paper and passed it to the Hoffmans. "We found this note when we arrived home from the ball early this morning. All her things are gone now, too. So is her cat."

This was news to Kristof and clapped his ears like blocks of wood. The finality of this information weighted his shoulders. No one needed to point out that if Rose was planning to return soon, she wouldn't need all her belongings, and especially not the cat.

He reached across the table and enfolded Sylvie's hand in his. Her fingers, far too cold for a summer's evening, squeezed his before she withdrew them to her lap.

"Well." Karl's voice was gruff with emotion. "We thank God for keeping her safe, ja?"

Cupping her hands around her mug, Anna's mouth pursed. "We can't know what she's thinking, and it's clear she doesn't want us to. But she knows you love her, dear. She knows you have a home for her to come back to. We'll keep praying for her, and for you. Perhaps that is all we can do?"

"She could be anywhere," Sylvie said. "Now that she has all she needs. She could have left the state and might be on her way . . . anywhere."

"Or perhaps she is still here in the city," Kristof said.

Sylvie's eyes flicked to his, so hungry for hope that it startled him.

He cleared his throat. "I learned something today." With as few words as possible, he relayed what Tiny O'Bannon had seen Rose do after her violin lesson on Monday. "So I went to the train terminal this afternoon and questioned the men in the ticket booths for all the lines. One of them remembered a young blond lady carrying a violin case. She bought a ticket and boarded a train alone. The elevated train. It was only headed to another station in Chicago."

"So she's still here in the city." Sylvie sat up straighter, leaning forward.

"It's possible. That's as much as we know for now."

She bit her bottom lip. "But how did you come by this information?"

Kristof shifted in his chair. He didn't want to tell her the truth, but he refused to lie. "I talked to someone who followed her."

"Ivan Mazurek? The young Polish man? He told me he didn't follow her into the fairgrounds."

Sun slanted across the table, gilding dust particles that danced in the air between them. "Not Ivan." He pinched the pleats of his trousers where they fell away from his knees. "Gregor owed a man some money after gambling and losing to him. When we couldn't pay it all back at once, a man followed us, and another man followed Rose."

"Why?" Sylvie nearly shouted. The color rushed back into her cheeks. She appeared as though she were on fire on the inside.

"I can only imagine that if we failed to pay the debt, they would have—" He hated the words before they even formed on his tongue. He brushed schnitzel crumbs from the yellow tablecloth into his hand, then didn't know what to do with them. He stuffed his fist into his pocket. "They would have held her to make sure we did."

Anna gasped, and Karl muttered an oath in German.

Sylvie's eyelids flared. "My daughter was in danger because of Gregor's gambling? That doesn't make sense."

"The man in question saw me talking with you the night of the fireworks on Wooded Island. He thought I cared about you, and about Rose." He swallowed. "He was right. And it didn't take much sleuthing for him to learn that we live in the same building. He was taking a precaution, but he never touched her."

"You believe him?" She was out of her chair, pacing the small kitchen, twisting her hands together.

"I do. He only wanted the money he was owed, and now he has it. Plus a little extra for sharing what he saw Rose do."

"You paid him extra to tell you that?" She rounded on him. "How do you know he didn't make it up, just to get the payment? He could be stringing you along for his own benefit and holding her just the same."

Kristof tilted his head, absorbing the wildness that had flooded her eyes. "Because I talked to the man at the train station. And before that, I talked to the ticket booth employee for the steamship that runs out of Casino Pier. Both of them corroborate his story." Slowly, he stood, careful lest he startle her further. "I know it isn't much to go on, but it's more than we had before."

Sylvie pressed shaking hands to her head and bent forward, rocking just slightly. If she'd felt as though she were coming undone at the ball, apparently he'd just unraveled her further. It was a blow, seeing what his words had done to her.

Anna reached up, placed her hand on Sylvie's back, and rubbed a slow circle.

"Ja," said Karl. "You know that Rose spoke with someone she knew. You know that during the one-hour boat ride, that someone may have convinced her to board a train that went somewhere else in Chicago."

"But after that she could have gotten on another and left the state. She could have . . ." Sylvie was pacing again, out of the kitchen and into the parlor, then back.

Sympathy for her sharpened Kristof's helplessness. She had been exhausted as it was before dinner, and now she was coming unglued. And it was he who had brought this on.

"Look." He stood in front of her so she would face him. Strands of hair had slipped from their pins and framed her careworn face. Silver streaks shone at her temples, more than he'd noticed before. "There are a lot of question marks. But the one thing we know for sure is in that note. We know she's safe."

She crossed her arms. "But do we?"

CHAPTER FOURTEEN

After dinner, Sylvie returned to her apartment and pulled Rose's diary from her parlor bookcase. She scoured the pages for secrets, for clues, and found both. Olive's words—*"She has always hated small men"*—hung like a banner in the room as Sylvie happened upon mention of the novel, in an entry written when Rose was sixteen.

> I think I know why Mimi likes *Little Men* so much. In the story, an orphan named Nat comes to stay at Plumfield School with Mrs. Jo, and he completely forgets about his own parents and never talks about them again. But that isn't how it works. You don't just forget where you came from. You don't just trade an old life for a new one like you're swapping out a wardrobe. My parents loved me, and I miss them both. They are woven into the fabric of who I am.
>
> There are twins who live at Plumfield, too, a boy and girl, but they aren't orphans at all. They just like being with their aunt and uncle, who run the school. If my parents were still alive, there is no way I

wouldn't live with them. Only when the twins' father dies do they go home to stay with their mother. Mimi cries at that part, but it serves those two ungrateful children right. If they loved their father, they wouldn't live anywhere else! Pinocchio is a much better story. There's a boy who had sense enough to try to get back to his father.

I do love Mimi with all my heart. I know she loves me with all of hers. She says I'm all she needs, but what if she's not all I need? I can't tell her that. It would break her heart. But someday I've just got to find more. I've got to get out of here. Her love for me is so constricting that sometimes I feel like I can hardly breathe.

Sylvie stared at the page, stunned. She read the passage again and again, as if torturing herself would atone for the mistakes she'd made with Rose.

From her pocket she withdrew the note left for her after the ball. The handwriting was the same. Only this time, Rose declared, *I have everything I need now.* Everything she needed did not include Sylvie.

She wondered who Rose's new life did include. Her most hopeful thought was that she'd moved into the apartment building that housed the Jane Club. Tessa had said she hadn't seen Rose at all, and Sylvie believed her. Rose wouldn't have put Tessa in that position, to have to lie to her employer about her daughter's whereabouts. But there were five other apartments with Jane Club girls.

Do not come looking for me, Sylvie read from the note again.

Ridiculous.

Friday, August 18, 1893

After a haunted night and a distracted day giving tours at the Fair, Sylvie pinned her hat in place, hooked the net below her chin, and left Corner Books & More.

Insects rattled the heavy evening air. Hoofbeats clip-clopped on the street, and her heels clicked over the sidewalk as she hurried east on Randolph Street. One-horse cabs and hansoms waited, empty, outside the six-story Sherman House at the corner of Randolph and Clark. But the coins in Sylvie's pocket felt light. It would cost a dollar fifty to get to Beth where she lived at the Hull House and back again, not to mention the time lost in rush-hour traffic, making the almost two-mile trip seem much longer.

Veering away from the cab, she entered the

grey sandstone Sherman House instead. Stores and offices lined the first floor of the building. A sign beside the elevator indicated that the public telephone was straight ahead.

Her footsteps echoed on the tiles as she made her way past a haberdashery and a cigar shop to the Chicago Telephone Company station. She paid ten cents for five minutes, stepped into a narrow booth, and closed the door while she called the Hull House. When Beth came to the phone, Sylvie filled her in on everything from the Midway Ball to the note Rose had left in place of her belongings.

"Rose isn't staying with Tessa," Sylvie added, "but maybe—"

"I'll check," Beth cut her off to say. The Jane Club building was just around the corner from Hull House. "I know all the young ladies there. If Rose is staying with them, those harboring her will have to answer to me for making you worry like this." Her voice crackled over the wire. "Give me an hour or so. I'll call you back at the Sherman House exchange and tell you what I learn."

An hour felt like three. At last the phone rang, jarring Sylvie's nerves, and the telephone company agent sent the call to the phone in the booth for her.

She held her breath while listening. Beth had been inside every apartment, searched every closet, and inspected the upholstery for cat hair, God bless her.

"She isn't there." Beth sounded almost as defeated as Sylvie felt. "I talked to Tessa, though. A couple of weeks ago, Rose told her that she wanted to prove to you that she could make it on her own. Maybe that's really what she's doing."

Silence buzzed on the line while Sylvie tried to make sense of this possibility. If Rose wasn't proving this point with the Jane Club, where else could she be? And if her goal was to demonstrate she could be on her own, why wouldn't she want Sylvie to see for herself? The pieces of this riddle scattered through Sylvie's mind, none of them fitting together.

"Sylvie? You still there?"

"I'm here." She rubbed the grooves on her forehead, then remembered to ask if Beth had learned anything from the Hull House Players.

"Nothing, or I would have told you. Apparently, they barely spoke to her when they weren't rehearsing lines. They accepted her acting—no one could deny she was gifted—but resented that she had so much more privilege than they did."

Sylvie swiveled slowly on the stool on which she sat. No wonder Rose had written that she knew what it was like not to belong. And yet . . . "I thought Rose was friends with a girl named

Gita." She'd talked about her more than any of the other players.

"Gita Górecki? She told me Rose had been to her home a few times but was more interested in her mother than in her."

Górecki. The woman Rose had mentioned in her diary. How had Sylvie missed that she was Gita's mother?

She pressed the handset tighter against her ear. "I need to talk to her, then. Gita's mother." She glanced at the clock on the wall outside the booth. They were running out of time.

"Bring your translator," Beth said, presumably referring to Kristof. "Gita was the only one in that household who spoke English, and she just traded her job at the knitting factory for a trial as a live-in domestic on the other side of the city. Or you could wait until Gita comes home on her half day off in a week or so."

But Sylvie couldn't wait.

Sunday, August 20, 1893

"Watch it." Kristof glared at the stubbled young man who had elbowed Sylvie without bothering to beg her pardon.

"Are you kidding me?" he shot back in thickly accented English, one lanky arm stretched over his head to grip a leather loop hanging from the electric streetcar's ceiling. Between his suspenders, his shirtfront was halfway untucked from his trousers.

"Do I look like I'm kidding?" Kristof replied in Czech.

Surprise flitted over the man's face before he stumbled toward the rear, bumping into more folks as the car sped along the street.

"It's a trolley, Kristof, on a Sunday afternoon," Sylvie said with a small smile, swaying with the car's rocking motion. "It's crowded."

The August heat stuck to his skin. "You hate crowds." His feet planted wide, he held the grip beside hers and angled himself to shield her from the press of bodies behind him.

He'd gone to the bookshop yesterday afternoon to check on her, content to wait while she steered patrons toward recommendations that led to sales. Between customers, she had told him about her telephone call with Beth. After sharing that she wanted to visit a Polish woman on DeKoven Street, she'd said, "I need to bring a translator. I want to bring a friend."

A friend, indeed.

Sylvie was still gazing at him. Wind puffed through an open window, sweeping a curl of hair across her neck. "Thanks for coming," she said. With a sudden glint in her dark eyes, she reached up and tugged the brim of his hat, rotating it off-center.

Hiding his amusement, he straightened it. "I ought to bump your hat askew and see if you don't cry . . ." *Drat!* The expression was on the tip of his tongue. Cry what? Not wolf, that was completely different. "Chicken?"

Sylvie's brow twisted before releasing in a burst of quiet laughter. "So close. Cry *foul*." The trolley jolted, and she steadied herself with a hand against his chest, then smoothed his lapel before tucking the errant strand of hair behind her ear.

Kristof shook his head. "I'd have an easier time remembering your idioms if they made any sense." His English mother had never said things like this.

"F-o-u-l, not f-o-w-l. It's a baseball term, I think, or maybe sports in general. Short for 'foul play.' You know, something out of bounds, off limits. Not fair play. As in, if Rose knew I had Beth search the Jane Club apartments, and that you and I are going to talk to Mrs. Górecki, she'd cry foul."

"For Rose to tell you she's safe with no other details and ask you not to look for her—*that's* foul play. You're doing the right thing. This isn't a game."

The streetcar slowed to a stop, and they got off, transferring to a southbound horse-drawn streetcar. After Sylvie slid onto a wooden bench, Kristof sat beside her.

"How often did Rose visit Mrs. Górecki?" he asked.

"At least a few times." Sylvie seemed to be guessing. "Judging from the address Beth gave me, she lives near the Mazureks, whom Rose and I have visited in the past. Mrs. Mazurek has been ill, so we've brought her bread and honey, a few tins of tea. A few times Rose went back to the Halsted Street neighborhood with Tessa after work to visit Mrs. Mazurek before Hull House Players' practice. It may be that she visited Mrs. Górecki, as well."

At the next stop, Kristof gave his seat to an elderly woman and remained standing. When it was time to disembark, he guided Sylvie to the exit, then hopped out first to help her down. Then, instead of drawing her gloved hand through the crook of his elbow, he simply held it and waited to see if she'd withdraw from his touch, as his own mother had.

She lifted her face toward his, surprise flashing for a moment before she smiled and gave his fingers a gentle squeeze. That was all, and yet it was enough to release the cinching in his chest.

They said little as they skirted the Maxwell Street market. Fish gleamed silver from ice-topped barrels fitted with pipes that fed waste-water into the street. Near them was a long table bearing prunes, raisins, nuts, soda water, candles, matches, and cakes covered with black flies.

Smells of raw chicken and fish mingled with those of ripening fruit. The air crackled with haggling, with neighborhood dogs barking and begging for scraps, and with children shrieking in play.

"This way," she said. They took a side road, then another until they reached DeKoven Street. A train chugged by a few blocks away. Though the factories and sugar refinery were closed today, the atmosphere remained thick with their fumes.

Sylvie nodded toward a steamship ticket agency edging up to the potholed road. "Beth said she lives above that." Greasy newspaper sheets blew across their path as they made their way to the alley's narrow stairs.

The hallway outside the door held the odor of the privies in the backyard, along with dill, caraway, and paprika from someone's cooking. Kristof knocked.

A woman he assumed was Mrs. Górecki answered with a baby of about four months on her hip. Three more children, all under the age of eight, streamed out from behind her and clambered down the steps. From below, a door squeaked on its hinges as they barreled outside to play.

"Mrs. Górecki?" Kristof gave a little bow and tipped his hat before introducing himself and Sylvie in Polish, adding that Sylvie volunteered with Hull House, and that her daughter, Rose, was in the Hull House Players with Mrs. Górecki's daughter, Gita.

Suspicion shadowed the woman's features as she bounced the fussing infant. "Gita isn't here."

"We understand Rose paid you a few visits. Would you mind if we speak with you about those?"

Sylvie laid a hand on Kristof's arm. "Tell her we don't need to come inside. She's probably wary of needing to feed us if we do."

At this, the woman visibly relaxed, shifting her baby to the opposite hip. Strands of fading brown hair escaped a red kerchief, framing a face lined by years of care. Still, she was clean, her fingernails trimmed, and her skirt and shirtwaist, though faded, were in good repair.

"There isn't much to tell." She swiped at a spider web in the corner of the doorframe and wiped it on her apron. "One day, I mentioned that I knew her father when he lived in the neighborhood. After that, she started coming with apples or cheese for us, books for Gita to borrow, but she asks all kinds of questions. Rozalia acts like we ought to be friends, wearing my poor Gita out with all the translating."

Kristof shared this with Sylvie. From the street below, a medley of Bohemian, Polish, and Italian voices rose and fell.

"She wanted to belong," Sylvie said quietly,

and Kristof repeated it in Polish. "I'm sure of it."

The baby whimpered, and Mrs. Górecki gave him a damp, twisted rag to suck on. "Well, she doesn't. Not here, and I told her that. She wanted to learn Polish cooking, Polish traditions, the language. Here I am, bending over my laundry tubs, the baby screaming, and she thinks I have time for all that. Me! Teach her! Her in her fancy clothes, with her shiny hair that smells like flowers, her perfect teeth and soft white hands. She's had better schooling than I ever had, and she comes in here like I could give her something she doesn't already have. 'Go on with you,' I finally told her. 'If there's one thing I know about Nikolai, it's that he wanted your life to be better than this, and it is. You're not one of us, you're *American.* So be happy, and go on to your acting practice with Gita, where you can *really* pretend to be someone you aren't.' "

Sylvie stepped a little closer to Kristof, almost as if bracing against the tirade. "Leave nothing out. Tell me every word she said."

So he did. He understood where Mrs. Górecki was coming from, yet still ached for Rose and Sylvie both.

"Oh. Oh no." Sylvie's nose turned pink, but she bridled the emotion pulsing just below the surface. "I wish she'd told me."

"She didn't want to hurt you," Kristof guessed,

then wondered what would have happened if Rose had confided in her. Most certainly, Sylvie would have tried to comfort her. But would Rose have accepted it or resisted it as counterfeit, hurting both Sylvie and herself?

Kristof knew what that was like. He'd done it himself.

He thought again of his own mother. When he was thirteen years old, he'd gone with his family to hear a Viennese symphony orchestra playing in Budapest. He had been so moved by the sublime music that he had reached for his mother's hand. She had startled, shocked. Glowering, Father had leaned forward, hissing that he was too old for "such nonsense." The music had played on, though for Kristof it had been ruined by this humiliation. Then small fingers found his, and it was Kristof's turn to be surprised that four-year-old Gregor had filled the emptiness his parents would not.

But he hadn't wanted his little brother, already a prodigy, already usurping Kristof in his parents' affections. He'd wanted his mother—and not even very much of her. Just a moment, just one beautiful shared experience. So he'd pulled away, hurting Gregor in exactly the same way his parents had just hurt him.

He still regretted that choice. He hoped Rozalia would not do the same to Sylvie.

All of this flashed through his mind in the time

it took to brush a loose thread from his jacket. Then Sylvie's hand pressed his once more, anchoring him to the present.

"Mrs. Górecki, did Rose ever talk to you or Gita about wanting to leave home?" Kristof asked. "Did she express any interest in becoming a domestic like Gita?"

"No." The woman chuckled. "She gave Gita her condolences, actually, over leaving me and serving in another household. Rozalia would never do the same."

Waiting in the doorway while Kristof filled Sylvie in, Mrs. Górecki gentled her swaying to a rhythmic pattern. She began to sing a lullaby. "*A-a-a, a-a-a, byly sobie kotki dwa . . .*" The child's eyelids fluttered closed, his dimpled fist tight on the rag in his mouth.

"Is there anything else you'd like to ask, Sylvie?" Kristof murmured, trying not to disturb the baby's drift to sleep.

She stared at Mrs. Górecki. "That song. I've heard Rose humming it at home. She said it was the lullaby her mother sang to her, but I only heard it for the first time a few months ago. Please, what does it mean?"

Turning back to Mrs. Górecki, Kristof explained that he was going to translate the lullaby into English for Sylvie, if she didn't mind. She didn't.

Kristof bowed his head closer to Sylvie's and

whispered the lyrics as Mrs. Górecki sang about two little kittens, both greyish-brown, who wouldn't settle down for the night.

Oh, sleep, my darling,
If you'd like a star from the sky, I'll give
    you one.
All children, even the bad ones,
Are already asleep,
Only you are not.

Mrs. Gorecki repeated the first verse, then ended with the last one, persuading the kittens to sleep because even the moon was yawning. The lullaby over, she continued to twist at the waist, one hand cupping her baby's head against her shoulder.

"Thank you," Sylvie said through Kristof. "That was charming. Beautiful. We won't disturb you further."

Mrs. Górecki waved a hand dismissively. "Rozalia asked Gita to teach her this song, too, the first time she heard me sing it."

Sylvie frowned. "Rose told me she learned it from her mother."

A shrug lifted Mrs. Górecki's shoulders as she backed into the apartment. "Her mother might have sung it to her, it's common enough. But if Rozalia learned it at all, it was from me and my Gita. Good afternoon."

The door closed.

"The poor child," Sylvie whispered. "She's just a child, longing for her mother."

But that didn't explain where she was.

CHAPTER FIFTEEN

Monday, August 21, 1893

It had happened over the weekend, this seismic shift within Sylvie that moved her toward a begrudging acceptance of the way things were. Rose wasn't a child anymore; she was seventeen. She wasn't living with the Jane Club girls. She hadn't told Mrs. Górecki of any plans to leave home, and after Sylvie and Kristof talked to more Polish neighbors, they learned nothing else. Whatever her motivation, she was gone, and she wasn't coming back.

The sooner Sylvie adjusted to this, the better, and the only way Sylvie knew how to manage the grief of loss was to bury it under work. Which was exactly what she was doing right now.

Fixing a smile in place, she regarded the group of five women, all English teachers from Indiana, who had hired her to guide them in a meaningful tour of the Fair, beginning with the Woman's Building. For lunch, she would take them to the Great White Horse Inn, designed to be an exact reproduction of the inn Charles Dickens made famous in *The Pickwick Papers*. What they would see first, however, was even better.

"Ladies," she said, "we are about to enter what

I believe will be the pinnacle of your experience in this building, and perhaps throughout the entire Fair." After a dramatic pause, she announced, "The Library."

"Is it true every book inside was written by a woman?" A lady named Mildred adjusted her spectacles.

"All seven thousand of them. I'm afraid you won't be able to handle the volumes, but I'm sure you'll be dazzled by the sheer number of them. In glass cases, you'll see manuscripts sent from England, written by Jane Austen, Charlotte Brontë, Elizabeth Gaskell, and George Eliot, also known as Mary Anne Evans."

"Oh my." A rotund woman named Mary dabbed a handkerchief to her nose. "To be so close to their genius, I just can't tell you what it means to me."

Sylvie smiled. "Be sure to visit the cabinet devoted to Harriet Beecher Stowe. It holds a rare first edition of *Uncle Tom's Cabin*, along with forty-two foreign translations." All of this information flew from Sylvie's tongue without thought. It was rote to her and required nothing of her to repeat it. "Let's go in, and you'll see for yourselves."

She followed her little flock of English teachers into the library and heard their gasps of awe, for it was the most beautiful room of the entire Fair. Above low bookcases, wainscoting

221

of old English oak graced the walls, taken from a seventeenth-century French cathedral. The mural on the ceiling, painted by a woman named Dora Wheeler Keith, showed medallions and allegorical figures representing Science, Art, and Imagination, all enclosed in a border of Venetian scrollwork.

The English teachers were visibly moved by the effect. But today, Sylvie did not feel their joy. She felt very little and was glad of it. She had prayed this morning to be numb.

Sunshine lit the stained-glass windows and the gilding throughout the otherwise subdued room of deep blues and greens. While Mrs. Fanning, the presiding librarian, welcomed the teachers and pointed out the highlights of the room, Sylvie slowly strolled the perimeter, past busts and portraits. Reaching a green leather armchair, she gripped the back of it, forcing herself to remain standing when her body begged to sink into the cushions.

Her mind winged over the White City, carrying her back to Mrs. Górecki's apartment yesterday and the lullaby Rose had claimed as her mother's own. Why would a girl so tender toward her mother's memory also walk away from the woman who raised her? Rose longed for a connection to her past, but did that mean she had to sever the bond she'd forged with Sylvie? *"Surely there is room in a woman's heart for more than one person,"* she'd mused to Kristof yesterday.

"Is there?" he'd replied. His fingers laced with hers.

He knew that Sylvie had been single-minded about caring for her own mother after Stephen came home from war, because no one else seemed to notice how Ruth struggled. After the Great Fire, Sylvie became Stephen's primary caregiver, a role that lasted until his death. And then there was Rose, the little girl Sylvie loved to love, the precious child who filled her life so completely that she had no need for a suitor. Besides, how would a man in Sylvie's life have affected Rose? No, carving out space for a man was far too complicated.

But it hadn't seemed complicated yesterday. Being with Kristof was natural and simple in the best sense. She was drawn to him in ways she was nearly ready to give up denying. But she didn't see how he could possibly feel the same way about her. Holding her hand like that, maybe it was only another Hungarian custom, like the habit he'd had to give up upon moving to America of kissing both cheeks of anyone he greeted. Or the tradition of a man walking on the left side of the woman, because long ago men wore swords on their left side, and this way he would be ready to draw the weapon and protect her.

Yes. Another Hungarian custom. That must be it.

She frowned. It hadn't felt like mere convention.

"Is there?" Kristof's voice echoed in her mind, entreating her all over again. One question, two words, an open door. At least, that had been her interpretation at the time. Was there room in her heart for him, and in a role that went beyond friendship?

She barely had the words to admit to herself, let alone to him, that somehow, he was already at that threshold, or dangerously near it. All she'd been able to do was blush beneath the warmth of his attention, not trusting herself to read his intention right. Worried that something had been lost in translation.

"If you'll direct your attention to where Miss Townsend is standing." Mrs. Fanning rescued Sylvie from further reflection. "Just behind her is a glass case of autographs you won't want to miss."

Sylvie stepped out of the way as the English teachers beat a straight path to view the autographs. Mildred held out her hand, fingertips nearly touching the glass. Mary blew her nose into her handkerchief as the others read aloud each name.

Catherine de Medici.
Mary, Queen of Scots.

"Sylvia Townsend."

She startled. "Jozefa," she said. "Are you lecturing again today?"

"No, this time I'm merely attending. You ladies have arranged such a fascinating array of topics, and I'm learning all I can. How are you?" The question was laden with meaning.

"Rose is fine, I'm glad to report." Sylvie forged a smile she didn't feel. "I do apologize for not letting you know earlier."

"Ah. That is excellent news. She's returned home, then, I take it."

Home. Sylvie had no idea where home was for Rose anymore, but she knew it wasn't the apartment above Corner Books & More. She hesitated. "Actually, she decided to move out on her own." She might as well have announced, *I have failed as an adoptive parent and have driven her away.*

Jozefa inclined her head, exuding grace and class. "Then I congratulate you for raising her to be independent enough to make that leap. The goal, from infancy, is always to guide children into adulthood so they can make their own contributions to society. That Rose is ready for this step tells me you have accomplished this. She is launched!" With a flourish, she flung out her arm as though releasing a bird once caged. Perhaps that was exactly how Rose had felt.

Sylvie didn't know what to say. She cast a

glance at her tour group to see if they were ready for her again. They weren't.

Jozefa squeezed Sylvie's hand. "I imagine this transition will be more difficult on you than it is for her. But don't be fooled. You are free now, too."

"Free?" Sylvie didn't feel free. She felt locked inside her regrets.

"Singleness is a gift, dear, and so is being childless. Don't waste it. Why, I'd never be able to do what I do if I were tied to a family of my own."

But Sylvie didn't want to be free of family. If she had the choice between having her name read aloud in a list of accomplished women or on the lips of the people she loved most, she would far prefer the latter.

"What am I supposed to do now?" she whispered.

"My dear." Jozefa leaned in, her floral-scented talcum powder choking the air between them. "Whatever you want."

Hacks and cabs lined Congress Street, arriving and departing with shoppers, businessmen, and tourists. Behind Kristof, above the alley between Wabash and State Streets, the elevated train roared along the trestle-like bridge, shuttling passengers to the Fair. Bicyclists zipped around omnibuses and streetcars.

Kristof, however, had walked the seven blocks south and four blocks east to get here from his apartment. Immune to the bustle around him, he paused on the sidewalk and peered at the tower topping the Auditorium Building's hotel. The immense granite building on the corner of Congress and Michigan Avenue had been home to the Chicago Symphony Orchestra since its founding two years ago. Squinting, he could make out tiny figures on the tower roof. Every day, more than a thousand visitors paid a quarter to ride the elevator up seventeen stories to the top for a view that reached to the lake and well beyond the city.

At a break in traffic, Kristof darted to the other side of the street and strode beneath the Coliseum-type arches that marked the building's theatre entrance.

He'd missed this place.

The saloon in the south lobby was empty this time of day. Kristof checked his pocket watch, confirming he had a full two hours before his lunch meeting, then crossed the saloon, passed the brass-barred box office windows, and strolled through the main lobby. Even without all the electric lights turned on, the mosaic tile floor shone in shades of white, black, and terra-cotta.

With one more push through a set of double doors, he stood at the rear of the stunning four-thousand-seat auditorium. A series of huge arches spanned the ceiling at intervals, each one studded with electric lights. Smaller arches flanked the stage like gilded rainbows. Sunshine fell through the skylight above.

Kristof marched down the crimson-carpeted aisle, passed the orchestra pit, and took the stage, which currently held an opera set for *Carmen*, complete with a faux stone fountain, pedestrian bridge, and painted backdrop of old Seville. There were practice rooms aplenty, but there was nothing like playing here, with perfect acoustics. The sound was heavenly when he played well, and painfully clear when he was in error. He welcomed the accountability. Just because the new season wouldn't open for three months was no excuse for getting sloppy.

A philosophy Gregor didn't share.

Kristof opened his case and rosined his bow. Despite what he'd said to Gregor about trading their father's timepiece for information about Rose, he couldn't deny that he felt its loss. It wouldn't have happened if Gregor hadn't gambled in the first place.

But then again, they'd know less about Rose, too.

Setting his jaw, Kristof lifted his instrument to his shoulder, tuned the A string, then intervals of perfect fifths between all four strings. He needed to concentrate on Mozart's "Rondo alla Turca," not the sins of his brother, or the mystery of

Rose's whereabouts, or the way Sylvie's hand fit so perfectly into his own.

Right. That was exactly what he needed to stop thinking about.

Kristof sharpened his focus, and his fingers danced over the strings, each sixteenth note and grace note ringing out over the auditorium. Every slur was smooth, every staccato sharp. In his ears, he could hear the rest of the orchestra playing with him, elevating the music to new heights.

After the third repeat, the melody changed to a steady rhythm of running sixteenth notes for nine solid lines, repeats included. He stumbled. Backed up a few measures and tried again. Drilled the line over and over, slowly at first, then with increasing speed until he played it *a tempo, allegretto*. Sweat dampening his forehead, he nailed the intonation. But with the smallest lapse in focus, he fumbled the fingering and lost the perfect rhythm when correcting it.

A child's error.

What was wrong with him? What kind of first violinist was he?

The distracted kind, obviously. The kind that needed more practice.

Shame whispered in his ear: *You're an imposter.*

It wasn't true. But his father had insisted upon it for years. It had taken Kristof too long to realize his father secretly felt the same way about himself. His compositions amounted to nothing.

He lived a lifestyle he couldn't afford, just to keep up the appearance of success. Any musical accomplishments in the Bartok family would have to be realized by the sons. Kristof and Gregor were both slaves to their father's failure, always being driven to compensate.

That was why Kristof worked as hard as he did. And why Gregor rebelled against it.

Between Mozart's rondo and drilling Beethoven's violin concerto, two hours of practice flew by. He could have doubled the time, easily. But he would not keep his maestro waiting.

Laying his instrument in its velvet-lined case, Kristof opened his watch once again and thought of the one so recently lost. The heirloom that skipped over the eldest son to show favor for the youngest, even beyond the grave. Honestly, he didn't know why he was sad to see it go.

After smoothing a hand over his hair, Kristof spotted Maestro Thomas already seated in the Grand Dining Room restaurant on the Auditorium's tenth floor. They might have saved money by simply meeting in the maestro's office downstairs, but from what Kristof could tell, Thomas was in no mood to be crossed. After pausing to allow a waiter to pass with a loaded tray, he wove between the tables and joined him.

"I took the liberty of ordering for you," Thomas said.

Odd. Kristof was five minutes early. "How efficient." He chuckled, sliding his violin case beneath the chair. "What am I having? I sincerely hope it isn't humble pie."

The maestro's ample mustache bent up with a grin. "Humble pie is an acquired taste. As it turns out, one I've never managed to acquire." He patted his belly. "I'm sick with it."

That didn't sound good. "Care to elaborate?" Kristof sipped the ice water in front of him and placed the goblet back on the ring it had already left on the tablecloth. Conversations among other diners were crystal clear, as well, thanks to the acoustics of the soaring arched ceiling.

"It's why you're here, Kristof. The lawyers have concluded the negotiations over the Exposition Orchestra's broken contract. The good news is that the Exposition Company has agreed to let the orchestra start twice-daily concerts again, at your original salary. The bad news is that it will only last two weeks. Then it's over, for good."

Kristof nodded slowly. Two weeks' more salary meant three hundred more dollars for Kristof, and another three hundred for Gregor. They'd be able to pay their rent without issue.

"You'll also be paid on concession. When folks purchase tickets at the gate, the Exposition Company keeps fifteen percent, and the musicians get the rest." He winced. "Those numbers won't add up to much, based on the audiences we've been drawing."

Pennies. They could literally be making pennies per performance. But at least they'd still be salaried.

"We could change the program," Kristof suggested. "If we play the more popular selections rather than the longer, wouldn't that drive up sales?"

"It might." Thomas grabbed a slice of steaming bread from a linen-draped basket and slathered it with honeyed butter. "But would the masses pay to hear those songs when they can hear marching bands for free throughout the day?" He took a bite and chewed. "You're set up for failure all over again. Bread?"

Kristof declined. Absently, he pushed the salt and pepper shakers toward the center of the table where they belonged. "You mean *we*. You mean *we're* set up . . . don't you?"

The maestro made a show of wiping his hands in front of him, allowing crumbs to drop from his fingers. "I've washed my hands of the entire affair, Kristof. They invited me to lead again, but I already resigned, and I won't go back on that. I'm a man of my word, even when they don't like it. That means you're in charge. You're conducting the Exposition Orchestra in my stead, for as long as the performances last."

Surprise snatched Kristof's speech.

232

The maestro leaned toward him. "I thought I was getting a stowaway in you when your brother convinced me to take you on in New York. He was the prized musician, I thought. Turns out you're the Bartok I rely on."

Cutlery clinked on china throughout the dining room while Kristof waited for the words to make sense. "Did you say Gregor convinced you to hire me on to the New York Philharmonic?"

Thomas sat back. "I thought you knew. His audition was spectacular. Yours was routine. But he refused to join unless I hired you, too. It was the best hire I made."

At the next table, a woman laughed in a cascading glissando. A ray of light shattered on the cut-glass pitcher of water, casting quivering rainbows all over the table. Kristof did not trust himself to frame a reply.

"Do you hear what I'm saying, Kristof? You discipline yourself more than I ever could. Your growth as a musician has outpaced Gregor's. He's no more sensational now than when I first met the both of you ten years ago. You demand perfection from yourself. Now is your chance to demand it from everyone else, too."

An hour ago, Kristof could barely manage his own playing. And now, suddenly, he was to manage one hundred fifty others besides. He took another drink of water. "When do we resume?"

"Day after next."

CHAPTER SIXTEEN

Tuesday, August 22, 1893

Beth was a force to be reckoned with. And just now, Sylvie was grateful to have her by her side.

After Sylvie had led the Readers Club at Hull House last night, she'd paid her friend a visit. "I keep thinking back to what we learned from the Hungarians who work at the Orpheum on the Midway," she'd said. "If they wanted their serving girls to speak Hungarian, especially after two Chicago girls had already been fired, Varga might have had a different purpose in mind for Rose from the beginning. Maybe he was working with someone else. . . ."

"The brothels." Beth had named Sylvie's worst fear.

Five days had passed since she'd argued with Kristof about visiting them, but now she could think of nothing else.

"Rose wrote that she's fine now," Sylvie had mentioned, "but she could have been coerced into writing that to throw us off the hunt."

"Absolutely she could have been forced. We should see for ourselves. I'll go with you."

With her entire being, Sylvie wanted to believe

that Rose was simply a successfully launched young woman, as Jozefa had said. If that were the case, Sylvie would find a way to adjust. But neither could she let go too easily. It would cost her nothing to knock on doors on South Clark, Custom House, and Dearborn Streets.

So this evening, after she and Tessa had closed the bookshop, Sylvie and Beth took to the most notorious streets in the city, armed with determination, caution, and an extra dose of courage. It was hard to believe the Levee district's northern border of Harrison Street was a mere eight blocks due south of Corner Books & More.

Broad sidewalks accommodated the busy, albeit disreputable, neighborhood. Long rows of buildings lined the street with so few spaces between them that any that existed drew notice, like dark gaps where missing teeth had been. Cable cars trundled north on South Clark Street, from the direction of the stockyards toward downtown.

The street cleaners performed their duties well enough, she supposed, but the very air here was unclean. The trains entering and leaving the station a block away pumped out sooty clouds. Sylvie's skin filmed with humidity mingled with the odor of cheap perfumes and cheap whiskey from nearby saloons.

"Apples! Oranges!" a woman cried. "Get your apples here! Two for a penny!" They smelled as though they might better be used for making cider.

Heading north on South Clark, Sylvie paused in front of the Pacific Garden Mission. Inside, a sea of chairs filled the great hall—five hundred, she guessed, perhaps more. She had heard the mission took in upwards of six hundred homeless every evening, and that after they listened to a sermon, they were permitted to sleep in the chairs overnight. Hand-painted Bible verses scrolled over the walls above a potbellied stove. *Therefore if any man be in Christ, he is a new creature: old things are passed away; behold, all things are become new.*

Turning to Beth, Sylvie asked, "Have you been here before?" Telegraph poles bristled overhead, their cables sagging against the sky.

Beth shook her head with a jerking motion. "But I read about it in one of those guidebooks you sell, *Chicago by Day and Night*. Surely you know what it says."

She did. There was an entire chapter on Cheyenne, which began with, *"This is an excellent neighborhood to let alone, however curious you may be."* It ended by calling it the Whitechapel of Chicago, a sensational reference to the area of London where Jack the Ripper killed his prey. The comparison was totally uncalled for, she was sure. Still, Sylvie shuddered at the sight of a shadowed alley, where unsavory characters were said to lie in wait, ready to steal, or kill, or worse.

A band of policemen, billy clubs in hand, pushed between pedestrians, street vendors, and hacks.

"Don't worry, I'm armed. With an umbrella." Beth lowered it from her shoulder and closed it, transforming it into a weapon as she stabbed an invisible foe. Beneath her hat, her russet hair curled even tighter in the damp air, springing about her face.

"And what do I have?" Sylvie asked with a chuckle.

"Me." The word burst from Beth with enough force to pull the cords of her neck tight.

Dear Beth. She was fierce because she was afraid. When they were girls together, Beth used to sing to herself when she was anxious, and whistle against the dark. Once they had hidden themselves in a closet, planning to jump out and surprise Beth's older brother. Instead, he had locked them inside for what felt like hours to teach them a lesson. Sylvie had told stories to fight the fear, all of them with happy endings. Lost children found. Maidens who married. An ugly duckling that became a swan. Beth just hugged her knees and rocked, a faltering tune on her lips.

She didn't sing anymore. She shouted and marched and, apparently, wielded umbrellas.

Beth shielded herself with a demeanor that tended toward the hard and unyielding. But Sylvie still saw the woman behind it, and the little girl still fighting the dark.

"Come on." Sylvie locked elbows with her oldest friend, and together they left the safe haven of the Pacific Garden Mission. Across the street were four brothels in adjoining row houses. Lace curtains framed empty windows. "We'll begin with Cora Clark's." She read the name from the sign out front.

"Cora Clark, here we come!" Beth said a little too loudly, then snorted with nervous laughter.

They crossed the road and climbed the steps. Sylvie knocked.

A few moments later, a shapely woman in a Japanese dressing gown answered. She surveyed Sylvie's straw boater hat, pleated shirtwaist, and navy skirt. "If you're selling religion, I'm not buying," she said.

"What? Oh," Sylvie stammered. "We're not from the Mission, if that's what you mean. I'm trying to find a young woman named Rozalia Dabrowski. I wondered if she might be in your employ." She showed the photograph that now went everywhere with her.

"Why? What's it to you?"

Beth pulled herself up tall. "Would you mind answering the question, ma'am? We just want to know if she works here."

The woman leaned a hip against the doorframe. "You two dames seem fun. I'd kind of like to pull your chain, but I haven't got the time. So I'll play nice and tell you she probably doesn't."

"Don't you know the names of the girls you work with?" Sylvie asked.

"Sure I do. Angel. Darling. Sweetheart. Doll-face. They forsake their given names as soon as they arrive. So no, I don't know any Rozalia. But we haven't hired on any new help in the last two weeks, so . . . does that answer your question?"

Sylvie exhaled. "It does. Thank you for your time." She nodded at Beth and turned to go.

The next establishment was Miss Lulu's, who also confirmed that Rose wasn't there.

And so it went, down the block, at Daisy Plant's, Kitty Plant's, and Candy Mollie Jones's. When they reached the famous Carrie Watson's brownstone house, Sylvie tried a different approach.

"She has blond hair, blue eyes, and she's a little shorter than me. And thinner," she added, holding up the sepia-toned image once again. "She's Polish but has no accent. She speaks English as well as I do."

"Lady," said a buxom woman who called herself Ida, "the girls we hire don't much resemble their old birthday photos, if you get my meaning. But we have several girls that fit your description."

"This one would have arrived in the last week or so. She would have arrived with nothing but the clothes on her back, and maybe her violin. But by Thursday morning, she would have had all her clothes again. Possibly, also, her cat."

The woman's red lips tipped with amusement. "Our girls don't keep pets."

"What about their own clothes?" Beth asked.

Long earrings sparkled against rouged cheeks. "I'm going to level with you two. Save you a little time and sweat. If this girl you're looking for has all her own clothes with her, I guarantee you she isn't here. She isn't in any house like ours in Cheyenne, nor anywhere else in the city, nor outside of it neither. Guaranteed."

A wave of relief rolled over Sylvie. "But how can you be sure? That she's not in this line of work at all?"

"You see what I'm wearing?" Ida opened her robe, revealing a low-cut, bright silk gown that left little to the imagination. She laughed at their shock and tied her robe closed again. Then her expression grew serious. "Listen. The way of the business is this. When a girl comes here, she loses everything she had before. Her name, her family, her friends, and her clothes. No madam would ever let her keep them. All she has is 'work attire,' so to speak. Do you know why? It's so that if she changes her mind about her life choice, decides to leave . . . well, she won't. She's not likely to run out into the street dressed like this, now, is she? Wardrobes like ours have a way of marking us for who we are. Girls who repent of this lifestyle are too humiliated to escape it, dressed like this. Who would give us a helping hand, knowing we've already been ruined?"

The Scarlet Letter flashed through Sylvie's mind, the character Hester Prynne forever marked and judged for previous sins. She swallowed a growing knot in her throat. She was overwhelmingly grateful to put fears of Rose's involvement in this to rest. But the thought of other girls trapped here opened an ache inside her.

"There is help, just there, at the Pacific Garden Mission." She pointed.

Ida raised thin eyebrows. "Those are church folks. We sinners aren't good enough for them, especially. None of us are likely to go anywhere we'd feel even worse about ourselves."

"It's not like that, I'm sure," Sylvie pressed. "That's why the Mission is there, to help anyone who needs it. Anyone. Jesus would turn none away."

Beth shot her a look, and Sylvie wondered if she'd overstepped.

Ida rolled her darkly outlined eyes. "Jesus wants nothing to do with us. And we get along fine without Him."

"Surely you don't mean that," Sylvie said.

"You know, I think she does." Beth tapped her umbrella's tip on the doorstep, rotating it by the handle.

"This is taking far too much of my time." Ida leaned out the door. "But because you could use an education, I'm going to tell you. A lot of us here are happy with our lot. We're eating better than we ever did before. Our clothes may not be up to your standards, but they're a whole lot better than the rags we used to wear. We get beauty treatments for our hair and skin all the time. That's instead of lice."

Sylvie grasped for something to say and came up with nothing better than, "I'm sorry."

"Don't be. We're better off. And with the Fair, business is so good we can hardly keep up with it. So if you see any young beauties needing work, send them our way, will you?"

The door shut soundly.

Beth blinked at Sylvie. "Well! That's one big question answered, at least." She led the way down the stairs.

Sylvie trailed her, a deep sadness weighting her steps as they crossed the street. "Oh, Beth," she said. "Sometimes I feel like we're doing some good at Hull House. But there's so much brokenness in this city. It breaks my heart."

Opening her umbrella against the slanting sun, Beth circled to stand in front of Sylvie. "Don't do that."

"Do what?"

"Don't feel guilty about all the lost sheep. You can't fix everyone. And you were right about the Pacific Garden Mission. It's *right there*"— she jabbed her finger in a forceful point—"and people *know* it's there. It's their choice to accept that help or not. It's not up to you. Just be glad we know Rose isn't mixed up in that."

"I am. I can't tell you how glad." Sylvie released a long, slow breath, expelling former fears and worries. "I just—" Frowning, she stepped aside to peek around her friend. "Beth! Isn't that Ladislava Mazurek? Ivan's little sister. Lottie."

Beth spun and gasped. "It is."

Lottie came toward them, a ragged bonnet half covering her raven-black hair. She focused on the signs hanging in front of each brothel. Still not noticing Beth or Sylvie, the fifteen-year-old stopped in front of Carrie Watson's, then slowly took that first step.

Beth was the first to reach her. Her long fingers encircled Lottie's wrist. "Lottie, dear, what are you doing?"

Sylvie flanked the girl's other side, her pulse thrumming.

Lottie blanched, then turned red from collar to hairline. "How did you know? How did you find me?"

Beth glanced at the brothel door. "We'll talk about it somewhere else, all right?"

243

Sylvie looped her arm around Lottie's waist, gently guiding her away. She didn't know the girl well. She wasn't in the Hull House Players and had never come to Readers Club. But there was no way on God's green earth she was about to let her hand her soul to Carrie Watson.

"I can't go home yet, I just can't," Lottie cried.

Tight-lipped, Sylvie caught Beth's attention over the girl's head. "Oh yes, you can. We're going with you."

"No!" Lottie twisted and broke away, bolting down the block.

"Stop!" Beth shouted and gave chase alongside Sylvie.

Sylvie's boot heels faltered on the uneven surface, cranking her ankle awry, but she felt nothing as she scrambled after Lottie. Strands of hair pulled free of their pins and whipped across her face. Lungs fighting against her corset, she followed Lottie north, past Polk Street, past the Salvation Army Hotel, a peep show, three saloons, and as many pawn shops. When the girl took a hard left behind Gypsy Vernon's, Beth pulled ahead of Sylvie, long legs pumping.

Sylvie rushed around the corner and pulled up short.

Lottie had stopped running, caught by a man who held her fast in his arms. He wore a billy-cock hat, and a cigarette drooped near his stubbly beard. His shirtsleeves were rolled up to his elbows, and his collar splayed open.

"What do we have here? You in some kind of trouble, sweetheart? I'm sure I can help you out." He tore Lottie's hat from her head, thrust his fingers into her hair, and dislodged the pins. Her dark tresses tumbled over her shoulders, and he took a hank, rubbing it between his fingers, then brought it to his nose and sniffed.

"Stop!" Sylvie shouted. "Police! Help!"

"Get away from me!" Lottie stomped on the man's foot, then lunged for the fire escape ladder on the side of the building, grasping the iron bars and kicking at him while Beth ran at him with her umbrella. She struck at his kidney just as the police came pounding toward them from Harrison Street, clubs aloft and handcuffs jangling.

CHAPTER SEVENTEEN

The smell inside Lottie's home was not her mother's fault, but Sylvie could think of no polite way to set the poor woman at ease about her housekeeping without edging too close to insult. Situated about a mile west of the Levee, four blocks west of Chicago River's south branch, all the rear tenements on West DeKoven Street were just as small, the walls as thin, and the air fouled by the outhouses and piles of refuse below the window.

"Please don't trouble yourself, Mrs. Mazurek." Sylvie laid her hand on the woman's shoulder, preventing her from stirring from the cot in the corner of the room. Two bedrolls peeked out from beneath it. The rest of the space was taken up with a table, two chairs, a stool, and stacked milk crates holding dishes and pantry stores. A few changes of clothing hung from nails driven into the wall. The room was bedchamber, parlor, and kitchen all in one. "We're only here to bring Lottie home."

Mrs. Mazurek wheezed, then surrendered to a rattling cough far too big for her frame. "And why should a girl her age need help finding her way home?" Poverty had etched more lines in her face, and deeper, too, than the passing years.

Lottie dug her fingernails into Sylvie's arm, silently reminding her of her promise not to reveal too much. But it was a promise made on one condition, a bargain not easily struck, and Sylvie still didn't feel right about concealing anything from another mother.

"Sylvie and I were out, and our paths crossed Lottie's this evening," Beth offered. "She mentioned you'd taken a turn for the worse, Mrs. Mazurek."

Lottie had also confessed that her mother's illness, which had prevented her from working at the feather brush factory for weeks, required medicine they couldn't afford.

"I don't need more charity," came the hoarse retort, even though Sylvie had come without any food this time. "My Ivan and Ladislava, they have jobs. Yes, Ivan found work again, praise the saints. They earn wages, even while I cannot. It is enough, I'm sure. We work for our own keeping."

Sylvie measured this against what Lottie had told them. The girl's wages were meager. Even though Ivan was working again, she doubted the combined pay would cover the deficit from their mother's unemployment. They were already in arears for rent and on the brink of being evicted. *"If it means we won't be homeless and might even have money for doctors and medicine for Matka, I would take any job,"* she'd said. *"My virtue is not so highly valued that I wouldn't sell it to save her."*

The door budged open, and Ivan ducked beneath the jamb to enter before wedging it shut again. "I didn't know we were expecting company." He went to his mother and kissed her forehead, adjusting the limp pillows behind her back. "My matka isn't up to entertaining just now."

Sylvie chafed at his censure. He knew she'd come before with Rose and had never expected to be *entertained*. "No, of course not. We have a different purpose in mind."

A few blocks east, trains roared by on the tracks shared by three different railroads, shaking the tenement building and rattling the window. Dingy grey smears flared upward on the wall where soot had seeped between pane and sill.

Whatever had been brewing in Ivan seemed to burn away, his tense shoulders drooping. "News of Rose?"

"Yes, actually," Sylvie said. "She's written to say she is fine."

"But that's not why we're here," Beth cut in, preventing further questions. "Sylvie has a job opening for Lottie, if she'll have it."

"But I wanted to discuss it with you—both of you—first." Mrs. Mazurek was Lottie's mother, but as Ivan was the man of the family, Sylvie wanted to honor his role, too. She knew how responsible he felt for his mother and sister.

He gestured to the table, and she found herself sitting across from him while Beth and Lottie sat on overturned milk crates.

Sylvie angled her chair so she could better see Mrs. Mazurek, too. "I need some domestic help in my building. I wish to hire Lottie as my house-keeper, for my own apartment and for the two others I manage, if the tenants desire it. Which I think likely. If Lottie doesn't mind giving up her work at the factory, she could have fewer hours and more pay by working for me."

"Like Gita Górecki?" Mrs. Mazurek asked. "She will live with you?"

"She would still live here, with her own family," Sylvie assured the woman, then dis-cussed the terms in detail, at the same time reminding herself she could afford it. With Rose gone, she had one fewer employee on the book-store payroll and one fewer mouth to feed. Gladly would she pay those costs, but the fact remained that Rose wasn't coming back, at least not in the near future. Lottie wasn't suited to work in the bookstore, as she might not even be literate. In time, perhaps, Sylvie could change that, too. But meanwhile, there was still work to be done, and Lottie could help.

Mrs. Mazurek coughed into a handkerchief but nodded to Ivan, who then addressed his much younger sister. "Ladislava, you will do this work for the family."

A rueful smile bent Sylvie's lips. She and Beth had saved a girl from the Levee district tonight after all. It just wasn't Rose.

Upon reaching home, Sylvie whisked into her bedroom and consulted the mirror to see the day's toll. The sight confronting her wasn't kind. Neither was the odor from the tenements, sunk deep into her clothing. All she wanted was a brief conversation with Kristof before she retired for the night, but she couldn't let him see her like this.

Casting her hat and gloves onto the bed, she quickly repaired the damage. She washed her face, donned a fresh shirtwaist and skirt, and brushed and re-pinned her hair. Several new grey strands winked at her. Given the fear and shock she'd entertained since Rose disappeared, she was surprised there weren't more.

Surely it was vanity to notice, especially when far greater matters pressed for attention. Above her, violin music began and halted, then started the same section again. Good. Kristof was home. Gregor never seemed to practice, at least not in this building. She hated to interrupt but decided not to delay.

Upstairs, Sylvie didn't have to wait long after knocking before he opened the door.

The expression on his face was unaccountable. Mild surprise, she expected. Perhaps even pleasant surprise, given how close they'd grown of late. Not this. Relief smoothed the ridges from his brow as he scanned her from head to hem.

"Sylvie," he breathed. "I have been wondering when you'd return." He rolled down his shirtsleeves and buttoned the cuffs.

"Were you watching for me?"

If Beth were here, she would cluck her tongue and say he was beginning to think he owned Sylvie and her time. That Sylvie had already given him too much.

But this didn't feel like too much. It felt like coming in out of the cold, her senses thawing by the fire after being numb too long.

He opened the door wider. "Come in, if you like."

She did, reminding herself she was here for Lottie's sake, not her own.

The apartment was as neat as it had been the last time she'd been inside. Mail and newspapers were stacked in separate baskets on a table inside the door. In the kitchen, no dirty dishes littered the counter, no jackets were draped over chairs. In the parlor, her father's memoir and *A Tale of Two Cities* rested on the tea table. Shelves of books remained as orderly as ever, alphabetized by author last name and arranged by genre.

Gregor sprawled over a wing chair, the only untidy sight in the apartment. Sylvie began to doubt whether Lottie could improve the place.

Kristof moved to the kitchen table and shuffled sheet music into a pile. Then, smelling faintly of coffee and shaving soap, he pulled out a chair for her.

Gregor called out from where he lounged, one arm flung over his eyes. "Oh, save me, Sylvie." His voice betrayed a cold, which was probably the only reason he wasn't out on the town right now. "My brother now fancies himself a maestro, and it is I who will pay for it."

She raised an eyebrow and slid into the proffered seat. "What's this?"

Kristof sat across from her, then stood again. "Drink?"

"No, thank you. Please sit."

"By all means," called Gregor, still not rousing from his repose. "Sit down and *compose* your-self, Maestro." He blew his nose into a handker-chief.

Sylvie hid a smile. "It looks like you've been working. Are the concerts back on?"

"As of tomorrow, yes." Kristof brushed a crumb from the oak table. "And since Maestro Thomas has resigned as musical director of the Fair and will not return, I am to conduct in his stead. Which means Gregor is now the concertmaster. If he can exert himself to the responsibility."

Gregor didn't appear to exert himself for any reason.

"What does it mean, to be concertmaster?"

252

Sylvie asked. A breeze moved through the apartment, feathering her face.

"It means that when the orchestra is in place and ready to begin, Gregor will walk out on stage and take a bow, and the entire audience will clap for him. Then he'll indicate that the oboist should play an A so the instruments can tune to it. That part I'm sure he'll enjoy."

Sylvie could see that. Even his refusal to conform to the polite convention of sitting up when one had a visitor was a way of drawing attention to himself. Suffering a cold was no excuse.

"If only that were all," Gregor groaned.

"But it isn't." Kristof gestured to the sheet music. "The concertmaster is to be a leader among musicians in both integrity and musicianship. He's also supposed to make sure all the music for every musician has the right markings on it and deliver it to them before the rehearsals so they can practice. And make sure they all have the schedule for section practices, rehearsals, and concerts."

Sylvie peered down at the scores crowded with notes, dynamic markings, and brief spelled-out directions. *Mezzo forte. Pianissimo. Anticipate*! "But that's your handwriting, Kristof."

Gregor pushed himself up on his elbow and faced her from the parlor. "He's so much better at it than I am."

"Only because I've been doing it for years,"

253

Kristof told Sylvie quietly. "He could do it if he would only apply himself."

"Then why doesn't he?" She looked from him to Gregor, who brought a finger to his lips with theatrical flair.

Then, sighing, Gregor said, "It's a proven fact. I was born with less patience and far less passion for detail than Kristof."

"I see," Sylvie said. "And why should he try when you do it so nicely for him?" As soon as the words left her, she feared she'd said too much. Then again, no one could say her question wasn't valid.

Lines bracketed Kristof's mouth. "As much as I would enjoy defending myself, I don't suppose this is the reason for your visit."

"Correct." Sylvie clasped her hands in her lap, rubbing at her cuticles beneath the table. "I've asked a young lady, fifteen years old, to be my general housekeeper. Her name is Lottie Mazurek, and she needs the work. I wondered if you might want her to clean and launder for the two of you, as we—"

"Yes!" Gregor shouted before she'd even finished. "She's hired, Sylvie."

"You don't actually seem to need the help," she said. Unless, of course, the bedrooms were hidden disasters.

"*Rend a lelke mindennek!*" Gregor called out. "Right, brother?" He sneezed, then announced he was retiring to his bedroom for the night.

Sylvie sent Kristof a questioning gaze once the door had firmly closed.

"It's a Hungarian saying," he explained, "that means 'Order is the soul of everything.' Not that he would know from experience." He rubbed a hand over his stubbled jaw. "You say Lottie needs the work? What would you consider a reasonable weekly wage, and what could we expect from that?"

Sylvie shared her recent calculations and the work it would cover.

"That's all she would be paid?" he asked.

"If this is how you maintain your apartment, you're not giving her much to do," she said. "What I'm suggesting is more than the going rate, and far more than she's been getting at the factory, but with fewer hours and an atmosphere that won't put feathers into her lungs as it has her mother. Not to mention that this is honest work that will preserve her virtue."

"What does that mean? Was she harassed at the factory?" Concern deepened Kristof's voice.

"I wouldn't doubt it, but I can't say for sure."

"Then why imply her virtue is at stake?"

"You must not think less of her. She's just a girl," Sylvie began. "But she was so desperate for income to help pay for her mother's medicine that she was willing to take a different position. In the Levee."

"How do you know?"

She hesitated. "Beth and I stopped her on the steps of Carrie Watson's this evening. She was on her way to apply, and we literally turned her away." She had told him she planned to go. He shouldn't be surprised.

Yet the color drained from his face. "You what? Unchaperoned, you did this?"

"Chaperone!" Sylvie nearly laughed. "I speak of a girl nearly ruined tonight, a girl we snatched from the clutches of vice, and you ask me about chaperones?"

"To the subject at hand, then. Yes, we will hire this Lottie, for our apartment and for the Hoffmans, too. I'll cover that expense myself, to ease Lottie's burden as well as our dear neighbors', who sorely need the help but may not have the income to pay for it. Does this suit you?"

It was twice the generosity she'd been hoping for. More than that, considering he kept his apartment in such order already. "Yes," she said quietly. "It suits very well. Thank you."

"You're welcome. Now, explain what in heaven's name you were thinking to visit the Levee alone."

Frustration kindled. "I was with Beth. I wasn't alone."

"You know what I mean."

"So you're saying if I'm not with a man, I'm

alone?" Her tongue grew sharp, and she heard Beth's attitude and offense in her tone.

"You were unprotected. What if something had happened?"

"Something did happen, Kristof. Lottie broke away from us, and she was caught by a man, exactly the sort you warn of. But Beth and I held fast, the police were nearby, and all ended well."

His color rushed back. "Sylvie." It was as much of a gasp as she'd ever heard from him. "It could have gone a different way. It could have been worse. I told you not to go there!"

"Yes!" she hissed. "You did! And I told you I was going anyway."

"I thought Rose's letter would have put the idea to rest."

Rest. She could barely remember what that was like. Exhaustion pulled her one way, then another, from being touched by his concern to denying it was necessary. "I wanted to be sure, and now I am, that she isn't there. I haven't forgotten our conversations with László Varga and Margit at the ball. Those waitresses he hired locally— Laura and Danielle? Varga says they were fired, but maybe they disappeared, too. Maybe Rose was part of a pattern. I had to go and see for myself."

"They did not disappear."

"We don't know that!"

"I do." He paused, forcing the conversation

to slow, to steady. "I went to the Hungarian Orpheum this afternoon because I, too, couldn't stop thinking of what Varga and Margit had said. I was going to ask more questions, dig deeper into what happened with Laura and Danielle, thinking it might shed light on Rose. Danielle was there, Sylvie. I talked to her."

Sylvie's mouth went dry. "What?"

"She had come to pick up her final paycheck from the restaurant. I saw her name on the check. She's working now at a café in the Manufactures Building. Laura works there, too. She's the one who helped Danielle get the job. What Varga told us about them was true. I don't believe he took Rose. I believe he honestly pulled her closer because of his hearing loss, and I believe she gasped in pain because Walter had already bruised her wrist, trying to keep her in the Ice Railway car."

"Thank God," she said. "Thank you."

"I wish I could have told you sooner, before you went to the Levee."

"I still would have gone," Sylvie told him. "I did what I had to do. You could have been that chaperone yourself, if you were so convinced that two old maids would need one in broad daylight. I would have welcomed you by my side."

Kristof pushed back from the table and stormed away, more upset than she'd ever seen him. Why? Because she'd disobeyed his wishes, though he had no right to impose them? Her own anger burned hotter at the thought.

Rising, she stared at his silhouette against the window. His shoulders rose with every slowly drawn breath and fell with each release. Light from the streetlamps below pushed darkness away, but only so far. Shadows crept into the parlor. A clock on the fireplace mantel shaved off seconds, and she felt them piling up, taking up space, until time became its own presence too large to ignore.

He turned around, opened his mouth to speak, then closed it.

She silently dared him to try again. Ready to contradict, to strike down any argument, she bridged the gap between them.

Kristof reached for her hands and took them. "You are not an old maid."

The words pierced the tension, and the fight drained from Sylvie's spirit.

"You are vibrant. Intelligent. You have more compassion than any other woman I've ever met. I'll say it until you believe me—you are not an old maid at all." His thumbs circled the backs of her hands.

She swallowed the dryness in her throat. "I'm forty-three and single. What would you call me, if not that?"

"I would call you beautiful. If you would allow it." His expression was serious, an invitation to

259

confirm or correct the liberty he'd just taken in making so personal a comment.

Speech fled, and she could do neither. Heat swept her as she realized the effect his words and touch had on her. The effect she seemed to have on him.

If they had been standing in the Rose Garden of the Wooded Island, fragrance perfuming the air about them, she wouldn't trust the moment rearranging itself about her. If they were riding in a gondola in one of the lagoons, even if they were strolling in the Court of Honor by the light of electric bulbs, she would call her feelings, and Kristof's, false. Any romance would be as fabricated and temporary as the Fair that inspired it.

But they weren't at the Fair. They were in an ordinary apartment with Gregor snoring in the next room. Her hair probably still smelled faintly of DeKoven Street. She'd just yelled at him. And this was the place and time he'd chosen to call her beautiful?

Whatever else was uncertain, this much was true. This was no manufactured moment, and no impulsive emotion carried Kristof away. She allowed her gaze to move slowly over his handsome face, from the impenetrable eyes to his strong nose and jaw, to his lips. There she lingered.

And teetered.

With just one nudge, their relationship might find its place. Step back, and she would find footing on solid ground again. She the landlady, he the tenant, comfortable friends but nothing more.

But step forward, tilt her face to his, and she would fall into a place she'd thought she'd never revisit. She stood to risk her heart again, but this time, so much more. She wasn't one to dabble in idle romance. If love grew, it would lead to either heartbreak or marriage.

Did she want that?

Kristof dared to pull her nearer. The idea of Sylvie courting danger in the Levee made him never want to let her go again. Calling her beautiful didn't begin to reach the depths of his feelings for her. He would call her far more than that, if he thought she'd let him. He'd call her his.

"Be angry with me, if you must," he said, although her ire had faded. "But understand that my telling you not to visit the Levee came not from a desire to control you, but to protect you."

"But you—"

He placed a finger against her lips to quiet her. "I know. I have no authority over you." He let his finger fall away and reclaimed her hand. "I only want to keep you from harm. If I had known your intention to visit the Levee hadn't changed even over my strenuous objections, I would have accompanied you. I'm disappointed you didn't come to me and ask."

Sylvie began to twist away.

"No," Kristof said more firmly, sliding one hand to the small of her back. "Not in you. I'm disappointed in myself for not making it clear to you that I would care for you in whatever way suited best."

Her lashes rose. A sconce on the wall bathed her skin in soft golden light. "You would care for me?"

Her question tightened his chest. Did she not believe it? Was she so convinced she was an old maid that she could not entertain the notion? "Sylvie." He ran his knuckles softly down the side of her face. "I do care for you. Very much." It had taken too long for him to admit it, even to himself. He hated gambling with every fiber in his being, and relationships were high-stake risks. They were messy and complicated, but the way he felt about her was simple.

He tipped her chin with the crook of his finger. "Tell me now if my feelings aren't welcome. Tell me never to touch you again, and I won't. Only don't tell me to stop caring for you, because I have already tried and failed."

Her lips parted with an intake of breath. "I—I didn't know. . . ."

"You don't need a man at your side. The

question is, do you *want* one? Do you want *this* one?"

Her glossy dark hair drew in the light and reflected it back. "I've given my heart away only once before," she said. "It ended badly."

Kristof wondered what this first love had done to her, and whether she was erecting barricades even now to prevent her heart from shattering twice. "I don't claim to be perfect, but I am honest and true. I'm already yours, if you'll have me."

Tears glazed her eyes. When she smiled, he bent his head toward hers in relief, gently drawing her closer, alert for any tension in her body that meant she would push him away.

She didn't. "Kristof," she whispered, "I have never kissed a man before."

Shock shuddered through him. Never? His conscience warned that if he kissed her now and treated her poorly later, he might hurt her irreparably. She might be in her forties, just as he was, but he saw in her the young girl she'd once been, full of hope and dreams, before those had burned away like chaff. He saw her resilience as she committed herself to her father and the store instead. She was an enigma of both strength and vulnerability.

Kristof swallowed and cupped her cheek with one hand. "I want to kiss you, but I will not take so precious a gift from you unless it is offered willingly." He searched her face as it lifted toward his, and struggled to master his pulse. He wanted her, and she knew it. How she responded to that was her decision alone.

"I—I do care for you, Kristof. More than you know. But this is all so new to me, and I don't quite know what to do."

He could take care of that. He was not so old that he didn't know what to do with a woman in his arms. He could kiss her soundly, guide her, lead her . . .

This was a symphony, the back and forth between them. Kristof felt music arcing in the narrow space between their bodies. Quiet and halting conversation, restrained passion, then soaring, sighing intervals before more ardent repetition. So clearly did he hear every note, he was tempted to lean into the music. To lean into her.

But her heart was not his to conduct.

Outside, the plosive rhythm of hoofbeats sounded on the street below. A breeze waltzed through the screened window and twirled a strand of Sylvie's hair. She was still waiting for him to play the next notes in this movement.

With all the self-possession he could muster, he kissed her cheek, then bade her good night.

"You want me to leave?" She took a half step back.

How little she understood him. "I want you

to stay." He brought her hand to his lips and pressed one more kiss to the valleys between her knuckles. "So I must ask you to go."

Her complexion deepened to a rosy hue. She left, and the music went with her.

CHAPTER EIGHTEEN

Thursday, August 24, 1893

Roses. They were everywhere.

Sylvie had forgotten that in the Tea Room of Marshall Field's department store, every place setting had a rose. Amid the din of conversation, her gaze attached to the crimson bud before her, and memory unfolded of the time a would-be suitor had come into her store bearing a dozen such long-stemmed flowers just for her. An extravagant gesture, especially for the time of year.

He had arrived just before closing, confessing he'd admired her from afar for months and had mustered all his courage to present his case for a speedy courtship. *"I have a child, Mr. Rosche,"* she'd told him and smirked at his hasty retreat.

Thirteen-year-old Rose had come out from the fiction stacks and wrapped slender arms around Sylvie's waist for a sideways squeeze. *"He probably figured that a single woman in possession of a good bookstore must be in want of a husband,"* Rose had joked. *"Too bad he didn't let you keep the roses, though. Do you mind very much?"*

Smiling, Sylvie had kissed her forehead. *"You're the only Rose I need."*

That night, as snow ticked against the windows, they'd popped corn on the stove and made hot chocolate and taken turns reading aloud from *Sense and Sensibility*, which they'd both concluded was even better than *Pride and Prejudice*. Rose's eyes had twinkled when Sylvie came to the line, *"I am convinced that I shall never see a man whom I can really love."* She'd snuggled deeper beneath the blanket they'd shared on the sofa and rested her head on Sylvie's shoulder.

Was that truly only four and a half years ago? It felt a lifetime.

Sylvie fingered the velvet petals on the table before her and prayed again that Rose was all right. Fresh relief that she wasn't in a brothel reminded her of Kristof's reaction to Sylvie's having gone to the Levee.

Her fingers went to her lips.

She took a drink of ice water to cool them.

At least Lottie had started working yesterday. She'd been half an hour late and eager about when she'd be paid, but by the time Sylvie had walked her through the apartment, showing her what she expected, those lapses of decorum had been excused. When she'd introduced Lottie to the Hoffmans, Anna had made it her personal mission to feed the girl at every opportunity.

"More water, ma'am?" A waiter in a white uniform held a pewter pitcher wrapped in a linen towel. His approach had been noiseless on the thick medallion-patterned Persian carpet.

"No, thank you." She glanced around the fourth-floor restaurant. Potted palms arched against pillars between tables, and floor-to-ceiling mirrors doubled the space. "We'll be ordering tea as soon as the rest of my party arrives."

He offered a little bow and receded from view. It was seven o'clock in the evening. No doubt the waiter preferred she order more than just tea, but her budget couldn't justify it. She wasn't here for the famous chicken potpie, though her mouth watered at the thought. She had come to visit with Meg, and with Hazel during her break from working in the millinery department. She'd come early to collect herself. The tea—and the ambience that came with it—was just a bonus.

"Aunt Sylvie!" Letting go of her mother's hand, Olive rushed to the table and claimed a seat beside her aunt. "Look!" She poked her tongue through a new gap in her smile. "See?"

As Sylvie assured her she did, Hazel sat on her other side, as starched and neat as Marshall Field demanded from his employees. Honeyed brown hair in a loose chignon softly framed her face.

Meg sat directly across the square table from Sylvie. "Nate and Walter are both working tonight. I hope you don't mind some extra company." She tilted her head toward Olive. Wisps of russet hair had escaped the child's braid, giving her a flyaway look despite wearing a Sunday dress.

Sylvie reached out both hands and squeezed those of her nieces. "Are you kidding? I'll take all the company I can get. So long as it's the three of you," she added. Her sister knew her too well to believe she'd outgrown her love for solitude.

"Waiter." Hazel signaled the man and ordered tea for four. "I'm on break from downstairs, so if you don't mind . . ." She waved him away with her fingers.

Sylvie held in a laugh at her take-charge personality, especially with a fellow employee of the same company. Hazel favored her father in that regard. "Meg, how is painting going?"

"I haven't been back to the Fair since last week." When she brushed a tendril of hair from her face, her unbuttoned cuff flapped open.

"Mother," Hazel whispered. "Your sleeve."

"Oh." Meg gave no sign of embarrassment. She shouldn't have been, of course, but it was the sort of thing that normally would have bothered her. She had long since accepted that her scarred right hand could not manage buttons, but she usually asked for help when she needed it.

"I'll do it!" Olive's small fingers worked at fitting the button through the hole. Her fingernails were clean but bitten short, making the task a challenge.

"You should have done it at home," Hazel said as Olive finished. "Don't let her leave the house looking like that."

Irritation grated at Sylvie. "Like what? A Gibson Girl?" It was true, after all. Even in her forties, Meg's style and grace proved just as charming as those famous illustrations.

"Ah." Hazel brightened as the tea cart rolled their way. "Here we are."

The white-gloved waiter carefully arranged the silver tea service on the table. A three-tiered platter held almond tea cakes, petit fours, and miniature strawberry tarts. Meg gazed at her youngest child with the countenance of one traveling back in her mind to some distant and painful place. Sylvie suspected that place was Louise.

The waiter left, and Hazel carried the conversation between sips of bergamot tea and bites of fondant-covered lemon sponge. Sylvie bit into a tart and watched her sister. All the things she'd planned to tell her—about Mrs. Górecki, the Levee district, Lottie, and her growing affection for Kristoff—all of that dissolved like the pastry in her mouth. None of it was as important as what Meg was feeling right now.

"Divine," Hazel pronounced, dabbing her napkin to her mouth. "It was good to see you, Aunt Sylvie. I hate to dash without hearing all your news, but you have no idea how strict my boss is." With a quick kiss to Sylvie's cheek, and one for Meg, Hazel swept away.

Olive seemed happy enough to have both adults to herself. She reached for another tea cake and nibbled its scalloped edge. "Is Rose home yet?" she asked. "She's nicer to me than Hazel. I miss her."

"Not yet," Sylvie replied quietly.

At this, Meg paused. "How are you, really?"

Sylvie brought a porcelain cup to her lips and savored the sharp taste before lowering it to the saucer. "Are you sure you want to talk about me? I'm more interested in you."

"Do me a favor and distract me from myself. Please."

Olive laid her dimpled hand on Sylvie's arm. "Or we could talk about my birthday."

"Oh, darling, not now," Meg pleaded. "Please, Sylvie. Anything else."

Sylvie squeezed her niece's shoulder. But she understood Meg, too.

There was no way she would discuss her experience at the Levee in Olive's presence. But there were other things she could talk about. So in the briefest terms possible, she told Meg about searching the Polish community and hiring Lottie as housekeeper. But after sharing how the young lady was getting on after her second day on the job, Sylvie could tell this was not the sort of news that captivated Meg's full attention.

"I also—" Good heavens, her face flushed just thinking about this.

Meg's eyebrows arched immediately. "Yes? You what? Is it Kristof?"

Sylvie gaped. "Why would you say that?"

"Just hoping, I suppose."

Sylvie folded her napkin and smoothed it over her lap. "He's conducting the Exposition Orchestra now, twice daily. I went to the noon concert today after finishing with my morning tour group. You should have seen him."

Kristof had been resplendent in his white bow tie and tuxedo. The way he sliced the baton through the air, using his other hand to cue, demand, and draw back the other sections of the orchestra was a language all its own, and one his musicians responded to. So had she. His entire body leaned into the music, guiding and leading, his expressions ranging from fierce to pure pleasure in the beauty of the piece.

"What else?" Meg leaned forward. "Tell me everything."

Laughter swelled inside Sylvie, threatening to burst out. She covered her mouth to trap it.

"Come on, Sylvie," Meg pleaded. "Please tell me the two of you have come to an understanding."

"Not exactly, although he's made his feelings clear."

Meg folded her arms. "I'll say his feelings are clear. And if you don't mind my saying so, yours are, too. To me, at least."

"Is that so? I'm all ears."

"You're attracted to him but afraid to admit it. You've spent so many years convincing yourself you don't need a man that you feel out of your depth now that you've—"

"Wait." Olive swiveled between her mother and aunt. "What are you talking about? Are you finally getting married, Aunt Sylvie?"

"What? No, dear. It's not that simple."

Olive's brows drew together. "Why not?"

"Yes." Meg dropped her hands below the table, and Sylvie could tell by the flexing of her arms that she was stretching her fingers to combat the scar tissue. She was agitated. "Why not, indeed?"

"Signing a marriage contract would be signing over all my property, relinquishing control over everything I've managed for decades. That's no small thing."

"If you're thinking of Beth Wright's late husband—"

"Not just him. Roger Bell only courted me for the property, not because he had any affection for me as a woman."

Meg laughed. "Roger Bell! You figured him out almost immediately and sent him on his way. The entire affair lasted less than a month. Now, tell me—in the years you've known Kristof, have you ever had the impression that he was anything like Amos Wright or Roger Bell?"

"It's not Kristof who concerns me. It's the law."

"That's an excuse." Meg punctuated her verdict with an emphatic nod.

It wasn't just that, but Sylvie didn't know how much more she wanted to share. She didn't want to make Meg feel guilty that for fourteen years of her life, while Meg was having babies and raising children with Nate, Sylvie was bringing her father's medicine to him, calming him after his nightmares, and supporting him on the days his courage failed him and he didn't want to get out of bed, let alone leave the apartment to face a city of strangers.

Sylvie also cherished warm memories of Stephen playing checkers with Karl by the fire while Sylvie and Anna kept them supplied with hot coffee. Of discussing Milton and Keats with him on the rooftop. Of rocking Rose to sleep while Stephen told the Grimm brothers' stories. He always changed them to softer versions that wouldn't terrify a child. Sylvie wouldn't erase the years she'd had with him, even if she could.

But after being tethered to Stephen for so long, she was reluctant to tie another knot, of any kind, to anyone.

Sylvie sipped her tea. "I like my life the way it is. I've always thought that Kristof and I were like Jo March and Laurie," she said. It was easier to believe when he wasn't holding her in his arms.

"You're more like Emma Woodhouse and Mr. Knightley. You just don't know it yet."

Breaking from her sister's scrutiny, Sylvie leaned back in her chair and let her gaze travel the room of shoppers enjoying corned beef or chicken salad or evening tea. Some ladies scooped small bites of rose punch ice cream. Waiters at the perimeter of the room stood ready to refill drinks.

"Rose," Sylvie gasped. She gripped the edge of the table, wrinkling the linen. "There, four tables away. Her back is to us, but I would know that ensemble anywhere." She had purchased it here in this department store. "Do you see her? Or am I going mad?"

Eyes wide, Meg turned to look. "I see a woman wearing an outfit just like one that belonged to Rose, yes. But, dear, I don't think that's her."

There was only one way to find out.

Without pausing to think it through, Sylvie rose and threaded between tables until she found herself standing, awkwardly, before a young lady who was not her daughter. "Oh." Disappointment slipped from her like a sigh.

"May I help you?" The young woman in Rose's clothing stared back at Sylvie.

"I beg your pardon. I just—couldn't help but admire your dress and hat. Would you mind if I asked you where you acquired them?" A nearby palm frond swayed, its spear tickling her neck. The tang of recently watered soil scented the air.

The young lady's friend sniffed. "You don't have to tell her anything, Gertrude."

The bodice didn't fit Gertrude as though it had been made to her measurements. There was the ink stain, no larger than a pinhead on the inside of one cuff, where Rose's careless gesture with a pen had left its mark. And the hat was exactly what she and Rose had requested be custom-made in the millinery department.

These were Rose's garments. Sylvie was sure of it. Dread spidered down her spine.

A waiter nudged behind Sylvie with a full cart, and she edged closer to the table. She was in the way and in danger of making a scene. "Please, Gertrude. I have a daughter your age, and I'm sure she would like this." It wasn't a lie, Sylvie reasoned.

"The tag says Marshall Field," she admitted.

Of course it did. "But is that where you got it? Did you find it in a pawn shop, by any chance? Or perhaps someone gave it to you—"

"What kind of a question is that?" Gertrude interrupted. A few diners paused in their conversation, spoons suspended above chicken pot-pies. Listening. "Leave me in peace and do your own shopping. This store has everything your daughter could ever need, I'm sure."

Her face ablaze with shame, Sylvie returned to Meg and Olive. She was mortified. Was she taking leave of her senses?

"What's wrong?" Olive asked, and Meg shushed her.

"Deep breath, Sylvie. Just drink your tea and compose yourself. It's all right."

But it wasn't all right. *She* wasn't all right. "Meg, I am absolutely positive that girl is wearing Rose's clothes. I just don't know how to find out *why* without getting thrown out on my ear."

Meg looked dubious. "You're sure?"

"Yes." Sylvie's appetite withered.

Olive reached for another treat, but Meg intervened, handing her one of the *Five Little Peppers* books she'd brought to keep her occupied instead.

While Olive turned the pages, Meg pushed her chair closer to Sylvie. "Sometimes we see what we don't want to see, and sometimes we see what we long for. It's nothing to be ashamed of. I do it, too. So did—" She swallowed the end of her sentence.

"So did Father," Sylvie finished for her. A chill prickled her skin, leaving gooseflesh in its wake. "What are you saying, that madness runs in the family?" She hated even saying it. Father hadn't been mad; he'd been wounded. It wasn't the same at all.

"I'm saying the mind and heart are complicated

organs. Grief is even more so. We can't begin to comprehend what it does to us. All I know is that it's a full-body experience that doesn't go away. Grief affects us in ways we don't even realize."

"I don't think this is grief, Meg."

"My jaws are sore all the time from clenching my teeth through the night," she whispered. "I don't even realize I'm doing it. I can barely see through my headaches sometimes, headaches that no doctor can treat."

An ache squeezed Sylvie's throat.

But her sister wasn't done. "Mother had those nosebleeds all the time—*all the time*—after Father came home from war, because she was grieving the husband who would never return to her. And Father, well, you understand more about him than any of us."

That was true. After the Great Fire, Sylvie had developed some symptoms in common with him. Bursts of unaccountable anger, panic, anxiety, and fear. For weeks, nightmares had plagued her when insomnia didn't.

"This is different," she said, silently begging Meg to believe her. "Father may have seen people who weren't there, but I never did. That's not what's happening now. You can see for yourself, that girl is wearing Rose's clothing. I'm not imagining this. This isn't grief. It's something else. Something very, very wrong."

And she wouldn't rest until she found out what.

Chapter Nineteen

Friday, August 25, 1893

It was nearly five o'clock when Kristof dashed into Corner Books & More after a full day of rehearsals and concerts at the Fair.

Tessa greeted him from behind the cash register. "Miss Townsend is upstairs paying Lottie for the week." Thunder rolled. "Can I help you with something?"

Before he could reply, the rear door opened and closed, and footfalls announced Sylvie's approach.

"Did the accounts reconcile, Tessa?" Sylvie asked, then stopped when she saw Kristof. A smile softened her face, along with the most becoming blush.

He tried to ignore the answering heat beneath his collar. She knew he cared for her and that his feelings wouldn't change. The rest of their story was up to her. He wouldn't push. Neither would he withdraw his friendship while she decided. Not now, while Rose was still missing.

Not ever. Or at least not until she asked him to.

"Kristof," she said. "Just getting home?"

"I am. And you're going out?" She smelled

fresh and clean, two things he was not. He couldn't wait to trade his tuxedo for different clothes.

"To the police station, yes. Beth has finally gotten herself arrested for marching for women's suffrage." The jacket Sylvie wore hugged her form and flared slightly over her hips, a style entirely too fetching for a visit to a jail.

The thunder crescendoed, taking on the sound of indistinct voices melding into one. Another protest, Kristof realized, and crossed to the front window. Sylvie and Tessa came beside him as a mass of men rounded the corner and marched past the courthouse. Working men pumped painted signs in English, Polish, and Czech.

Jobs!

We want work!

Decent wages for decent hours!

They moved in groups of dozens, scores, hundreds. Kristof stopped estimating their numbers when he figured they'd reached the thousands.

Other men inserted themselves into the throng, fists curled, teeth bared. "Communists!" one snarled. "If you don't like the way capitalism works, go back where you came from!"

This was going to get ugly fast. Kristof regarded both women. "Neither of you are going anywhere right now."

Sylvie agreed. "Yesterday a fight broke out on the City Hall steps. I don't want you getting caught in any of that, Tessa. Ivan came to pick up Lottie, at least."

"If the two of you will wait for me, I need just a few minutes upstairs, and then we'll see about getting you both where you need to go." The crowd choked the street, spilling onto the sidewalks, and pressed close—too close—to the bookshop.

"We'll wait." Sylvie backed away from the window.

Upstairs, Kristof entered his apartment and began stripping off his tuxedo. Only after he'd rinsed off and dressed again did he think to check on Gregor. He'd gone straight home following their afternoon concert, complaining of his cold. He must have been feeling poorly indeed to give up a Friday night.

But Gregor's room was empty.

If Kristof was exhausted, as he ought to be, he hid it well. He smelled of clean, warm linen as he walked beside Sylvie, and the faintest hint of balsam. Dusk gathered around them.

"You seem unsettled. Is it the protest that's bothering you?" Kristof asked above the sound of hacks and hoofbeats on the cobblestones. Now that they'd seen Tessa safely to the streetcar stop, they were on their way, at last, to the police station where Beth waited.

"Yes, but not just that," Sylvie admitted. "Meg

and I went to Festival Hall this afternoon to hear Frederick Douglass speak in honor of Colored American Day at the Fair. Our father heard him once, and it spurred him to enlist."

"I would have been there if we hadn't had a concert at the same time. So what troubled you?"

Sylvie was almost embarrassed to tell him. "Some white people in attendance shouted the most terrible insults at this seventy-five-year-old man. Mr. Douglass took control of the situation, but it was so discouraging. Our Declaration of Independence says all men are created equal, but we still don't treat all men equally, three decades after the Civil War ended. The Fair celebrates man's progress in the four hundred years since Columbus's arrival here. But we still have such a long way to go. Women want to vote. Immigrants want jobs. Black Americans want to be treated like full and equal citizens. These seem like such basic things."

"They are," Kristof agreed. "And each one is worth fighting for. Do what you can in your areas of influence but remember that the outcome is not your responsibility alone."

She stepped around a crushed tin can. "When I see a need, I want to meet it, if at all possible."

Shadows from lampposts and telegraph poles leaned down the street. "We should. You do. Just keep in mind, for example, that you can give Lottie a job, but you can't be the fiscal savior of that entire family, let alone their neighborhood. You can march for equal rights and speak up for the voiceless, but you can't force everyone to agree with you."

The police station loomed before them, an old newssheet stuck in one corner of the stone stairs. "And I can bail Beth out of jail, but I can't prevent her from getting arrested again."

He sent her a wry smile. "Exactly."

Gripping her reticule in one hand, Sylvie slid her other into the crook of Kristof's arm and entered the building.

An officer sat behind a wide, battle-scarred desk facing the front doors. Behind him, a door led to what Sylvie imagined were offices and records rooms. To either side of the lobby, short stone staircases led to wings buried half underground, each barred with an iron gate. From one of them came women's voices. From the other, the deeper timbre of men.

Sylvie was close enough to see down the stairs to a corridor that ran between a stone wall and a row of cages. The floor moved with homeless men—toughs and decent out-of-works alike— getting comfortable for the night. Smells of tobacco, cigarette smoke, and liquor combined with that of the sanitation gutter she knew ran the length of the cells.

After stating her business, waiting for a matron to bring Beth out was only a matter of paperwork, payment, and patience. In fifteen minutes, she emerged.

At the sight of Kristof standing near Sylvie, Beth's expression compressed into a hard knot of disapproval. "Now I see why you were too busy to come get me out of jail." Untidy ringlets of hair pointed in various directions from her head. The matron returned to the women's wing, and Beth jumped when the iron gate clanged shut, echoing across the tiled floor.

Guilt needled Sylvie. "Beth," she said, "I tried to come sooner—"

Beth raised a hand while the policeman shuffled paperwork at his desk. "I see very well, thank you." She smashed her hat back on and adjusted the wrinkled sash across her torso, emblazoned with *Votes for Women*. "I see I've been replaced."

Sylvie was too surprised to respond.

"Come now, Beth." Kristof's polite tone was as brittle as glass. "I make a poor replacement for a friend like you. Isn't Sylvie allowed to have more than one?"

"I'll thank you to stay out of this, sir," Beth told him. To Sylvie, she said, "It's been a long day. I could have used a friend on the streets and in that cell. Now I'd like to go home."

Sylvie squared her shoulders. "You knew I had to work this morning and that I wanted to hear Frederick Douglass this afternoon, and you decided to march without me. You knew, and I daresay hoped for, your own arrest. I imagine some of the other suffragettes kept you in fine company back there."

"They did. Until they were released hours ago by people who actually care about them."

Sylvie ignored the implication. This had far less to do with bail, she realized, than with Kristof. But she refused to bow to baseless insults. "We'll walk with you to the streetcar, but first—"

"*We?*" Beth blurted. "*We* used to mean you and me. Not you and a man. I have no interest in being the third wheel."

Sylvie stepped closer, wishing they were somewhere more private. "Stop being ridiculous. There's no need to be jealous."

"I'm not jealous, Sylvie. I am betrayed. There is a difference. *I'm* betrayed because *you* are betraying our ideal of life without men. I can see what's happening," she hissed, fierce again. Afraid.

Understanding blunted Sylvie's irritation, even as she wondered what Kristof must think. "Our ideal was a fulfilling life, regardless of marital status. I never committed to life without men. I only said I wouldn't waste time pining away for one. Let's talk about it later, all right? I want to see if any progress has been made on Rose's case."

"Forget it, Sylvie. You do your thing, I'll do mine. I can get along just fine—"

"Miss Wright," Kristof cut in. "I suggest you go home before you say anything else you'll regret. I'll escort you to the streetcar if you wish."

Beth snorted and wiped her nose with the back of her hand. "Not a chance. I don't need your help. And you know what? Neither does Sylvie." She wheeled and walked away, her heels clicking a strident rhythm until she pushed outside.

A breeze slipped in, stirring the fetid air. Sylvie crossed her arms, biting back a roiling frustration. "I'm sorry she was so rude to you."

"That's her business. Not yours."

Sylvie hesitated. "The people who are closest to us sometimes hurt us the most."

He bent his head to hers so the policeman couldn't hear. "The people closest to us shouldn't want to. They should be the first ones to lift us up, cheer us on, forgive our faults, and believe we can do better."

She felt again that the moment was bigger than their surroundings. She knew without him saying it that he would be the one to lift her up, forgive her, believe in her. If she would only let him.

"Excuse me," the officer called from his desk. "Is there something else I can help you with?" Coarse grey eyebrows overhung his close-set eyes. Narrow shoulders beneath his uniform made his protruding belly all the more pronounced.

"Oh. Yes. Thank you, Officer Thornhill." Sylvie read his name from his uniform. "I'd like to check the status of a missing person case. I reported Rozalia Dabrowski missing on August sixteenth. She's been missing since the four-teenth. Could you please let me know if anything has turned up?"

Gaslight from the wall sconce blinked on his badge. "How old is she?"

"Seventeen." Sylvie reached up to shove a loose hat pin back in.

Officer Thornhill made a clucking sound against his teeth. "We get a lot of these cases, ma'am. Twenty percent of girls in this age bracket, we never hear from again."

"We're aware of the statistics," Kristof cut in. "Please check the file and let us know what you find."

The policeman held up his hands in mock surrender and rolled back in his chair. His feet slurred over the floor and down a corridor, keys jangling the handcuffs at his hip.

When he returned minutes later, he laid a file folder on the desk and slapped it triumphantly. "Case closed. Lucky we still have the file."

"What? You found her? Why on earth wasn't I informed?" Sylvie strained to make sense of the news.

Thornhill picked up his coffee mug and threw back the swill before slamming it back on the desk. "It appears this entire case was a mis-understanding." He opened the file and pulled out an envelope. "I have here a letter from one Rozalia Dabrowski notifying us that she was never lost, she just moved out, and that no police resources ought to be expended to find her. See for yourself. At the bottom, she wrote that she notified you, as well." He handed the envelope to her.

With trembling hands, she removed the piece of paper inside.

This letter serves as proof of my well-being. I've left home of my own accord for personal reasons. . . .

Kristof read over her shoulder. "Is that her handwriting?"

"It is. And it's the same paper she used to write me." There was no use keeping it hidden, now. To Thornhill, she confessed, "A similar note to this one was hand-delivered to my apartment the night of August sixteenth or the early morning of August seventeenth."

"Well, there you have it," the officer said. "According to the file, this letter was delivered to the station in person on Thursday, August seventeenth. Yeah, that's right. I was working that day. Case closed."

"Who delivered the message?" Kristof asked.

"She did. Rozalia delivered it herself."

Letter creasing in her hand, Sylvie pressed a

fist to her chest. "What did she look like? What was she wearing?"

Laughing, Officer Thornhill tugged the letter from her grip and slipped it back into the file. "Lady, I have no recollection of what she wore that day. But I do remember that she matched the description you gave, if you were the one to report her missing." He consulted the folder again. "Blond hair, blue eyes, five foot five, about one hundred twenty-five pounds. Same birth date and background story. It all checked out."

There must be thousands of girls in Chicago like that. She showed him the photograph. "Was it her?"

"If that's Rozalia, then apparently so."

Kristof looked skeptical. "Was anyone with her when she came to deliver the letter?"

"Nope." Officer Thornhill crossed his arms, resting them atop his paunch. "I'd think you'd be pleased. This is good news I'm giving you, considering the alternatives."

"I just—" Sylvie fought to regain her composure as she looked at the image of Rose's smiling face the day she turned seventeen. The photograph had been taken just after she'd received what she'd most wanted: a first-edition copy of Jane Austen's *Mansfield Park*. *"I can't believe it!"* Rose had exclaimed and wrapped Sylvie in a fierce hug. *"It must have cost a fortune. I'll work a month for free to help pay for it!"* When Sylvie had refused the offer, Rose had vowed to channel her enthusiasm to turning book browsers into purchasers. It was a promise she'd kept.

Voices ricocheted from the two wings on either side of Sylvie. "I just don't understand."

"There's not a lot to it. This is the best possible outcome. Be happy!" Out of nowhere, a brown tabby cat leapt onto his desk and waved its tail beneath Thornhill's chin. He scratched the cat behind its ears. "Isn't that right, Sergeant Whiskers?" He chuckled. "This is what happens when you feed an alley cat. He thinks he owns the place."

The cat came up to Sylvie and nuzzled its head beneath her hand. As she stroked its silken fur, she couldn't help but think of Tiny Tim and wonder if he was still with Rose.

"People say cats are aloof," said Thornhill, "but not this one. He's never met a stranger. Not that the feeling is always mutual. Your daughter, for instance, couldn't stand him."

Sylvie balked. "Really?"

"Oh, yes. As soon as Sergeant Whiskers appeared, her eyes started watering, she started sneezing, and she said her throat would close up if I didn't shut him away. She tried being polite about it, saying he was a handsome cat but they had always made her sick."

Sylvie's fingers dug into Kristof's arm before

290

she realized what she was doing and released him. Something new was coursing through her, a cocktail of justified suspicion and fear searching for a release that could not be had.

"I don't know who came here with that letter," she said, "but I know it wasn't my Rozalia. Which means even if Rose wrote it, someone else pretended to be her in order to close the case."

Thornhill squinted. "A lookalike, you say? I can't see why that young woman would come here acting like someone she's not."

"Rose loved cats. They never made her sick," said Kristof. "The young lady posing as her was hired for her physical likeness, no doubt. But by whom?"

Sylvie rubbed the goose bumps on her arms. "Someone who doesn't want Rose to be found."

Sylvie wasn't crazy. But she felt like she was coming out of her skin.

She and Kristof had stayed at the police station until Officer Thornhill agreed to talk to his superior about reopening the case. Even that meager concession had taken far too long.

She paced her apartment, looking out the windows, though night had fallen and all she could see were coronas encircling the lampposts and the shadows that sometimes moved beneath them. Suspicion was the lens through which she heard and saw. Every man coming back to the Sherman

House hotel down the block was a man to be investigated. Footsteps belonged to stalkers. Every couple returning from the theater district might be accomplices, villains in their own drama. Closed carriages held secrets and vice. Barking dogs clawed her unraveling nerves.

The clock in the parlor struck midnight. Another hour gone, and Rose still lost. Another day done, and her daughter still in trouble, wondering why Sylvie had believed the note she'd clearly been forced to write. *Dear Mimi . . . Your loving Rose.* She should have known by those clues alone. She should have done something, anything. She ought to have acted on her doubts instead of reasoning them away.

Her father would have believed her. Stephen would not have slept but would have taken up arms and gone after Rose. There was nothing he would not have done—but even so, would he have found her? Could anyone now, or was it too late to hope?

The clock ticked on. More time spent.

Shadows gathered inside her.

Chapter Twenty

"No." Kristof dropped his hands, and the orchestra dropped the concerto with a discordant crash, notes from strings and winds falling into each other. He looked pointedly at Gregor, who stood apart, in front. As first violin, he had the solo in Beethoven's concerto for violin and orchestra. "Your attention, gentlemen. Watch my cues. Anticipate."

It was eight o'clock in the morning, and he knew full well most of his musicians didn't want to be there. But he wouldn't have called this rehearsal if they didn't need it. They had one more week of concerts to perform at the World's Fair, and if he had anything to do with it, they would give their absolute best.

He raised his baton. "Measure eighty-seven." He cued the strings, *pianissimo*, a delicate support to the beginning of Gregor's solo. His brother's bow flew as he ascended the scale with eighth notes and sixteenth notes. The articulation was perfect, exquisite. But he was *fortissimo* when he should have been *pianissimo*, which meant a crescendo had nowhere to go.

293

Frustration boiled in Kristof's veins, but for the sake of the orchestra, he let it go.

Until Gregor decided to rush the solo, forcing the rest of the musicians to choose—follow Gregor's unreliable rhythm to stay in synchronization, or follow their conductor's leading and sound like they couldn't keep up.

"Enough!" Kristof bellowed. Again, the music smashed to a halt.

All except for Gregor. "Just wait, this part is so beautiful, and you haven't let me get through it once today," he said, keeping his jaw firmly on the chin rest.

Kristof could not remember being angrier than he was right now. He stormed off his conductor's box and clamped his hand around the neck of Gregor's violin, choking off the solo. "I am your conductor," he seethed. "Any more insubordination, and you will not be playing that solo at all."

Gregor seemed unimpressed. And unpersuaded.

Kristof wanted to throttle him. Gregor still hadn't come clean about where he'd gone last night when he'd said he was headed straight home.

"Calm down, brother," Gregor muttered. "I know what's really bothering you, but it won't do to take it out on me. Now, if you don't mind, shall we get on with it?"

Just who was conducting whom here? Kristof

turned his back on his brother and took the box once more. "Change of plans," he announced. "We're taking the concerto off the program. Take out your music for Liszt's Hungarian Rhapsody No. 2." A lovely piece with zero violin solos. "Cymbals, be ready for your cue."

They began.

This was better. Baton in hand, Kristof felt the music flowing through his outspread arms. This was the piece for his mood, full of angst and drama.

Gregor was right. Kristof was angry, and though his brother was certainly part of the cause, he wasn't the entire sum of it.

The music slowed, punctuated by a brief silence, and began again with bright flutes. Then bows sawed across strings in monotone repetition, the epitome of panic. Of pacing. Of Sylvie as she'd tried to cope last night.

He'd heard her crying in her apartment, and he hadn't been able to do a thing about it. Their visit to the police station had shaken her, for good reason. And he found that she could not be stricken without him feeling the blow himself.

Baton in hand, he waved that aside and poured himself into channeling the rhapsody, conducting it from a walking pace to a robust frenzy up and down the scale, cymbals crashing. Then, putting his finger to his lips, he slowed and quieted them for a few measures before bringing the piece to its rousing, climactic end.

He was sweating by the time they finished. Mopping his brow with a folded handkerchief, Kristof allowed himself a small smile. "Yes. That ought to please the masses."

They sent up a cheer in response. All of them, he noticed, save Gregor.

At ten o'clock, Kristof finally concluded the rehearsal with a command to be back in their chairs no later than twenty minutes to noon.

When the hall had mostly cleared, Gregor approached him, and Kristof stepped off the box. "That was a mean trick," Gregor said. "Taking away my solo."

"That's what happens when the soloist can't be trusted to follow his conductor."

Gregor shrugged. "Maybe the conductor is a little too confining for everyone."

Kristof doubted that. "How about you master your job before telling me how to do mine?"

"Does that mean you don't still want to do both?" Gregor kept his face perfectly serious, then broke into a laugh. "Never mind that now. I have a surprise for you."

"Does this have anything to do with where you were last night?"

Grinning, Gregor punched his arm. "Come on, I'll show you. But we'll have to hurry if we're going to be back here on time."

After locking their instruments in the rehearsal hall, they went out into the summer morning. The white buildings surrounding the basin in the Court of Honor reflected the dazzling sun. Kristof tugged down the brim of his hat.

"Where are we going?"

"Off the fairgrounds. Trust me."

Tall order. Especially when the mystery journey included taking a streetcar north, to the corner of Harrison and South Clark. It was the outer edge of the Levee.

Disappointment sank to the bottom of Kristof's gut. "Tell me this is not where you've been spending your free time."

"Suspend your judgment, oh holy one, and follow me. And we ought to hurry. I'd check the time, but I don't have a watch." He waggled his eyebrows and trotted across the street to a pawn shop on the corner. Turning back, he said, "Yet."

Kristof's dread dissolved as he followed his brother inside. Tables of secondhand goods crowded the small establishment with everything a household might need—or in this case, might need to trade for cash. Furniture, candlesticks, clothing, pots and pans, crockery. Mediocre landscapes in oil hung from the walls in cheap frames. The space was stale and humid, not to mention a nightmare of disorganization.

"This way." Gregor threaded between a rack

of cast-off gowns and some kind of rusting farm implement.

Kristof followed him to the rear. There, on the top shelf inside a glass case, was their father's pocket watch, shining among a display of gold rings and bracelets.

"Mr. Goldstein?" Gregor called. "A little help over here, if you please."

With a flick of his wrist, the proprietor finished dusting a cuckoo clock on the wall, then tossed the rag over one shoulder and shuffled to where the Bartoks waited. "Yes?"

Gregor pointed to the timepiece. "If you please. I'd like to show this to my brother."

Mr. Goldstein unlocked the case and withdrew the item, then laid it on a square of green felt atop the case. His balding head shone in the fractured sun slanting through a cracked windowpane.

"I told you I'd find it," Gregor said.

Kristof ran a fingertip over the engraved surface, then opened it to see the diamonds in its face. "So you did." It seemed no worse for wear either, thank goodness. He eyed Mr. Goldstein. "What are you asking for it?"

The man named his price. For what the piece was worth, it was only slightly north of fair. But even if they managed to haggle him down, it was more than they could afford. "It will be a while before we can claim it." But for that price, hopefully no one else would beat them to it.

Beside him, Gregor deflated. "Can't you at least be happy that we *found* it? For once in your life, can you enjoy the victory without thinking about what's next?"

Irritation crawled over Kristof's skin. "Not thinking about what's next is exactly what gets you into trouble."

Gregor scowled.

"If there be nothing else, then, gentlemen . . ." With fingers stained with silver polish, Mr. Goldstein replaced the watch in the case and locked it.

"How about a deposit?" Gregor asked him. "We'll pay what we can now, and the rest later. You keep it for us until then."

"Sorry, mister. That's against store policy. We don't hold things back from customers willing to pay in full."

Kristof folded his arms. "How long does something like that typically last before someone takes it off your hands?"

"Depends. The more expensive items sit longer, sometimes. Then again, discerning shoppers check pawnshops first for hidden gems like this." Sliding the dusting rag from his shoulder, he resumed dusting his wares.

Gregor's lips drew a thin line across his face. "I'll get it back, Kristof. That's a promise you can count on. Don't worry about how. I'll take care of it."

But Kristoff had stopped listening after the word *promise*. He cringed at the rough way Mr. Goldstein was dusting a violin and bow hanging on the wall. "Stop."

The man turned. "Yes?"

"You're transferring whatever is on that filthy rag onto a delicate instrument. You'll damage it if you're not careful." The violin swayed where it hung, knocking into another one beside it. Kristof squinted at the second instrument. "May I see that one please?"

"Really?" Gregor huffed. "Of all the things you need, a violin from a pawnshop is not on the list. No offense, Goldstein."

Grunting, Mr. Goldstein took it down anyway and laid it before Kristof.

"The bow, too, please." He ran his fingers lightly over the violin's contours, then lifted it to his shoulder and began to tune the strings, only to find they were barely out of tune at all. The horsehairs on the bow were a little too loose, but they weren't dry. They'd recently been rosined. He knew this sound. He knew this violin. "This belonged to Rose."

Gregor stared at the instrument. "You're sure?"

"I've handled it before. I've listened to it every week during our lessons, watching Rose's fingers intently as she played, taking note of every imperfection in the instrument. This scratch on the fingerboard. This nick on the scroll. Even this streak here, on the back, where either the wood was stained unevenly, or it simply amplifies a natural variation in the grain." Taken together, it was as distinct as a fingerprint. "It's hers. Or it was."

By degrees, Gregor's expression had shifted from doubt to genuine concern. He looked at Goldstein. "When was this brought in, and by whom?"

The proprietor hesitated, kindling Kristof's impatience. "Do you always dust from left to right, Mr. Goldstein, as you were doing when we came in? You stopped just before reaching this instrument, and yet it carries no dust." He wiped a finger on the bridge and held it up, clean. "And unless you tune the instruments and rosin the bowstrings daily, I'd say it came to you very recently." Otherwise the pegbox would have swollen around the tuning pegs, making them impossible to turn without brute force.

Mr. Goldstein slapped his rag on the counter. "Why? You interested?"

"Just answer the questions." Gregor leaned forward, elbows on the glass. "Who brought this in, and when?"

Kristof pulled out his wallet. "I'm interested."

Shrugging, Mr. Goldstein pressed the back of his hand to his perspiring brow. "A man brought it in this morning."

That wasn't much to go on. "What did he look

like?" Gregor pressed. "Old, young, tall, short, thin, stocky? Did you catch a name?"

Mr. Goldstein took a step back from the counter. "I don't want any trouble. You've got business with someone, I don't get involved. You got it? I've said all I'm going to say about it. Do you want the fiddle or not?"

Kristof swallowed his frustration. "Do you have the case it came in?"

Mr. Goldstein pulled it up from behind the glass case and set it on the counter. The tag with Rose's name and address was absent from the handle, but it was hers.

"I'll take it."

Monday, August 28, 1893

Sylvie raised her closed parasol above her head, the signal to her group of ladies from Canada that she was about to speak. She'd tied a broad, red satin ribbon around it, its ends floating down in conspicuous streamers.

"Ladies," she called out, "welcome to the largest building in the world and the largest roofed building that was ever erected. St. Peter's Cathedral in Vatican City could fit inside this space three times over. The old Roman Coliseum could seat eighty thousand people. The Manufactures Building is four times larger. The largest building we have in Chicago, outside of the Fair, is the Auditorium. Twenty of those could fit inside the Manufactures."

She could do this. She had given this speech so many times that she could do it without thinking, which was good, since her thoughts remained tethered to Rose's violin, now in Kristof's apartment. The case, she'd found on closer inspection, had been threaded with Tiny Tim's black hair, evidence that the cat had been with her, wherever she was. No doubt he'd made a bed in her case while she played. Why she'd pawned the violin now, Sylvie had no idea, especially since they'd learned from Mr. Janik that Rose's mother played the violin, too, increasing its sentimental value. Nor could she guess who the man was who'd made the trade. All she knew for sure was that Rose was here in Chicago—or at least, she had been on Saturday.

She pointed upward with her parasol. "Look above, ladies. There is enough iron and steel in the roof to build not one, but two Brooklyn Bridges. Those red-and-white-striped awnings running the length of the ceiling filter the sunlight that pours through eleven acres of glass. Now look around." As she had dozens of times before, Sylvie explained the layout of the ground floor of the building. "Aisles between the pavilions are laid out as streets, with ornamental streetlamps along the way. We are standing in the middle of Columbia Avenue, the fifty-foot-wide main thoroughfare that stretches from the north end to the south." All down the center of it, rows of chairs sat back to back for the weary. Lining the avenue were gilded domes, minarets, mosques, palaces, kiosks, and pavilions, all in miniature to represent thirty different nations.

"Just behind me, at the crossroads with the east-to-west avenue, is the clock tower, which will serve as a reference point for our day here in this building." It was one hundred and twenty feet high and couldn't be missed.

"Excuse me, Miss Townsend?" A petite red-haired woman named Marie raised her hand. Her fair cheeks were florid already, and it was not yet eleven in the morning. "I read in my guidebook that we could spend a month in this building alone and still not see everything. I'm already overwhelmed. Could you bring it down to a scale we can manage?"

"With pleasure," Sylvie said. "That's what you've hired me for. Now, as I understand it, some in your group are of French descent, am I right?"

Five of the seven women nodded.

"Then you'll have special interest in France's pavilion, right next to us. To my mind, it is the most expertly done of all the nations represented here. Would you like to see it with me?"

They said they would. She reminded them

once more where the closest toilet facilities were located, then led them beneath the arched façade and inside.

Gasps rose up from her little group, just as she expected. "That's right, ladies," she told them. "This fountain is not of water, but of French perfume. You are all invited to dip your hand-kerchief into the pool for a free sample."

She led them from one marble-columned salon to the next, designed in the Louis XIV and Louis XV style, containing rich furniture and silver from Versailles. They also saw a carpet made of otter fur, luxurious Gobelin tapestries, and a display of the latest Parisian bridal fashions, worn by life-size wax figures.

Before long, the strong jasmine-and-orange perfume of the French pavilion inspired a head-ache between Sylvie's temples. "Marie." She pulled the woman aside. "Why don't you ladies work through this pavilion and the Belgian one adjoining it at your own pace. Meet me beneath the clock tower when you're finished, all right?"

Marie agreed, and Sylvie escaped the maze of French salons until she was back on Columbia Avenue. A sparrow swooped beneath the clock tower before soaring up again toward the light. Sylvie lost sight of it behind one of the American flags hanging from the skylights more than two hundred feet above her. But she knew it was trapped. She wondered if it longed for its mother or simply for freedom.

She needed more sleep.

No. What she needed was to find Rose.

Then there she was, materializing out of the crowd, her back to Sylvie as she headed north, her hand in the crook of a gentleman's elbow. Gasping, Sylvie followed her with her gaze. The honey-colored gown was unmistakable, though, with black lace trim at the collar, puffed sleeves that ended just below the elbow, black tulle ruffles at the cuffs, and matching ruffles on the skirt at the hem and about the knees.

With a chill, Sylvie recalled "The Yellow Wallpaper," which had been published in *The New England Monthly* magazine last year. In that short story, the narrator had descended into madness, seeing women trapped behind layers of wallpaper, then finally believing she was one of them herself.

Sylvie shuddered. This was completely different. She was not hallucinating. She was not insane. Her sight had not betrayed her. She had been right about Gertrude, after all.

The clock tower above her chimed eleven times. The Canadian ladies could spend another hour, at least, between the French and Belgian displays. Pulse rushing in her ears, Sylvie watched the hem of Rose's skirt recede into the German pavilion.

There was no choice but to follow. Leaving the clock tower behind, Sylvie darted between other fairgoers as she crossed the avenue. Towering black wrought-iron gates swung open to admit her into a German garden, and she hurried under the arch of a sixteenth-century Renaissance façade and into a courtyard that held several pavilions. She whirled around. Rose—or the girl in her gown—was gone.

Sylvie hurried through displays of porcelain, past the altar-like structure that housed an eighteen-foot by twelve-foot painting of German industry on more than a thousand tiles. In the next pavilion, she was surrounded by thousands of German dolls of every size and variety. Roped off in the center of the room was a life-size model horse in fine livery, hitched to an ornate carriage filled to overflowing with toys from Sonneberg, Germany, and topped with a Christmas tree. Sylvie felt as though she could sense every false eye upon her. She shivered.

She hastened out of Germany and into the adjoining Austria. A couple stood admiring Vienna wood carvings. Others bent over goods of pearl and shell, mosaics, amber work, silks, and velvets.

Panic threatened. "Rose!" she called out, knowing the girl she followed might be someone else entirely. But her daughter's name burst from her in spite of all logic.

Palms sweating, she emerged from Austria and spun in a circle. Where could she have gone? Japan was next to Austria, and on the other side of the avenue stood the United States pavilion, featuring Tiffany & Co. in the corner.

Of course. What young lady wouldn't feel drawn to view the creations of the famous jeweler?

Sylvie checked the clock tower, shocked at how much time had already passed. But she didn't see her group below it. She hurried back across the avenue, her strides so long as to be unseemly if they weren't concealed beneath her skirt.

A Columbian Guard stood with his back to one of the Corinthian pillars flanking the entrance. American flags artfully draped the imposing façade above the engraved words: THE UNITED STATES OF AMERICA BIDS THE WHOLE WORLD WELCOME.

Stepping inside was like walking into Tiffany & Co.'s New York City gallery. Chandeliers with globe-shaped hurricanes hung from a paneled ceiling that was open in the middle to allow natural light to fall through. Glass cases lined the dark wainscoted walls and studded the exhibit floor, bearing watches, silverware, smelling bottles, vases, Viking punch bowls, love cups, and, above all, jewelry of every kind imaginable mounted on black velvet.

And there she was, the young woman in Rose's

gown, gazing at the inch-wide canary-yellow Tiffany Diamond. The gem slowly revolved in a case all its own, so people could view it from all four sides. Sylvie's breath hitched as she approached the case, and she willed her heart to calm.

While the young lady remained entranced with the diamond, Sylvie studied her through the glass from the other side. The bodice of the dress was exactly as she had suspected. Lace trim to match the high collar was sewn in straight lines angling from the shoulders to the center of the waist.

There was no perfect way to proceed from here.

Sylvie stepped around the display case until she stood almost shoulder to shoulder with her. "Excuse me," she began. "I couldn't help but notice your gown. It's beautiful."

The young woman looked up. "Thank you. But I'm surprised it was my gown that caught your eye when we're standing in front of the Tiffany Diamond. But then, I suppose you've seen it, haven't you?" A silver badge pinned to Sylvie's shirtwaist identified her as an employee of the World's Columbian Exposition.

"Oh. Yes, I have. I'm a tour guide here, so I've seen most of these exhibits already. Actually, I thought I'd seen your dress before, too. Do you mind telling me where you got it?"

The young woman set her small black hat to

a jaunty angle. "It was a gift. From my father."

A few yards away, a man studied the enameled dials and ornately carved case of the eight-foot-tall Louis XV astronomical clock. "Is that him?" Sylvie asked.

She said it was.

Sylvie thanked the young woman and moved to join her father, the many ticks and clicks of the clock tweaking her nerves. "Pardon me, sir. Your daughter told me you gave her that gown as a gift. Would you be willing to tell me where you found it?"

Eyes narrow beneath the brim of his bowler hat, he turned to her. "Why do you ask?"

There was nothing for it but the truth. "Because I think it once belonged to my daughter."

"Shh!" He guided Sylvie to another glass case, farther away, where electric light from the chandeliers gleamed on a variety of tea sets. "Keep your voice down," he said.

"I don't need the dress," she whispered. "I just want to know where you found it."

"Why should you care?" The Tiffany & Co. catalogue wrinkled in his grip.

"I realize we're complete strangers to each other, but you're a parent, so to that sensibility I make my appeal. My daughter may have run away." It was the simplest reason she could offer. "I thought she took her clothes with her, but now I am finding them on other young ladies in

Chicago. I don't understand why. I'm trying to piece the puzzle together."

He moved along the glass case, gaze traveling from a silver etched coffeepot to his daughter, who was now mesmerized by a Marie-Antoinette diamond collar. He must think Sylvie mad to have just revealed such personal information, but she could think of no other course to reach him.

"I'm sorry to hear about your daughter," he said, coming back toward her. "I found that dress in a secondhand clothing shop on Clark Street last week."

"Which one?"

He told her, and she locked the name of the establishment into a mental file. "Please, don't say anything to her about it, all right? Times are hard, you know. She doesn't know it's second-hand. I just wanted to give her something special for her birthday."

Sylvie wondered if he was a bank manager whose bank had closed this summer, or a busi-nessman laid off and afraid to tell his family. "It becomes her," she offered sincerely. "Whatever happens, whatever she learns, she will still love you. She will love you no matter what." It was not her place to say it, but she'd already shared more than propriety condoned.

His brows snapped together. "Do you think so?"

"I know it. I had my own father once."

Her throat closed as she realized how much she still missed him. Yet she'd been fortunate to have as many years as she did with both of her parents, when Rose had lost hers so young. No wonder she'd been searching.

A whirring sounded from the astronomical clock on the other side of the room as it geared up to chime the hour. Sylvie thanked the father, cast one more glance at his daughter, and hurried back to the clock tower on Columbia Avenue just as it finished striking twelve.

CHAPTER TWENTY-ONE

Wednesday, August 30, 1893

By the looks of his apartment, Kristof wasn't convinced he was getting his money's worth from Lottie's housekeeping. He hadn't hired her because he needed the help, but he did hope she served the Hoffmans better.

Exhausted from another day of rehearsal and two afternoon concerts, he set his violin case in its spot by the music stand in the corner of the parlor.

Gregor dropped his by the door. "Come out to dinner with us tonight."

Kristof swiped a finger through a fuzzy strip of dust on the edge of the mantel. "Who are you going with, and where?"

"Neil and Geoffrey." A cellist and the pianist from the orchestra. "Plus some ladies who work in the typewriters exhibit in the Manufactures Building. Three of them, to be exact. It would do you good to get out."

"You mean it would do you good to have evenly matched pairs," Kristof replied. "No, thanks. Dining out with you is one thing, but I'd rather avoid the appearance of favoritism with anyone else in the orchestra."

Gregor laughed as he freed the tail of his shirt from his waistband. "Because you're the maestro?"

"Conductor," he corrected. He'd never deign to use the more formal term reserved for men far more experienced than him. "And yes."

"There's a rule somewhere about it, is there?"

If there wasn't, there ought to be.

"In all seriousness, Kristof, you're doing great," Gregor offered. "You work us at least as hard as Thomas did, if not harder, which is a cross to bear, but the performances are better than ever, and ticket sales prove it. Do you enjoy it? Commanding everyone else, telling them exactly what to do, and telling them when they're not good enough?" He smirked.

"Actually, I do," Kristof admitted. He'd been surprised how much. The precision that drove him to hours of practice had channeled into making the orchestra everything it could be. When they stumbled, he tried not to lose his temper as much as he would have if he'd been the one making the mistake. When his musicians got it right, however, the music transcended everything. It was sublime. And Gregor may have been teasing, but he was right that Kristof's strict standards were paying off.

Kristof moved into the kitchen to pour himself a glass of water. The tumbler he pulled from the cabinet, however, still had a trace of dried lemonade filming the bottom of it. He pointed the glass at Gregor. "Did you put this away dirty?"

"Do I ever put dishes away at all?"

"Excellent point." Kristof unbuttoned his cuffs, rolled them to the elbows, and ran water and soap into the sink while he methodically inspected every dish in the cupboard, dunking into the suds those that didn't pass muster.

Gregor raised his eyebrows, lips twisting. "So now you're paying her, *and* you're doing her work." Shaking his head, he sauntered away to his bedroom.

His words stuck where they landed. Gregor was being paid to be concertmaster, and he wasn't doing his work either. Kristof's hands stilled beneath the water. Sylvie had admitted she had trouble drawing a line between her responsibility and someone else's. But here Kristof was doing the same thing, redoing tasks that weren't his to begin with.

Sylvie had hinted at that, too, and he'd shut her down.

Hang it all. She'd been right.

Should he find Lottie elsewhere in the building and make her come back to finish washing? That would only take her away from cleaning for Sylvie or Karl and Anna. No good. Next time he saw her, he decided, he would gently explain that she needed to raise her standard if she hoped to be a domestic elsewhere. She could have been dismissed for her negligence.

Minutes passed. The skin on his finger pads wrinkled while he washed and rinsed every dish. Done at last, he withdrew from the sink and dried his hands on a towel before hanging it back on its hook. Absently, he watched the soapy water whirl down the drain. Finishing Lottie's job was one thing—he couldn't very well eat off dirty dishes. But what would happen if he didn't do Gregor's work for him? It would affect the entire orchestra. Was that a risk he was willing to take? Would he give Gregor a chance to rise to the challenge, or was he so convinced his brother would fail that he didn't allow him room to succeed?

Kristof dropped into a chair at the kitchen table. As a young man, he'd felt nearly crushed by his father's low expectations for him. How could he do the same to Gregor? He raked his fingers through his hair. This was different, he told himself. There was more at stake. If Gregor didn't do his job correctly, then . . .

Then Kristof would decide what to do at that point. Enough quibbling.

He stood. "Gregor," he called. "We need to talk."

Gregor emerged from his room freshly shaven, in a crisp white shirt he was still buttoning. "Yes?"

"I'm done being concertmaster and conductor both. It's time for you to step up."

"Not a good idea. You won't like how I do it." He pressed his arm against his middle and buttoned the cuff.

"I write the musical phrasing in the master score, and you copy it into each musician's copy, exactly as I've done it for each section. That's all you have to do. Copy."

"Copying, dear brother, is not my style."

Typical. "Your style has nothing to do with it." Annoyance surged. "For once, don't concern yourself with being special and instead be concerned about doing this right. Not everything you do needs to be about your own glory."

"It hurts!" Gregor slapped his chest. "Oh, how the truth hurts!" Laughing, he tucked his shirt into his trousers.

Kristof waited for a more satisfying response. It didn't come. "I need you to take this seriously. I need you to prove you're capable of the honor of being concertmaster and first chair." He opened his leather valise and pulled out a folder fat with sheet music. "I've already marked my scores for the pieces in Friday's program. You need to copy the rest, tonight, to hand to the orchestra at tomorrow's rehearsal. They need time with the music before we perform on Friday."

The humor fled Gregor's eyes. "There are one

hundred and fifty members. You expect me to mark everything before morning?"

"Perhaps I won't be the only one staying home tonight." It was all he could do to keep from demanding Gregor cancel his plans.

"Not a chance. I'm going. If I need to stay up late to get it done, I will, but I won't back out of my evening plans. They're counting on me."

"I'm counting on you."

"Are you?" A glint of mischief entered Gregor's eye. "I'd wager that by the time I get home tonight, my work will magically be done for me. As always."

That was Kristof's fault. Sylvie had been right. Gregor had no reason to feel accountable, none at all, based on their previous pattern. That all changed now. "No more wagering, remember? Especially not on this."

Gregor disappeared into his room again. "Whatever you say, Maestro."

Kristof's jaw hardened, and he ducked into the bathroom to wash his face and neck. The cool water soothed his warm skin but did little to abate the heat within. Returning to his bedroom, he removed his own shirt, now damp with the day's perspiration, and pulled out his bureau drawer for a fresh undershirt. At least the bureau was free of dust, he noted.

And the top drawer was free of something else. His heart skipped a beat as he felt beneath the stacks of undershirts for last week's wages. With so many banks failing these days, Kristof wasn't eager to put all of his salary into the bank anymore. After cashing the check, he was sure he'd put the cash right here. One hundred and fifty dollars.

Gone.

He slammed the drawer shut and opened the next, then the next, until he'd rummaged through every one of them.

Gregor appeared in the doorway, his hair shining with pomade, a dinner jacket draped over an arm. "Do you have something to say to me?"

"My wages from last week are gone."

"Are you sure?"

"Help yourself." Kristof gestured toward the ransacked bureau. "I hope you find it."

He didn't.

"Please tell me that at least your wages are safe," Kristof said.

"They were right where I put them this morning."

"And now?"

Frowning, Gregor marched back to his room, Kristof on his heels, watching as he opened a cigar box he kept on his nightstand. He saw cuff links and matchsticks inside, a ticket stub or coat check claim. But no money.

"Three hundred dollars." Kristof felt as though he'd been punched. "It didn't vanish into thin air." He sank to the edge of the bed. "Only one other person comes in here." And she was desperate for money by her own admission.

Gregor hooked a thumb in his trouser pocket, shifting his weight where he stood. "Lottie might have moved the money while cleaning and just didn't put it back. It could be around here somewhere. Listen, I've got to go. I'll help you sort this out when I get back."

Kristof barely heard him leave. He was already back in his own room, pulling on a fresh shirt, putting to rights the clothing he'd rumpled in his search, and at the same time reordering his thoughts. Lottie had no business even opening Gregor's cigar box. As for his bureau drawers, she only opened those to put away cleaned and folded clothes, but she hadn't done laundry today.

Rose's violin case remained on the floor, since Sylvie couldn't bear to have the reminder in her apartment. Kneeling beside it, he unfastened the buckles to reassure himself it was there. It was, thank goodness. Perhaps Lottie hadn't realized she could get money for the instrument, as well.

Sitting on his heels, he rubbed a hand over his face, trying not to feel the theft as a personal betrayal. He was already paying Lottie, who had no references or experience. He was patient, or trying to be. And this was how she repaid him.

Did she not know any better? Was her mother truly on death's doorstep? *Three hundred dollars!*

It was a staggering amount of cash, far more than a doctor's visit and medicine would amount to. Exactly what kind of girl was this housekeeper?

Sylvie locked up the bookstore twenty minutes early. All she wanted to do was curl up in her apartment with a cup of peppermint tea. The headache pushing against skin and bone hadn't released her since she'd seen Rose's gown at the Fair on Monday.

That afternoon, she'd gone directly to the clothing shop on Clark Street and inquired about when the dress had come in and who had brought it. The manager had laughed at her. *"You expect me to remember who brings in what, and when, with a full description of their physical appearance?"* he had said. *"Why not ask their birthdates and addresses along with their names?"* His sarcasm had stung. It was another dead end. She was surrounded by them.

Removing the pins from the base of her skull, she freed the lower portions of her hair and massaged her scalp, hoping to relieve some pressure. It helped, some.

In the corner, the fern drooped, its arms hanging over its pedestal, as if it were as utterly spent as she was. The brittle edges of the leaves were curling. She couldn't bring herself to care. Instead, she put the teakettle on to boil, sank into a chair, and measured the emptiness around her.

Flanking the fireplace in the parlor, bookcases leaned against walls papered with blushing peonies on a ground of sage-green vines. A leather armchair her father had favored still bore a depression where he'd sat with books or newspapers. A clock clicked on the mantel beside a framed photograph from Meg and Nate's wedding and a vase of dried roses left over from the occasion. The only other decoration in the room was a portrait Meg had painted for her of Lucy Snowe, the heroine in Charlotte Bronte's *Villette*, and a stuffed bird in a cage on a stand in the corner.

She owned nothing from her childhood and certainly nothing from generations past. No quilt passed down from her mother, no cross-stitched sampler from her grandmother. She had very little from before October 1871, and those few treasures she kept in her bedroom. She did not even own doilies to spread over the green upholstered sofa and wingback chair. There was something about losing almost everything in a fire that made her resist acquiring material possessions that could burn.

Except for books, which had always been faithful companions. But just now she was so lonely she could scarcely draw air around the hollow between her ribs.

A light knock sounded at the door, and the hinge squeaked as Lottie let herself in. "Oh! Miss

Townsend. I didn't know you'd be here. I just came to pick up my bonnet. It's right over there on the sofa."

Sylvie gasped. "Lottie!" she cried. "What are you wearing?"

Startled, Lottie looked down at the dress beneath her apron. "I didn't steal it, if that's what you mean! And why shouldn't I have a nice dress to wear?"

Either Sylvie was genuinely losing her wits, or that dress was Rose's navy-and-white gingham day dress, with a ruffle at each shoulder above sleeves that were barely puffed at all. It had been the simplest Rose had owned but remained in excellent condition. "Where did you get it? When?"

"A charity bin at St. Michael's, on Sunday. The nicest I ever did wear, even if it is a little too long in the hem. I'm sure I can fix that, but I didn't have time and I—I wanted to look nice for work." Her cheeks flushed with the confession. Her neatly plaited hair bore testimony that she had indeed taken extra effort. "Some ladies say that we are what we wear. I only wanted to be decent for once. Almost pretty." She spread out the skirt. "No one could tell I live in a rear tenement on DeKoven Street from this, could they? Don't you like it?"

"Of course I do." Sylvie choked on the words. "You look lovely. And if I remember correctly, the hem shouldn't be challenging to rip out and re-sew."

"How do you know?"

"Because I hemmed it myself."

"This was yours?"

"Rozalia's." It was excruciating, seeing pieces of Rose over and over like this and still having no idea where she was sixteen days after she went missing. So much could happen in that time. Too much.

Lottie's countenance clouded. "Don't tell Ivan that. He'd probably take it right back and say I'm not good enough to wear it. He was the one who found it for me in the church charity bin. I don't recall the last time he gave me a present."

Sylvie crossed to the sofa in the parlor and sat, the champagne folds of her dress spreading about her. "Is his new job working out?"

Lottie sat beside her. "He won't say much about it, but the hours are good, and he is bringing home more cash. He doesn't say much of anything."

"I see." Sylvie fingered the crocheted trim at her elbow. "Are the two of you close?"

"The thing about Ivan is that you don't know what he's thinking or feeling, sometimes, until he's yelling about it. He hasn't hurt Matka or me, but sometimes I worry he might. He told me once that when a person loves something, they hold on to it to keep it safe. To keep it from running away and getting hurt. Like that." Lottie nodded to the stuffed bird in the cage. "Once, after I told him he was scaring me, he said that if scaring me was what it took, then he didn't mind doing it because he was protecting me from myself. From my own ideas and plans. He said if it took more than scaring me, he'd do that too. Like our father did." She shrugged again, as if to dismiss the entire conversation.

A chill raced up Sylvie's spine as each revelation unfolded. Could Ivan, the son of an abusive father, be holding tight to Rose even now? He'd said he didn't know where Rose was, but he could have been lying.

The teakettle whistled in the kitchen. Only when it reached a frenzied pitch did Sylvie register the sound and excuse herself to set her tea to brew. When she returned to the parlor, Lottie looked like a bird ready to take flight. Sylvie ought not ask more questions. She ought not push her further today.

Lowering herself beside the young woman, she offered a reassuring smile. "Let's see about that hem." She made no remark on the worn and tattered condition of Lottie's boots, string in place of shoelaces, as she turned up the hem to inspect the seam. "Just as I thought," she said. "I hand-stitched this, so the stitches aren't very small. You'll have no trouble slipping a ripper beneath the thread."

Lottie flipped up another portion of the skirt,

exposing a petticoat beneath. She ran her finger along the hem. "What's this?" She unpinned a small white tag from where the hem met the seam that ran to the waist.

"May I see?"

Lottie handed it over, and Sylvie read aloud. " 'Laundered by the staff at—' " She lost her breath.

"What is it? What does it say?"

Sylvie was already on her feet when a knock on the door jolted through her. Laundry ticket clutched in one hand, she opened it to find Kristof, his hair disheveled, face drawn. As eager as she was to blurt out what she'd just discovered, the seriousness of his expression stopped her cold. Something was dreadfully wrong.

His gaze went immediately to her hair. Though silver combs still held it back from her face at the sides, the rest fell in waves down her back. "I'm intruding," he said. "But I'm afraid I must, if Lottie is here. I thought I heard you talking, and I have a serious matter to discuss with her. You may as well be part of it. I'm sorry, Sylvie. I wish this weren't the case."

Bewildered, Sylvie closed the door behind him.

Lottie stood beside the sofa, clutching her bonnet. "What is it, Mr. Bartok?"

He marched toward her, but when the girl shrank back, Kristof went no farther, allowing several feet to remain between him and their young housekeeper. "Lottie, I need to ask you something, and I want you to be honest. Tell the truth, and we'll work it out, I promise." He paused. "My wages from last week are missing. So are my brother's. That's three hundred dollars."

Lottie dropped the bonnet and covered her mouth. "You think I stole three hundred dollars?"

Shock stole Sylvie's speech. Memories assaulted her of how destitute Lottie had been when she and Beth had found her on the steps of Carrie Watson's, of her insistent questions about when she'd be paid, even before she'd done any work. Lottie had forgotten to lock the apartment door before, so perhaps the same neglect at the Bartoks' had allowed a thief easy access. Sylvie hated to think so. She didn't want to imagine that Lottie had anything to do with this, by accident or intention.

"That's what I wanted to ask you. I don't want to assume anything," he went on, "but you are the only person who comes into our apartment, and you are in there, alone, for hours. Now, I realize your mother's declining health generates expenses, but—"

Tears filled Lottie's eyes. "I wouldn't do that, Mr. Bartok. I never stole a thing from you. Why would I, when you're the one who pays me?"

A cloud passed over the sun, muting every color. "What about Ivan?" Sylvie asked quietly.

"On occasion you've forgotten to lock the door when you finish cleaning. Did Ivan tell you to do that? Could he have come in and taken the money?" Even suggesting the idea was abhorrent to her, but she had to ask.

Thunder grumbled in the distance. "He's working now. And he never said to do any such thing, I swear it." Lottie lifted the hem of her apron to her nose. "And if he had, I wouldn't have done it. I can't blame you for not thinking much of my morals after the way you found me, but all I have is my word."

Was that enough?

Tension charged the atmosphere. The wind sweeping through the window and ruffling through the fern in the corner did nothing to thin it.

"There must be some misunderstanding," Sylvie ventured at last. "May I speak with you, Kristof?"

He followed her into the kitchen. The rumbling outside grew louder, and plates rattled in the cupboard. Kristof looked haggard and wary. Her fingers itched to smooth both the worry and suspicion from his brow.

"Remember the bail money I paid to release Beth from jail?" she whispered. "Beth came to repay me one day when I wasn't here. She left the money on the kitchen table while Lottie was cleaning my apartment. She could have taken it before I returned from work, and I never would have known. Why would Lottie leave that alone and then steal from you and Gregor?"

"Her family needs money. She's loyal to them. It's not unthinkable."

Sylvie walked back and beckoned Lottie closer. "Could you have moved the money or misplaced it? Can you offer any ideas as to what might have happened?"

"No, Miss Townsend! I never even saw that much money all at once in my life. I don't snoop around. I only check your pockets when it's wash day and I need to empty them first. And whatever I find in the pockets, I don't throw away either. I just put the coins and bits of paper on your dressers."

Sylvie believed her. She wanted to believe her.

"Do you?" Kristof challenged. "I didn't notice any such pile on my bureau this week."

"Oh no." Lottie slapped at the pocket of her apron. "I must have forgotten, but it's all right here." She scooped out the contents and released them into Kristof's cupped hands. A few quarters, a dime, restaurant receipts for Kinsley's and the Chicago Oyster House, and something else Sylvie couldn't quite decipher.

Kristof plucked it out. His complexion paled, then fired to a livid red. "A receipt from the Garfield Racing Association. Gregor's been gambling again. Of course the money disappeared." He crumpled it in his fist. "I owe you an apology, Lottie. I'm sorry you had to defend yourself like that. Your honesty has proven your innocence. And my brother's guilt," he added quietly to Sylvie, steel in his tone.

Sylvie picked up Lottie's bonnet and placed it on her head. "You've been very helpful, and we've kept you long enough. See you tomorrow."

With a small, awkward curtsy, Lottie scurried from the apartment and down the stairs.

"I apologize for barging in like that." Kristof exuded frustration. "But she cleared her name quicker than I thought possible. I'm glad she's blameless. . . ." His voice trailing away, he clenched the back of a chair and leaned on it. "I hate that my brother isn't. Three hundred dollars! I noticed it was missing before he left this evening. He knew I suspected Lottie, must have known I would question her. He could have cleared her name himself and didn't."

Peppermint tea infused the air, but Sylvie let it turn tepid. She laid a hand on Kristof's back and felt his muscle tense. "I can only imagine the confrontation you have ahead of you with your brother," she said. "But right now I have one of my own."

Lightning flashed outside in a bank of clouds

hovering over the courthouse. "Not with me, I hope?"

She opened her hand to show the laundry tag within. "At the Palmer House. With the guest in room 423."

CHAPTER TWENTY-TWO

The hansom cab lurched, and Sylvie clutched the leather bench. Kristof peeled her fingers away, enclosing them in his. "We're close," he said. "Just a few more minutes, and we'll have some answers."

Rain dropped on the roof of the cab in fat, loud drops. "I want more than answers. I want Rose. I want whoever is in room 423 to—" *Suffer,* she'd almost said. She'd never felt this vindictive before. She ought to be ashamed, but she was too preoccupied to manage it. "I just want this to be over. The mystery, the suspense, the hope and fear. If I don't even recognize myself right now—and I don't—will I recognize Rose?" She squeezed his hand. "I have no idea what she's been through, but I'm sure it's changed her."

"I'm sure it has." He angled toward her, his knee brushing hers and disappearing in the folds of her skirt. His nearness, the shadows, the vulnerability she felt just now, all combined to form a startling degree of intimacy. She wanted to be strong. But at the moment she didn't mind if that strength came from him.

"Kristof." She spoke his name as much to reassure herself that she was not alone as to ask for attention that was already hers. "When she went missing, my world broke into pieces, and she and I were no longer in the same piece. What if, when we come together again, the rift doesn't disappear, and the jagged edges between us won't align?"

In her mind, she begged him not to point out that Rose's return was still not guaranteed. She knew what she'd said and implied. *When,* not *if.* It was a hope she had to cling to.

Rain blew through the windows, misting her skin. A wheel caught in a gap between cobblestones, rocking the cab to one side. Sylvie swayed against Kristof, and he draped his arm around her shoulders to hold her there. She had no desire to shrug away. Indeed, his arms were shelter, his presence security. His brown eyes held the warmth of a fire as he looked at her.

"You're right," he said. "Things may not snap back into place exactly as they once were."

She glanced past him to the silver streams outside. "The way things were right before she left weren't what I wanted either," she confessed. "I love her with everything I am, and yet I feel inadequate to help her."

"We are all imperfect, despite every effort."

"Except for you." She couldn't resist.

"No," he said. "Especially me. I'm worn out with striving to achieve an impossible ideal."

Sylvie read a struggle in the lines of his face

and considered this. "In your music?" she asked, all teasing erased.

"Music is only part of it. I grew up trying to be good enough and find it's a hard habit to break."

"But good enough for whom? For yourself? For others?"

"That is the question, isn't it? God says that as His child, I am good enough for Him—not because of what I've done, but because of what Christ has done on my behalf. For some reason, I often forget that."

"Shall I remind you on occasion?"

He smiled. Behind the stubbled jaw and the silver glinting in his brown hair, she saw in him the little boy he'd once been, a child who had craved belonging and never felt secure in it.

Without thinking, she lifted a hand to his cheek as though she could console a wound long buried. "You are good enough, Kristof. You are more than good enough."

He took her hand and pressed a kiss to its palm before lowering it. The gesture was so quick and artless, it failed to register a shock. In that instant, nothing in the world could have been more natural.

"You see how this works, don't you?" he said. "If there is grace for me, there is grace for you, too. You worry about your ability to reconcile with Rose and help heal her after whatever ordeal she's endured. Correct?"

"Exactly." The cab turned. In a matter of blocks, they would arrive at the Palmer. Her stomach contracted in anticipation.

"Where we are weak, God is strong. He can take our smallest offerings and make of them a feast. But for now, we focus on finding her."

The heavens opened wide, and drops became a driving torrent just as Sylvie and Kristof stepped inside the Palmer House hotel. Even with him beside her, her nerves buzzed. She couldn't imagine doing this without him.

The two-story lobby had been designed to awe its guests and visitors. Beyond red velvet seating and marble-topped tables, a grand staircase led the eye to a fresco mural on the ceiling taken from Greek mythology. Garnet-draped chandeliers glowed above them.

None of this interested Sylvie.

Kristof's hand warmed the small of her back as she made her way between men in dark suits and women in dinner gowns and matching elbow-length gloves to the long reception desk against one wall.

A man stuffed into his brass-buttoned uniform scribbled on some kind of ticket while Sylvie mustered all the patience she could find. "I'll be with you shortly." The name on his straining blue jacket said Tom.

Sylvie surveyed the lobby while she waited.

The air was thick with the smells of perfumes, colognes, and the restaurant adjoining the lobby. Gilded frames held artwork Bertha Palmer had brought home from France by a painter she'd befriended named Claude Monet. At a time like this, it was impossible to enjoy a single one of them.

"Excuse me, Tom," Kristoff said to the receptionist, tapping his umbrella lightly on the floor. "We have a pressing matter, and it won't take much of your time."

The receptionist's eyebrows plunged but quickly smoothed back into placid arcs. "Yes, sir. How can I help you?"

Sylvie produced the laundry ticket. "Somehow I have ended up with the laundry belonging to the guest in room 423," she said. It wasn't a lie.

Color deepened in Tom's already ruddy cheeks. "I'm sorry to hear it. I'll find out where the mistake was made and report it immediately." His chin lowered, flattening against his neck.

"Your guest ought to be notified at once, as well." Kristof's demeanor was a thin veneer of nonchalance. Beneath it, the tendons in his neck pulled taut.

"But of course," Tom said. "You have the article with you?"

Sylvie swallowed. "Not at present. I first wanted to see if the guest is still staying in that room. You'll see the date on the ticket is from last week."

With an ink-stained finger, the receptionist spun the ticket to face him, then consulted a ledger book. "The guest checked out last Friday. The room is occupied by someone else now, a guest who has specifically asked not to be disturbed."

"Who was it?" Kristof asked. "We'll try contacting him or her ourselves."

"I'm not at liberty to release that information to you," Tom hedged. "We pride ourselves on preserving our guests' privacy even after they've gone."

Sylvie had never heard such a ridiculous notion. She touched Kristof's shoulder, and he bent his ear to her. "I'm going to sit down. Stay and finish your conversation."

He nodded. He was still arguing with the receptionist when she strolled away, circling through the lobby. She took a seat in one of the plush velvet chairs and watched the bank of receptionists at the long mahogany desk. Rain pounded outside, mingling with the steady drone in the lobby. Bits and pieces of other people's conversations floated to her, and she discarded the fragments as quickly as they fell upon her ears. She was focused on one thing only.

"I said I want to speak to your supervisor," she thought she heard Kristof say.

Tom straightened and stalked away.

As soon as he did, Sylvie whisked over to the other end of the desk. "Pardon me," she said quietly. "Could you send up two extra pillows to 423, please?"

"Certainly. I'll have a maid bring those to you shortly."

"Thank you."

Heart hammering, she walked through the lobby with a purposeful stride and, unwilling to speak to an elevator operator, ascended the stairs. Gloved hand gliding over the railing, she answered Kristof's questioning gaze by staying him with her palm. She would do this alone. All she wanted was to speak to the maid.

Her headache swelled with every step. *I didn't lie,* she told her conscience. Even so, her own actions surprised her. But what wouldn't she do to get to the bottom of this? She was too close now to give up. If the new guest had asked not to be disturbed, perhaps he—or she—had secluded himself enough so the hotel staff wouldn't recognize him anyway. There were hundreds of rooms, after all. The staff might never realize she wasn't actually a guest.

On the fourth floor, she hurried down the corridor toward room 423. Electric light from the wall sconces reflected off the crown molding and absorbed into the carpet cushioning her feet. She had to wait only five minutes before a maid appeared at the other end of the hall, pushing a cart topped with pillows in starched white cases.

Sylvie walked toward her. "For room 423? Thank you." She met the maid halfway down the corridor and read the name embroidered on her shirtwaist. *Jenny.* "I'll take them from here." Her legs were shaking, but her voice did not. It was a gamble, wagering that the maid either had not yet met the room's new occupant or would assume that Sylvie was a visiting friend or relative. "Have you serviced this room for long?"

"Yes, ma'am, this is one of the floors I'm assigned to. If there's ever anything I can do for you, just let the front desk know, and I'll get the message." She bobbed in a curtsy, then stood there expectantly, most likely waiting for a tip.

Sylvie dug into her reticule for a coin but held it while her mind raced. Questions tangled on her tongue. "I understand the last guest in 423 was here for some time," she began. Her mouth went dry. She licked her lips. "Jozefa Zielinksi? Since August 14, if I'm not mistaken."

"I'm not at liberty to say, ma'am." Jenny adjusted the ruffled cap over her blond hair. She could not be more than eighteen years old. So very like Rose.

"Of course, I understand." Sylvie's conscience pricked at what she was about to say, but she silenced it. She had to know. "It's just that she mentioned that her maid was extremely helpful, and I wanted to pay you the compliment of hearing that. That is, if it was you she meant. After that mix-up with her room not being ready until a week after she came, it was especially important that the service here was good."

"She was always kind to me. I was happy to serve."

The words clanged like cymbals in Sylvie's ears. Her palms began sweating through her gloves. "It was kind of you not to report that she kept a cat in the room. A little black one with a white chest and paws."

Recognition flickered across Jenny's face.

Emboldened, Sylvie pressed harder. "Didn't you feel like you were coming down with a cold every time you came into the room? At least, that's what she told me."

Jenny rubbed a finger below the tip of her nose. "If there was a cat, it must have been hiding whenever I was in there. And any mix-up with the dates of her lodging wasn't the Palmer's fault. Room 423 waited for her, empty, for an entire week before she showed up. All I know is that she asked us to hold it for her, paying the full price even though—"

"The room was available right away? You didn't refer her to the Sherman House?"

"Land sakes, no, ma'am! We were ready. She just wasn't ready for us."

Pieces of memory slammed together. Jozefa had seen Rose's notice in the Polish bulletin. She had come to find *her* at the bookstore, not Sylvie. The week she'd spent in their apartment had been based on a ruse. And all those things Jozefa had said so calmly, so deceptively, now slithered through Sylvie's mind.

"I congratulate you."

"You are free now, too."

"Singleness is a gift, dear, and so is being childless. Don't waste it. Why, I'd never be able to do what I do if I were tied to a family of my own."

And Sylvie had believed her.

A coldness clutched her. She had missed them. She'd come too late. The realization jarred her into a clawing urgency. "Where did she go? She and Rose—did they leave the city?"

The maid eyed the coin still in her grip. Ah, yes. Jenny could be bought. Jozefa had already done it.

"I heard them talking. There are plans." Jenny's tone teased. Taunted. She took pleasure in holding information and clearly expected a reward.

Whatever apprehension and guilt had plagued Sylvie burned away, leaving something stronger, sharper, in its place. "Jenny." Sylvie stepped closer, clenching the cart between them. She bridled her voice to a low rumble, while lightning flashed outside. "Listen to me carefully. I know you were paid to impersonate Rozalia

Dabrowski at the police station. That's a crime. You obstructed an investigation. Losing your job for that is the least of your worries."

The maid's face washed clean of its color. She was shaken now. She ought to be.

"Now, I'll ask you again. Where did the two of them go?"

Chapter Twenty-Three

Thursday, August 31, 1893

Morning had come too early. And Gregor hadn't come at all.

The sunlight infusing the rehearsal room was weak and pale, the sky still overcast after last night's rain. Fog wrapped Music Hall, hovering just outside the closed windows.

All through the early rehearsal, it had taken Kristof every ounce of discipline to focus on the program at hand. His brother's absence wasn't what troubled him. No, he'd decided what to do about that ten minutes into the practice.

It was Sylvie, Rose, Jenny, and Jozefa who frayed the edges of his concentration. Last night, he and Sylvie had escorted Jenny to the police station, where she'd confessed to Officer Thornhill exactly what she'd done. But it failed to instill a sense of urgency in the police. After all, Officer Thornhill pointed out, Jenny was an eyewitness that Rose had not been harmed. She'd been staying at the Palmer, for pity's sake, which didn't exactly sound like a hardship.

It was what they still didn't know that haunted most.

Where was Rose now? Jenny didn't know.

Were Jozefa and Rose preparing to leave Chicago? Jenny had a hunch they were. New gowns had been made for Rose in European styles, and more linens had been piling up in the room. Enough underthings to last quite a while without washing, as if they were readying for a trip.

If Jenny was correct, a clock was ticking down to their departure, only no one but Jozefa knew how much time was left. If they left the city, there was no chance of finding Rose again, Thornhill said, statistically speaking.

Dvořák's Symphony No. 9 in E minor commanded Kristof's attention as he conducted the orchestra along its strains and swells. He pulled and pushed at the music as if it were a living, breathing thing to be tamed and set free in turns. The rests were pure, the strings clear on their cue, the timpani rolling like summer thunder. The music reached every corner of the room in whispers, then in magnificent shouts.

Baton slicing through the air, Kristof brought one hundred and fifty musicians through a stirring climax, bows sawing away on strings, percussion the very heartbeat of the symphony, woodwinds and brass intent on long-held notes, until Dvořák's Symphony No. 9 ended with its distinctive, repetitive, resounding chords.

When the last note faded, he closed his eyes and smiled before raising a triumphant fist in the air. "Bravo," he told his orchestra, and he meant it. For a piece named "From the New World" to honor Columbus's discovery, it was as dramatic and moving as it should be and was sure to thrill the audience later today.

The musicians broke into applause, congratulating each other on their feat. While red-faced woodwind and brass players mopped their brows, Kristof glanced at the clock. It was half past ten. By now Sylvie would have left a note for Tessa to manage the bookstore without her, and would have already been to the Woman's Building.

He pulled his focus back to the rehearsal. It was time to dismiss the orchestra so they'd have a break before the noon concert, but he couldn't do that yet. After stepping down from his podium and crossing to a table, Kristof began spreading out the scores for the music they were to perform tomorrow.

"Section leaders," he called, "meet me up here and bring a pencil. The rest of you, take a break for a few minutes." He extended a hand toward the second violin, since Gregor was still not present. "Charles, you're up."

Charles Krueger was twenty-six years old, young enough to be Kristof's son. But he was always on time and didn't complain. Kristof had no doubt he was capable.

Once all the section leaders had assembled, Kristof handed each of them a stack of music.

"The former concertmaster failed to mark your music for you. So if you would, please refer to my master score, mark up one copy, and then take the rest for your section and see that each one is marked with the same phrasings." He didn't like keeping everyone here when they would normally be released, and inviting so many hands to mark the music almost guaranteed variation. This wasn't going to be perfect, but they'd work that out. "I want everyone to be able to take their music home with them and practice tonight before tomorrow morning's rehearsal."

Charles's pencil stilled. "Pardon me. Did you say *former* concertmaster?"

Footsteps announced Gregor's approach. "Exactly what I'd like to know, Charlie." His violin case dangled from his hand.

Gritting his teeth, Kristof clapped his hands to gain the orchestra's attention. "Once you have your music for tomorrow and you've copied all the markings, you're dismissed. See you in your places at 11:40. Good work this morning, everyone."

Gregor stalked to a window and set his case on the floor. He folded his arms and planted his feet in a wide stance, eyebrows nearing his hairline.

After a few more words to the section leaders, Kristof told Charles, "You're first violin and concertmaster now."

The young man's thanks came immediately. "I won't let you down, sir."

"No. I don't think you will." Why had he waited so long to give Charles a chance?

How many chances had he given Gregor?

Rolling back his shoulders, Kristof joined his brother near the window. "You're fired, Gregor."

A laugh burst from him. "Fired? You can't be serious." His face flushed, and he tugged his bow tie loose and unfastened the top collar button behind it.

"I'm very serious. For years I have protected you from your own consequences. Off and on I've wondered what it would feel like to finally let you experience the same laws of cause and effect the rest of us face. I thought I would feel guilty, as if I were failing our parents by not taking care of you." He paused, allowing the weight of his words to transfer to Gregor's shoulders. His brother was not a burden he needed to bear any longer.

"You're saying you don't feel guilty, then." Gregor scratched his arm. "After all I've done for you."

What Kristof felt was liberation. "I've done us both a disservice by allowing you to skate through life. So I spoke with Maestro Thomas this morning before rehearsal and told him what I thought should be done if you didn't fulfill your responsibilities. He agreed. You're done in the orchestra."

Shrugging, Gregor shifted his weight to his other foot. "There's only one more week of concerts anyway."

Kristof took a deep breath. "You're done in the Chicago Symphony Orchestra, too. Maestro says if you want a job, you'll have to re-audition."

Shock registered in Gregor's eyes, his pupils unusually small. His hand trembled as he raked it through his hair, which bounced back without any pomade to hold it. "That's it, then? Just like that?"

"No. We're just getting started." It was a mercy to both of them that Kristof had had time to consider his response to the gambling receipt Lottie had shown him last night. He didn't want to speak out of anger, although that emotion wasn't far beneath the surface. Anger was not enough for the situation. This called for nothing less than logic, reason, and a firm resolve to do the right thing.

The room was emptying now. Musicians cast backward glances as they placed their instruments in a large locker and filed through the door. Metal clanged together as Charles closed the gates and locked them, then made a hasty retreat.

"What, then?" Gregor nearly shouted, throwing his arms wide. "I would think that after Lottie stole last week's wages, you'd want *both* of us earning to help make up for it."

Now this was too much. Kristof walked away, mastering himself before rounding on Gregor again. "How dare you pin your own theft on a fifteen-year-old girl?"

Gregor blanched. "Let me guess—you talked to her, she denied it. Did you think she would outright admit it? She'll lose her job over this."

"The only one losing their job today is you." Kristof withdrew the receipt from the Garfield Racing Association from his pocket and held it up. "How much did you lose this time?"

Blood rushed back to Gregor's complexion, and he squeezed his eyes tight. For all the world, he resembled the child who played seek-and-hide this way when they were growing up. *"Closing your eyes doesn't mean I can't see you,"* Kristof had repeatedly told him.

Gregor slumped into a nearby chair and groaned, holding his head in his hands. "I was trying to get Father's timepiece back. I told you I would take care of it."

Kristof sat beside him. "You also told me you were done gambling, and I told *you* I don't need that watch." They had drilled these lines repeatedly, with no progress to show for it. He leaned forward, elbows on his knees, hands clasped. "You stole from me, you tried to blame Lottie, and if we don't have enough left to pay the rent, that affects Sylvie and the bookshop, too. She doesn't charge us enough as it is."

"You have a savings account, don't you? In the bank. You can just use that."

"Unless you found a way to clean that out, too."

"I did this for us! For our family!" Gregor was on his feet now, shouting. "It was just bad luck that my horse didn't win. But my motives were noble. I wanted to surprise you."

Balderdash.

Kristof stood, folding his arms to keep his fists from curling into weapons. "If you don't have enough money to cover half the rent, it's time for you to move out."

"You wouldn't."

"I would. I will." The only way for Gregor to grow up was if Kristof let him.

"Kristof!" Gregor exploded. "I don't have a job, thanks to you, and now you want money or you'll throw me out. Is that what brothers do? I'm all you have left! You can't do this. You can't just turn your back on me."

"What happens next is up to you," Kristof said.

And then he walked away.

Sylvie leaned on the Check and Guide Services counter at the Woman's Building, scanning the schedule in *The Daily Columbian* once again. Not that she could retain a single thing she'd read.

"I don't know what else to tell you." Dorothy

peered through her spectacles. "Miss Zielinski has been here every day for three weeks, eager to hear every presentation. But today she hasn't shown up yet."

"Would you know if she were here, though?"

Dorothy sneezed into her handkerchief. "All I can say is that every day so far, this has been her first stop so she can check her parasol. I don't see why she would break that pattern. What's this all about, anyway?"

Setting down the paper, Sylvie looked up. "I have reason to believe Rose is with her."

"Your daughter, right?"

In her heart, Rose was. And yet Sylvie had begun to wonder if claiming that sacred relationship was as insensitive as it was inaccurate. "I've raised her since she was four. But I'm not her mother, really."

"Sounds like a technicality to me. Why is Rose with Miss Zielinski? Is she her mother?"

"No." Sylvie shook her head and immediately regretted it. Her headache had only gotten worse, and every movement was a torture. "No, Rose's mother perished on the voyage to America. Her name was Magdalena, and she must have been a beauty."

Dorothy's smile flashed. "Miss Zielinksi is striking, too. Even if she couldn't act a whit, I bet she'd have been successful on the stage."

But Jozefa Zielinksi could act, Sylvie was

absolutely certain. It was a talent Sylvie did not possess. Neither had her reflection this morning been able to hide the state of her inner disrepair.

Even with Jenny confessing what she'd done, Officer Thornhill had the audacity to ask things Sylvie never would have thought of. *"Did Rose seem to enjoy her time at the Palmer? Was she ever in need of anything? Did she order room service? Did she ever try to send a note out with the dirty dishes?"*

Sylvie had lashed out at him. *"You're implying she was on an all-expense paid vacation!"*

"What makes you think she isn't?"

Sylvie had wanted to scream. *"Because Jozefa hired a maid to impersonate her!"*

Officer Thornhill still maintained that Rose might be in on the entire charade. Perhaps she'd sanctioned the deception, he'd suggested. Perhaps she was content and simply unwilling to be found by anyone else. *"That doesn't make her missing,"* he'd said.

Perhaps, perhaps, perhaps. A wide trail of *perhaps* led them nowhere.

In the end, it was Kristof who had convinced the police to put out an alert so they could keep an eye out for either woman. Sylvie had persuaded the Columbian Guard at the Fair this morning.

"You unwell, Sylvie?" Dorothy's gentle voice pursued her. "Need some water? Or a seat?"

She needed so much more than that. "Thanks, Dorothy. I'll take a walk instead. Just to see if Jozefa is anywhere in the building."

Sylvie began winding her way through the gift shop just as Beth scurried into it and blocked her path. They hadn't seen each other since the night Sylvie had bailed her out of jail.

"Oh." Beth clutched her umbrella in both hands. "Sylvie. I forgot you were working today."

"My group canceled, but it's just as well," she said. "Have you seen Jozefa today?"

"No, I haven't. You look awful. Just terrible."

"Pardon me." Sylvie squeezed past her. She didn't make friends easily, which made conflict with the ones she had so disagreeable. But she didn't have the time or focus to set everything back to rights just now.

Beth followed. "Look, I'm sorry for what I said at the station. You can be mad at me if it makes you feel better, but I can tell something else is under your skin today." When they emerged into the Gallery of Honor beneath the rotunda, Beth caught up to Sylvie. "Will you tell me what's going on if I promise to behave?"

Sylvie glanced at her, then paused to allow a rolling chair to wheel past them toward the display of laces sent by the queen of Italy.

"Walter?" she called.

Her nephew turned to her, gripping the handles of the chair he pushed. He was being paid by

353

the hour, Sylvie knew, and that didn't include personal conversations.

Still, she couldn't help but ask if Meg happened to be at the Fair today.

Sunshine bounced off the shiny brim of Walter's cap. "Set up inside Horticulture," he tossed over his shoulder. With the smallest of waves, he faced forward again and asked the elderly woman in his care which exhibit she'd like to see next.

"Well? What's going on?" Beth prodded with an elbow to her side, and Sylvie told her in hushed tones everything that had happened last night, from the laundry tag in Lottie's gown to her escapade at the Palmer to Jenny's confession at the police station.

"My, my. Doesn't Kristof figure nicely as a hero from one of those novels you sell. What I can't figure out is why you're in the market for one."

Frustration stilled Sylvie's steps. Visitors parted and flowed about them like a stream around unmoving rocks. "Have you so little imagination, Beth? This is Rose we're talking about. I know you've never wanted children and you're through with men completely, but try to understand where I'm coming from." One of the guards nearby raised his blue-black eyebrows. If Sylvie had spoken too loudly, she hadn't realized it.

Beth's shoulders slumped. "Sylvie, Jozefa is gone."

"What?" All other noise dimmed into an indistinct blur in the background.

"She's gone. And if Rose was with her, I imagine that she's gone, too." Beth's hand came under Sylvie's elbow and guided her to sit in one of the chairs encircling a statuary fountain.

Mist sprayed Sylvie's neck from behind. Questions staggered around on her tongue, which grew thick and dry in her mouth. "Start over," she forced out. "Tell me everything."

"I sat with her at one of the lectures here last week. I invited her to the upcoming performance of the Hull House Players, and she said she'd love to but she wouldn't be in town anymore. For all the hardships of living in partitioned Poland, where women are much further behind in their quest for equality than we are, she misses it. She's seen enough of the Fair, enough of Chicago, and she's ready to go home."

"With Rose?" The words skittered out on a breath.

"She didn't say that. You're the one who said Rose was staying with her at the Palmer and that she checked out recently. Why else would she check out unless she was headed home?"

Sylvie tried to breathe, tried to think. Was this something Rose would have agreed to, returning to the land of her parents? She knew so little of the language, but she was young and smart and could quickly learn.

"The police said they would notify all the ports and train stations to keep an eye out for Jozefa or Rose." But even as Sylvie said it, she felt the ineptitude of such a promise. Between commuters and fairgoers from all over the world, tens of thousands came in and out of the city every day. The idea that they could pinpoint two blond women— and the right two, at that—was ludicrous.

And Sylvie was only one person. Even if Kristof and every member of her family helped her, she couldn't possibly hope to patrol every train station, livery, and port in the city.

"I am sorry, you know," Beth replied. "Sorry about Rose, and sorry for not knowing what to say."

Sylvie nodded but could think of nothing to say herself. What was she supposed to do now?

Sylvie wasn't sure how long she sat in front of the fountain, staring vacantly up at a mural by Mary Cassatt that filled the arch above the north gallery. But by the time she rose to go, the back of her jacket was soaked through to her skin from splashing droplets. The damp clinging of fabric was the only thing she felt as she left the Woman's Building. It was all she could stand to feel.

She had planned to return to the bookstore but found herself heading south instead, to the Horticulture Building. If it had been a different day, she would have admired the Venetian Renaissance architecture of the long structure. A huge central glass dome dominated its otherwise long, low silhouette, and it glittered and sparkled as the sun climbed toward its zenith. Its front steps led down to the lagoon where Venetian gondoliers ferried visitors.

Sylvie closed her umbrella and entered beneath a frieze of cupids and garlands. Immediately to her left, a garden of hollyhocks, asters, and clematis exploded with color. The concentrated fragrances of exotic flowers and tropical fruits filled her nose. Prisms fell from the many-paned glass roof. Beneath the dome, ivy and other vines Sylvie didn't recognize obscured balcony railings and cascaded in thirty-foot curtains. The building was a thousand feet long and swathed in light now that the fog had burned away. Courtyards, greenhouses, pavilions, and exhibits featured nations from every corner of the world.

Walter hadn't said exactly where Meg would be, but Sylvie knew her sister. She would be amused by California's tower of fourteen thousand oranges, impressed by the giant cider press in daily operation with fresh apples, and interested in the many educational wine exhibits. But she wouldn't want to paint them.

Rainbows rippling over her skirt, Sylvie circled the area beneath the central dome until she spotted Meg's easel just off the main walkway.

The canvas was a study in lush shades of green and gold. The towering cacti, bamboo, and palm trees were only the background, however, to the people craning to see.

"Meg," Sylvie said when she was close enough to be heard.

Meg twisted toward her, a streak of flake white paint on her chin. Her smile slipped as soon as she saw Sylvie. "Oh no," she said. "What's happened?"

Covering her mouth with one hand, Sylvie waited until she could speak without falling to pieces. Then, while Meg's paint dried on the canvas and stiffened the bristles of her brushes, she told her sister everything.

Meg gripped both of Sylvie's hands. "Oh, my dear. What you must be going through. But I don't believe Beth's version of this tale. Remember what Dorothy said? That up until this morning, Jozefa had come to the Woman's Building daily. That means yesterday she was still in town. But when did she check out of the Palmer?"

"Last Friday." The pressure in her head mounting, Sylvie brought to mind everything she'd learned from Tom and Jenny. "Yes, I'm sure that's what they said."

Eyebrows lifted, Meg paused as though waiting for Sylvie to catch up. "So why would she have left the Palmer any sooner than the day she planned to leave town?"

"Perhaps she was running out of money and needed cheaper lodging. Maybe the ticket home was more expensive than she'd anticipated and this was a way to compensate."

Meg pumped her hands. "Or it could be that they checked out of the Palmer and intended to leave town but couldn't get a ticket that fast. The trains were full, possibly, with all the traffic for the Fair. And that's not all. Think of Rose. She sent you a note telling you not to worry. Would she truly leave the country without at least sending another to say good-bye?"

"We have no proof of any of this." Still, hope flickered in Sylvie.

Meg released Sylvie's hands. "It's only a hunch, but I think we have as much reason to think she's still in town as reason to think she isn't."

Sylvie hoped she was right. But even if Rose was still in Chicago, there was no way to guess for how long.

Chapter Twenty-Four

Friday, September 1, 1893

"For you." Kristof held out a box of Van Houten chocolates he'd picked up at the Fair before returning to his apartment building. "It's my turn to bring the treats, wouldn't you say?"

Anna Hoffman's laughter was a merry tune to his ears and a balm to his spirit after the day he'd had. Right in the doorway, she wrapped her soft arms around him in an embrace that smelled of warm yeast and sugar.

Standing back, she regarded him with a twinkle in her crinkling blue eyes. "Such a good boy, you are."

Suddenly he felt like a child who had delighted his mother with the smallest gesture, though he was a bachelor of forty-four. He didn't mind. Once he'd given his mother a bouquet of flowers carefully chosen for their bright yellow color. He'd thought it would please her, which was what he'd most wanted in the world. Instead, she'd told him that he'd picked common weeds and that his father would not like to see dirt beneath his fingernails when he played violin. Kristof had watched her cast the weeds out a rear window where they would be trampled in the alley below.

Absently, Kristof checked his fingernails. They were clean.

"Come in, come in!" Karl called from the kitchen. He folded a newspaper and set it beneath his chair. "Nate's here, too. You must partake with us whatever you've brought. It's only right."

"Oh, yes, you must!" Anna pulled him inside and shut the door behind him.

Nate rose and shook Kristof's hand before sitting again. "I see I picked the right time to drop by. We don't have to tell the other ladies about this, do we?" His lips slanted in a mischievous grin. "Meg is downstairs with Sylvie. I figured they needed some sister time. Our youngest is home with our oldest."

"Ja, this is good," Karl said, clapping Nate on the shoulder. "I'd say you figured right."

Adding his own agreement, Kristof set the box of chocolates on the table, opening the lid to reveal the smooth, shining treasures inside. "The man who sold them to me said they're filled with different things. Raspberry, caramel, hazelnut mousse, and a few are solid chocolate. There's a key written inside the lid so you know what you're getting before blindly taking a bite." He tugged his trousers up at the knees and sat across from Nate.

Anna set four small plates around the table before sitting. They were white, painted with pale blue flowers and grey-green vines twining around the edge. The one in front of Kristof had a small chip on the rim.

"What a shame," he murmured. The pattern looked old-fashioned and German. Not something they'd picked up at Marshall Field's. "I don't suppose you're able to replace this with a new one, are you?"

"Replace it?" Anna's tone implied she'd never considered it. "Oh, because of that tiny notch. No, dear, there's no need. It's not sharp enough to hurt anyone, and I've grown rather fond of that chip, to tell you the truth."

Intriguing. "Tell me more." The chocolate that melted on Kristof's tongue was creamy, the raspberry center cool and sharp.

While Karl helped himself to a chocolate, Anna leaned back in her chair. "These plates are some of the only things Karl and I saved from the Great Fire of 1871. They were my mother's back in Germany. That little chip on the rim is a reminder of what the plates have been through. They've crossed an ocean, carrying memories of generations past, and they've survived a fire, too. We bundled them together in such haste that night, packing them in a trunk with precious little else. Karl was able to load them onto a train that rolled out of town before the fire destroyed this neighborhood. That we have them back at all is such a blessing, I don't mind the flaw."

Nate turned solemn. "I'm sure the plates are

more precious to you now than they ever were. In terms of material possessions, I lost everything that night except the clothes on my back and a few mementos of my parents. But thank God I didn't lose what was most important: people."

"Meg," Kristoff prompted, thinking of her burned hands. It could have been so much worse.

"Yes, Meg, and Sylvie, and their father. My stepsiblings were never in harm's way, thank goodness." He took a chocolate and popped it in his mouth.

In 1871, Kristof had been twenty-two years old and trying to keep Gregor in check at school in Vienna so that both of them could graduate. "I can't fathom what you all have been through. I've never had to run for my life. I've never lost all my worldly goods. I can't begin to understand what it was like for Meg to learn to paint again." Instinctively, he flexed his hands beneath the table. If they were disfigured, what kind of music could he ever hope to play?

"She had to set a different standard for herself, that's for certain," said Nate. "She had to stop thinking in terms of perfect and imperfect and see things in a new way. There is room, in art, for all kinds of interpretation, as the French impressionists are proving. It's subjective. A matter of perspective."

Perspective. That was certainly something Kristof was trying to learn.

Anna dabbed a napkin to her mouth. "I hear you practicing so much, Kristof. But I rarely hear your brother."

"Rarely see him about either." Karl took another chocolate. "I begin to think he is a ghost!"

Kristof tried to smile. "You may see him even less, actually." He didn't want to think about Gregor just now, nor of the row they'd had at the rehearsal yesterday morning. But it had been more than just an argument. It was a Rubicon. There was no going back.

As Kristof had suspected, Gregor hadn't been able to pay his full share of the rent today, so Kristof had covered the rest. Gregor paid a small portion of it and promised to get the rest to him within a week. Kristof had agreed to the grace period against his better judgment. But after that, if Gregor failed to pay, he'd have to move out, and that was that.

"Trouble?" Nate folded his arms across the table. "I don't mean to pry, but if you need to talk, I hear I'm pretty good at listening."

"It may do you good to unburden yourself." Anna squeezed Kristof's hand. "We won't break your confidences."

Kristof ran a hand over his stubbled jaw. "I suddenly find myself unwilling to continue compensating for Gregor's mistakes." He brushed his fingertip along the chip in the china again. "It's time for him to change his ways. If he doesn't come up with the rest of his share of the rent by Friday, he'll no longer be sharing my apartment." He deflated, shoulders slumping as if he'd just confessed his own sin.

Nate removed his glasses and massaged the bridge of his nose. "That's tough. Really tough." He exhaled. "But it's the right decision. I had to come to a similar breaking point with my stepbrother, Andrew, many years ago. I used to think it was my fault, but I've come to realize we all own our choices. He's made his, over and over, not to reconcile with me. I regret it, but I don't lose sleep at night over it anymore. We are grown men, all of us. There comes a time when we have to say, 'I am not my brother's keeper.' "

"That's exactly what I've been, though," Kristof blurted before he could consider his words. "Since I was a child and my parents realized he had more musical talent than I did, my job was to keep him in line, protect him from his own bad choices so his music could flourish."

"Your parents said that to you?" Karl muttered an oath in German, perhaps forgetting that Kristof understood.

"Oh no," Anna said, "I'm sure they loved you dearly." Concern filled the cadence of her words.

"If they did, it was kept secret." Kristof's laugh came out hollow and bitter. But that was not who he wanted to be. "I never lacked food, shelter, or education. For that, I'll always be grateful. And Gregor and I had our moments. Good ones," he clarified. "Since our parents died, he's all the family I have left. That's why I've waited so long to hold him accountable, I suppose. Deep down, I knew that meant we'd have to part ways. And what do I have, if not family?"

Anna clasped Kristof's hand between both of hers. "Oh, my boy."

The endearment went straight to the dry place in Kristof's spirit, the desert that had never been watered with motherly affection before he'd met Anna Hoffman. He allowed himself to soak it in.

She patted his hand. "The psalmist wrote, 'God setteth the solitary in families.' And it's true. Having you and Sylvie, Meg, and Nate in our lives has made the two of us feel like we have family again. Imagine, at our old age! We left many kin in Germany when we came to America to build a better life for our children. Children that never came. I wonder if you understand that you've become like a son to us. Blood has nothing to do with it."

"No." Kristof swallowed the wedge in his throat. "No, I don't suppose it does." He lifted her hand and kissed it. Color infused her cheeks.

"Ja." Karl spread his arms, squeezing Kristof's shoulder and Nate's. "We have two good boys here, don't we, Anna? And they take good care of our girls, too. Don't you?"

The question was clearly directed at Kristof. "As far as she'll let me, yes. With all that I am."

Nate replaced his spectacles and leaned forward, hands folded on the table. "You have to understand something about Sylvie. She's a romantic deep down, but she fights it because she got her heart broken by the first man she loved."

"If you're unsure, son, do not toy with her." Karl's voice was gruff, but Kristof detected no anger in it. "She is precious beyond all measure."

"However"—Anna laid a hand on her husband's shoulder—"if you're earnest in your suit, be patient. Don't give up on her. You are precious, too. Both of you deserve to be cherished." Releasing Karl, she took Kristof's hand again. "But, dear, you must realize that you already are. By us, but more importantly, by your heavenly Father, who sings over you with rejoicing."

Kristof considered this picture of God so unlike his own father. It seemed impossible, and yet his spirit reached toward it like a willow bending to water.

Gathering himself again, he looked from one face to another, taking in all three surrounding him at the table. Rather than feeling as though he were being interrogated, he could almost believe he was part of a team. No, a family. That was what this was. He met each steady gaze, understanding that Nate stood in for Sylvie's brother, and Karl and Anna for her parents.

Kristof was no expert in romance, but he was learning a lot about love.

Ever since Meg and Sylvie had adopted Oliver Twist, the buff tabby cat they'd found in the rubble after the Great Fire, a cat's presence had always had a soothing effect on Sylvie. The silky fur between her fingers and soft vibration of purring had set her more at ease. Somehow, stroking a cat that enjoyed the attention seemed to promote contentment.

Not today.

"I don't understand." Meg sat on the parlor sofa beside Sylvie, a tray of tea service still untouched on the table. "He just magically showed up? Out of nowhere?"

Sylvie's hand rested on Tiny Tim, who was curled into a ball on her lap. Her pulse throbbed. "That's certainly what it seemed like. When I arrived home today, he just walked right up to greet me as if he'd never been gone at all. He was hungry, but other than that, he seems no worse for wear. Not like he'd been scraping by on the streets, fending for himself these last few weeks."

Meg frowned. "And the door was locked when you got here."

"It was. Whoever brought him back to me had a key, and Rose is the only other person who has one, besides you. When Lottie comes to work,

I let her into the apartments with my own keys, and she locks up on her way out. If I had come home earlier from the Fair, I could have been here. I could have seen Rose, talked to her. . . ." Her voice cracked with regret.

"Don't torture yourself over this." Meg sat up straighter, adjusting her skirts over her knees. "Rose could have given her key to someone else to use, too. Jozefa hired Jenny to impersonate her, so she would not have been above this. Or, what about Lottie? She has forgotten to lock the door before. She could have left it open, then remembered later and come back to fix her mistake. Someone could have brought Tiny Tim back while your door was unlocked. He's wearing a tag on his collar saying this address is his home."

Sylvie rubbed beneath the little cat's chin. "Lottie wasn't here when I arrived home after work. If I'd seen her, I'd have asked about the door. But I don't need to. It was Rose. Or someone acting on her instructions. The family picture from her baptism is gone, too." Sylvie still kept the image of Rose on her seventeenth birthday in her reticule or chatelaine bag.

Meg inhaled sharply. The clock ticked on the mantel while the tea cooled, untouched.

"She hasn't left Chicago yet," Sylvie guessed, "but this can only mean she's leaving soon. Perhaps she wanted something to remember us by, since we were all in that photograph with her. Tiny Tim would not have been able to make a transcontinental trip."

"But no note?" Meg asked.

"Nothing. I searched before you got here."

Quiet dropped in the room like a curtain and hung there limp for an unbearable stretch of time. Sylvie was at war with her own thoughts, first refusing to believe Rose would willingly leave like this, then forcing herself to recognize that her daughter was of age now and could decide these things for herself. She'd chosen Jozefa. She'd chosen Poland. She had chosen to leave Sylvie without saying good-bye.

But then, why on earth would she have wanted that picture? If Rose wanted a clean break from her life in America and hadn't even seen fit to pen a word of explanation, Sylvie was hard-pressed to imagine that she could harbor any sentiment for the photo.

Shadows stretched long outside, reaching for that which was just beyond their grasp. Tiny Tim yawned and walked away, leaping onto the windowsill and scaring a pair of pigeons off their roost.

At last Meg stretched her hands, then stood and carefully poured the tea. "Drink," she said as she handed Sylvie the cup and saucer, as if this were medicine that could heal. But it wasn't. It couldn't.

Sylvie stared at the amber liquid, now luke-warm in a cup that had never touched her mother's hands. Since no cups or saucers had survived the Great Fire, she'd purchased these at a discount from Marshall Field's. They meant nothing to her. She did not crave material possessions for their own sake. But just now, she longed to draw comfort from a teacup that had brought comfort to her mother, since she could not have her mother back to do the solacing herself.

Sylvie had so few connections to her past, and even fewer now that Rose had taken the photo and all her own things away. She could imagine herself like a character in the middle of a book, with the first half of the chapters wiped out, and the rest of the chapters yet unwritten. It was disorienting, being so untethered to either past or future.

This wouldn't do. She felt herself spiraling downward. She reached out and touched Meg's knee, the simple touch anchoring her to the present and to the only close family member she had. Meg had been part of her past, but Sylvie had no claim on her sister's future. That belonged to Nate and to their children.

"Remember what Mother used to say," Meg said. " 'I am not afraid of storms, for the One who made the sea is in my boat with me.' " She paused to take a drink. "That's the marvelous thing about God, isn't it? He is with me in my grief, He is with you in yours, and wherever Rose is, I am convinced He is with her, too."

"Yes." Sylvie's finger curled through the handle of her teacup, and she chided herself for not feeling more at ease with this truth. But feelings, especially hers, were not to be trusted.

From the second floor, a violin melody began. She knew this song. It was a waltz, slow and haunting, that Rose used to play, only it had never sounded quite this polished. Sylvie cocked her head, listening.

That wasn't just Rose's piece. That was her violin.

For one irrational moment, Sylvie's mind leapt over the fact that Kristof had purchased it at a pawnshop, and conjured an image of Rose upstairs, having a lesson with her instructor as if nothing uncommon had ever happened.

Then she blinked, and found Meg looking up at her, eyes wide. Sylvie hadn't recalled standing, but there she was, her teacup rolling to a stop against the rug's edge, its contents puddling on the floor.

Meg set her cup on the tray, dropped a couple of napkins atop the spilled tea, and touched Sylvie's elbow. "What is it?"

"That song," she said. "Why must he play that song with Rose's instrument? He has his own! What is he doing?"

She fled her apartment and bounded up the

372

stairs. The music grew louder, then halted just before she banged on Kristof's door.

It took him too long to open it. When he appeared, Sylvie could barely maintain her composure.

"Please," she said, "for pity's sake, must you play that song? And you were using Rose's violin, too, weren't you? I'd so much rather you didn't."

His hair looked rumpled, as if he'd just run his hands through it. "Sylvie. You'd better come in. You too, Meg. Please."

Sylvie hadn't even noticed her sister had followed. They both stepped inside, and Kristof shut the door.

"Nate's still upstairs." Kristof rubbed the back of his neck. Rose's violin lay beside its case on the kitchen table.

"And your brother?" Meg asked.

"Out." He waved a hand dismissively. "I was thinking about how odd it was to find Rose's violin. I opened the case to look at it again, and I couldn't help but play it. I'm sorry if hearing it upset you, Sylvie. But I just noticed something." He ran his finger along the velvet lining, pausing where it sagged away from the inside of the case. "This is loose." He slid two fingers inside.

Sylvie's mouth felt lined with flannel. She sat, and Meg did the same.

"You didn't notice it until tonight?" Meg asked.

Kristof's lips pressed into a thin line as he reached deeper between the case and the fabric. "No. This is the first time I've taken the violin out since bringing it home from the pawnshop."

At last he pulled something free—a folded piece of paper. He handed it to Sylvie, whose breath caught and flipped like something hooked.

Her fingers trembled as she accepted it, hope warring against caution. It was a letter, dated August 25.

" 'Dear Mimi,' " she read aloud, and her voice collapsed. Squeezing back a rush of tears, she tried again, Meg's hand on her back in solidarity. " 'Dear Mimi, I guess I don't blame you for being mad at me, but I didn't think your anger would last this long. I wanted to at least let you know we've moved in case you decide to write or visit. Now we're—' "

There it ended.

Bewildered, Sylvie turned the paper over and back again, finding no other words. "That's all," she rasped. Suddenly feeling the paper was too heavy to hold, she lowered it to the table. What could the unfinished note mean? What had Rose tried to say, and what on earth had she meant about Sylvie being mad at her?

What, what, what?

"She was interrupted," Meg said. "She was trying to send word of her new address and something—someone—stopped her before she could finish."

"I'm not mad at her," Sylvie gasped. "She says 'in case' I decide to write or visit—as though I could have all this time and chose not to! She doesn't know how we've been searching." The idea lanced her.

"But she was trying to reach you. She'll try again," Meg crooned.

"There's some kind of watermark on it from the stationery company." Kristof slanted the paper toward the light, then pointed to the image, his eyes alight. "That's no stationer's brand. That's the logo of the Auditorium Hotel."

"She's there." Sylvie's heartbeat slammed. "That's where she is. Don't you think?"

Kristof ran a hand over his jaw. "She was, when she wrote that note. It's the best lead we have, even though we have no idea which room she was in or if she's still there."

Meg turned to Sylvie. "Remind me when Jozefa checked out of the Palmer."

"Friday, August 25. The same day Rose wrote this note. And when did you go to the pawn shop?" she asked Kristof.

"The next day," he answered. "The proprietor said it had been dropped off that morning."

"So we know that before the violin came to the pawnshop, it was with Rose, and she parted with it after they checked out of the Palmer," Meg said. "They needed a place to go Friday night. It's not difficult to believe that place was the Auditorium."

"I don't know how Jozefa got a room without a reservation booked months in advance, but there's no arguing with that paper." Kristof held it up again.

Sylvie stood, every nerve awake. "There's one way to find out. It's time to bring Rose home."

CHAPTER TWENTY-FIVE

While Meg and Nate returned home to their children, Kristof escorted Sylvie straight to the police station for help locating Jozefa inside the Auditorium Hotel. It was the only logical move, and Sylvie still needed to be convinced of it. Her plan had been no plan at all. Just go to the Auditorium and start knocking on doors? If Jozefa caught wind of such a thing, she and Rose would pack up and disappear, possibly forever.

No, Kristof insisted on doing things according to the rules. The law was on the side of the innocent, after all.

At least, it ought to be.

Officer Thornhill wasn't cooperating the way Kristof had hoped he would. Sylvie seemed to be barely keeping a lid on her emotions. Not that he could blame her.

"An unfinished note with no address. It isn't even signed." Officer Thornhill pinched it between two fingers. "This is your justification for searching every room at the Auditorium? Do you have any idea how many rooms they have?"

"Of course we do," Kristof said. "Which is why we have no intention of doing such a thing ourselves. But you could demand the front desk staff tell you exactly which room Jozefa Zielinski is staying in, and go search the room yourself."

The paper fluttered to the top of the officer's cluttered desk. Sylvie snatched it up and tucked it into her reticule. The amused bounce of Thornhill's wiry grey eyebrows seemed to ignite her ire even more.

"Ever heard of a search warrant?" Thornhill scratched behind his ear, then took a swig of coffee that smelled as if it had been scraped from the bottom of the pot. "I can't get one based on a scrap of paper in a pawned violin case."

Sylvie threw up her hands. "Then what do you need from us?"

"The Fourth Amendment says I need probable cause. And, ma'am, this sure ain't it."

"Coming here was a mistake," Sylvie muttered and walked away.

Kristof set his jaw, folded his arms. "Send a patrol, then. At least ask the hotel staff if they've heard sounds of anyone being kept against their will. Any banging on doors or walls, shouting, screaming, that sort of thing. Will you do that much, at least?"

From the corner of his eye, he noticed Sylvie bend over. Sergeant Whiskers, the resident brown tabby, had ambled over to greet her, and she scooped him up in her arms, swaying slightly as she held him. She was made to love, even now, when she was livid and afraid. Perhaps especially now.

Thornhill rose, crossing his arms over his rounded middle. "Do you have any idea how thinly stretched our resources are? Crime is up, and I'm not just talking about pickpockets at the Fair. And here you two keep coming back, asking me to send my men on a wild goose chase."

"We've done no such thing." What did wild geese have to do with it?

"There are thieves to catch, actual murders to investigate—with real bodies, mind you—and immigrant communist rioters to lock up before we have another Haymarket on our hands. So, yeah, I'll send an officer to the Auditorium and have him ask the staff if there is anything fishy."

Kristof had hoped for more than that. He started to say so, but Thornhill cut him off with an outstretched palm.

"And you know what else I'm going to do?" His jowls wobbled as he spoke.

A gust of foul-smelling air swirled into the station as more homeless men came seeking a place to sleep for the night. Thornhill waved them through to the men's wing, where the warden admitted them through the iron gate, then clanged it shut again.

"I'll have the staff notified about the two of you and your interest in searching their guest rooms. If they see you on the property, they'll have permission to detain you until an officer can come make an official arrest for trespassing."

Kristof hardly believed anyone would recognize them based on physical description alone, but he wasn't about to point that out. "I work there, Officer Thornhill. In the theatre side with the Chicago Symphony Orchestra. Surely you've no intention of arresting a man for rehearsing Mozart."

Before the officer could respond, Sylvie came marching back, and Sergeant Whiskers darted toward the men who'd just arrived. "Your policemen should be searching for Jozefa Zielinksi and Rozalia Dabrowski. Not the two of us." She slipped her hand into the crook of Kristof's elbow, closing ranks with him, warming a cold spot inside him. "They're in there right now but could leave at any time."

Tapping the badge on his uniform, the officer sneered. "I don't take orders from you or any citizen, least of all a woman. Now, as your business here is done, it's time you both take your leave."

Kristof made no move to go. "First tell me when you'll send an officer to the hotel."

Thornhill expelled a long-suffering sigh. "By half past eleven. Let me get my night shift officers up to speed, and I'll send someone over."

"See that you do," Kristof said. "I'll be watching from across the street, waiting. If I don't see any police patrols enter the building by then, I'm coming right back here to haunt you. Good night. At least, for now."

Sylvie squeezed his arm as they left the station. "Were you serious about waiting outside the Auditorium to be sure he keeps his word?"

"I'm not a man given to empty threats."

The crease between her brows began to ease. "I didn't think so. I'm coming with you."

He looked down at her and smiled. "I expected nothing less."

Sylvie paced the sidewalk on Michigan Avenue across from the Auditorium Hotel, unable to contain the energy coursing through her. Kristof leaned against the lamppost at the streetcar stop, watching the hotel doors, the street, and the sidewalks. It was ten o'clock, or something like it, and the broad avenue separating her from Rose rumbled with traffic, most of it from theatergoers on their way to late dinners or cocktails.

The night was warm but cooling quickly, and Sylvie could not blame her fine sheen of perspiration on the humidity. She searched for a policeman who might have come early, or for Jozefa, or even Rose herself. Guests coming from the Auditorium Theatre filled the spacious balcony above the hotel's main entrance. They were silhouetted against glowing windows, but Sylvie could still see their sparkling opera attire and glinting champagne flutes as they laughed and talked. She doubted Rose would be among them. Not if Jozefa was keeping her locked up. It would be too easy for her to shout for help or whisper in someone's ear.

Frustration boiled inside Sylvie. She marched back toward Kristof. "See anything?"

"Nothing yet."

"This is madness," she replied. "Thornhill said no police officer could be spared until after the eleven o'clock shift begins. That's another hour at least to wait. Meanwhile, Rose is inside, wondering if anyone got her message, if anyone can rescue her. I could go in right now. She thinks I'm staying away on purpose." She still couldn't stomach the thought.

"Sylvie." Disapproval laced his tone. "Even if we set aside the fact that we said we wouldn't do that, what would you do once inside?"

"I—I would do what I did at the Palmer. Act like any other guest. There's no way the staff can remember all their faces and names. I would find a maid to talk to, at any rate."

"A maid. One maid."

"It worked at the Palmer."

"Because you knew which room you wanted. Here, you'd be walking in blind. Even worse than not finding Jozefa at all would be coming close enough for her to hear or see you, giving her reason to whisk Rose away without a trace. Is it worth that risk to you?"

She watched the hotel windows, hoping and praying one of them would open and Rose's blue shawl would be hung out of it. "I know how you feel about risk, Kristof. But sometimes one must take a chance."

"These stakes are too high. And the odds are not in your favor."

"I—" But she had no rebuttal. He was right, and she hated that he was right. "She's right there." She pointed across the street. "She's just a girl, and she must feel so alone. I have to *do* something, Kristof. Anything would be better than this agonizing wait and see. If we don't help her, who will?"

Kristof brushed off the bench beside the lamppost, then sat and patted the space next to him. "Come here."

She did. Wind teased a strand of hair from beneath her hat, and it swayed beside her cheek.

He covered her hands and lowered them to his knee, where he broke their clasp and laced his fingers through hers. The faint smells of chocolate and coffee and balsam cologne wafted between them. "Sometimes we do all we can, and still it is not enough."

She blinked in surprise. "And here I thought you might attempt to console me."

His mouth tilted. "I still might." The lamplight above him called out every line framing his eyes, his brow, and his mouth. Some men wore masks of charm and flattery, but Kristof's face, Sylvie could tell, was a map of his own sincerity, every ridge and groove born from care. "Just because you can't control everything doesn't mean it isn't being handled. Trust the One who is far better at orchestrating every detail than we could ever be."

A spark of irritation fanned to flame. "Are you saying I don't have enough faith? Or that I should just pray and hope for the best?"

"What I'm saying is that we are, all of us, far less independent than you may want to admit. Life is not a solo performance." His strong, lean hands tightened on hers, as if anticipating his words would make her want to take flight.

She broke from his gaze instead, scanning the Auditorium Hotel again. "I didn't come here so you could scold me like a child."

"You are accustomed to solving your own problems. You're an excellent manager of your time, money, and the people you love."

She snapped her attention back to him. "I don't *manage* the people I love."

He hesitated. "You prompted Meg to paint at the Fair to take her mind off her grief. You gave Lottie a job to keep her out of the Levee. You bailed Beth out of jail, and Rose—well, until a month ago, you held a pretty tight rein on her."

"And look what happened when I let go!" Sylvie cried. "You see? What you call managing, I call caring."

384

"From here, it looks like fear." His voice held no judgment or condemnation. Only compassion, which might have been worse.

Sylvie yanked her hands from his and covered her face. If she could trust her legs to hold her, she would walk away. Away from Kristof, away from the truth. But she could not leave fear behind her.

His hand settled on her back. "Forgive me. I'm bungling this. All I mean to say is that sometimes we can fool ourselves into believing we don't need God's help. But we do. We always do, but in a crisis it's more obvious. God can solve this puzzle, Sylvie."

"I know He can. But will He? And when? Being locked away affects a person. My father was changed unalterably by it. I know Rose isn't in a Civil War prison camp or an asylum, but she's trapped and can't see the way out. It's a trauma layered on top of the trauma of losing her parents, of wanting to connect with her biological family and not being able to find them. By the time God orchestrates her rescue, as you put it, what invisible wounds will she have suffered?" She shook her head. "I don't doubt God's ability. But sometimes I struggle to trust His timing."

As she leaned back against the bench, Kristof slipped his arm around her shoulders. His warmth radiated into her as they sat side by side, her skirt brushing his trousers.

"Waiting is such hard work," he said. "But remember, just because we are still doesn't mean that God is. We can rely on Him."

Be still, and know that I am God. The verse scrolled through Sylvie's mind.

Kristof's fingers cupped her shoulder, pressing her more firmly into his side. Quiet surrounded them, punctuated by the occasional passing carriage. Dew thickened in the night air, chilling her skin, and she rubbed her arms. Her eyelids and limbs grew weighted with fatigue of body, mind, and spirit.

"Rest your eyes," Kristof urged. "I'll keep watch." Before she realized he'd taken off his jacket, he draped it around her, enveloping her with his warmth, his scent.

What a strange and welcome sensation, to be cared for.

Drowsiness filled every inch of her. A sigh brushing past her lips, she took off her hat so she could rest her head on his shoulder. "Do you mind?" she murmured. "My leaning on you, I mean."

"That's what I'm here for." He kissed her temple, his arm gathering her close.

The last thing she remembered was the rumble of his voice as he prayed, beseeching the Almighty for help.

CHAPTER TWENTY-SIX

Saturday, September 2, 1893

Whiskers tickled Sylvie's nose and cheek, stirring her to wakefulness. Tiny Tim pushed his head beneath her hand, meowing insistently.

"All right." Wincing at her corset's pinch, she pushed herself up on the bed and oriented herself, trying to remember why she'd slept in her clothes last night. Her hairpins were placed neatly on the table, between the photograph of her father and her mother's copy of *Little Women*. She expected to see her boots splayed on the rug by the bed, but instead they stood upright against the wall beside her bureau. She was still wearing Kristof's jacket.

Ah. No wonder she'd dreamed she was in his arms. She'd fallen asleep nestled into his side. The police had come later, as promised, had checked inside and outside the hotel, and reported nothing unusual, which was discouraging but not surprising. She'd fallen asleep again during the cab ride home. Kristof had roused her enough for her to climb the stairs, unlock the apartment door, and make it to her room before collapsing into bed.

She considered the pins on the table, the

boots against the wall. Even her hat was on the bureau. He'd been here, in her bedroom. He'd pulled the shoes from her feet, and the pins from her hair. A flush of heat climbed up her throat at the thought of such intimate acts, his fingers searching through her hair, pulling out each pin so it wouldn't bother her while she slept. And performing the task so gently that she couldn't recall it now.

She almost wished she could.

"Balderdash." She banished the sentiment, removed his jacket, and fed the cat, who was now noisily protesting her delay.

She'd slept too long and too deeply. And felt more rested than she had in quite some time, despite sore ribs from sleeping in her corset. She needed to be in the bookstore in half an hour.

Twenty minutes sufficed for her to wash, dress, and repair her hair before breaking her fast on a thick slice of bread slathered with butter and strawberry preserves. Sun poured through the parlor window, bringing with it the sounds of a city in motion. A train whistled in the distance, sending alarm through Sylvie.

Was Rose on that train? Would she board another before Sylvie could reach her? Was she already too late? Any peace she'd felt during those fleeting hours of slumber vanished, leaving nothing but questions in its place.

Unable to finish her bread, she pushed it away.

Be still, and know that I am God, she repeated to herself. She persuaded her pulse to slow, and begged God to show Himself trustworthy. Perhaps it was not a proper prayer, for the Bible already said He was. But right now, it was all she could manage.

Tiny Tim batted at something on the floor near the front door. Sylvie left the kitchen table and bent to retrieve it. It was an envelope, and the handwriting on the outside was Kristof's.

She withdrew a note.

> *Dear Sylvie,*
>
> *I pray your dreams were sweet.*
>
> *I have two concerts today but will return home as soon as I can. Please don't do anything rash without me, or I'll cry chicken. Once I return, we can talk about doing something rash together. Or even better, something reasonable.*
>
> *Wait for me.*
>
> *Yours,*
> *Kristof*

Her lips curved at Kristof's attempt to make her smile by mangling the idiom she was certain he now understood.

A knock on the door jolted through her. Gritting her teeth, she set the note on the table and smoothed her hair. She hated how easily she startled lately. The only other times her nerves had been this fragile were after the Great Fire, then after Louise and Father died in the same season. Loss, she supposed, stripped her ability to cope. How maddening it was that at the times she needed her wits the most, they scattered.

The knock again, louder this time. "Miss Townsend?" Lottie called.

She opened the door, surprised to see both Lottie and Ivan, the ten-year age difference between them sharply pronounced.

"Come in," she said. "I wasn't expecting to see you today, but I'm glad you're here."

"Well, so is Ivan." Lottie glanced up at her brother. Her black hair was braided into a crown that encircled her head, her face scrubbed to a healthy pink shine. She wore Rose's blue-and-white gingham dress again, this time hemmed properly. "We're here to collect my wages. You weren't here yesterday when I was finished."

"Of course." Sylvie should have remembered this. "It's good to see you too, Ivan. You get the weekends off from your new job, I take it?"

"I don't work today."

"Is it going well? Your employment?" she prodded.

Ivan hooked his thumbs behind his suspenders. His brown hair curled over the tops of his ears and his collar. "If you wouldn't mind, Miss Townsend, the wages? I know you've got to get downstairs and open the bookshop. We won't keep you."

Sylvie glanced at the clock, annoyed that he was right. Time was slipping away from her. "Lottie, did you happen to leave my apartment door unlocked yesterday for any length of time?"

The girl paled. "No, ma'am. Did someone steal your money, too? Am I not getting paid today?" She looked up at Ivan. "I swear I kept everything locked up, even while I was inside, just like you told me to."

"I haven't been robbed," Sylvie assured her. "It's just that Tiny Tim has come home. The cat. He was here, inside the locked apartment, when I arrived home yesterday, and I wondered if you knew anything about that. Was he here when you were cleaning?"

"You have a cat now?" She spied the little black-and-white furball in the corner of the parlor. "Oh, there he is! No, he wasn't here when I was yesterday. Is he friendly? Can I pet him?"

"Of course you may. What time did you leave?"

"I finished here around noon and finished at the Hoffmans' around three o'clock," Lottie tossed over her shoulder. She approached Tiny Tim slowly, then crouched and scratched between his ears.

"I'll be right back with your wages, Lottie." She nodded to Ivan, who remained by the door.

As Sylvie returned with the money, Lottie

pinched a small object out from under one of Tiny Tim's paws and stood.

"He shouldn't play with this," she said. "He could swallow it if he isn't careful." She frowned as she examined it.

"I'll take it." Sylvie held out her hand.

Wordlessly, Lottie dropped a button into Sylvie's palm, jutting her chin at Ivan.

He was staring at the birdcage on the stand. Something about it seemed to trouble him.

"Ivan?" Sylvie tried. "You disapprove of the bird?"

"At least it's in a cage where it belongs, right, Ivan?" A trace of sarcasm threaded Lottie's tone.

"Enough." He strode over to them both, his worn-out boots imprinting the rug. "We should be going. Matka is grateful, thank you. So is the doctor who needs to be paid." He reached for Lottie's money.

Sylvie bristled at his grab for wages his sister had earned, even though she understood the money was for the family's welfare. If Lottie didn't complain about it, Sylvie wouldn't make things worse by doing so either.

Then she saw that his sleeve cuff was pinned together in the absence of a button. The one closed in her fist matched the one on his other sleeve.

A chill washed over her. She stepped back.

"Miss Townsend. It's getting late." Ivan

reached farther, almost lunging for the money. In doing so, his sleeve inched up on his wrist, revealing bright red scratches. Cat scratches.

"Oh, Ivan," she whispered. "What have you done?"

His jaw hardened. But surely he could see that she wouldn't be fooled any longer. It was Ivan who had brought Tiny Tim back. Ivan knew where Rose was.

"Are you helping her?" Sylvie asked. "Or are you hiding her?"

Lottie's lips parted. "Rose. You know where she is."

The air thinned, and time stretched as she awaited his response. Answers were so close she could almost taste them. She clenched her cold fingers at her side, crumpling Lottie's money.

"I did what I had to do," Ivan said at last, "for my family."

"But is she safe?" Sylvie pressed, the need to know billowing hot inside her. She passed Lottie's earnings to her and clutched Ivan's rough, calloused hands. She searched his face for the person he'd been before his father died and he'd been forced to grow up overnight.

"Ivan." She called to the tenderness buried inside him still. "I have known you since you were small. You have always been responsible, loyal to your family. And you have always been kind to Rose."

Hadn't he? Doubt wound around Sylvie and squeezed. These hands that had grown broad and strong at the stockyards could break her bones. She had no idea who he was or why. She had misjudged men before.

Sweat pricked her skin. "Tell me the truth. Help me understand what's happening."

"You think I understand what's happening?" he growled.

"I think you understand far more than you're letting on, and infinitely more than I do. Please. At least tell me if she's safe. Is she still in Chicago?" Desperation serrated her voice.

The movement was so slight, it was almost imperceptible. But it was a nod. His stiffness faltered, and the ice in his eyes began to melt.

"Thank God." Sylvie squeezed his hands. "Where?"

At once, his face shuttered. "It's time to go." He broke free of her and turned to Lottie, reaching for her money.

"No!" Lottie shouted. "Not until you tell her the truth!"

He pried the money from his sister's fist. She clung to his arm, trying to make him stay.

Sylvie planted herself between Ivan and the doorway to block his retreat. "Rose tried to tell me where she was. She tried writing me a note but couldn't finish it. Help me find her!"

He wasn't listening. With his back to her, he

was struggling with Lottie. His elbow thrust backward, splitting Sylvie's lip.

"I said it's time to go!" Ivan shoved Sylvie out of his path, sending her sprawling. The single thought racing through her mind was Rose. Had he done this to her? Had he done worse?

He may have. And he could do it again.

Lottie was shouting, grasping his arm again, pulling him backward.

"Let me go, Lottie." Ivan brimmed with warning.

Jaw throbbing, Sylvie pushed herself up. She had to stop him, stop this. Ivan could easily injure Lottie in his urgency to leave. There was no way she could prevent it, and yet she had to. Kristof was gone. The Hoffmans wouldn't even hear them from the fourth floor, and no one was in the bookstore below.

"Ivan, don't hurt her!" Sylvie's protest fell to the floor, powerless.

Then footsteps sounded, and a man strode through the door and straight to Ivan, who still had both hands on Lottie. The man slammed his fist into Ivan's nose with a sickening crunch, then twisted the young man's arms behind him and held him fast.

Sylvie gasped, and the good Samaritan turned, his eyebrows spiking, then plunging before he tightened his grip on Ivan's arms. "You've assaulted my maid and my landlady. And you've woken me up on a Saturday morning when I could have been sleeping!" Unshaven, rumpled, and smelling like stale perfume and last night's whiskey, Gregor winked at Sylvie. Lipstick smudged his ear, and his complexion was almost as ruddy.

She was stunned. Tasting blood from her lip, she hurried to Lottie. "Are you all right?" she asked.

Lottie sniffed, swiping the back of her hand beneath her nose. "He tore my dress. My best dress."

"We'll mend it," Sylvie promised. "We can mend it together right here if you like."

"Excuse me, ladies," Gregor said above Ivan's groaning. "Anyone care to tell me what I've walked into here? Quietly, though. You wouldn't believe the size of the elephant sitting on my head just now."

Lottie scowled. "My brother—"

"Hold on," Gregor said. "This is your brother? Don't tell me I got up for a sibling squabble."

"No." Sylvie held out a hand to stop Gregor from releasing his captive. "Ivan knows where Rose is. He won't tell me."

All levity fled Gregor's expression. "Is that right? Need a little convincing, is that it, Ivan?" His eyes were almost all pale blue, his pupils alarmingly small.

"Please." Sylvie took her handkerchief from

her pocket and wiped the blood from Ivan's face. His nose was already swollen and purpling.

He winced. "It's broken!"

She feared it was. "Please," she said again.

"Hear that, Ivan?" Gregor asked. "That was your conscience speaking. Let's have a seat, and you tell us what you know."

Sylvie dabbed at Ivan's neck, catching the blood before it stained his collar. "Wouldn't Rose want you to?"

He and Gregor sat. Lottie took the armchair, and Sylvie stayed on her feet, glancing at the clock, then back to Gregor, wondering why he wasn't at Music Hall right now.

"Ah," Gregor said. "Lucky for you, Miss Townsend, my brother fired me Thursday and threatened to evict me yesterday. So, Lottie, you're not the only one in disagreement with your brother, eh?"

Kristof hadn't said anything about this to her. "You're not serious," Sylvie said.

"Not usually, no." Gregor chuckled. "This time, I'm afraid I am."

This didn't feel right. None of it. She set aside her disappointment that Kristof hadn't shared this news with her himself. Set aside her regret at not giving him the chance, spending all their conversation on her own concerns, instead. What she was left with in this moment was a pair of men who both happened to be desperate in their own ways. And desperate men made reckless decisions.

So did desperate women.

Memories of last night surfaced, and she saw herself then as Kristof must have. He'd been right to hold her back, talk her down, before she had done anything she might regret. What would he do in this situation? She was sure he would use words, not fists, not force.

But Ivan was subdued now. She sat on the other side of him, holding the handkerchief to his nose once more.

"I didn't mean to hurt you, Miss Townsend," he said gruffly. "Or you, Lottie."

Lottie's mouth was a stitch on her face as she pinched the tear in her sleeve together. Tiny Tim leapt onto her lap and batted at a lock of hair that had fallen out of her braid. Releasing her sleeve, she stroked his back.

"I'm out of my head, sometimes," Ivan said. "We need that money, is all. And I needed us to leave. I'm not supposed to say . . ."

"Ooh, that's a bad sign, Ivan." Gregor clucked his tongue. "Secrets are dangerous. Especially the kind you're keeping. Am I right?"

From the street below, someone knocked on the locked door to the bookshop and called out. Sylvie ignored her customer, studying Ivan instead. He shifted on the sofa, gaze riveted on the birdcage.

"What is it?" she prompted.

Lottie curled her legs beneath her, nestling deeper in the armchair. "You're thinking of the bird you caught when I was too little to remember, aren't you? Matka told me the story."

Ivan skewered her with a glare.

"Go on, tell them about it. If you don't, I will." Lottie continued petting Tiny Tim, who rested contentedly in her lap, purring. "Ivan found a sparrow that had gotten into our tenement building. He was thirteen. He and his friends had nothing better to do than torture the poor thing, so they—"

"That's not at all what happened," Ivan blurted. "You trapped it."

"I was trying to help."

"Well, that didn't work out, did it?"

Ivan's face darkened to a deep red. "Nothing better to do, you say. When I was thirteen, I had just become the man of the house and was working to support you and Matka. When I found that bird, yes, I put it in a box. The other boys wanted to pluck out its feathers or feed it terrible things, but I wouldn't let them. I kept it *safe* in that box, not letting anyone else get near it."

"It would have been safer if you had just let it go." Lottie looked at Sylvie. "It couldn't breathe, and it died."

"That's not true either." But the slant of Ivan's shoulders hinted at guilt. "I'm not stupid, and I'm not cruel. I cut holes in the box and put grass and leaves in it, and worms for it to eat. But when I finally decided to let it go, it wouldn't leave. It just stayed in a corner of that box even though the lid was off."

"And it died," Lottie said. "That's the end of the story, no matter what the middle is. Birds were never meant to be shut away."

The parlor warmed. A breeze reached through the room, and a dried petal from the bouquet on the mantel twirled off and landed near Ivan's feet.

Sylvie picked it up, fingering its brittle edge. "Neither were roses." She waited until he finally met her gaze. "You can set her free, Ivan. Can't you?"

Silence swelled thick and dense, until Gregor spoke into it. "The police are already investigating. I could tell them to investigate you, and you know how they feel about immigrant troublemakers. How would it help your family if you're arrested?"

Placing the rose petal on Ivan's knee, Sylvie wiped his neck one more time with her handkerchief. "It's not too late for you to do the right thing on your own."

Ivan huffed a dark laugh. "Right for her or for me?"

"For both of you," Sylvie said, heart in her throat. "Rewrite the ending of this story. The captor can become the savior."

Chapter Twenty-Seven

Sylvie let Ivan go.

Someone else might call it naïveté, a reckless hope, or an abiding belief in mankind. But she had seen the dark corners of the human heart, including her own, and couldn't explain her action in any of those ways. The only way she could account for it was faith. The opposite of fear, just as Kristof had said. Faith not in man, but in God.

If faith was blind, it was only in the sense that she could not see the ways God would choose to work in the future. But she'd seen Him work in the past. How else could she reconcile every small step that had led to what transpired in her parlor this morning? She didn't believe in luck, nor did she hold with coincidence. There were too many of them to call it anything other than Providence orchestrating the details.

The bookstore was all but empty now. Tessa had the day off. A pair of sisters pulled apart one of Anna's soft pretzels in the bistro area, each of them reading their newly acquired novels. Another customer, Mrs. Murphy, deliberated in the poetry section, purple ostrich feather quivering from her hatband as she scanned the spines. Sylvie returned to the counter to unpack the most recent box of inventory, reconciling each title against the packing list.

That finished, she set the empty box on the floor, and Tiny Tim promptly jumped into it. She fingered the gilt-edged pages of *A Tale of Two Cities* and thought of the character Lucie Manette Darnay. Lucie was the only one able to pull her father back to reality after his years in a French prison wounded his mind. For this alone Sylvie could relate to her, having done the same for her own father. Now, as she considered the months Lucie spent waiting and worrying while her husband was locked away, and otherwise doing nothing, Sylvie had new insights to add to such an experience.

Kristof had been right last night. *"Just because we are still doesn't mean that God is. We can rely on Him."* Letting Ivan go was her acknowledgment of this truth. When Rose left, it wasn't the first time Sylvie's world had spun out of control. It only reminded her that she was never in charge of it to begin with. It was a lesson she'd learned when the Great Fire took nearly everything from her in one night. A lesson too easily forgotten, she supposed, when she and Chicago rebuilt.

Mrs. Murphy beckoned.

Sylvie met her at the counter. "Did you find what you were looking for?"

"Even more." She slid two volumes toward Sylvie, one of Elizabeth Barrett Browning's poems and another of Walt Whitman's. "The trouble is deciding which to leave behind for next time."

"Did you see the special we're running right now? Get a free souvenir ticket to the World's Fair for Chicago Day with a purchase of three dollars or more. The celebration will be October 9, in honor of the anniversary of the Great Fire. You wouldn't believe how many special events are planned."

"Well!" Mrs. Murphy chuckled. "In that case, I'll take them both!"

It was a genius sales strategy, even if it wasn't Sylvie's idea. Clothing stores, wine shops, and millineries were all doing the same thing. And it was working.

Sylvie placed Mrs. Murphy's books in a paper bag stamped with the store's name, then handed her the ticket for the Fair.

After the older woman left, the sisters in the bistro followed. Sylvie busied herself shelving the rest of the inventory.

When the bell chimed over the door, she emerged from the fiction section to greet a late afternoon customer.

But it was Kristof in his concert attire. Doffing his hat, he looked dashing, and concerned, and unspeakably dear. "I came home as soon as I could. Any news?"

"More than you can imagine." But she could

wait to tell him all that had happened since Lottie and Ivan's visit. "I understand you have news of your own. You fired Gregor?" She walked toward him.

His eyebrows lifted. "Ah. You spoke to him. It was overdue. He's on probation this week to see if I'll let him stay in the apartment with me, too. But we can talk about all this later, Sylvie. What you have to share is more important and pressing."

When she reached him, his gaze swept over her, catching on her swollen lip. Instantly, his face darkened. His fingers went to the bruised edge of her jaw, which she'd meant to conceal with powder. "What happened?"

She told him everything, gauging his reactions in every shifting line of his face.

"You cannot know how much I've wanted to keep you safe from harm," he said when she was finished, "and here it came to you in your own apartment."

"Not very much harm," she reminded him, slipping away to lock the shop door and turn the sign to announce it was closed. "Gregor came almost right away."

"I'll thank him later," Kristof murmured.

Sylvie pushed the switch near the door, extinguishing the lights throughout the shop. Then she stepped to the front window and stood on her toes to reach up and pull the shade.

Kristof came alongside her and brought it down with ease, surrounding them in deeper shadows. And privacy. "If anything had happened to you—anything worse than what already did—I don't know what I would have done. I—"

"Shh, it's all right. I'm all right," she told him. "If God can take care of Rose without my help, He can take care of me without your presence, too." She winced. "That didn't come out the way I hoped."

He laughed quietly. "No, it's true. It serves me and my pride right that God should choose my brother to come to your aid instead of me."

"As to that." She slid her hand into his. "I'd choose you by my side any day."

A slow smile spread over his face. "Sylvie. You are so dear to me."

The way his voice cradled her name would have been enough to melt her last defenses. But the tender confession that followed unlocked an awareness in her that she was fast losing her ability to resist him. The reasons she ought to were fading.

"It's been a long day," she whispered. "Would you like to come up for tea?"

Sylvie turned the key in the lock and entered her apartment, Kristof following, and gasped. "Ivan!" Had she failed to lock the door this morning?

He stood in the parlor, shoulders squared, arms

crossed. Dark purple crescents on either side of his nose marked their earlier encounter. Lottie didn't appear to be with him.

Kristof moved as though to place himself in front of Sylvie.

"Wait, Kristof." She had no idea what Ivan planned to do or say, but there was something in his expression that gave her pause. "You cannot keep coming into my apartment like this," she told the young man. "You could have found me in the store and we could have talked, either there or here. But coming in as you have without me, this is trespassing."

"Mimi."

Ivan stepped aside, and there was Rose on the sofa, unfolding her legs from where she had curled against the armrest.

Sylvie's knees buckled, and Kristof's arm came around her waist. "Rose?"

"Thank God," Kristof said.

Clutching her mother's shawl around her, Rose stood in an aura of uncertainty. Years peeled away, and Sylvie saw Rozalia the child, shaken after her father's death. *"Will you keep me for always now?"* she had asked then, wrapped in the same blue shawl.

"You're home." Sylvie flew to her, gathering her close. "I love you." Those five small words had to carry everything else she couldn't say while questions caught in her throat like bones.

Rose returned the fierce embrace. "I thought you didn't want to see me."

"I've been searching for you since the day we parted. Why on earth would you think I wouldn't?" Releasing her, Sylvie stepped back.

Confusion wrinkled Rose's brow. "I wrote to you. Many times. You never replied."

"I only received one note, the one in which you said not to look for you. Which I didn't obey, by the way."

"There were others. You didn't get any of them?" Rose's complexion clouded. "Not one?"

Sylvie could only shake her head and stare.

Paling, Rose pinned Ivan with her gaze. Her silence was more condemning than a scream.

Ivan's face was blank as he stood his ground.

"Did you have anything to do with Rose's letters not reaching me?" Sylvie hissed. The anger blasting through her was immediate and complete. "Did Jozefa?"

"I had my reasons," Ivan said. "Rose, we needed more time together. I can explain—"

Rose walked away from him, cradling her elbows in her palms. "I trusted you."

"I brought you back, didn't I? Isn't that what you wanted? If I made other mistakes, this has to make up for it. In the end, I did what you asked."

The end, indeed. "You're right about that, Ivan. Whatever you've done, whatever nightmare Rose has endured these last three weeks," Sylvie said, "it's over now."

"Not a nightmare," he muttered, shoving his fists into his trouser pockets. "A dream."

"Either way, I woke up, didn't I?" Rose swiped a handkerchief beneath her nose. She leaned against the wall beside the mantel.

"Are you hurt? Injured? Ill?" Kristof asked her. Rose denied any of that.

Ivan watched her with regret and something that looked suspiciously possessive. Sylvie didn't trust him, didn't want him in their home. He had deceived her the evening she and Beth offered Lottie a job. He'd asked about Rose, implying he knew nothing.

"Ivan," she said, "thank you for bringing her back. Now it's time for you to go."

At the first hint of defiance, Kristof stepped in, escorting him away.

"Rose, dear." Sylvie spoke quietly while the men exchanged words at the door. "Rozalia. I love you, and I've missed you so much. I need to understand what happened, but no matter what, you're where you belong now."

"Oh, Mimi." Rose's voice was so heavy, each syllable a soft mallet upon a drum, each drumbeat a tocsin. "I don't know where I belong."

Chapter Twenty-Eight

Kristof had been right when he'd guessed that Ivan wouldn't refuse a free meal. He watched the young man finish his sandwich at the coffee shop next to Sylvie's building, then offered dessert. Anything to keep him here and answering questions.

Ivan ordered a slice of chocolate cake.

"So you were working with Jozefa the entire time," Kristof said. They spoke in Polish for extra privacy. "But I take it you don't agree with her on all accounts. Otherwise, you wouldn't have brought Rose home."

"True." Ivan took a drink of coffee. Outside, fat drops of rain darkened the sidewalk. Umbrellas popped open, and women's skirts blew in the wind. "Jozefa won't be happy about me letting Rose out, but what can she do? If she crosses me, she knows she'd lose. She's lost already."

"Start over. From the beginning."

A twisted story began to emerge from Ivan's faltering, nonlinear narrative. Jozefa had hired Ivan as a guardian for Rose and paid him handsomely. He was to stay in the hotel with her during the day while Jozefa enjoyed the Fair. Once Jozefa came home, he was free to go.

"How did she choose you for the job?" Kristof asked.

"Jozefa came to the coffeehouse where the Hull House Players practice. I was there, watching for Rose. She asked if I knew anyone who might be interested in work as a bodyguard at the Palmer for good pay. I took it, supposing the person I would be guarding would be her. I didn't know when she hired me it had anything to do with Rose."

"But when you saw her," Kristof said, "didn't you ask what was going on?" On the other side of the window, the coffee shop's shingle whined as it swayed on its rusty hinge.

Ivan downed the rest of his coffee, thumping the mug back on the table. "I'm not stupid. It seemed too good to be true, spending that much time with Rose every day, so I kept my mouth shut about knowing her already. I didn't know if Jozefa would like that we had a connection. Rose was smart enough to keep it quiet, too."

"How long have you cared for her?"

Ivan's mouth hooked up at the corner and then down again. "Years."

"Did you ever tell her how you felt?"

"I must have tried a hundred times." The normally quiet young man was obviously uncomfortable answering so many questions. "But yes, finally, at the Palmer, I did. We had a lot of time together when I was keeping her safe. She said she cared for me, too."

"But she couldn't have been happy with the confinement," Kristof broke in.

"No. When Jozefa announced her plan to take Rose back to Poland with her, neither Rose nor I was happy. Fate brought us together, Mr. Bartok. I wasn't about to let us be torn apart by Jozefa."

"Or by Miss Townsend," Kristof said. "Rose asked you to mail letters for her, to let Miss Townsend know where she was, and you didn't. Explain."

The waitress arrived with a plate of chocolate cake topped with an unnaturally red cherry in a cloud of whipped cream. She refilled Kristof's coffee and whisked away.

A strange smile crimped Ivan's mouth. He took a bite of his dessert and washed it down with water. "When you love someone, you do whatever it takes to be with her. I was getting paid—good money, too—to be the only person Rose ever saw, aside from Jozefa. I brought her anything she asked for. I gave her companionship when she was lonely. She *needed* me. I didn't want anyone to interrupt that, but I'd never let her go to Poland. I would have gotten her away from Jozefa before they got on the train. The only reason I decided to do it today was that Miss Townsend and the man who broke my nose were on to me. The last thing I need is to get mixed up with the police."

There was so much wrong about what Ivan had

said that Kristof hardly knew where to begin. The rain had strengthened into a steady slurring just beneath the din of the other diners. He cupped his hands around the mug of coffee from which steam rose and divided and curled without any kind of pattern. Chaos.

"Ivan, did you read *A Tale of Two Cities* for the Hull House Readers Club? Or did you only attend to see Rose?"

He said he'd read it.

"Then you know who the real hero in the story is. It's Sydney Carton, the man who loved Lucie so much that he let her go. He sacrificed his own life so she could be happy in hers, even though her happiness wasn't tied to his." Kristof waited for his point to sink in. When Ivan made no sign of understanding, he drove it further. "I would hope that you helped Rose escape for her own sake, not just for yours."

"I liked Sydney. I felt for him. But that's not our story. I couldn't give Rose up like that."

Kristof stifled a sigh. "The police, then," he said. "Fear of getting caught was the only reason you brought Rose home?" If Ivan was so enamored with her, he could have run off with her, away from Chicago, cutting her off from anyone who wanted to find her. He could have kept her completely to himself if he'd had a mind to. "That's not very romantic."

Ivan forked another piece of cake into his

mouth, chewed, and swallowed. After three more bites, he spoke. "If I get arrested, I can't earn wages for Matka and Lottie. If I run off with Rose, I also abandon them. I can't do that. I want Rose, but I want her right here in Chicago. I want her to want me, even when she isn't locked in the same room with me."

"That makes sense. But it's quite a test, isn't it?" Secretly, Kristof wondered just how honest Rose had been about her feelings for Ivan. What choice had she had? He'd been her jailer. It was in her interest to appease him, lest he take what he wanted by force.

Oh no.

Ivan and Rose had spent nearly every day together for three weeks, alone in a hotel room. Ivan wanted nothing more than to possess her. Would do anything to keep her with him. It was too early to tell what the results had been, but the possibility was enough to make Kristof sick.

"Ivan." Kristof leaned over the table toward him. "Did you take advantage of the situation? Of Rose?"

"What do you think?"

"Can we talk?" Sylvie hugged Rose's diary to her chest, then handed it to its owner.

Rose accepted it from her seat on the parlor sofa, Tiny Tim sleeping beside her. Darkness had fallen, and rain purred against the window. "I was wondering where this was. I told Ivan to get it for me the night he came for everything else. He couldn't find it." She looked up. "You read it?"

Sylvie lowered herself to the other end of the sofa. "Yes. I was searching for clues as to what happened to you. What I found along the way—" She blinked back tears. "I've made so many mistakes, Rose. I was insensitive to your feelings. I'm sorry I made you feel like you couldn't trust me with them. You should never have had to worry about hurting me by missing your parents." Fingertips biting into the cushion, she crossed her ankles, then uncrossed them. "I'm not sorry for reading the diary. I am deeply, truly sorry for not being what you needed."

She'd had weeks to rehearse this apology, and still it came out sounding a little petty. All she could think was that she'd hurt Rose by not being enough for her. Just like she hadn't been enough to heal her mother's pain after the war. When Ruth wanted to clean, Sylvie cleaned with her until her knuckles were chapped red, but the next day Ruth redid the work Sylvie had done. It was never enough. The sadness never left Ruth, the nosebleeds didn't stop. Sylvie hadn't been enough for Meg either, not that she could blame her sister for marrying Nate. That left Sylvie to care for Stephen, and after her own traumatic experience during the Great Fire, she understood him better than ever. But even so, there were times when she hadn't been able to chase the wildness from his eyes, or the trembling from his hands.

"I never meant for you to read these words." Rose spread a hand atop the diary. "It must have sounded so hateful. I wish you hadn't."

"You were *missing*. Your safety was more important to me than your privacy."

Rose tucked the diary between the armrest and her leg. "I sent word, or thought I had. I thought you were angry with me and that's why you didn't write back. Which made me upset with you."

"I had no idea. I don't understand what happened." Something fundamental had changed between them, had changed each of them as people. How was she to navigate such unmapped territory?

Rose rested her head against the dark wood trim of the sofa, then straightened up once more, fingers twining in the shawl's fringe. "It all started when Jozefa found me after my violin lesson at the Fair. She took me on a ride out on the lake and invited me to stay at the Palmer overnight with her. I did."

"Without telling me?"

"Jozefa told me she'd sent word to you—"

"She didn't! I don't understand why she took you at all. Why *you*, out of a million people?"

Rose's face pinched. "This will go better if you don't interrupt me. Please. This isn't easy for me either."

Sylvie clamped her lips shut and waited.

"A few days after Ivan took the note to our apartment and collected my things and the cat, I started feeling smothered. I decided to write to you and asked Jozefa to send the letters. I must have given her five of them before I suspected she wasn't mailing them. She grew angry every time I handed her another one, telling me I ought to give it up, that you were set on not responding. That's when I started giving letters to Ivan instead. But as you know, he kept them for his own reasons."

Sylvie's next question could not wait. "Do you think Jozefa will come for you? If she thinks I'm working at the Fair or in the bookstore? Do you suppose she'll come back?"

Rose shook her head. "I don't think so. I wrote her a note telling her I left with Ivan of my own free will and that she should not come after me."

That sounded all too familiar. "A note," Sylvie repeated. "A note didn't stop me. Just the opposite, in fact. When I got your message, I searched all the harder."

"I thought you might."

"So you wanted to be found."

"Not the first or second day. And then I did. And

then I didn't." She settled deeper into the corner of the sofa. "It's all been so confusing, Mimi. She treated me so well, ordering new dresses made, bringing Ivan to keep me company. She let me have Tiny Tim and all my things from home. It was a grand adventure. The Palmer House! You can't imagine the luxury there."

"Rozalia." Sylvie could barely contain her amazement. "You were kidnapped." And Sylvie still didn't know why.

"Not technically. I went with her willingly to prove to you that I would be all right even when you couldn't personally safeguard me. Then, when I'd had enough of proving my point, Jozefa kept coming up with reasons for me to remain. She told me all about my people—the Polish people. My homeland. Every day she shared something new and precious, and I felt like I was being handed pieces to the puzzle of who I was, and that I might finally be whole again if I stayed a little longer, learned a little more."

Tiny Tim stretched out beside Rose, and she buried her fingers in the soft fur on his chest.

Sylvie inhaled deeply in an effort to calm her nerves while waiting for answers that still hadn't come. Could Rose not see that she'd been held hostage for almost three weeks? "I didn't know what had happened to you," she choked out. "I almost wished for a ransom note so I could do something to bring you home safely."

A smile touched Rose's lips. "Jozefa didn't want money. She wanted me."

"But *why?*"

"I'll get to that." Rose looked at the cat as she said this, as if unwilling to witness the wreck Sylvie's composure had become.

Again, Sylvie strove to be patient. Again, she failed. "You say she wanted you. So did I. So *do* I. And she nearly took you out of the country, didn't she?"

"But she didn't. Ivan let me go."

Thunder rattled the china, startling Sylvie into an awareness of just how dark the room had grown. She turned on the lamp. "Just how close did the two of you become?"

"Quite. He rescued me. And he saved me from boredom and loneliness before that."

"He also made you stay! He didn't mail the letters to me that you asked him to!"

Rose rubbed her forehead. "He was confused. We've both been so confused. I still am, if I'm honest. You're right, he didn't mail those letters, but he meant no harm by it. You heard him. He only wanted more time with me."

Alarm bells rang in Sylvie's head, competing with the storm outside. "Exactly how much time did he want?"

A moment stretched long and empty, then another, and one more. Finally, Rose met Sylvie's gaze. *All of it,* her eyes seemed to say.

"Has he spoken of marriage with you?" The question staggered from Sylvie without permission.

"Don't be cross. Just because he's ready for that doesn't mean I am."

Sylvie trapped a groan in her throat. To even think of marriage at this age was un—oh no. Her stomach hollowed. "Rose. I need to ask you something else, and I want you to trust that my love for you won't change at all based on your answer. But in all that time you had alone with Ivan, did he—try anything?"

"Nothing I didn't allow. He only—he . . ." Her complexion burned a florid red. But from embarrassment or pleasure? "He kissed me."

"Did he do more than that? Did you two . . ." Sylvie covered her own blazing cheek with one hand.

"No," Rose said quickly, loudly, and Tiny Tim flinched beneath her hand. "I'm only seventeen, after all, and I'm not that kind of girl. Even if I didn't mind the immorality of it—which I *do* mind, very much—what would I do with a baby right now? What would *he* do?"

Relief flooded Sylvie. "Exactly. Thank God."

Silence hung in the room, dimpled by the pattering rain. All of this talk of Ivan had led them away from the path she most wanted to take. The one which led, she hoped, to answers about Jozefa.

"Jozefa never should have put you in that position. Did you know she hired your hotel maid to impersonate you and tell the police you were fine so they would close your missing person case?"

Rose raised her eyebrows. "Jenny?" Her surprise could not have been manufactured. "I did write the letter to the police, but I thought she'd mailed it."

"Of all the dangers I imagined for you, a Polish actress older than I am never crossed my mind. I don't know why she singled you out, Rose. But she might do it again to another unsuspecting girl she finds. You ought to press charges so she doesn't get away with this."

"I'm not going to press charges. I don't want her to get in any trouble."

"Rose!" The admonition flew out of Sylvie's mouth before she could moderate her tone. "She entrapped you and obstructed an investigation. She lied to the police. There are consequences."

"I don't see her as a criminal, and I never will. That's not who she is." Rose's chin quivered. Tears welled and spilled over.

Sylvie was dumbstruck. "Then who is she? You haven't reached the age of adulthood, and she tried to take you out of the country. Why?"

Sniffing, Rose swiped the back of her hand beneath her nose. "She's my aunt."

Shock exploded through Sylvie.

"Jozefa is my mother's sister. Zielinski is her stage name. All she wanted was to reunite with the only family she has left. How can I blame her, when finding my real family has been my quest, as well?"

Real family. The words opened a vein in Sylvie, and all her relief bled away. The truth that should have staunched the flow—that Rose had returned to her anyway—rattled through her mind but found no purchase in her heart.

"Jozefa knew my parents had come to Chicago with me, but after my father died, no more letters crossed the ocean. She'd always wondered if I was still here. Then, when she came for the Fair, she saw my notice in the bulletin for Polish visitors. She came to the bookstore to find me that day. But when she met you, she was afraid to say who she was, convinced you wouldn't believe her because she had no proof. But she couldn't have known to bring records with her from Poland to verify that we're related. You see now, don't you, Mimi? I felt sorry for her. My aunt. We both wanted the same thing."

Sylvie stared at Rose until her young, smooth face rippled and shimmered. "Your aunt." She tried to swallow the stone in her throat. "You found your family, at last."

CHAPTER TWENTY-NINE

Sunday, September 3, 1893

Never mind that the tap water was too cool for proper shaving. The anger simmering beneath Kristof's skin warmed it up just fine.

He lathered his face with balsam shaving soap, then pulled the razor down his cheek and over the angle of his jaw, distracted by the fact that Gregor hadn't come home last night. The shirt he'd left for Lottie to wash had lipstick stains on the collar and smelled of alcohol and sweat and stale perfume. This was how he spent his time, now that he was unemployed?

Kristof rinsed the blade in the water and finished shaving, then wiped his face with a clean towel before throwing on a shirt. It was Sunday morning, and he ought to be preparing for worship. Instead, he was counting the ways his brother fell short and despairing that he would ever reform.

Dawn came misty and grey this morning, bringing none of its usual cheer. After buttoning his collar and cuffs, Kristof headed to the kitchen, drawn by the bolstering aroma of brewing coffee. Strong coffee. He needed his wits about him now more than ever. Gregor wasn't the only person on his mind. He wondered how Sylvie and Rose were doing but wanted to give them space and time together. He also wondered whether Sylvie would even want his company, now that Rose was safely home. Would she choose him if she didn't need him?

But there was far more at stake now than his feelings. Ivan couldn't be trusted, Rose might still be in some kind of trouble, and Gregor might have gotten himself beaten and left in some dark alley.

Pushing fear beneath his anger, he tucked his shirt into his trousers, poured a cup of coffee, and settled at the kitchen table with the morning paper.

Someone fumbled at the door. When the knob didn't turn, Kristof rose and opened it himself.

Perspiration beaded Karl Hoffman's brow. He had one arm around Gregor's waist, while Gregor's arm was draped over the seventy-year-old man's stooped shoulders. Kristof's pulse skidded at the sight of both men. They stumbled inside, and Kristof detached his brother from their elderly neighbor just before Gregor collapsed to the floor. His skin was yellow and filmed with sweat.

"Karl." Kristof helped him into a chair before his knees gave way, as well. "What—"

"It's all right, son," Karl heaved. "That is, I'm all right. It's your brother who isn't."

"Gregor," Kristof called to him.

His brother rolled onto his side. The buttons on his shirt were misaligned. The smell of opium and illness exuded from his person like an atmosphere.

Staggering back, Kristof held a handkerchief to his nose. "Gregor, can you hear me? I'm calling a doctor."

"No," Gregor rasped. "It wears off. Just wait."

Kristof was stunned motionless. So this wasn't the first time Gregor had been in this condition. Only the first time Kristof had seen it. He sank into a chair beside Karl, then recalled his manners. He brought his neighbor a glass of water and mug of black coffee before retaking his chair.

"I'm sorry, Karl." He wiped a hand over his smooth jaw. "Can you tell me what happened?"

"I am up, getting ready for church, ja? Then I hear a commotion down on the street. From my window I see a man being pulled out of a hansom cab, the driver fishing in his pockets for money. I think he has been assaulted. I think he is being robbed, so I go downstairs to see what I can do. It takes me a while, this is true, but I get outdoors, and there he is, nearly insensible."

"Like this," Kristof said.

"Ja, just so. Like this. I cannot leave him there, so I help him up the stairs, and here we are."

Kristof rested a hand on his neighbor's back.

"I wish you'd pounded on my door on the way down. You shouldn't have done all that yourself."

"You were bathing, I think. I hear the water in the pipes. Anyhow, I don't know it is Gregor until I roll him over outside."

Kristof couldn't imagine the effort this must have taken. "Did you hurt yourself, helping him up here?"

"Oof." Karl's chuckle ended in a spate of coughing. "Please, do not tell my beautiful bride, and all will be well. At least for me." He took a drink of coffee. "By the time I reached him, he had vomited in the street. It is good for him, to get that out of his system."

Kristof regarded his brother. A deep sadness replaced his anger, filling every crack in his soul. A feeling much like mourning twisted his middle, for though Gregor wasn't dead, he was the image of something lost. This would be far easier if, when Kristof looked at him, he didn't also see the bright-eyed boy who had been the darling of his mother, the hope of his father, and, for many years, the constant companion of his older brother.

But none of that excused his choices. The habitually poor decisions that put others at risk as well as himself.

"This is it." Kristof cleared the regret from his throat. "He can't live here anymore. I told him he could have until the end of the week to come up with the rent money he owed me, but even if he does manage that somehow . . . This is it, Karl. He has to go."

Part of him wanted Karl's confirmation that this wasn't cruelty, but consequence. But he didn't need it. There was no other possible conclusion, and yet guilt stabbed him. His father's dying request was that he take care of his prodigy brother. And now he was deliberately, coldly planning not to.

Karl exhaled. He cupped his large-knuckled hands around the mug, his skin marked with pale brown spots. "Last night you told us Rose is home. Is this true?"

Kristof glanced at him, disoriented by the change of subject. "It is."

"Everything you told Sylvie about Rose is true for Gregor, too. God loves him. God knows exactly where he is. You can't save him, but God can. His well-being is not up to you, Kristof. He is a grown man. It's up to him, and to God. Sometimes the best thing we can do is simply get out of the way of that."

Gregor moaned and folded his arm beneath his head for a pillow. An oily smear of lipstick glistened on his stubbled jaw. One would never believe how much talent had been given to this man, nor how bent he was on wasting it.

Karl rubbed at the silver whiskers on his chin. "There is a man called Moody preaching all over

Chicago this summer on an evangelistic crusade. I have gone to hear him three times, and every time he preaches on the prodigal son. You know the story."

Kristof nodded.

"Then you know the younger brother left home and spent his inheritance. He came back at the end, but why? The older brother didn't bring him back. The father didn't go get him and bring him home. No. That young man had to wallow with pigs before he decided to come home again. Nothing else would do. Sometimes you just have to let a man live with his decisions. This is not your burden to bear."

"Thank you, Karl," Kristof said. "In my family, growing up, it was. We had to be perfect to win our father's approval. Gregor excelled in music, I was blameless in behavior, and only when taken together did he say he had one whole son he could be proud of." The memory still stung.

"Ach." The older man shook his head. "A grave mistake, a corruption of what our heavenly Father intended. I hope you have since learned you can stop striving to earn a place you've already been given. You're already a beloved child of God. You can't perform your way into or out of His family. It's grace, son." His voice was thick with conviction, touching a chord in Kristof's spirit that had been silent for far too long.

"Amazing grace, indeed." The old hymn

echoed in Kristof's mind, its lyrics as profound as the melody was simple. He bent and, with his handkerchief, wiped the spittle from the corner of his brother's mouth. "And now grace—not me—will have to lead Gregor home."

Monday, September 4, 1893

Sylvie relished the balmy morning air freshened by the breeze coming off Lake Michigan. Summer, at last, was beginning to bow to fall. Checking the timepiece pinned to her bodice, she climbed the stairs to the Woman's Building. Her heels clicked over the marble floor as she entered the sun-splashed rotunda, then veered left into the gift shop and continued to the Check and Guide Services counter tucked into the back.

Dorothy smiled when she saw her.

Briefly, Sylvie told her that Rose was now safe at home. "I've actually come early to see about rearranging the schedule," she added. "I need to spend the day with Rose."

Beth bustled in through the gift shop, adjusting the mauve hat on her deep red hair. "Well? How is she?"

Sylvie had used the phone at Sherman House to call Beth over the weekend and let her know that Rose had returned. She'd also reached Meg late Saturday night, thankful that Nate's job as

Tribune editor meant they had a telephone in their house. Meg had brought her entire family to join Sylvie and Rose for lunch after church. Rose had seemed genuinely glad to see them but also flustered by the attention.

"Better than I had any right to hope." Sylvie straightened a stack of Mary Wollstonecraft's *A Vindication of the Rights of Woman* pamphlets. "Still, I'd like to have today off. I can make up for it later."

Dorothy slid her glasses up her nose and consulted the schedule. "You're both in luck. Beth's group canceled. Beth, you're now the proud tour guide of a group of New York ladies arriving in roughly an hour."

"Thanks, ladies," Sylvie said. "Beth, if you need time off later, please let me know."

Right now, Rose was with Meg and Olive, waiting for Sylvie in the Austrian Village on the Midway.

Beth agreed and turned back to Dorothy, her elbow brushing a pile of *The Daily Columbian* and knocking one to the floor. Sylvie picked it up, scanning the day's schedule. She took a second look.

"Jozefa Zielinski is speaking again this morning?" she asked. "She was only invited to speak twice, and she did that weeks ago. Is this a misprint?"

Dorothy wound her beads around one finger.

"She's filling in today. One of the speakers had to cancel due to a death in the family, and she volunteered to take the slot. It's a topic she's already covered, but chances are no one here today heard it the first time. She seemed delighted for the opportunity."

Heat, then chills, cycled through Sylvie. "This says she speaks at ten. Is she already here?"

"As usual." Dorothy pointed up with one slender finger. "In one of the parlors."

Sylvie was already walking away.

By the time she found Jozefa in the Japanese parlor and seated herself across from her, her middle was a tangle of pity and fury. She clasped her shaking fingers on her lap.

Jozefa raised her head slowly, regally. "I've been waiting for you." She was as composed as if she'd arranged this meeting herself. "She has made her choice. You've won. I congratulate you."

"Jozefa," Sylvie began. Her throat dried. Everything she'd thought of saying to this woman dissolved at the sight of her tears. Was she truly so lonely? Compassion flared in Sylvie, unbidden. How much easier this would be if she could only be filled with rage. "You could have told us you were her aunt from the beginning. Did you honestly think I would shut you out at a time when Rose wanted you most?"

Light danced on the gemstones in Jozefa's

hair combs. "Do you not recall? The first day I met you, you learned about Rose's notice in the Polish bulletin. You made it clear that anyone claiming to be a relative would need to prove it. And proof I could not offer. Besides, it was clear to me that I also came at a time when you wanted me the least. No, do not pretend I'm wrong. You wanted her to yourself. I could not blame you. I wanted the same."

"No." Sylvie's tone was abrupt and resounding, like something slamming shut. "We aren't the same at all. You deceived Rose."

"How?"

"You—you tricked her into staying with you."

Jozefa's lace collar moved with her even breaths. "If that's what she told you, she's the one deceiving you, not me. I invited her into my life, and she leapt at the chance. You can understand why. The pull of family is strong for an orphan."

It had been years since Sylvie had thought of Rose in those terms. "Then why did you hire Ivan to keep her locked up while you were enjoying the Fair? Why not let her come with you?"

A few women strolled by, pointing at etchings of mountains and waves, and admiring folding silk screens of iridescent blues and greens. A kimono displayed in the corner drew their attention, magnificent in shades of fire.

"She felt no lack," Jozefa said when they passed. She spread her hands over her knees, rings sparkling. "I understood that she had already seen every inch that she wanted to see with you. It was obvious she enjoyed her time with Ivan. She loved being pampered. Everything she desired was brought to her."

"But when she gave you letters for me, you didn't mail them."

Jozefa flicked her wrist, discarding the challenge. "As I said, dear, she made her choice, and she chose you. It's over." She retrieved her handbag from the floor and withdrew two railroad tickets. "She could have taken this ticket and started a life with me in Europe full of every comfort and experience a young girl could wish for. She didn't. I beg of you, be good to her."

Sylvie didn't need to be begged on that score. She studied the tickets. "You're leaving this afternoon?"

"My trunks have already been sent to the station." Jozefa's eyes misted. "I'll speak here one last time, and then yes, I'm leaving. Alone."

It was a straight walk of nine blocks from the Woman's Building, at the western edge of the fairgrounds, to the Austrian Village on the Midway. But stepping inside, Sylvie felt a world away in both time and space, transported to Old Vienna as it appeared in the 1700s. Thirty-six buildings, all in a state of elegant and artificial decay, surrounded a central plaza and included shops and houses leaning against each other, a functioning church, a one-thousand-seat restaurant, a beer garden, and the spired City Hall.

Still, it was easy to find Meg. As expected, she had set up her easel in the middle of a courtyard, where she could see the most. The canvas reflected the crisp blue sky, the terra-cotta rooftops, and the grey-brown buildings around them. Potted trees and windowsill boxes spilling over with flowers popped with color.

Sylvie spotted Olive and Rose at a table beneath a red-and-white-striped awning and waved.

"Oh!" Meg startled. "Sylvie. I wondered when you'd come. I had no idea all these shops actually have the tradesmen and women inside, producing the goods they sell. Lace, embroidery, carving, ivory-turning. I tried talking to some of them but didn't get far."

Sylvie laughed. There were five hundred Austrians here to populate this village for the Fair, and she wasn't surprised they didn't all speak English. "I'm sure they understood and appreciated your interest in their work, all the same."

The Austrian band struck up their next piece on the opposite side of the plaza.

"Charming," Meg murmured. "I can see why this is one of the most popular sites to visit, even though the wares are marked with 'World's Fair prices.' The ambience is worth it."

"I saw Jozefa." Sylvie could hold the news in no longer.

Meg's paintbrush suspended in the air. "This morning?"

Sylvie told her what had transpired, then checked her timepiece again. "In three hours, she'll be gone."

A sigh lifted and released Meg's shoulders. "I hate to say good riddance, but . . . well. I still can't believe what she did, even if she *is* Rose's aunt. Does Rose know she's leaving today?"

"She must. Jozefa said she chose not to accept her train ticket." Sylvie squinted toward the girls again. "Who's that with them?" But as soon as she asked, she knew.

Ivan.

Excusing herself from Meg, Sylvie threaded between tables and Austrian waitresses in starched white aprons. Beneath the awning, her vision adjusted to the shade.

Rose jumped up and hugged her. "I didn't invite him, Mimi," she whispered in her ear. "Please don't be rude. He missed me. I kind of missed him, too."

"Rude, me?" Sylvie tried to sound casual, but resentment twitched inside her. She wanted this time together to be special. Without Ivan. Nonetheless, she assured Rose she knew how to be civil.

She sat in a slatted wood folding chair beside

Olive, across from where Rose settled next to Ivan.

"Aunt Sylvie!" Olive lisped through the gap in her teeth. A small checkerboard on the table between her and Rose held a game half played. "Rose has a new friend, and his name is Ivan. Do you know him?"

"I do. Hello, Ivan. I didn't know you'd be here today."

A waitress set a basket of rye bread on the table and poured Sylvie a mug of rich, dark coffee topped with hot foamed milk. The girls didn't care for it, but she noticed Ivan wasn't drinking any either, and supposed he was trying to save money.

"Please." She gestured to the basket. "Help yourself."

Thanking her, he tore off a chunk of bread and ate it without butter.

"How did you find us?" She brought her mug to her mouth and licked the foam from her lips.

"I went to the apartment this morning. Thought I'd visit Rose while Lottie cleaned. Lottie told me where you'd gone."

Sylvie should have guessed.

Rose kinged one of Olive's checkers. "It feels like we're in the pages of one of Olive's storybooks, doesn't it? If I can ignore the tourists, everything else is enchanting."

"Yes, it is," Ivan said archly, watching her. For

a man of few words, he certainly knew how to make them count.

Sylvie ripped a hunk of bread from the loaf, then pinched off a smaller piece and ate it, the bitter taste filling her mouth. Her gaze returned to Rose, wearing another dress that Sylvie hadn't seen before today. "You never told me what happened to your clothes," she said. "I saw other young ladies wearing your dresses while you were gone."

"That must have been so strange for you. I had no idea you'd ever see those again. Aunt Jozefa wanted to give me all new fashions, so she gave my old things to Ivan to dispose of."

"She told me to burn them behind the tenement," he said. "But I saw no reason for such waste. I couldn't do it. Couldn't even cut them up for rags, there was so much use left in them. So I dropped the clothes off at a few different pawnshops and church charity bins instead."

Sylvie considered this. "Including your own, St. Michael's."

"I saw no harm in it. My sister hasn't had a new dress in far too long."

"But did you know the laundry tag was still in it?" Sylvie asked. "Did Jozefa?"

He took another bite of bread, swallowing quickly. "I didn't. She realized it had been left in it later, but it didn't bother her until she learned I didn't burn it. You should have seen how upset she was when she heard Lottie had the dress."

Rose looked up from the checkerboard. "She *really* came unglued when you mentioned that Lottie was doing housekeeping for Mimi, remember? That's when we started packing."

So that explained the sudden move out of the Palmer House. Jozefa figured Sylvie would recognize the dress and inspect it, find the tag, and track them to their room. "But Ivan, if she asked you to burn the clothes, why did you tell her you didn't?"

He ran a hand over his hair, but the waves bounced back over his forehead just the same. "She kept saying she knew best, better than us. I wanted her to know I do my own thinking."

"A point you have fully proven," Rose said. She turned her face toward the sky peeking between the awnings over the tables. Seagulls flapped and soared toward Lake Michigan.

With Olive paying far too much attention, Sylvie changed the subject. "Have you thought of where you'll seek employment next?"

"There's always the docks," Ivan said, "but you never know until you show up in the morning whether or not you'll get a day's work. So I'm going to apply at the Polish restaurant at the Fair. It'll close at the end of October, but in the meantime it might not be so bad. Being Polish ought to give me a leg up. I heard they have waiters from Cleveland and the guests are disappointed."

That sounded familiar. "Do you have any experience in food service?" Sylvie asked.

"No, but I'm learning I can act my way through a lot. 'All the world's a stage, and all the men and women merely players; they have their exits and their entrances; and one man in his time plays many parts.' "

Rose sent him a smile, and Olive reminded her to take her turn.

Sylvie gaped. "I had no idea you were a student of Shakespeare, Ivan."

"It's a recent thing. Over the last few weeks, Jozefa asked me to help Rose with her lines. Rose helped me understand what the lines mean, too. We've been practicing *As You Like It* together. And *Romeo and Juliet*."

Sylvie nearly spit out her coffee. Then she drank, and drank again, disguising her absolute speechlessness. Had this been a genuine kindness on Jozefa's part, giving the couple something constructive to fill their time? But surely she, an actress herself, would have realized the danger of putting two young people in such a position. Acting out lines of love and romance, unchaperoned in a hotel room . . .

"I win!" Olive cried. "Aunt Sylvie, will you play with me next?"

Sylvie nodded as Olive reset the checkerboard, strains of Austrian band music floating around them.

Soon the waitress returned, and Sylvie stumbled through her order. *All the world's a stage, indeed!* Jozefa hadn't known what she was doing with these two. Or worse, she had.

When Olive slipped out of her chair and scampered off to see Meg, Rose leaned forward. "In a way, I feel sorry for my aunt. She tried so hard to keep me."

A month ago, Rose had said Sylvie's boundaries were so confining they felt like a cage. And now she felt sorry for Jozefa, who had literally penned her up?

"Possession," Sylvie said quietly, "is not the same as love."

Ivan needed to hear that as much as anyone. Only grudgingly did she remind herself that he had, in fact, freed Rose, hoping to win her even when she had more choices, according to Kristof's report.

Still. Sylvie had so little trust to spare, she couldn't bear to part with much for him.

Rose reached across the table and touched Sylvie's hand. "I was hard on you before. For all the rules and guidelines. But I've come to realize you meant them for my own good. Aunt Jozefa meant them for hers." She leaned back in her chair. "To her credit, she let me go my own way in the end, didn't she? She didn't come back for me, when she certainly knew where I was."

Ivan folded his arms. "She 'let you go' because

you were already gone by the time she returned to the Auditorium Hotel on Saturday."

"She's my only blood relative in the world." Rose's chin trembled. "Now I'll never see her again."

A pang of compassion swelled in Sylvie. "It could have been different. If she hadn't resorted to deception, she could have been part of your life in an honest way. I would have welcomed her. Her choices were—"

"Please, Mimi. Speak no ill of my aunt, especially when she's not here to defend herself."

The Vienna sausages and potato salad arrived, drawing Olive and Meg from the easel. By the time they'd finished *sachertorte* for dessert, Sylvie had checked her watch three more times. Not until after they had browsed through shops of Austrian linens and market tables of silver and amber jewelry did Sylvie relax. At last, Jozefa was on her train and speeding away from Chicago, out of their lives. It fell to Sylvie to pick up the pieces she'd left behind.

Chapter Thirty

Tuesday, September 5, 1893

Tying her hat ribbons firmly beneath her chin, Sylvie emerged onto her building's rooftop, though she'd never been fond of heights. There was Rose, reading in a folding chair beneath the open sky. Wind pulling at her skirt, Sylvie pressed a hand to her flipping stomach and passed the terra-cotta pots of red geraniums.

"Thanks for leaving a note to find you here." She sat in the chair beside Rose. Two sparrows landed nearby, pecking at seed and bread crumbs Rose must have scattered when she arrived.

"I didn't want you to worry when you came home from work to an empty apartment." The broad brim of her straw hat undulated. Her shawl had fallen behind her back, the ends looped over her elbows.

"Worry, me?" Sylvie teased, glad her hat covered her hair, which showed far more grey than it had a month ago.

After slipping a ribbon into her book, Rose closed it. "I'm serious, Mimi. I've caused you more distress than you ever deserved. I'm sorry about that. It's not your fault we're not related by blood. I wish we were. You don't know how much I do. I don't know how to explain why it matters at all."

"You don't have to explain that, Rozalia."

"I want to try." She tapped the cover of *Mansfield Park*. "Do you know why this story means so much to me?"

Sylvie could guess. "I'd rather hear it from you." Warmth soaked through her hat and dress to her skin, the parting caress of a mild day.

"It's about finding one's true home, and Fanny Price has so much trouble. She's a monster, you know." Rose's hair draped over her shoulder in a long thick braid, the ends of which flirted with the wind.

"The literary trope?" Sylvie clarified. The character type was most often associated with Mary Shelley's novel, in which the monster Dr. Frankenstein created didn't fit or belong in the world he inhabited.

"Right." Rose shifted in her chair, and it creaked. "Fanny doesn't fit anywhere. She doesn't belong with her natural parents in Portsmouth, and she doesn't really belong with her adoptive family, the relatives who have raised her in Mansfield Park. It's incredibly sad when you think about it."

Sylvie watched her intently, suspecting that she was talking about herself as much as she was of Fanny.

Rose opened the novel on her lap and read.

" 'When she had been coming to Portsmouth, she had loved to call it her home, had been fond of saying that she was going home; the word had been very dear to her, and so it still was, but it must be applied to Mansfield. *That* was now the home.' "

"What does that mean to you?" Sylvie prompted.

Rose sighed. "Fanny Price is basically homeless. She feels like she belongs wherever she *isn't*. She doesn't belong anywhere at all."

Sylvie reached out and cupped her slender shoulder. "You aren't Fanny Price. You aren't homeless. Your home is here, for as long as you want it to be. I can't answer why God allowed both your parents to die. But I've always counted it my deepest joy that I got to be the one to raise you in their stead. It was love, not obligation, that bound us together. I love you more than you know."

She paused, wondering if her words were having any effect at all. If words alone could make Rose secure, she would surround her with them, wrap her as tight as the shawl Rose now drew around her shoulders. Instead, she feared what she'd said had made no more impression than the butterfly that landed on the nearby geranium and fluttered off again without even making the blossom sway.

Rose watched its looping flight. "Honestly, I

don't even think she belongs with Edmund. She married him because he just happened to be the one closest to her."

Sylvie pondered this. If Rose saw herself in Fanny Price, was she saying her attachment to Ivan was unraveling? She had to ask. "Has your view of Ivan changed?"

Rose shut the book. The traffic from the street below mingled with the bright notes of the wind chime hung outside the Hoffmans' window. "I don't know how I view Ivan anymore. Everything is different. He seems to care for me as much as ever, but now that I'm free, I don't fancy being smothered, even by his affection." She spoke quietly, as if only to herself.

"Jozefa dangled outings in front of me, chances to see you at the Fair." Rose had obviously leapt to the parallel track in her train of thought, for Jozefa and Ivan were the two rails of her captivity. "But every promise proved false. She kept putting it off. *'Tomorrow,'* she said. *'Tomorrow. Today will not work after all.'* And I already told you about the letters."

The letters. Sylvie's hand went to her pocket, stiff with today's mail. Something had come for Rose today. She withdrew the envelopes and flipped through them until she came to it. The handwriting seemed feminine and vaguely familiar. Perhaps Hazel had—

No. Sylvie examined the script again. That was

Jozefa's hand. She glanced at Rose, who was looking off into some unseen distance again. If Sylvie kept the letter back, Rose would never know it. And why shouldn't she, when Jozefa had kept so many letters from Sylvie?

Her conscience cracked. To mimic another's wrong was never right.

Besides, Jozefa was already gone. Rose had chosen Sylvie. The letter was either a good-bye, an apology, or an invitation to correspond. Sylvie had no right to keep it.

"Rose," she said. "This is for you. I think it might be from Jozefa."

"And you're giving it to me anyway? I'm impressed."

"So am I." Sylvie tried to laugh as Rose opened it and began to read.

"You're right, it's from her. Long, too." She smoothed the page on her book, bending over it as she read.

All at once, she stood, *Mansfield Park* falling from her lap. She paced, one hand over her mouth, then turned her back to the wind and stood still. Sylvie pushed out of her chair. Warning licked through her.

When Rose cried out, Sylvie could bear the suspense no longer. "What is it?" she pleaded. She could not survive any more secrets.

Rose spun to face her. "Jozefa is not my aunt. She lied."

"What?" Sylvie gasped. "*Now* will you press charges? If you won't, I will. The woman is mad!"

But Rose was already shaking her head, tears rolling free from her lashes, holding up the letter. "She isn't my aunt. She's my mother."

Her shawl slipped to the ground.

"I don't understand," Sylvie said again. She sat opposite Rose at their kitchen table, having taken refuge from the wind when it threatened to snatch the letter. Nothing Rose had said since reading it made sense. "Your mother was Magdalena Dabrowski."

Rose pressed a handkerchief to her mottled face. "You haven't read this."

Sylvie braced herself.

"Jozefa had a baby when she was twenty-nine years old. She wasn't married, and she was already an actress. She named me Rozalia and gave me up for adoption, requesting a few things regarding the people who adopted me. She asked that I be adopted by a couple who lived in a small town and could have no children of their own. She wanted me to be cherished as a miracle. From what Mr. Janik told me, I was."

Sylvie pressed her fingers to her temples, willing the room to stop spinning.

"But she always regretted giving me up. She tried for years to track me down, but the orphanage wouldn't cooperate. It was only after my father—" She stopped, stricken.

"Nikolai was your father," Sylvie said. "Go on."

Rose balled a handkerchief against a fresh wave of tears. "Well, only after he left for America did they tell her I'd been placed with him and my—and Magdalena." She paused, stumbling, it seemed, over calling the woman something other than her mother. "She sent a letter to the house in Wloclawek, but by then Magdalena and I had moved out of it. It's just like Mr. Janik said. When Nikolai left to make a home for us here, Magdalena took me somewhere else so we wouldn't be alone with the Russian soldiers billeted with us."

If Sylvie had doubted the power of words before, she knew what they were now. They were blows that bruised. They were blades, scraping away at everything she thought she knew, whittling the foundation out from under her feet, and Rose's. The poor girl was falling apart right in front of her.

"Rose," she said. "Jozefa has already confessed to lying. Why should we think she is not lying now? Did you tell her what we learned from Mr. Janik?"

"I didn't. Well, maybe just a tiny bit. I told her my mother played the violin, so she'd understand why it was important to me to keep playing mine.

She seemed genuinely surprised by that information, and I wondered why she didn't already know it, as my mother's sister. Mr. Janik said Magdalena learned to play the fiddle from her father. But Jozefa wouldn't have known that if this letter is true. If I was adopted by a couple she never met."

As if on cue, Kristof's violin began to sing in the apartment above them. "Did she pawn your violin because she didn't want you to play it?" Sylvie asked. "Or for money?"

Rose swiped at her tears once more. "She told me she was going to trade it in for a better, more expensive one. But she didn't. That was another promise that went unfulfilled."

"Why do you think she didn't want you to have it anymore, especially when she knew you loved it?" Sylvie had her own guesses. But it would be so much better if Rose could reach the same conclusion herself.

Bending, Rose scooped Tiny Tim from the floor and buried a kiss between his ears before settling him on her lap. "For a while I thought she was worried someone would hear me playing and it might be a clue for anyone trying to find me. But now—I don't think she liked the connection to Magdalena it represented. I told her that when I played it, I thought of my mother. It sounds strange to say it, but maybe she was jealous."

"That's not a strange thing to say, at all," Sylvie

said. "She clearly wanted you all to herself. Away from me, away from your own memories, even. If she could have done it without a guard, she wouldn't have hired Ivan, either." Sylvie stopped just short of calling Jozefa manipulative, though she had more than earned the label. "Does she say why she told you she was your aunt?"

"She does." Rose flipped to the second page of the letter and began to read. " 'You must wonder why I told you I was your aunt. Forgive me for that, but I thought it would be less of a shock to you, to adjust to that relationship first. If I had told you from the beginning I was your mother, without any documents to back it up, would you have believed me? Be honest, now.' "

Rose looked up. "She's right. If she had said she was my mother right away, I would have called her a liar and run the other direction. I certainly wouldn't have wanted to spend a few weeks with her."

The calculation on Jozefa's part was truly staggering. Rose folded the bright blue shawl threaded with dove grey into a triangle and set it on the table, pushing it toward the center. What a horrible thing to do, corrupting the precious memories Rose had of Nikolai and Magdalena, memories Rose had fought to preserve her entire life.

"So you believe her?" Sylvie dared to ask.

"You have to admit, her behavior makes more

sense if she really is my mother. She had to win my affections and trust before admitting who she was—because admitting she's my mother is also a confession that she gave me away. She gave me up to an orphanage, not knowing what kind of family would take me in, if any. No wonder she didn't want to tell me that. No one wants to hear that her mother didn't want her. But, Mimi"— she bit her lip, reached across the table, and took Sylvie's hand—"she wants me now."

Sylvie could summon no reply. Her breath came quick and shallow.

"She says she'll be in New York City until the end of October to see the sights there before sailing back to Poland. She—" Rose referred to the letter once more and read, " 'I want you to come home with me, but this time I won't trick you or force you. Take your time to think about what I offer. A life with your own true mother in Europe. No one can love you more than I do. Allow me to make up for all the years we lost, years we should have been together. If you decide to come, write to me at my hotel, and I'll wire money for a rail ticket. The ship leaves on October 30. I pray that you will be on it with me. But if you aren't, I wish you all the happiness one life can hold. If you never respond to this letter, I will understand that, too. I have much to be forgiven for. In case this is my last letter to you, I will leave you with the same words I left you with when I made the worst mistake of my life and gave you up.' "

Rose's face clouded. Then, with a broken voice, she sang. *"A-a-a, a-a-a, byly sobie kotki dwa . . ."*

The lullaby. The song Kristof had translated from Mrs. Górecki.

"I thought Mrs. Górecki taught you that song." Sylvie had already admitted to visiting her during her search.

"She only taught me the words. The tune was already embedded in my memory. My mother put it there." A shuddering sob escaped Rose. "I have to go. I mean, to my room. I'm sorry, Mimi, I need to be alone and think."

She took the letter with her, Tiny Tim at her heels, and the music upstairs stopped, too.

The composure Sylvie wore grew thin and loose as she stared at the vacant chair.

Emptiness magnified the erratic creaks and clicks of the building. Minutes slid out from under her as she replayed every word spoken since Rose had read the letter. Was this the truth, at last? Ought she to rejoice for Rose's long-lost mother's return? Just now, she couldn't.

A knock on the door.

She opened it. "Kristof," she breathed.

Instantly, the faint lines on his brow deepened. "What is it?"

"Ivan?" Rose emerged from the hallway, her

face still blotched and streaked. "Oh, hi, Mr. Bartok."

"I've interrupted something," he said, concern filling his eyes. "I only came to see if you'd like to start up your lessons again. I'll come back later."

"It's all right, don't go. Mimi, you might as well tell him. I don't mean to be rude, Mr. Bartok, but I've a terrible headache. Please excuse me." She receded from view.

Sylvie sank into her chair at the table, faltering. "Jozefa—" She struggled to regain herself.

Kristof moved a chair closer to Sylvie's and sat. "I thought she left yesterday."

"She did. Rose received a letter from her today. Jozefa says she's Rose's mother." Vertigo swept through her. The world was cracking and shifting beneath her.

Eyebrows drawing together, he dropped his voice low. "Explain." The way his gaze held hers felt to Sylvie like a hand to the elbow, helping her keep her balance.

Through the push and pull of his prompts and her answers, she recounted the news. From the parlor, the clock on the mantel struck six o'clock. When it chimed seven, they were still talking. In the end, it came down to a question.

"Are you afraid Jozefa is lying again?"

Sylvie whispered her confession. "I'm most afraid she isn't."

• • •

Streetlamps washed all the starlight from the sky and sent a dim glow between Sylvie's curtains. Quiet pulsed as she lay on her bed, listening for any sounds that signaled Rose was awake. She heard nothing but the sighs of the wind.

When four-year-old Rose had first moved in with Sylvie, she had strained her ears for the slightest whimper coming from the other side of the wall. During storms and after nightmares, Sylvie had rushed to the terrified child. She'd gathered her close and rocked her, smoothing the feathery, silken hair that still smelled of soap from her bath. Rose hadn't known much English yet. Sylvie had kept talking to her, anyway. Kept singing. Praying that some ray of tenderness would break through. *"I'm here. You're safe,"* Sylvie had said. *"It's going to be all right."* But Sylvie understood that perhaps Rose didn't want to be there. She didn't want to be merely safe. She wanted to be with her parents.

If Sylvie could have absorbed every ounce of Rose's grief, she would have done so. *"Help us, God,"* she had prayed aloud, pushing back against the shadows. *"I don't know what to do. Help her. Help me help her."* She knew two things only. That God had entrusted Rose to her care, and that she was wholly unequal to the task.

Neither of those things had changed.

Kristof had asked her tonight what she would

do if she decided Jozefa was telling the truth. She hadn't been able to form a response then. But it was a question she needed to answer. Would Sylvie place her own love for Rose above Rose's longing to reunite with her mother? Or would she, like the mother of King Solomon's time, let another woman have Rose even though it meant her own sorrow?

She'd always known her stewardship of Rose was a temporary assignment. She just hadn't expected to give her up so completely, or so soon. Every fiber in her being cried out to deny Jozefa's claim, to convince Rose to stay home. Stay safe.

But lines from Rose's diary stopped her. *She tries to control me now, but is she trying to protect me, or only herself? I want to be loved for who I am, but sometimes I wonder if she needs me to feel better about who she is.* Sylvie had to ask herself if those words were closer to the truth than she'd ever wanted to admit.

"Lord," she pleaded, "I don't know what to do. Help me. Help her. Help us."

Kristof had prayed with Sylvie, too, before he returned to his apartment. They'd been standing at the door, and she'd rested her forehead on his shoulder. His arms had formed a loose circle around her, but not like a cage. Like a shield.

"I'm here," he had whispered after she'd joined her *amen* with his. *"It's going to be all right."*

If Jozefa was Rose's mother, what right did Sylvie have to stand between them?

She wanted to do the right thing.

No. She wanted to *want* to do the right thing.

"Oh, God," she prayed, "I will never stop needing your help."

Chapter Thirty-One

Wednesday, September 6, 1893

It was over.

Sweat trickling down the sides of his face, Kristof kept his arms upraised for another beat after the end of the last piece the Exposition Orchestra would ever play at the World's Fair. In the silence that followed the last note, gratitude and satisfaction swelled his chest. *Bravo,* he mouthed to his musicians. They had followed him through the heights and depths of Strauss, Liszt, and Tchaikovsky, and they had brought the audience with them. Charles, his new concertmaster and first violinist in Gregor's place, had proven himself worthy of the role. Kristof hoped his parents had been here to see him.

He lowered his arms, and applause erupted behind him. It may not have been a perfect performance, but it had resonated with their listeners, and that was more than enough. He walked off stage, allowing the praise to lavish the orchestra, and paused in the wings, watching.

He would miss this. Conducting was so much different from playing. Conducting was connecting. Connecting himself to the entire piece, connecting the sections to one another in a coherent whole, connecting the music to the audience. There was such freedom and fulfillment in that. Come November, when the Chicago Symphony Orchestra season began, he hoped he could channel some of this satisfaction into being first violin again.

Kristof walked back on stage and took a bow. When he straightened and viewed the audience for the first time, his breath caught. Sylvie stood in the front row, her eyes glossy, clapping for him. Despite the staggering news from Jozefa delivered just last night. He'd been sure she had to work at the bookshop today, but there she was, wiping a tear from her glistening cheek. He bowed to her alone.

Only when he straightened did he see that she hadn't come by herself. Standing in a long line beside her were Rose, Olive, Meg, Nate, Anna, Karl, and Walter. Two rolling chairs rested in the aisle, no doubt for the Hoffmans. They could have no idea how deeply moved he was.

Throat tight, he smiled his thanks to each of them before gesturing to the orchestra once more.

When at last the ovations were finished and he'd shaken hands with the musicians, he joined Sylvie and her family. Her smile was radiant, even with the cares he knew were riding just below the surface. "I didn't expect you to be here," he said.

"I wouldn't miss it," she told him. "You were marvelous."

Compliments assailed him from Rose, Walter, and everyone in between. He was so unused to this that he hardly knew how to accept it.

"Hazel was sorry she couldn't be here," Meg said, "but she couldn't get off work."

"Here, Mr. Bartok!" Olive thrust a fistful of yellow wildflowers toward him, bits of grass and clover mixed in. "Don't worry, I didn't pick them at the Fair, because that's against the rules. I brought them all the way from my own yard."

Kristof bent one knee to accept the precious gift. "Did you know that no one has ever brought me flowers before?"

Olive beamed when he tucked their stems into the buttonhole of his lapel. The little blossoms drooped against his tuxedo, but he wouldn't trade them for the most prized bloom from the Rose Garden.

"Perfect," he said, and he meant it.

When he stood, Karl clapped his shoulder and shook his hand with an affectionate grunt. Anna reached up and took his face in her papery-dry hands. "I'm so proud of you."

Kristof bent and kissed her cheek, and she circled her arms around him in a motherly embrace. "God setteth the solitary in families, indeed," he said to her and was rewarded with an extra squeeze.

Sylvie came alongside him. "Tessa is minding the store today, and we all have time to help you celebrate. How does Blooker's sound?"

"Blookers?" Olive laughed. "What are blookers?"

Kristof chuckled with her. "Blooker's Dutch Cocoa Mill is a place where you can get fresh hot chocolate. It's a replica of an old Holland windmill, but this one uses its giant blades to grate chocolate instead of grinding meal. In all the months I've spent at the Fair, I've never been."

"Oh, you must!" Sylvie said.

"Then by all means," Kristof replied. She could have told him to hop on a camel in Cairo Street, and he would have. "If it's agreeable to the rest of the party, let's go."

Outside, Nate and Walter pushed Karl and Anna in their rolling chairs, Meg beside them. Olive held fast to Rose's hand, and Kristof drew Sylvie's through his arm. Together, they strolled southeast, around the edge of the Grand Basin, past the Agriculture Building with its shining Diana at its pinnacle, and skirted the South Pond. From the right, the telltale odors of cattle, horses, sheep, and pigs wafted from the Stock Pavilion. An electric elevated train clattered by on the track over their heads. A moment later, they passed the French Bakery exhibit just before Blooker's.

"Did you sleep last night?" Kristof quietly

asked Sylvie. "Did you tell Meg about . . . ?" He tipped his head toward Rose.

"Not well, and yes, I did," she replied. "We spoke before the concert began. But let's not allow that to overshadow your well-deserved celebration, all right?"

He smiled. If she could muster enthusiasm for hot chocolate, he'd let her. It was somewhere to put her mind other than on that bruised and tender place.

The wooden windmill's rotating blades cast a giant pinwheel of light and shadow on the ground. The rich fragrance of warm chocolate reached Kristof even before he opened the large wooden door, allowing the rest of the family to enter ahead of him. But inside, it was overwhelming.

A frolicking fire greeted them, along with a Dutch maiden in wooden shoes. None of the tables could seat all nine of them, and Kristof didn't complain when he and Sylvie were shown to a cozy table for two.

"I can't tell you how much it means to me that you came today. That you all came," he told Sylvie.

"Of course I came." She unbuttoned her jacket, and he moved behind her, sliding it down her arms. He draped it over the chair, which he pulled out for her. "All of us were looking forward to it, especially Karl and Anna. This will probably be the highlight of several months for them. I don't know if you realize what a gift your music is. It was so good for Rose, too. I could tell she was enjoying it immensely."

A smile edged his lips as he sat across from her. "I'm glad to hear that. See much of Ivan these days?"

Sylvie lowered her voice, though Rose was two tables away. "Not since Monday. He started work yesterday at the Polish Café, at the other end of the Fair. I wondered if she would protest when I told her we didn't have time to visit him today, but she understood. I think she's anxious about telling him of Jozefa and her offer to join her. Even if she's not as fond of him as he wishes, she still doesn't like the idea of hurting him."

Kristof wanted to ask if Rose liked the idea of hurting Sylvie, but that wasn't fair. It was Jozefa who had blown into Sylvie's household like a dignified hurricane, tearing her relationship with Rose up by the roots.

A bright-cheeked waitress arrived, and they placed their order. The young woman's wooden shoes clopped as she returned to the kitchen.

"If Jozefa were truly her mother," Kristof said, "she should have been happy to see that she's been so well cared for all these years, and should have let her feel secure in the Dabrowskis' love and in yours. All she's done is cause turmoil."

Sylvie leaned forward. "Believe me, I've

thought the same thing. But she saw how aggressively Rose was searching for her family, and Jozefa had been searching for her, too. How could she possibly resist?"

Kristof frowned. "Does it bother you that you still have no proof of her identity?"

Her mouth screwed to one side. "It does. I talked to Rose about it this morning. She said Jozefa had to sign over her rights to the baby when she surrendered it to the orphanage, and she has a dated copy of that, but she didn't bring it to America. Other than that, all she has is a lock of hair from Rose as a newborn. Apparently, she has worn it in a locket all these years."

A lock of hair didn't prove anything. "We need to talk to Mr. Janik again. He may be able to confirm some of these details."

Sylvie agreed. "Could you contact him for another meeting when you have a chance? I'd do it myself if he spoke English. But we don't have to talk about this anymore. This is your day." She smiled. "Yellow becomes you. It's really sweet of you to wear them." She nodded to Olive's wilted flowers in his jacket.

"Glad you approve."

"I do."

The waitress returned, setting cups of cocoa in front of each of them. Kristof watched Sylvie blow on its surface to cool it, then slowly take her first sip. "Good?" he asked.

"Mm-hmm." She closed her eyes in unabashed pleasure.

A smile curved Kristof's mouth. He wondered when he could hold her hand again. Or if, perhaps, she might reach for his.

Sylvie looked at him then. Enchanted him without even realizing it. "Don't you like it?"

He took his first taste of cocoa and licked the froth from his burning lips. "I do."

Thursday, September 7, 1893

Inside the Polish Café, Sylvie and Rose were shown to a table with a view of the lagoon framed by the eastern pavilion of the nearby Fisheries Building. A lazy breeze struggled through the open window, laden with the songs of gondoliers as they glided over the water. Sunshine caught on dragon-headed vessels painted purple, orange, and green.

Sylvie fixed her attention on the menu, though food was not her priority. She'd expected Rose would want to see Ivan. She was shocked that she'd been invited to come along.

"Do you see him?" Rose asked, peering over the top of her menu. "Lottie was supposed to tell him I'd come today."

The café was full, even though they'd come in the middle of the afternoon, after Sylvie's tours for the day were done. She scanned the servers carrying platters of steaming, savory dishes throughout the sunlit space.

"There he is!" Rose whispered. "I almost didn't recognize him."

Twenty paces away, a clean-shaven Ivan Mazurek wore a spotless white shirt beneath a long black vest that reached almost to his knees. Red tassels trimmed the belted vest, matching the red-and-white-striped trousers he wore tucked into black leather boots.

He was coming toward them. Of all the tables in the café, they'd been seated at one of his.

"I was hoping I'd see you soon," he said upon reaching them.

"Well, here we are!" Rose's laugh betrayed her nerves.

"Yes, I see that." He gave a stiff greeting to Sylvie. "Can we go somewhere after my shift?"

"Oh. I don't think so, Ivan." Rose knotted her fingers together. "But I was hoping I could speak to you here. Could you spare a few minutes?"

"I'd rather talk when I'm done working. We could ride a gondola." He gestured toward the window. "Every time one of them passes, I think of you. Of us, together, in one of those."

Rose blushed. Sylvie studied her menu, which was the only measure of privacy Ivan was going to get right now.

"That's a nice thought," Rose said. "But really, just sit with us when you can."

He didn't seem happy about it but agreed. "Do you know what you want to order yet?"

Predictably, Rose ordered pierogis, adding that Jozefa's version was awful. Sylvie requested only a side dish of potato pancakes.

When he took their order to the kitchen, Rose said, "He isn't going to like this. But the sooner I tell him about Jozefa's letter, the better."

"Of course," Sylvie assured her.

Rose leaned forward. "Remember, Mimi, your job is to make sure I go through with this. If you weren't here, I might not have the courage to do it. And if I were alone with him, I—" She pursed her lips. "He can be very persuasive. He'll try to talk me out of anything that would take me away from him. He does have a bit of a temper, but with you here, and with all these people . . ."

"If he wants to keep this job," Sylvie said, "he'll find a way to control his reaction."

Not ten minutes later, Ivan returned and took the seat beside Rose. "All right, what's this all about?" He draped his arm across the back of her wooden chair, claiming her.

A deep inhale seemed to steady Rose as she faced him. "Do you remember the locket Jozefa wore all the time? It had a lock of hair inside from her baby."

His brows knit together. "So?"

465

Rose sent a glance toward Sylvie before continuing. "Jozefa and I had long talks about that baby, a daughter she gave up for adoption when the baby was just a week old."

Sylvie straightened. She'd thought Jozefa had only mentioned the locket for the first time in the letter.

"I heard some of that story," Ivan said. "She wasn't married, and she wanted to keep acting. So somewhere out there you have a long-lost cousin. Is that what she was telling you?"

"I thought so," Rose said. "She asked me if I thought she should try to contact her daughter, or if she should just leave her alone. I told her that if she knew where she was, she ought to at least try."

Understanding filtered through Sylvie like a wave of nausea. Jozefa had been preparing Rose, step by calculated step, the entire time.

"But what if the daughter was happy where she was?" Ivan asked. "What if she didn't even know she'd been adopted? It seems like Jozefa should have decided when she gave birth what she really wanted."

Color stained Rose's cheeks. "Jozefa asked me those questions, too."

"And?" He was growing impatient, either with the story, or with Jozefa, or both.

"And I said I didn't know the answer. But she kept talking about it, almost every evening after you'd gone home for the day. She told me how miserable she was for what she'd done, how she longed to make things right somehow. I felt truly sorry for her."

Which was exactly what Jozefa wanted. Sylvie bit her tongue to keep from saying anything. This was another layer of manipulation, but the motivation, at least, was understandable. Jozefa needed to know if Rose could see the situation from her perspective before risking the unvarnished truth.

"I don't feel sorry for her," Ivan said. "My mother would never do that, no matter what. What kind of mother gives her own baby away, for any reason?"

"She didn't think she could give her a good home without a father." Defensiveness climbed into Rose's voice.

A short laugh burst from Ivan. "That's an excuse if I ever heard one. How many families do you know that still have fathers? How many of those fathers make it a 'good' home? No, she gets no sympathy from me. It's ironic, though. You lost both your parents, and she willingly gave up a perfectly healthy baby. So what did you tell her to do?"

Rose took a drink of water, clearly stalling. Wavering. Sylvie nodded for her to continue.

"I—" Rose dabbed a napkin to her lips. "I told her if she ever found her daughter again, then it was meant to be, given how little information she had about her. If Jozefa found her, she could try contacting her. She'd regret it for her entire life if she didn't."

Sylvie's mouth went dry. It was the perfect setup, and Rose had responded exactly the way Jozefa had hoped.

Ivan shrugged. "Makes no difference to me. I don't understand what Jozefa's baby has to do with you either, especially if you have no idea where she is."

Rose's nostrils flared. Color bloomed on her neck. "But I do know, Ivan. She's right here. It's me. The hair in the locket is mine."

He frowned. "You just said that was Jozefa's baby's."

A lump bobbed behind Rose's collar. "Yes." She hesitated. "Jozefa wrote me after she left. She isn't my aunt. She's my mother. She named me Rozalia. I was the baby she gave away."

Sylvie listened intently to Rose's tone, her words, the spaces between the words. She hadn't said, *"She thinks she is my mother,"* or *"She says she is my mother."* She had presented the statement as fact. The realization tore a fissure somewhere inside Sylvie. It was small, and halfway expected. But now that it was there, she could feel herself deflating, releasing every breath she'd held.

"She could be lying again." Ivan glowered.

"Miss Townsend, do you believe this? You can't."

Sylvie's throat scratched like sand when she swallowed. "I have no proof either way." She twisted the linen napkin in her lap.

"Jozefa might have given up a baby girl named Rozalia," Ivan argued, "but there must be thousands of girls with your name out there."

Sylvie listened as Rose supplied more details to convince him. Then she lifted her chin. "She asked me to reconsider her invitation to go to Poland with her. She'll be in New York City for several weeks before setting sail."

Ivan stood, the blood-red tassels on his vest swaying with the abrupt movement. "And?"

"And I'm considering it. I wanted to let you know."

"You've already considered it. Say no. I don't want you to go."

Rose's eyes glittered with irritation. "What about what I want? If I decide not to reunite with my mother, it won't be to cater to your whim. Why can't you be the least bit happy for me? Don't you understand? *I found my mother.*"

Whirling from her, Ivan marched away.

Slouching, Rose rested her forehead in her hand. "He's angry."

"It's a shock," Sylvie managed to say. "It's understandable, given how he feels about you."

"If he loved me, wouldn't he want what I want for myself?"

469

Somewhere else in the restaurant, a server dropped a tray of dishes. Sylvie barely noticed. "So you've decided already?" She turned to the window, unable to keep the pain from her expression.

"Sometimes I think I have. How could I do otherwise, when I advised her to tell her daughter what happened? When I fed her hope that any daughter would find a way to forgive her?" But then she moaned. "That was before I knew that daughter was me. Oh, Mimi, I'm so tired of people telling me what to do. And then, sometimes, I just wish someone would tell me what to do!" The laugh that followed was cheerless.

Sylvie faced her and watched a tear trace her cheek.

Rose wiped it away with a fingertip. "Aren't you going to tell me what to do?"

Stay here, Sylvie's battered heart cried. *Stay safe, stay with me!* But she trapped the words in her throat. Instead, she forced a smile. "Not this time, dear. This choice is yours alone."

Ivan returned with a tray. The surface of the small table disappeared beneath dishes Sylvie had never seen before. No pierogis or potato pancakes were among them.

"What's this?" Rose asked.

"Polish food. What else?" Ivan tucked his tray beneath his arm. "If you're going to move there, you'll need to get used to it. In front of

Miss Townsend is *kaszanka*." He pointed to fat sausage links. "Made from pig's blood and buckwheat *kasza*, fried with onions and stuffed in pig intestines, with horseradish on the side." Then he described a soup called *czernina*, made with duck blood and poultry broth.

"And for you, Rose, the real specialty." Ivan pinched the edge of the plate set before her and shook it, jiggling the gelatinous mound it held. "*Nóżki w galarecie*." Through the clear molded gelatin, chopped carrots and peas were layered over jellied cow's feet.

Rose covered her mouth and pushed it away. "You deliberately brought us the only dishes I wouldn't like."

"Are you sure?" Ivan opened a menu and held it at her eye level. "Take a look."

"You're being ridiculous." Rose's complexion burned red. "You know I can't eat this, just like you know I can't read that menu."

"I'm the ridiculous one?" He laughed. "Listen to yourself. You can't read Polish aside from the word *pierogi*. You can't speak or understand it. Don't assume Jozefa will teach you either. You asked her to at the Palmer. She knew she would invite you to go to Poland with her, and she still didn't teach you any of the language. She wants you to depend on her. For everything." The vein at his temple throbbed.

Sylvie's mind spun, searching for any other

reason Jozefa hadn't taught Rose Polish. Did she consider it premature? Was she superstitious enough to believe it might bring bad luck?

"Things will be different if I move there," Rose insisted. "I'll learn it on my own if I have to."

Ivan folded his arms. "Miss Townsend, you can't let her do this."

A wedge of helplessness slid between Sylvie's ribs. "If she wants to go, I won't stop her."

Friday, September 8, 1893

The fact that Kristof had known this day was coming didn't make it any easier when it arrived.

Outside, rain fell from swagged clouds suspended just over the courthouse and city hall. It tapped the windows in sliding, silver beads.

Gregor sat across the kitchen table, a lock of hair escaping his pomade and curling at his temple. "I don't understand why you can't give me a little more time. We're family." His belongings were packed and by the door.

"Come on, Gregor. I've already given you a week's extension, and you know it isn't just about the money."

"Are you still sore about Sunday? I could have gotten home just fine even if Karl hadn't come to get me."

Excuses were so ingrained in Gregor's

reasoning that Kristof doubted he even realized what he was doing. They had talked about this multiple times without traction. Gregor's answer for the drugs, the women, and the gambling had been insincere apologies, empty promises to reform, and declarations that Kristof wasn't perfect either—a fact Kristof already knew and was learning to accept. They were dogs chasing their own tails.

"You aren't fine." Kristof looped his thumb through the handle of his coffee mug. "You need help, and all I've done is hinder you from growing up."

Gregor smoothed his hair back into place. "We're brothers. Doesn't that mean anything to you?" His pupils were pinpoints, his complexion flushed. Both were signs, Kristof had learned, that opium was in his brother's system even now, discounting everything Gregor was saying.

"It's because I love you that I'm letting you go," Kristof explained. Gregor would probably hit rock bottom, but he needed to in order to finally look up and see how low he'd sunk, and that there was Light above, if only he would reach for it.

"Letting me go," Gregor scoffed. "You're literally kicking me out into the rain." As if on cue, thunder clapped, shaking the windowpanes and the dishes in the cupboard.

"You've had time to arrange employment and

lodging," Kristof said. "Did you check with the Austrian or Hungarian orchestras at the Fair? Either might be interested in another violinist, especially one of your talent, and they have space for you to lodge with them, as well. It might hold you over until you can audition again for the Chicago Symphony Orchestra." If he could humble himself to do so.

Gregor waved a hand dismissively. He scratched his neck and behind his ear, the itching skin another drug-induced symptom. "I heard you the first time you suggested it. No, I haven't gone begging for crumbs. That's not my style. You know that."

"If you keep up this dissolute lifestyle, begging for crumbs is exactly what you'll be doing."

"Oh, really? Would a beggar be able to afford this?" Reaching into a pocket, Gregor produced their father's gold pocket watch with the flourish of one who'd been keeping an ace up his sleeve. By his triumphant smirk, he appeared to believe he was calling Kristof's bluff. That this one card would change everything.

Kristof picked up the watch, rubbing his thumb over the cold, smooth surface. He unlatched the cover, and two small diamonds winked at him. This piece cost far more than a month's rent, even at the pawnshop's price.

"Do you see?" Gregor leaned back in his chair, inclining his head. He was completely at ease now. "I told you I'd get that back. I said you could count on me, and I came through. For you. This is what brothers do. I know you've always wanted it."

The weight in Kristof's hand as he held it was so much lighter than the memories attached to it. Vividly he recalled trying to talk to his father about some childhood concern. Instead of looking at Kristof's face, his father's attention had been fixed on the watch's. *"Time is precious,"* his father would say, pointing to the ticking second hand. By the time Kristof reached adolescence, he'd learned a dual lesson: that time was precious, and that he wasn't. Gregor was precious, but not Kristof.

But his heavenly Father said he was, imperfections and all. Thanks to Sylvie and the Hoffmans, he finally believed it.

Kristof snapped the cover back into place. "It wasn't Father's timepiece I wanted. It was his time." He slid the watch back across the table, releasing everything it represented. "I have no need of this."

Gregor stared. "You jest. This is a symbol of Father's approval, the one thing you've wanted your whole life. You can hold on to it now, wear it like a badge!"

"I might have envied your possession of it once, but no more. Keep it. Father wanted you to have it, after all." And at this rate, Gregor might need to pawn it himself. Kristof folded his hands and studied his brother. "I do find it odd that you found enough money to purchase this but not enough to pay half of this month's rent."

Grimacing, Gregor massaged the back of his neck. "So you noticed." He laughed. "Funny thing, that. As it turns out, Johnny Friendly extended me a loan so I could secure it before anyone else did. Time was of the essence, you know."

A coldness spread from the center of Kristof's chest. "Johnny Friendly," he repeated, incredulous.

"Why not? I had a need, and he had the resources. It worked out." But the tic near his eye betrayed him.

"Next you'll tell me he did this out of the kindness of his heart."

Gregor laughed again. "No, nothing so sentimental as that. He calls it an investment."

Kristof clenched his jaw. "Of what sort?" This didn't sound like conventional gambling.

"The profitable kind. For him. I'll pay him back one way or another. Either with cash, or—" Gregor rubbed the side of his nose. "If not cash, I'll pay him in kind."

Questions and conclusions exploded in Kristof's mind. "How exactly will you do that? Play the violin for him until your debt is paid?"

"Ah, if only he appreciated my talent."

Gregor's smile played false. He was nervous. Scared? "Alas, I'll provide services of a different variety."

The words strung out upon a thin, taut wire, unfurling the dread in Kristof's middle. Covering his face with his hand, he groaned. "You're working for him now. You're not just stuck in his web, you're part of it."

"Only if I'm unlucky! And it would be temporary. Nothing for you to be so worried about."

Kristof's fingers curled into fists. "How in heaven's name could you agree to this, for any reason? Do you have any idea what you've done?"

Darkness flattened against the window, transforming the view to a reflection of two brothers at odds. Lightning forked the roiling clouds.

Gregor's mottled complexion turned sallow in the gaslight. "I did it for you, Kristof."

But such blame found no purchase. "You cannot pin this on me. You know I never would have approved."

"No. You rarely do."

Kristof bristled. "It's your risks I take issue with, Gregor, and your reckless disregard for how they affect other people. You're the only one who hasn't noticed how destructive your pattern of behavior is."

Scooping their father's timepiece back into his

pocket, Gregor pushed back from the table and stood. "I can't help myself."

"Maybe that's true, maybe it isn't." Kristof rose, as well. "Either way, God can."

"You imply I want to be helped." Gregor settled his hat on his head and shrugged his jacket over his shoulders. "You don't understand the thrill of laying it all on the line, riding that razor-thin edge between winning and losing. There's nothing like it in the world. I'd suggest you try it sometime instead of judging me for it, but I know you won't."

He was right about that. If Kristof had harbored any qualms about evicting his brother, they would have shattered beneath Gregor's last speech. He would never change as long as he had no desire to repent.

"You don't think you're in trouble now," Kristof said, "but one day you'll realize the depth of your need."

"When that day comes, you'll be the first to know." Gregor bounced a finger off the brim of his hat.

"That's not what I had in mind." Kristof grasped his brother's shoulder. "The folks at Pacific Garden Mission on South Clark Street are there to help. They'll know what to do. Promise me you'll remember that."

Gregor's bravado slipped, and Kristof glimpsed genuine surprise that Kristof wasn't offering a future rescue himself. In the next instant, it was up again. "Sure," Gregor said. "Whatever you say."

His throat aching with unspoken words and wishes, Kristof offered his hand. When Gregor shook it, Kristof pulled him close, clapping him twice on the back. "Take care of yourself."

He released his brother, and Gregor left.

Wind moaned outside the building. Kristof went to the window, watching for Gregor through rain that had thinned to a drizzle. Suitcase in tow, Gregor appeared below, umbrella swinging from his other hand. A calculated distance behind him, another man stepped away from a lamppost and followed, the light of a cigar flaring and fading as he went.

Chapter Thirty-Two

Saturday, September 9, 1893

The smell of fresh-brewed coffee permeated the not-yet-open Corner Books & More. Sunlight slanted between the orange velvet drapes, spilling golden ribbons across the floor. On her way to check the cash register, Sylvie smiled in silent greeting at familiar characters framed against the deep purple walls. No wonder she never felt alone here. Then she stilled before the portrait of Fanny Price. *"She's a monster, you know,"* Rose had said of Jane Austen's favorite heroine. *"She doesn't belong anywhere."*

"You do belong," Sylvie said aloud, an echo of what she'd told Rose again last night. She'd received the same wordless, thoughtful gaze in response. Rose already seemed to be traveling away from her.

A creak sounded from the back of the store, followed by footfalls. "Sylvie?" Kristof called.

"Yes, here." Brushing out her skirt from her belted waist, she met him in the bistro area.

The shadows weren't strong enough to hide the creases on his brow, nor the dark crescents that hung below his eyes. "I did it." He cleared his throat. "I sent Gregor away last night." His tone was that of a person announcing the death of a loved one. Full and yet broken.

Sympathy filled Sylvie. "I'm so sorry it came to this."

"I had to." He swallowed. "I had to let him go."

She tangled her fingers with his, wishing she could press into him the empathy she struggled to express in words. She was beginning to feel the tear of letting go herself.

"Doing the right thing," she said at length, "often means doing the hard thing. That takes courage. And faith to believe that he'll be all right without you there to make sure of it." As soon as she heard the words, she feared she needed them as much as he did.

Kristof entwined her fingers more securely with his own. "Thank you. He's at the start of a long and winding journey, but you're right. God can work in his life without my help."

"He can," Sylvie agreed. "He will." It was so easy to say when it came to Gregor. Would she sound so sure of herself when it was time to release Rose?

"I'm keeping you from opening the store." Kristof released her hand. "Can I help?"

Sylvie asked him to open all the drapes while she unlocked the front door and flipped the sign. "Have you heard anything back from Mr. Janik?" She blinked at the light suddenly filling the shop and grabbed a dust rag from under the counter.

"Not directly. I stopped at his hotel to see if I had his room number correct and found they had forwarded my note to a different address."

Disappointment stung as Sylvie ran the cloth over the window display table. "So he's returned to Poland already?" It had been a few weeks since they met him. She wouldn't be surprised.

"I don't think a hotel or the postal service would pay to forward a letter overseas. My guess is he's sightseeing somewhere else in the U.S. If he gets my letter, I'm sure he'll respond. We just have to wait and see."

Wait. Again. Sylvie tried not to show her impatience as she went to the biography section.

Kristof joined her. "Has Rose given any thought to resuming her violin lessons?" He took the rag from her hand and wiped down the tops of the cases where she couldn't reach.

"She hasn't so much as touched her instrument since receiving the letter in which Jozefa said she was her mother. I suspect she's honoring Jozefa's wishes that she not pursue it because it was a shared interest with Magdalena."

"That's a shame." He kept dusting the tops of the shelves, from biography to history.

When he moved to the domestic science section, Sylvie stole back the rag. "I have an idea, Kristof. If she isn't taking violin from you, could she—would you be willing to teach her Polish?"

"Mimi!" Rose's voice soared over the towering

bookshelves from some unseen place. "Do you mean it?"

Chuckling, Sylvie threaded between the cases to the checkout counter, where Rose stood bearing pastries from the Hoffmans.

"Are you going to drop that?" Sylvie gestured to the tilting platter.

"Oh!" Rose set it down and began arranging sugar-dusted Berliners on the pedestals on the refreshment table. "But did I hear you right? Polish lessons?"

"You asked Mrs. Górecki for help, and you asked Jozefa," Sylvie said. "This is obviously important to you."

Besides, Ivan's point at the restaurant, while distastefully made, had hit its mark. If Rose was set on going to Poland, Sylvie wanted her to understand as much of the language as possible. If she decided to stay in Chicago, having a grasp of her native tongue would still be fulfilling and useful in a city of immigrants.

"Will you teach me, Mr. Bartok? Please?"

Kristof placed the glass domes over the pastry-laden platters, a task clearly beyond Rose's attention. "We'd need to meet often in order to make real progress in the next several weeks. Would you be up for daily lessons?"

"Absolutely. I'll work harder than you've ever seen me do before."

He agreed, and Sylvie smiled her thanks at

Kristof. This was the right thing to do for Rose. That didn't mean reaching this conclusion had been easy.

The bell chimed over the door when Tessa arrived, unpinning her hat from her dark hair. As Rose glided over to chat with her, a customer entered.

"Rose!" Mrs. Abbott called loudly. "It's so good to see you again. I've been wondering where you've been this last month. Where have you been hiding?"

"Nice to see you, too, Mrs. Abbott." Despite Rose's polite greeting, she stepped back, away from the well-meaning woman and the question she had no desire to answer.

While Tessa informed Mrs. Abbott about the special offer for Chicago Day tickets to the Fair, Kristof quietly called to Rose. "I've got a date with Karl and Anna in a few minutes to play their favorite board game. Play on my team?"

Rose brightened. "I saw they kept back some Berliners. We should probably help them take care of those. They're best when they're fresh, you know."

"Ah. The Hoffmans never fail to feed my sweet teeth."

A giggle tripped out of Rose. "Um. That's sweet *tooth,* Mr. Bartok. Let's not keep them waiting."

Kristof winked over her head at Sylvie, then left with Rose.

Sylvie was still smiling when she rang up the purchases Tessa had helped Mrs. Abbott select.

The rest of the day drifted by on a string of pleasant conversations with beloved customers and friends. Tessa mentioned that Rose was welcome to join her roommates for dinner any time. Meg stopped by to invite Sylvie, Rose, and Kristof to Olive's birthday party. She also extended an invitation from Hazel for Rose to lunch with her after church tomorrow. Beth visited, too, sharing stories from the Fair and inquiring about Rose. Her lips all but disappeared in a thin line when Sylvie shared briefly about the incident at the Polish Café.

"Quite right that she wanted you with her," Beth replied gruffly, her complexion pale on Rose's behalf. "If she steers clear of him altogether from now on, it won't be too soon."

Closing time came, Tessa left, and Sylvie locked up the store. Before she headed upstairs for the evening, she paused at the portrait of Fanny Price and saw Rose in her troubled face. "You are loved," Sylvie whispered. "You belong. You're already home."

Saturday, September 23, 1893

"Are you sure you don't want to go?" Kristof craned his neck to take in Mr. Ferris's colossal steel wheel. He and Sylvie were here to celebrate Olive's birthday, and the adventurous eight-year-old wanted nothing more than to spend a few hours on the Midway, including a trip around the giant wheel. The entire Pierce family, along with Rose, was already in line to buy tickets.

Sylvie wrinkled her nose. "I'm staying right here on solid ground. But if you've never been, don't stay behind on my account." A tendril of her rich brown hair swayed against her cheek.

"And miss out on twenty minutes I could be spending with you?"

She peered at him from beneath the brim of her straw hat. "I've seen you every day for the last two weeks."

Every evening, Kristof had tutored Rose in Polish at Sylvie's kitchen table. Sylvie brought them mugs of steaming hot chocolate—*"for your sweet teeth"*—and then read in the parlor. Rose was progressing quickly, and he enjoyed teaching her. But it wasn't an adequate substitute for spending time with Sylvie. To say that he missed her sounded ridiculous. But it was no less true.

With a gleam in her eye, Sylvie pinched his necktie and skewed it slightly off-center behind his vest. He straightened it with an extra show of precision to draw that particular smile that bloomed only for him.

There.

He chuckled, even as he felt the returning

ache of wanting more than just her smile. Their friendship had become a suspended chord unresolved, a fermata held too long.

From the line ahead of them, Meg turned and beckoned, and Kristof waited while Sylvie hurried to her sister, her hips twisting as she set a brisk pace. "We're sitting this one out," he heard her say. "My stomach will thank me for it. You doing all right?"

He knew she was asking if Meg was able to enjoy Olive and set aside thoughts of Louise's death. Meg nodded and replied too quietly for him to hear. Sylvie kissed her cheek, bent to speak to Olive, then returned to Kristof's side.

"How is she?" He guided her to a bench. "How's Nate?"

"Both well." Sylvie adjusted her plum-colored skirt over her knees as she sat. "The Midway is a merciful distraction. And, of course, Olive's enthusiasm for it all is contagious."

Behind them, an orchestra played on the second floor of the Vienna Café, the music cascading from the open windows. To their right was a model of St. Peter's basilica, whose spire pointed to the purpling evening sky. Thrilled screams of Ice Railway riders floated over its top. From where they sat, he could see the minarets of Cairo Street on the left and the great blue dome of the Moorish Palace on the right. Aromas of coffee and sausage mixed with those of cumin, coriander, and slow-roasting lamb.

"Still," Sylvie murmured, "I should have checked on her more these last couple of weeks. It's a difficult time of year."

"You visited her twice," he gently reminded her. Meanwhile, Kristof hadn't heard from Gregor since the day he left the apartment. Not that he expected to. He had hoped, however, to see his brother playing the violin somewhere on the Midway and at least find out how he was. Kristof had checked with the Hungarian Orpheum, the Vienna Café, the German Village, and every other concession that featured a stringed instrument. He'd even asked Maestro Thomas if Gregor had been in touch to re-audition.

No sign of him.

Kristof had stopped himself from checking the opium dens. Old habits of keeping watch on his brother proved painfully hard to break.

A camel walked by with its driver. Bells jingled from the animal's tasseled bridle, snapping Kristof's line of thought. He turned back to Sylvie.

"Meg understands you've had your own cares, too," he said. From what Sylvie had told him, Rose had received at least four more letters from Jozefa in the last two weeks. And up until last week, Ivan had been sending her messages through Lottie.

Thankfully, Wiktor Janik had finally replied.

Sylvie had been thrilled to learn that Janik would be coming back through Chicago and would meet with them, and with Rose, on Monday, October 9. Because that date was Chicago Day and full of special events at the Fair, no tours would be scheduled.

In a break between pieces played by the Vienna Café's orchestra, Kristof heard the distinctive notes of a snake charmer's *pungi*. He scanned the main thoroughfare outside Cairo Street until he found a cobra rising from a wicker basket. Onlookers gathered in a wide circle.

One of them disregarded the snake. Thumbs hooked in his belt, Ivan Mazurek watched the wheel ascend toward the sky. A muscle bunched in Kristof's jaw. The realization that Ivan had been following Rose again lined his gut with lead. What would he do if he got her alone?

Eventually the young man noticed Kristof. Shoulders slumping, he walked away.

"Has Ivan sent any notes to Rose lately?" Keeping his tone casual, Kristof watched Ivan until he was out of sight.

"Since you threw him out on his ear?" Sylvie laughed.

He wasn't sure what *on his ear* meant exactly, but he'd gotten pretty good at guessing. "At least I didn't break his nose."

"You looked like you were thinking about it."

"Don't pretend you blame me."

489

"I don't." She inched closer to him on the bench, the folds of her swagged skirt brushing his knee, draping him with warmth on this mild September evening.

Kristof stretched his arm on the bench behind her, feeling again the protective instinct that had fired through him on Rose's behalf last Friday. During their Polish lesson, Ivan had burst into the apartment, at first claiming he was there to escort Lottie and her weekly wages home. Then he'd demanded to be alone with Rose, becoming more irate with her refusal.

"You're making a huge mistake," Ivan had growled when he found her preparing to live in Poland.

"This is my decision, my life, we're talking about," Rose had spat back.

"You make it sound like your life is completely separate from mine."

"It is," she had replied, and Ivan had stepped back as though struck, then lunged.

Kristof hated to think what would have happened next if he hadn't been there to block Ivan and see him out. On his ear. Apparently, Kristof's remark about Sydney Carton's heroics had missed its mark if Ivan was still pursuing her.

"No," Sylvie said, "Ivan hasn't sent any more notes that I'm aware of. She told me she wouldn't read them if he did. He's in her way, she says, and she doesn't have time for that." She traced the wheel's gigantic revolution, her gaze fixed on the car carrying her entire family. Up, up, she followed the movement, until her head rested lightly on his outstretched arm. "I'm watching her float away, Kristof." Heartbreak spilled from the cracks in her voice.

He was tempted to point to the apex and tell her the car was coming back to her. But the wheel was not a trustworthy metaphor.

"You're giving her wings and the freedom to use them," he told her. "Choice is one of the greatest gifts there is." He'd tried to give Sylvie freedom, too. He was still waiting to see if she would ever choose him, the way he'd long ago chosen her.

Straightening, she angled to face him, her eyes glassy. "Who could have guessed what this summer held? Will we both lose the ones we love most in the same short span of time?"

Kristof shook his head. He twirled Sylvie's wayward lock of hair around his finger. "I love Gregor. He'll always be my brother. But he's not the one I love most." He cupped her smooth, sun-warmed cheek and held his breath while she took this in, wondering if he'd played a wrong note.

Her lips parted in surprise. "Kristof," she whispered, tears lining her lashes. She covered his hand with hers and leaned into it. Her smile held a symphony of hope.

After Olive's birthday party, once Sylvie was alone in her room, she still held the feeling of Kristof's touch, still heard the words he'd said and the words he hadn't.

He loved her. There was no mistaking this translation. Kristof loved her in a way that no one else ever had before. Knees going soft, she sank onto the edge of her bed. Her own eyes stared back at her from a portrait Meg had painted right after her hands healed from the burns she'd suffered during the Great Fire. The girl in the portrait was so young, her eyes bright and eager with what she thought was true, exhilarating love. Twenty-two years had passed since then.

Sylvie removed her hat. Before the looking glass on the wall, she inspected the coarse grey hairs sparkling at her part, the softening of her jawline. The fine webs at her eyes when she smiled.

The girl in the portrait knew nothing of love.

The woman in the mirror did.

A knock tapped her door. "Mimi? Can we talk?"

"Of course." Sylvie followed Rose into the parlor.

Rose had changed into a nightdress embroidered with little blue flowers. Magdalena's shawl draped her shoulders. It was the first time she'd worn it since that first letter arrived from Jozefa more than two weeks ago.

She settled into the sofa. "Sit with me."

After turning on a lamp, Sylvie joined her. "Did you have fun today?" Tiny Tim stretched out on the rug at their feet.

"Mmm. Loads." Lips tilted, Rose worked on braiding her hair for sleep. "I saw you and Mr. Bartok."

Instantly, Sylvie's cheeks flamed hot. Especially the one Kristof had touched so tenderly. Her hand went to the spot, as though she could hide that sweet moment or keep it for herself. "On the bench, you mean?"

"Everywhere. I see you together and I wonder why I never noticed it before. He's nice, Mimi. I like him. I like him for *you.*"

Sylvie allowed a small smile. "I like him, too." She fumbled for words. *I think he loves me,* she didn't say. *I think I love him. I think this love may be greater than the sum of my objections.* It was too grand a revelation to confess right now, one she would take to bed with her and ponder while crickets played outside, and she would wonder if Kristof in his room directly above hers was thinking of her, too. She wondered if he worried he'd said too much.

He had not.

And she had said too little.

Vexed at herself, she began pulling pins from

her hair and raked her fingers over her scalp, massaging the places that had been pulled too tight. "We care for each other a great deal."

Laughter tumbled out of Rose. "Obviously." She held up a hand when Sylvie opened her mouth to speak. "It's all right, Mimi. Your heart is so big. I know there's room in there for both of us." Her slender fingers flashed over her hair, tying the braid's end with a blue ribbon.

"Thank you," Sylvie said quietly. "I think you're right."

"Of course I am." But the smirk Sylvie expected didn't follow. Instead, Rose's countenance sagged.

"What is it?"

Rose crossed her arms. "Hazel and I had such a scare today. We lost Olive at Hagenbeck's Animal Show."

"What?" Confusion kept alarm at bay. Sylvie, Kristof, Meg, and Nate had waited outside the animal enclosure, saving on the fares. Forty minutes after Walter, Hazel, Rose, and Olive had entered, they had all returned.

Rose bit her lower lip and burrowed deeper into the corner of the sofa, folding her legs beneath her. "She was with Hazel and me for a while, and then she went to join Walter instead. Or we thought she did. Later we found Walter, but she wasn't with him. I was terrified. I didn't even think my legs would carry me as we frantically searched for her. It wasn't five minutes later that we found her, but, Mimi, I keep thinking that panic was what you felt when you thought I was missing, too. Only you felt it for weeks, not just minutes." Tears spilled down her cheeks. "I'm so sorry for doing that to you. I'm so very sorry. Will you forgive me?"

The words spread over a wound in Sylvie that had so far been untended. A balm. A promise of healing to come. "Of course, dear. I already have." She pulled out her handkerchief and wiped Rose's face. "It's all right now. You're safe. Olive is safe."

Nodding, Rose drew a shuddering breath.

"Olive loves exploring, just as much as you did when you were a child." Sylvie asked if Rose remembered the two times she'd slipped away.

"I remember." Her expression pulled into grave lines. "I wasn't just exploring. I was searching for my father. I wasn't lost. I was trying to find my family."

Sylvie felt a melting in her spine.

Rose had never stopped searching. She had never been truly lost. She had only been lost to Sylvie.

And Sylvie had lost sight of something else. The knowledge that she had only ever been a steward of this child's life. A temporary way-station. Nothing more. She tried to nod in acknowledgment of Rose's confession, but her head, unbearably heavy, would not lift after it dipped.

Tears clotted in her throat. "Magdalena's shawl," she said at last. "Why are you wearing it again?"

Rose brushed the fringe with her fingertips. "It wasn't Magdalena's. Not at first. Mother told me in her last letter that this was the shawl she wrapped me in when she surrendered me to the orphanage. That's how she knew, when she saw this shawl, that I was the Rozalia she'd given up. And the one she can no longer live without."

Ah. A great, long sigh exhaled from Sylvie through the fissure that had opened at the Polish Café when Rose first called Jozefa her mother. She emptied herself through this tear, pushing out every expectation and false hope until there was nothing left but a vacuum. Closing her eyes, Sylvie opened her palms in a gesture of release. She gave up clutching, grasping, seizing. She gave up filling herself with Rose.

It was over. She was empty. *Fill me, Lord,* she prayed. *Fill me with Your love for her. Not mine.*

Sylvie opened her eyes and found herself stretching her fingers backward, just as Meg did to combat the contracture of scar tissue that would otherwise shape her hands into claws. Sylvie's heart was not so different. Its natural bent was to hold. Letting go, she knew, would not be a onetime exercise, but a habitual fight. But for Rose's good, she would do it.

All of this she realized with a clarity so sharp it brought physical pain.

Banishing her own desires, Sylvie steadied herself to speak. "I love you, Rose," she began. "More than I ever thought possible. Selfishly, I want you to be here in my life." But she would not manipulate and trap like Jozefa had, or use feelings like weapons, like Ivan. Nor would she march and shout like Beth. "But you're old enough to decide the course of your own future. I'm grateful for the time God gave me with you. You have my blessing." She nearly choked on the words. "You're free. You're free to choose your mother."

Chapter Thirty-Three

Monday, October 9, 1893

Lake Michigan at his back, Kristof planted his feet wide while wind gusted at him from behind. Sylvie's green wool skirt billowed before her, and long strands of her hair whipped about her face. She reached for his hand, and he held it fast. He would hold it—hold her—every day, if she'd let him.

He was beginning to think she might.

But right now wasn't the time to push for any sort of declaration, not with her mind so occupied with her dwindling time with Rose. During the past two weeks, between his own violin practicing and meetings with the maestro about the fast-approaching symphony season, Kristof had doubled his Polish lessons with Rose. In less than two weeks, she would very likely board a train for New York and join Jozefa of her own free will. The long good-bye between Sylvie and Rose had already begun.

Breakers from the lake splashed against the back of the Peristyle, tossing white spray toward circling grey gulls. Kristof and Sylvie faced the Court of Honor, watching for both Rose and Wiktor Janik among the ever-growing throng pouring in between the Grand Basin and the buildings surrounding it. A fifteen-foot-wide path had been cordoned off for the Night Pageant in honor of Chicago Day, and already the Columbian Guards needed to hold those lines.

When they passed through the gates at noon, the ticket taker told Sylvie that sales had already shattered the Paris World's Fair record for attendance in a single day—and that had been nearly four hundred thousand. And the people kept on coming.

"I'm sure these crowds will slow Rose down." Sylvie's cheeks pinked in the crisp, sixty-degree weather. "As soon as we see Mr. Janik, let's take him inside. Rose will know where to find us."

He agreed. Rose had spent the afternoon with Hazel and Walter. Kristof hoped she would meet Janik as planned but suspected the urgency had dimmed. She wanted Jozefa, not more stories of Magdalena and Nikolai.

Kristof checked his timepiece. Quarter to six. The sky blushed at the coming night.

"There he is." Kristof pointed out Mr. Janik to Sylvie, then muscled a path down the steps and through a sea of black derby hats to meet him.

"Good evening!" Kristof said in Polish, grasping the older man's elbow as much to keep track of him as to hold him steady. Sylvie looped her hand through Janik's other arm. "How about a quieter place to talk?"

Nodding, Janik apologized for his delay and allowed Kristof to lead him into Music Hall.

Shadows and bunting draped the dim, cavernous hall. What the gigantic venue lacked in coziness and charm, it made up for in the ability to be heard.

"Please." Kristof gestured to the back row of seats in the auditorium.

Janik sat between him and Sylvie. After placing his derby on his knee, he brushed some kind of confetti from his lapels.

"Thank you so much for agreeing to meet with us again," Sylvie began. Kristof translated her gratitude, followed by inquiries as to his health and recent travels.

"But I suspect you did not ask me here to find out about my relatives in St. Louis." Janik winked.

Sylvie glanced at the door. Still no sign of Rose. "You're right," she said anyway. "We recently learned that Rozalia was adopted by Magdalena and Nikolai Dabrowski, most likely when she was an infant. You didn't mention it last time we spoke. We wondered if you knew anything about it."

As Kristof translated, grooves chiseled Janik's brow.

"No," he said. "This is not possible. Who told you such a lie?"

500

Prompted by Sylvie, Kristof explained everything he knew about Jozefa.

"Not possible," Janik said again.

Sylvie's lips pinched at one corner. "Kristof, I wonder just how close he was with the Dabrowskis," she murmured. "If Magdalena and Nikolai wanted everyone to believe Rozalia was their biological child, they could have lied about it or just let neighbors assume incorrectly."

He turned back to Janik. "Respectfully, sir, how can you be certain?"

The older man's wiry eyebrows bounced, then drew together. "I was Magdalena's doctor. I delivered the baby."

Sure he'd heard incorrectly, Kristof asked him to repeat himself before interpreting.

She gasped. "Why didn't he tell us this before?"

Janik spread his hands. "Why should I think it mattered? I was their friend and neighbor first. Their doctor second. Besides, I've been retired these many years."

Kristof pondered this as he shared it with Sylvie. She looked as confused as he felt.

"Please," she said. "Your story contradicts what Jozefa has told us. How do we know who to believe?"

Dr. Janik huffed. "I can't account for this other story. But I can tell you that delivering Rozalia nearly took Magdalena's life. Soon afterward,

I performed a surgery to make sure she never conceived again."

How Kristof wished Rose was here as he told Sylvie exactly what Dr. Janik had said.

Bewilderment flashed over Sylvie's face. "There must be some misunderstanding."

"I tell you God's truth," the doctor insisted. "After Rozalia was born, when I told my wife I'd have to perform the surgery, my wife crocheted a shawl and gave it to Magdalena for her recovery. I don't know who this Jozefa woman is, but she most certainly is not Rozalia Dabrowski's mother." Concern carved deep seams in his face.

"Tell me." Sylvie seemed to be winding tighter by the minute. "Don't change anything or try to explain it, just tell me exactly what he said."

Kristof obliged, implications and questions swirling in his mind like scattered notes unbound by a score.

"This can't be true." But the vibrato in Sylvie's voice belied the words.

Janik pulled up one leg of his trousers and pointed below the cuff. "Look, my wife also made socks for me of the same blend of her favorite yarns. I would know it anywhere. We own many items made from this wool." A peacock-blue, with soft dove-grey peeking between the rows. There was no mistaking the match with Rose's shawl. "Is Rozalia in some kind of trouble?"

Sylvie leapt up, blanching.

The door burst open behind them, the shudder echoing throughout the enormous hall.

Ivan Mazurek surged toward them on a tide of noise from the clamoring mob outside, shirt rumpled behind his suspenders. "Rose," he gasped, then rested his hands on his knees, panting.

A chill spidered over Kristof's scalp as he went to Ivan. "What's going on?"

"I was hoping she'd be here. Lottie overheard the plan for you all to meet with Mr. Janik."

The boy still hadn't given up following her. "So you came to talk," Kristof guessed. Sylvie remained rooted where she stood.

"I came to stop her. She's with Jozefa."

"What?" Sylvie rushed toward them. "No. Jozefa is in New York."

"You didn't know?" Ivan straightened and returned her wide-eyed stare. "Lottie found a note while cleaning Rose's room. Jozefa came back. She told Rose to meet her tonight on the roof of the Woman's Building. She told her to come alone."

Sylvie's world collapsed into a single imperative. *Get there.*

Leaving Kristof to bid Dr. Janik a hasty good-bye, she rushed with Ivan to the front of Music Hall. Sweat dripped from his temples as he leaned into the door, shouting to the masses on the other side to stand back so he could open it.

"It's no use." He wrung his hat. "Everyone is packed like sardines to see the parade. I had to beat my way into the building, and now it's even worse."

"Back door." Kristof, who had caught up with them, took Sylvie's hand, and the three of them ran through the lobby, down the corridor parallel to the auditorium, and into one of the stage wings, until Kristof slammed against the door that exited onto the Peristyle. Both he and Ivan wrestled it open for Sylvie to push through first.

Night was falling, and the temperature with it. Cool air splashed over her, along with the nearly deafening cacophony of tens of thousands of voices. Sylvie's chest constricted as she took in the Court of Honor. It wasn't just the ground level that was full. Rooftops and balconies on the surrounding buildings bristled with spectators. Others had wedged themselves between the columns of the Peristyle on which she stood. She could barely breathe in the crush of people.

Kristof reclaimed her hand, and she held fast. Ivan shouted to clear a path, but his voice was swallowed up. By the light of incandescent lights, men clambered up ropes and makeshift ladders for a better view of the parade from the top of Machinery Hall and the Agriculture Building. Some were even standing on the pedestal of the

Statue of the Republic in the middle of the Grand Basin.

The Woman's Building was at the opposite corner of the fairgrounds. They could barely move an inch.

Get there.

"It's starting!" a man beside Sylvie cried out. "I see the Hussars leading the way!"

Another man called from the Peristyle's roof that the crowd had broken the lines and was blocking the horses' path.

The crowd jostled around Sylvie, becoming all elbows and feet. Somewhere a child cried and a woman screamed. Another fainted.

"Ivan," Kristof called. "Can you plow a path to the water?"

Ivan set his jaw, then used all his brawn to part the sea, Kristof ushering Sylvie in his wake. "There's no way we can get there on foot," he told her, half shouting to be heard.

"I'll swim if I have to," she replied, doubting there were any vessels left.

By the time they reached the wide steps that led down to the Grand Basin, her hat was gone, and her hair was tumbling down her back. Just as Sylvie feared, no vessel waited at the landing. Every one of them already carried people and colored lanterns over water that reflected the Fair's white lights.

"Wait here." Kristof waded into the water

and grabbed the first gondola he came to. Then another vessel blocked her view.

"He's paying them," Ivan told her. "He's paying the passengers and the gondoliers."

Moments later, two gondolas glided up to the landing. As four people debarked, Ivan climbed into one of them while Kristof helped Sylvie into the other. It swayed as he stepped in after her and guided her onto a velvet-covered bench.

"Race you to the Woman's Building," Kristof called to Ivan.

With a terse nod, he accepted the challenge.

Kristof wedged himself beside Sylvie. Water from his dripping trousers seeped through her wool skirt. She didn't feel it.

"We're in a hurry," she called to the gondolier. "Can you get us to the Woman's Building?"

Kristof added something in Italian.

The dark-haired gondoliers on bow and stern answered with their long oars, sending the gondola forward.

Haltingly, they swung around the forty-foot-tall pedestal that held the Statue of the Republic and several daring spectators, then continued toward the opposite end of the Basin. At a snail's pace, it seemed to Sylvie, they angled beneath a bridge connecting the Electricity and Manufactures Buildings.

Sylvie followed the sound of cheers until she spotted a giant parade float depicting the Great

Fire that had taken place twenty-two years ago today. She had run from that fire and survived it. Even so, the reminder pressed a bruised spot in her memory, and she quickly looked away.

Kristof called out in Italian again, spurring the gondoliers on as they steered around electric launches, dugout canoes, and other watercraft.

She grasped his hands to warm them. "I don't understand why Jozefa came back. Rose has been writing to her. She planned to join her in New York, I'm sure." On land, people roared for a float of Columbus at the Court of Isabella.

"Jozefa is a proven manipulator. That's hard to do from a distance." He put his arm around her rigid shoulders. "We'll get there."

At this rate, it wouldn't be soon. Sylvie could only pray it would be soon enough.

CHAPTER THIRTY-FOUR

Twin lines of crimson light ripped through the sky just as Sylvie and Kristof gained the rooftop of the Woman's Building. The parade was over, the fireworks begun. Across the lagoon, fifteen thousand fairy lamps lit all at once in the trees.

"Ivan? Rose?" Sylvie called into the darkness. Trails of smoke striped the sky.

"Mimi." The searchlight swept over the roof, illuminating the empty chairs and tables of a deserted café, and Rose, who stood near the waist-high railing. Ivan, thank goodness, was with her. Jozefa presided, as still and pale as a sculpture. Beyond them, past the lagoon and Fisheries Building, showers of red and green burst over the lake.

"I'm here," Sylvie said. "Kristof and I are both here. But Jozefa, why are you?"

"I just got here myself," Rose said. "Ivan says he arrived a couple minutes before me."

His gondoliers had been more aggressive than Kristof and Sylvie's.

"What's going on?" Rose asked.

"This would have been easier if you'd come alone." Jozefa pushed back her shoulders, dignifying her silhouette. "But you didn't. As I was just explaining to Ivan, I missed you. I supposed you might want my company on the long journey to New York."

"Didn't she already tell you she would meet you there?" Kristof asked. "Why couldn't you trust her?"

"I—I wrote I would *probably* come," Rose stammered. "It was all but certain. But it's no small thing, leaving this way. How can I say good-bye to Mimi forever?" She faced Sylvie. "I wish I could take back every cruel and wicked thing I ever said to you. I shudder when I think of all the times I glibly pointed out that you were not my mother. You've been more of a mother to me for all these years than I had any right to. You shaped your entire life around me, though I was an orphan and you could have handed me to an institution."

"Like I did, you mean." Jozefa's veneer of control began to peel away. "Is that what you're trying to say? Have I not told you I'm sorry enough times? How many more apologies do you require, darling?" But the endearment rang hollow and cold.

"This isn't about you," Rose said. "This is my apology to make. I love you, Mimi. And during the past few weeks, whenever I've imagined myself far away from you—" She pressed a fist to her mouth. The edge of her shawl riffled in the wind. "It isn't guilt I feel, for you've given me your blessing. But how can I cut ties with you and not grieve? Since Nikolai died, *you* are the only family I've had. You and Papa Stephen, Aunt Meg, Uncle Nate, Hazel, Walter, Olive. Mr. Bartok, too. The Hoffmans. I've belonged with *you*. I'm sorry I ever lost sight of that."

A burden Sylvie hadn't realized she still carried suddenly lifted, the relief of it like a hundred birds taking flight from her body. "Yes," she managed around the hard wedge in her throat. "You belong."

More explosions spangled the sky.

"My dear, you begin to scare me. If I leave here without you, I don't know what I'll do. We stand atop a monument to what Woman has done, what Woman can do. But for all my accomplishments and fame, my life has failed to satisfy me. I need my daughter for that. I need you to prove that you've forgiven me."

Rose turned back to Jozefa, and Sylvie imagined she could see her mind sway as she leaned toward her. "I do forgive you. And I love you, too. I want you to be happy, you must believe that."

Even in the hazy glow cast from the bulbs lining the rooftop, the cords of Ivan's neck were visibly taut. "Be wary, Rose. She wants to use you for her own happiness. I should know. I've been guilty of the same. Beware of people like us." It was the truest thing he could have said, and it sent a shudder of surprise through Sylvie.

"She's my mother," Rose insisted. As if this alone might outweigh everything else in the balance.

She still didn't know it was a lie.

Sylvie slowly walked toward her, then hesitated, searching for the words that would right her world again—and bring Rose's world crashing down. Her lungs grew thick with dread. Sylvie didn't want it to be this way. She didn't want to have to crush Rose in order to save her.

"The truth," Kristof said above the distant but raucous crowd. "Just tell her the truth."

Wind whipped Sylvie's hair about her face and neck. "Rozalia, we met with Dr. Janik this evening. I wish you'd been there."

"I'm sorry, Mimi. I didn't mean to keep another secret from you."

"Wiktor Janik wasn't just the Dabrowskis' friend and neighbor. He was the doctor who delivered you." Sylvie's voice was steadier than her stomach. Kristof pressed reassurance into the small of her back with his hand. "He delivered you from Magdalena. She was your mother, and Nikolai your father. Jozefa lied to you."

Anger flashed over Jozefa, there and then gone. Mastered.

"What?" Rose frowned.

A strange laugh escaped Jozefa, scraped from some dark and hidden place. "Don't listen to her, dear. I wouldn't do that to you."

"You did." Ivan's defiance resounded over the continual blast of fireworks. There was no break, no respite between explosions now, but one piled on another, layering the sky with color and foul-smelling smoke. The searchlight swung back to them, lighting him from behind. "You lied to Rose over and over. You admitted it yourself."

"Miss Townsend is desperate." Jozefa raked a hand over the pearl strands draping her bodice. "What lie would she not utter, if it meant keeping you to herself? Of course she wants to deceive you. She'll say anything. Anything at all."

"No." Sylvie's middle roiled, her pulse thrummed in her ears. "That's your tactic, not mine. Listen to me, Rose. Your shawl was crocheted by Dr. Janik's wife as a gift to Magdalena soon after you were born." Rockets exploded in the night from a dozen different places about the Fair.

"You can't prove any of this." Jozefa's tone turned as dark as her face.

"I can." Kristof reached into his pocket and pulled out what appeared to be a rag. Metal chair legs scraped the pebbly rooftop as he pushed them out of his path. "Look," he said. "It's the same yarn."

Then Sylvie understood. Somewhere on the fairgrounds, an elderly Polish doctor was walking around without one of his socks so that Rose could see the evidence.

Light suddenly blasted away the dark all over the White City as five hundred-pound magnesium bombs detonated on the Wooded Island, in the Court of Honor, and at the lakefront all at once. In this gift of illumination, Rose gasped at the sock Kristof held, pairing it with the shawl that was tied over her shoulders.

"It's a match," she choked out from the brink of a dangerous height.

Sympathy throbbed through Sylvie. Dizziness shook her.

This moment—the wind, the rooftop, the dark, the smell of smoke—whisked her back to the weeks following the Great Fire. In the rush to reconstruct the city, the mortar between bricks had frozen before it had time to dry. Strong gusts toppled many-storied structures. Sylvie and Meg had stood on the top floor of one of those buildings, coaxing Stephen to come down from his soldier's-heart-induced patrol. Terrified, she had felt the floor shift and creak beneath her feet, had heard bricks slipping loose and tumbling to the ground. Just after they'd all left the building and crossed the street, it had collapsed.

Sylvie stood on such scaffolding again right now with Rose, who had hastily constructed her dreams and plans upon every word Jozefa had told her. It would not hold. And now, instead of coaxing Rose to climb down from the dizzying height, Sylvie was knocking away the bricks herself, until nothing remained but the joyless conclusion that Jozefa was an imposter and Rose's real mother was still dead in her watery grave.

Her heart kicked at its cage. "Dr. Janik is telling the truth, Rozalia," Sylvie said. "Jozefa isn't."

Rose twisted toward the woman she'd been calling Mother. "I don't understand. Explain it to me. The truth." She sagged against the railing, her skirt snapping at the rungs.

"I had a baby." Regret oozed from Jozefa's words. "I named her Rozalia and gave her up for adoption, regretting it for the rest of my life. I told you all of this, and it's absolutely true!" Strands of hair spun in the gusting wind, defying her tidy coiffure.

"Perhaps you did," Kristof said. "But your baby was not *this* Rozalia. Was it?"

Sylvie searched herself for some pang of sympathy but found none.

"I have been searching for so long, and so has she," Jozefa argued. "Fate brought us together, and I won't lose her now. Not after everything I've done."

It was Ivan's turn to laugh. "You mean not after trapping her, lying to her, and feeding her stories you thought she'd want to hear?"

"The lullaby?" Rose's voice was small and cracked. Parched, Sylvie thought, for nourishment Jozefa could not give.

"I sang that to you," Jozefa insisted.

"What lullaby?" asked Ivan.

Rose hummed the first line.

Ivan picked up the tune and sang it in Polish. "Rose, that song has been around for ages. Every Polish mother, mine included, has sung it to her children for generations. Go to any tenement in my neighborhood and you'll hear the same thing. This means nothing."

Rose slid along the railing away from Jozefa, her expression that of one plummeting.

"She isn't your mother." Sylvie hooked her arm through Rose's elbow. She would break her fall, be a soft landing if she could. But she could feel the cracking of Rose's heart in her own chest.

"Don't listen to her!" Jozefa bleated. "She's just being selfish. See how she pulls you away from me."

Rose stiffened, and Sylvie felt a bolt go through her. "Selfish? Mimi has done nothing but support me. She let me correspond with you, even after you destroyed the letters you said you'd mail her on my behalf. It was her idea to give me Polish lessons, and Mr. Bartok has given hours out of every day to make sure I learn the language. She told me I was free. *Free* to choose you. And I'm just as free not to."

"But don't you see?" Jozefa's eyes went round and wild. "It's perfect. You wanted your mother. I was trying to find my daughter. You even have

515

the same name she did. Surely that's a sign. Come back with me. I don't want to keep living alone. I'm weary of bearing the guilt for a single mistake I made twenty years ago."

"Twenty?" Rose rasped. Another flare overhead cast her face in blue and green.

"What difference does it make that you're a few years younger than my daughter? What does it matter that we don't share the same blood? I can't find my own Rozalia. But I found you. It's good enough."

Sylvie's blood went cold, icing her veins. Only when Kristof's hand settled in the hollow of her waist did she realize she was shaking. "So you confess the entire deception. You knew she wasn't yours the entire time?"

"No." The actress twisted a ring on her finger. Perhaps she was still performing. "At first, I really thought she might be mine. Then we bonded. Didn't we, Rozalia? The dates not working out mattered less and less." Ever graceful, even in her madness, she fluttered toward Rose, reaching.

"Miss Zielinski." Kristof stepped between them. Ivan went to his side, a bulwark. "Do not touch her. She is not your property." He looked over his shoulder at Sylvie and Rose. "Do either of you ladies have anything you wish to say, or are you ready to leave?"

Rose inhaled, then controlled her breath's

release. "My parents died while trying to give me a life in America. I'm not going anywhere with you."

An eerie smile crept over Jozefa's face, like a mask changing shape. "I see. And what about the baby?"

Rose peered around Ivan to see Jozefa. "What baby?" The wind all but snatched her question.

"Yours."

Shock spilled down Sylvie's collar. Her thoughts jumped so far, she reined them back, forcing herself to focus on much smaller things. The pebbles beneath her soles. The sour odor of fireworks, the ghosts of smoke they left behind. The cold Kristof endured in the dropping temperature, his clothing still wet and clinging to his skin.

Rose's hand went to her flat middle. "I am not with child."

"You don't expect me to believe that. I left you alone in a hotel room with a young man who adored you. Stalked you, even, which is how I knew he'd be perfect. I fed you lines from *Romeo and Juliet*. Who can resist forbidden love?"

"I tell you, I couldn't possibly be with child." She looked to Sylvie. "Believe me!"

Sylvie's knees felt loose as she stepped sideways, the better to see Jozefa around the barricade formed by the men. The barrage of heavenly explosions dimmed as she called

517

up the last five weeks that Rose had been home.

She hadn't complained of her monthly cramps. She hadn't taken to bed with a hot water bottle and a bar of chocolate, as she had every month since she was fourteen. Sylvie's mind conjured Rose with a baby, shunned, her place in good society gone. She saw herself helping Rose with the infant, the toddler, the growing child, as Sylvie's hair turned the color of stone.

An explosion shattered the visions. Rose had given her word that nothing had happened beyond a kiss.

Jozefa crooked a finger at Ivan. "Remember what we talked about."

His face latched shut against her. Fireworks burst into shapes of dolphins, fountains, and flying fish, but proved no more astounding or impossible than these rooftop revelations.

"Ivan, tell her. Tell them!" Rose cried. She stepped out from behind him to stand at his side. The broad beam of the searchlight veered over the four of them, and then over Jozefa, apart and alone.

In Ivan's hesitation, Jozefa clucked her tongue. "What do you think of your precious Rose now, Miss Townsend? Just when you finished raising her, she brings a baby into the world, unwed. You wouldn't force her into an unfit marriage. But are you ready to give another eighteen years toward helping her raise this child? I think not."

Sweat filmed Sylvie's skin. They were all too close to the edge. "I believe Rose," she said. "But even if she were with child, I would not send her or the babe away."

"Don't be ridiculous. You've already given half your life to her." Jozefa leaned toward Rose. "Come with me to Poland. I'll atone for my sin of abandoning my daughter by helping you raise yours. Just because you don't have a husband doesn't mean you can't keep your baby and your reputation, too. We'll tell everyone you're a widow. I'll make sure both of you are cared for. I'll redeem my past mistakes."

This was madness.

Kristof angled toward Ivan. "You have something to say. There's still time to be the real hero."

Ivan clenched fists at his sides. "There's no baby. There's no way she could be pregnant. I would never do that to her. And I would never lie about it. Not even if someone offered enough money to keep my family well fed and healthy for a year." He directed a scalding gaze at Jozefa.

Rose gasped. "How could you?" Her voice shook with disbelief and sorrow. "You *wanted* to *ruin* me! You orchestrated the entire thing, so that even if I was tempted to reject you, you hoped Mimi would reject me!"

"I love you, Rozalia," Jozefa crooned. But she was backing up, away from all of them, bumping and scraping chairs and tables. "I would do anything to have you with me until the end of my days. It doesn't matter to Miss Townsend that you're not her blood relation. Neither does it matter to me." She gripped the railing at the edge of the roof.

Rose shook her head. "I thought you were my mother. But no mother would do what you've done and tried to do."

"You're missing the point, dear. Everything I've done just proves how much I love you."

"That's not love. I don't know what it is, but it isn't love. Even if you were my mother, I wouldn't go with you now."

"But Miss Townsend is not your mother!" Jozefa's breath sawed in and out. "And you gave her thirteen years!"

"Magdalena Dabrowski is my mother," Rose said, and it seemed to Sylvie that she drew strength, grew taller, just naming her. "Nikolai Dabrowski is my father. And Mimi is my family. Nothing you can say will change that."

Sylvie's vision wavered and blurred. If Kristof's arm had not come around her, she might have sunk into the chair beside her.

Jozefa opened her mouth, then closed it. She clutched at her chest, where the locket lay hidden against her skin. "Rozalia," she wheezed, "my Rozalia." Then her face went vacant, her hand dropped. She listed, unmoored, against the railing at her elbow. The searchlight rolled over her as she swooned.

Rose screamed, pebbles sprayed, and Ivan and Kristof lunged, catching Jozefa before she capsized over the edge of the roof.

The night exploded again. Rose flung her arms around Sylvie's neck, shoulders shaking in a sob that could not be heard. Her own cheeks wet, Sylvie returned the fierce embrace. "It's all right," she told her. "You're safe. I'm still here."

Rose shuddered on a muffled cry. "So am I."

CHAPTER THIRTY-FIVE

Sunday, October 15, 1893

Sylvie shielded her eyes from the light bouncing off Lake Michigan. Leaves turned and fell against a cerulean sky. The air was apple-crisp. Three-quarters of a million people had been at the World's Fair on Monday, but here in a quiet stretch of Lincoln Park, the biggest crowd was the one she'd brought with her.

Meg and Sylvie packed up the picnic basket with the scant leftovers from lunch while Hazel and Rose strolled down to the shore, Olive chasing after them. Walter, already ankle-deep in the water despite the cold, held out a shell or fossil he'd found as they approached.

When Karl and Anna stiffly rose from the nearby bench, Nate and Kristof steadied them. "Ready to stretch those legs?" Nate asked.

"Go on, Anna. We'll take care of this." Sylvie waved her away and smiled when she took Kristof's arm. Nate walked at Karl's side, ready to support him if needed.

Latching the basket closed, Meg sat back on the plaid blanket they'd brought and unfolded her legs, the tips of her shoes poking out from beneath her grey wool skirt. "How is she, Sylvie?

I still can't believe all that poor girl has been through. All *you* have been through, for that matter."

Sylvie shifted to sit beside her. "We've had our share of tears this past week, that's for sure." The Hoffmans had added their own, Karl's few just as moving as Anna's many. Then they'd showered Rose with pastries and hugs that smelled of yeast and coffee. "Dr. Janik stopped by on Tuesday afternoon," she added.

"Did he come for his sock?" Meg teased.

"Quite." Sylvie chuckled. "Kristof came down right away to help translate. Dr. Janik spent another hour with Rose, maybe longer, telling her more about Magdalena and Nikolai, restoring memories she'd recently discarded. He reminded her that her parents cherished her, always. She had never been unwanted. You should have seen how tender he was with her, how pleased that she had learned some Polish and practiced it with him. It was good for her. *This*"—she nodded toward the cousins on the shore—"*this* is good for her." This outing after church had been Rose's idea. Instead of breaking her connections with all those who loved her, she was strengthening them, daring to believe they'd hold.

Blond tendrils of hair twirled by Meg's jaw. "Any word from Jozefa since then?"

"None." Kristof and Ivan had taken her to the hospital on the fairgrounds after catching her.

Rose had gone to the police this week, filing for a restraining order she hoped would be rendered unnecessary by Jozefa's departure. "I understand from the authorities that she's sailing, right now, for Poland."

At the lake's edge, Walter handed the shell to Olive, then bent as though to pick up another. Instead, he splashed water up at his sisters and Rose. All three shrieked, to his apparent satisfaction. Their laughter somersaulted across the beach.

"So it's over now," Meg said.

But Sylvie wondered.

Meg's natural bent was to paint with a broad brush of optimism. Though life experience had tempered this tendency, Sylvie still felt a gap in how they viewed the world. In the same autumn sky, Meg would see dazzling blue, and Sylvie the clouds bringing rain.

But not all rain was bad. Twenty-two years ago last week, right here in Lincoln Park, Meg, Sylvie, and Nate had praised God for it when the heavens dumped their cargo over the Great Fire. Rain stopped the burning. Rain cleansed. But first, it made a mess of the ashes.

Sylvie bent her knees, clasping her hands atop them, watching Rose. She would be all right. But when? Sylvie's imagination could not plumb the depths to which Rose had been hurt, nor how long it would take for her to recover.

"I mean, the wounding is over." Meg laid her disfigured hand on Sylvie's. "The healing has just begun."

Sylvie held her sister's scars—at least, the ones that were visible. "Have you?" she dared to ask. "Healed from losing Louise?"

Meg's gaze rested on her children, and Sylvie wondered if she saw not just three but four. A sad smile tipped her lips. "There will always be a spot in my heart contracting over her absence," she said. "The sharp edges have dulled to a chronic ache that is easier some days to bear than others. But that doesn't mean I can't hold on to joy at the same time, too. Healing doesn't mean forgetting the loss, nor does it mean enshrining it. Healing, at least for me, has meant holding both the blessings I once had and the blessings I still do, but holding them loosely in open hands." She turned palms to the sky in a gesture that appeared remarkably like surrender.

Sylvie's throat tightened as she nodded. They hadn't always seen eye to eye on things, but at forty-three years old, she still looked up to her older sister.

Meg stood, helped Sylvie do the same, then captured her in a sideways hug as Olive scrambled toward them, kicking up sand behind her.

"Come on, you have to see this!" the child lisped through her missing front teeth and pulled at Meg's arm. "See what I found. I couldn't bring it up here to show you. It was too wiggly."

Laughing, Meg followed her daughter just as Rose arrived. She looked pink from the sun and windblown, and something approaching happy.

"Do you have something wiggly to show me, too?" Sylvie teased, opening a parasol against the light.

"Lucky for you, no." Rose looped her arm in Sylvie's and guided her on a path that followed Kristof, Nate, and the Hoffmans. "Hazel was asking me what I plan to do now, and I'm sure you've been wondering, too. There's a lot I'm still thinking about, but I'd like to resume my violin lessons with Kristof." Kristof had invited Rose to use his Christian name after Monday, and she'd warmed to it immediately.

"I think that's a fine idea," Sylvie affirmed.

"But I want to pay for them myself. And I'd like to keep learning Polish, but Kristof is going to be busy with the symphony soon. If he doesn't have time, I'll see about hiring a different tutor, or maybe there are classes I could take. But I insist on paying for these out of my salary."

Sylvie quietly considered this. She could only afford to pay Rose for part-time hours at Corner Books & More. That wasn't going to add up very fast compared to the cost of formal education. "I want you to have those classes," she said. "If that's what you want."

"I do, Mimi. Which is why I don't think I'll be working for you anymore." Rose bit her lower lip and pushed a strand of hair away behind her ear. "Hazel says they're hiring at Marshall Field's. Business there hasn't slowed down, even with the recession. I can get plenty of hours there. Please don't be upset, Mimi. I've loved working at the bookshop, but it's time I start earning my own way without it costing you."

Sylvie's steps slowed, her boots sinking a little in the sand. "Sweetheart, you work wherever you want. I never meant to trap you in a life that was not of your own making." She adjusted the parasol to shade Rose, too.

"Good. I thought so. Even if I get the job, though, I won't try to move into one of the Jane Club apartments."

Sylvie waited for her to explain. Overhead, a formation of Canada geese honked as they winged southward.

"Those apartments are for young working ladies who have no other place to go. They'd be turned out and adrift if they lost their jobs and they weren't in the club. I don't want to take one of those spots from someone who needs it more. After all, I have a home still. With you. Even though I'll be eighteen next month, I'd still—" She paused, gaze settling on Meg, who was bending over Olive's treasure, while Hazel laughed a few feet away. Walter skipped a stone across the water, then joined the men and Anna.

When a strong gust nearly blew the parasol out of Sylvie's hands, she closed it.

"I'm saying, Mimi, that I'd still like to live with you."

Sylvie smiled. "I would like that very much. You have your own life, I understand that. But you don't have to worry about outgrowing your home, no matter how old you are." Wind swirled between them, tugging at their hair. "Now I need to apologize to you, Rose, for all those times I called you my daughter without first making sure you were comfortable with it. It was insensitive of me, and I don't want to be careless of your feelings like that again."

"Oh, Mimi. You've cared for mine far better than I've cared for yours lately."

"But if it bothered you, I'm sorry for that."

She tilted her head. "It wouldn't bother me now. I realize I've been doubly blessed. I had a mother by birth, and a mother by choice. I know I've said before that I had no role in that decision, but I have one now, and I choose you. I choose both of you."

Sylvie inhaled. "Thank you." Those two small words buckled beneath the weight of all she felt.

"I choose to be yours," Rose said again, "even if that means sharing you with someone else." She turned Sylvie around. Kristof walked toward them, his jacket flapping in the breeze. Rose gave her a little shove. "A very worthy someone else. He's been waiting long enough."

Kristof's smile brought the warmth of the October sun to full blaze in Sylvie's cheeks. Had it been confident or carefree, it would not have affected her so. But this one hinted at hope.

Hope was catching.

She reached for his hand as soon as they met on the shore of the lapping lake. A glance over his shoulder showed that Nate and Walter were helping Karl and Anna toward a bench. Behind her, Meg and Rose had gathered Hazel and Olive and were strolling in the opposite direction. My, but her family knew how to make themselves scarce.

Kristof cleared his throat. "I've been meaning to ask—has Ivan tried making contact with Rose since Monday?"

"Oh." It was not what she'd expected him to say. "He sent a message through Lottie—verbally this time. He said, *'I finally figured out what Mr. Bartok meant about Sydney. Good-bye, Rose. I wish you well.'*" She raised an eyebrow. "Care to explain?"

A satisfied grin stole over his face. "Just a little chat we had about *A Tale of Two Cities*."

She could guess the rest. "Ah. The unlikely hero who loved by letting go." It was brilliant.

So was the glare off the water. Braving the

wind once more, she opened the parasol so she could talk to Kristof without squinting. A pair of sandpipers raced by.

"Thankfully, there are other ways to love." His fingers—those magnificent fingers that could make a violin sing and draw a symphony from the air—twined with hers, their gentle pressure a resounding chord inside her. "A man might love by hanging on, for example. By waiting for a heroine who needed time and space. A heroine worth waiting for." His expression was stamped with an earnestness that made her heartbeat stutter.

Of all the ironies. While she had feared being hemmed in by marriage laws, and while Jozefa and Ivan had literally locked Rose away and called it love, Kristof wanted to give Sylvie room to do as she pleased. After the confines of caring for an aging parent, and on the heels of raising a child, it was what she'd thought she wanted. But the space she'd fancied as freedom would be empty without him.

"Oh, Kristof." Her eyes shimmered. "I love my life. But I love life most when you are in it. I love *you*."

"Sylvie . . ." His throat contracted around a swallow. "You've held my heart since before I even understood that I'd given it up. But I've never once wanted it back. I love you more than words can say. More than music can express."

Smiling, he settled his hands on her waist and bowed his head toward her. "I'd really like to kiss you now. May I?"

Every nerve awakened, every sense heightened. Longings she hadn't dared to name came rushing into recognition. It wasn't romance she craved, but love, belonging, knowing and being known. It was Kristof.

Drawing closer to him, she positioned the parasol to shield their moment from family and friends. Still he remained unwilling to take from her what she wouldn't freely give. At last she was ready for him to be the first—and, God willing, the only—man she ever kissed.

His hand curved behind her neck. She lifted her chin, and his mouth met hers, warm and sweet and certain. Sylvie pressed herself closer, melting into his embrace. This was not the tentative kiss of an unsure suitor, but the kiss of a man who knew what he wanted and had found it at last.

The parasol slipped from her grip. Shadows rolled away as she let it drop to the sand, and she felt the light of the sun on her face.

Epilogue

November 1895

"More tea?" Sylvie topped off Beth's cup and then her own, then slid the plate of shortbread cookies toward her friend. "Don't let me eat all these by myself."

Beth eagerly obliged. "Happy to help." She sank back in her chair with a contented sigh. "I thought that husband of yours would be home by now."

Sylvie checked a laugh while replacing the kettle on the warm stove. Beth would never admit it, but she'd grown fond of Kristof and likely hoped she'd see him tonight. "Any minute now. There's a vacancy in the violin section at the symphony, and he's one of the jurors for the auditions. They're running late, I guess." She drew curtains against the night before returning to the table.

Beth took another cookie. "Well, it's a good thing I came, then."

"A very good thing," Sylvie agreed, though she knew how to spend an evening alone. Two newly released books had arrived today and remained unopened on the parlor tea table: *The Red Badge of Courage* by Stephen Crane and *The Time Machine* by H. G. Wells. She'd been itching to read them all day. Still, after almost losing Beth's friendship over Sylvie's marriage to Kristof, she welcomed her visit, grateful for the connection that stretched back decades.

Footfalls sounded in the hall before the door opened and Kristof stepped inside. While Sylvie poured him a steaming cup of tea, he kissed her cheek, then hung up his hat and coat and joined them at the table.

"Beth!" he said. "Glad you stopped by. Work doesn't normally keep me this late." He wrapped his long fingers around the cup, warming them.

"It was fine, really," Sylvie told him. "I had dinner with Rose." And if she hadn't, she would have been happily reading.

"Is she staying out of trouble?"

Sylvie told him she was, adding the regards Rose sent for him.

Nodding, Kristof helped himself to a short-bread cookie. "You wouldn't believe it, Beth. Rose moved out a year ago, and she doesn't call, she doesn't write."

Beth pushed a russet curl from her forehead and stared down her nose at him. "She lives right above you."

"Ah. That must be it." He winked at Sylvie. Overhead, floorboards creaked, a door opened and closed. Water rushed through the pipes. "She seems so far away."

Sylvie rolled her eyes and chuckled as Kristof

reached for the *Tribune* and browsed the head-lines.

Taking one more cookie, Beth layered a spoonful of strawberry jam onto it. "Your niece Hazel rooms with her, doesn't she? Spreading the ol' wings just a bit?"

"She does." More footsteps sounded, more hinges squeaked, along with muffled feminine voices. "Along with two other friends of theirs who recently moved in. Twins named Holly and Ivy. Yes, they were born on Christmas."

Beth brushed the crumbs from her shirtfront. "Is that the Holly who works for you now that Tessa has married and moved away?"

"The same. Ivy is a clerk at the courthouse, where Rose serves as a court observer and translator." Rose had worked so hard these last two years, full-time at Marshall Field's during the day, then taking night classes from the lan-guage school. Now she worked part-time at the department store, using the rest of her time to help Polish immigrants at the courthouse. She helped them complete legal documents and trans-lated for them in court. It was a testament to her unfailing energy that she'd had time to make friends, too. She no longer took violin lessons, but she often played duets with Kristof after they shared a meal together.

"It's like a regular Jane Club up there, then," Beth said.

"It is. But they're calling themselves the Garden Club. Can you beat that?"

"Ha!" Beth snorted, wrinkling her nose. "Rose, Holly, Ivy—and Hazel? What is she, an honorary member?"

"Her middle name is Eden," Sylvie told her, "so she fits right in. Though the personalities up there are . . . diverse."

"Uh-oh. Sounds like trouble."

"Not trouble, exactly." Sylvie lifted her teacup, savoring the orange-and-cloves scent. "How would you describe the girls, Kristof?"

The newspaper crinkled as he folded down the corner and looked at her. "Like apples and cherries."

A grin bloomed on her face. "Oh, stop."

"Blueberries and bananas. Watermelon and rhubarb? Apricots and strawberries. Say, are you saving any of that jam for me, Beth?"

Beth threw up her hands in mock despair. "Apples and oranges! I get it!"

Sylvie's full-throated laughter filled the kitchen.

"You're both ridiculous." But a hint of a smile softened Beth's angular face. "I'm leaving."

Kristof rose when she did, and helped her into her coat. "It's a cold one tonight," he told her. "Shall I hail you a cab?"

"I'll hail it myself."

He insisted on walking her out and waiting with

her until she'd secured her ride home. When he returned, he came up behind Sylvie, who stood at the sink, washing dishes. His lips pressed warmth to the nape of her neck, and then he turned her around to face him, eyes alight.

"What's going on?" She dried her hands on a towel, then reached for a jar of lemon hand cream.

Kristof took it from her and began massaging the cream into her skin. "Guess who won the chair."

She frowned. Then gasped. "You're kidding."

"I'm serious."

"Gregor?"

He nodded, and she read the wonder in the lines framing his smile. "The auditions are completely anonymous. All the candidates played behind a screen."

"But could you tell by the music that it was your brother?"

"Something in his audition did make me hope it was him. But where he would have taken outrageous liberties with a piece a few years ago, he played with a restrained and polished musicality. It was like the piece evolved, but in line with the composer's intention. So I assumed it couldn't be him, after all."

"But it was." She squeezed his hands.

"It is. He's starting at the bottom of the section, and the position is probationary for a full year, but he's back, Sylvie. My brother is back."

Her husband's palpable relief touched a familiar chord. "That's wonderful. I'm so glad. What did he tell you?" They hadn't seen or heard from him in more than two years.

"Not much, except that he took the long way home, and that he'd tell me more later. He apologized, though, for his past behaviors and mistakes. And then added that he couldn't guarantee he'd be perfect from now on."

"Ah, perfection," Sylvie said, understanding this lifelong struggle in Kristof's family. She untied his necktie and pulled it free of his collar, then unfastened the top button. There. Better.

"Right. I told him I didn't expect perfection. I only want his best. The best for him, the best from him. Which, now that I hear myself say it, is still a pretty high standard. His best would be phenomenal." His lips curved in a rueful grin. "He asked me why I wasn't conductor of the orchestra yet."

"The maestro isn't old enough to retire," Sylvie said, perhaps a little defensively on her husband's behalf. Kristof adored conducting and could have taken that position at a different orchestra, but he and Sylvie weren't willing to leave Chicago. "And Thomas has been letting you stand in for him quite a bit these last few seasons." Kristof was on track to replace him, but the time had not yet come. "Was Gregor disappointed to hear you'd found a new roommate?"

Kristof laughed. "He was surprised. He thought music had always been enough for me. I told him it had been until I met you. And nothing was the same after that."

"It was better," Sylvie teased.

"In every way. You, Mrs. Bartok, are the heroine of my story." Gold flecks glinted in his deep brown eyes as he gathered her close and kissed her with a tenderness that took her breath away.

She laid a hand on his chest and felt the beat beneath her palm. "And you, my dear husband, are the conductor of my heart."

She could feel his smile and the scruff of his jaw as he kissed her again and then conducted her toward the bedroom, right past the novels she'd thought she'd been dying to read.

Books, she had learned, would wait.

Author's Note

I hope you've enjoyed spending time at Chicago's World's Fair of 1893 as much as I have. I only had room to share with you a small fraction of what I learned in my research, so if you're hungry for more, I encourage you to dive into further study on your own. There are plenty of websites and books to choose from, including one of the 1893 guidebooks mentioned in this novel, *Chicago by Day and Night: The Pleasure Seeker's Guide to the Paris of America.*

The main characters of this story are fictional, but as ever, they interacted with real historical events and settings. The descriptions of the Midway and of the Fair buildings, exhibits, and restaurants are as accurate as I could make them without bogging you down with dimensions and details. Beyond that, the following aspects of the novel are also true to history: the recession of 1893, the protests outside City Hall, the Exposition Orchestra and its broken contract with the Exposition Company, Hull House and its Readers Club and Hull House Players, the plight for women's suffrage and the evolving image of the New Woman, the Pacific Garden Mission and the Cheyenne neighborhood of the Levee district, and Chicago Day and its record-smashing crowd of 751,026 people. Over the six-month course of the Fair, 27 million visitors attended. The White City was so magical, it served as the inspiration for L. Frank Baum's Emerald City in his novel *The Wonderful Wizard of Oz*. Another fun fact: Wellesley College English professor Katharine Lee Bates's visit to the Fair inspired her to write the line "thine alabaster cities gleam" in the patriotic anthem "America the Beautiful."

Historical figures who appeared in or were referenced in *Shadows of the White City* include Maestro Theodore Thomas, founding director of the Chicago Symphony Orchestra and musical director for the Columbian Exposition; Frederick Law Olmsted, the landscape architect who was working on the Biltmore Estate landscaping in North Carolina at the same time he worked on the Fair's; Antonín Dvořák, composer and guest conductor of the Exposition Orchestra; Frederick Douglass; Helen Keller, the thirteen-year-old who met the inventor of the braille typewriter; Harry Houdini; Jane Addams and Ellen Gates Starr, founders of Hull House; Sophia Hayden, who designed the Woman's Building when she was in her early twenties; Kate Marsden, British missionary to leper colonies in Siberia; Josephine Cochran, inventor of the first automatic dishwasher; Susan B. Anthony; Buffalo Bill Cody; George Francis Train, a.k.a. Citizen Train; Sioux Chief Rain-in-the-Face; Mary Cassatt; Dora

Wheeler Keither, painter of the mural in the library of the Woman's Building; Carrie Watson, famed brothel madam, and all the other brothel owners mentioned; evangelist D. L. Moody; Claude Monet; and Bertha Palmer, whom readers met in *Veiled in Smoke*. Bertha was much more than just hotelier Potter Palmer's wife. She served as president of the Fair's Board of Lady Managers and is credited with introducing Chicago to French Impressionism by bringing paintings back from France and hanging them in the Palmer House hotel and her own home. She eventually amassed one of the largest collections of Impressionist art outside of France. Visit the Art Institute of Chicago to see several of them.

The name of this series of novels, THE WINDY CITY SAGA, comes from Chicago's nickname as the Windy City. The origins of this moniker aren't entirely clear, but most agree it refers to the boastful "hot air" claims made by politicians and city boosters, particularly while competing with other cities to host the 1893 World's Fair.

Chicago remains a fascinating city to visit for so many reasons. If you have a chance, consider including any of the following places on your itinerary, all of which have connections to the 1893 World's Fair and *Shadows of the White City*:

- **The Auditorium Building.** Take the historic building tour of this place if you can. This was the original home for the Chicago Symphony Orchestra. The CSO later moved to its current home, Orchestra Hall, which was designed by Daniel Burnham, chief architect of the 1893 World's Fair.
- **The Rookery, 209 South La Salle Street.** Daniel Burnham and his business partner John Root completed this office building in 1888. As chief architect for the Fair, Burnham met with the nation's top builders and drafted blueprints for the Fair in his eleventh-floor office.
- **The Art Institute of Chicago.** The Columbian Exposition Company funded one-third of the construction cost in exchange for using it during the Fair. Its function was that of an auxiliary building that housed assemblies, lectures, and conferences. After the Fair closed, it was converted to its long-term use of housing the Art Institute's collection.
- **The Museum of Science and Industry.** This was the only permanent building of the Fair, built to house the Palace of Fine Arts. After the Fair, the building became the Field Museum until 1921, when the Field moved to its current location.
- **The Field Museum.** Named for Marshall

Field for his generous donation to the venture, it was originally founded as a permanent memorial to the World's Columbian Exposition and held fifty thousand objects from the Fair, many of which can still be seen today (ask at the information desk for details).

- **Jackson Park.** At 6401 S. Stony Island Avenue, you'll find a replica of the Statue of the Republic (much smaller than the original) that towered over the Grand Basin. It was designed by sculptor Daniel Chester French, who also designed the figure of Abraham Lincoln for the Lincoln Memorial. You'll also find in Jackson Park the Wooded Island, which includes a Japanese garden that started with the Phoenix Temple built there for the World's Fair, and the burr oak tree mentioned in Chapter Five of *Shadows of the White City*, which has a spread of nine hundred feet.
- **Midway Plaisance.** You'll have to use your imagination here, but the grassy median called Midway Plaisance on the University of Chicago campus runs through what was once the center of the Midway.
- **Macy's at 111 North State Street.** Before this was Macy's, it was Marshall Field's Department Store. This location was built after 1893, but visit anyway. On one of the

upper floors, you can dine in the Walnut Room or the Narcissus Tea Room. The same floor showcases historic photos, artifacts, and clothing that was once displayed in Marshall Field's windows.

- **Palmer House, 17 East Monroe Street.** This location wasn't built yet during the 1893 World's Fair, but it is still worth your time. Bertha Palmer asked the cook at the Palmer House restaurant to invent a new chocolate dessert in honor of the World's Fair—and voilà, the brownie was born! So make sure you order Bertha Palmer's original brownie at the Palmer House restaurant.

ACKNOWLEDGMENTS

A novel is never the product of just one person working alone. I owe a debt of thanks to the following people:

To my editors, Dave Long and Jessica Barnes, for investing in this story and series, and for sticking with me even though this is the second book I turned in without an ending (in its first-draft form). Thanks for your patience, graciousness, and all-around brilliance. You're a joy to work with.

To copy editor Elisa Tally, and to Noelle Chew, Amy Lokkesmoe, Brooke Vikla, Serena Hanson, and all the marketing, publicity, and author support staff at Bethany House who have a hand in helping the novels reach readers.

To my agent, Tim Beals of Credo Communications, Inc., for his faithful support of my work.

To Kevin Doerksen, owner of Wild Onion Walks in Chicago, for another personalized tour of the city to aid me in my research of this time period.

To Michael A. Ramirez and the staff at Jane Addams Hull-House Museum, for an insightful tour and for helping me secure further research materials afterward.

To the staff at the Chicago Historical Society

and the Newberry Library, for accommodating all my in-person research requests.

To the Auditorium Building staff, for the insightful historic building tour of your beautiful theatre.

To Susie Finkbeiner, my personal cheerleader and very dear friend. I'm so glad I get to do this writing and publishing journey alongside you.

To Mindelynn Young Godbout, for research assistance and general enthusiasm.

To my husband, Rob, and children, Elsa and Ethan, for their evolved understanding and support (including the custom map of the Fair Rob designed for the front of this novel), and to Elsa in particular for being my partner for my research trip to Chicago in February 2020. That was so fun. Let's do it again. Only next time, not at the start of a global pandemic. Maybe also when it's warmer.

To God, whose love is so great that we get to be called His children.

Dear reader, thank you for coming with me on yet another journey. The World's Fair was spectacular, but if you only remember one thing from this story of found family, I hope it's this: If you're a believer, God lavishes His love on you and calls you His child. You cannot earn or perform your way into His love. You cannot lose His love by stumbling or making mistakes. He has grafted you into His family. You belong.

Discussion Questions

1. Echoes of the Great Fire of 1871 can be found throughout the story, even though it took place twenty-two years before the World's Fair. What significant event in your life still influences you today?
2. Chapter Two ends with the line, "Kristof wouldn't give up on family." Do you think Kristof's decisions regarding Gregor at the end of the story were the equivalent of giving up on him? Why or why not?
3. Jozefa and Sylvie each wanted Rose to be part of their families. In what ways were the two women similar? How were they different?
4. Beth comes across as abrasive at times, but Sylvie remains friends with her. Have you had a friendship that was difficult to maintain? If so, did you continue to invest in it or decide to move on? What factored into that decision?
5. Kristof and Sylvie each had relationships with their fathers that profoundly shaped who they were. How has your relationship with either of your parents affected you, even as an adult?
6. At one point in the story, Kristof tells Sylvie

that we are all more dependent on God than we may want to admit. Would you agree? Why or why not? Does this encourage or discourage you?

7. During her search for Rose, Sylvie confesses that while she doesn't doubt God's ability, it's difficult for her to trust His timing. Can you relate to this? When has God's timing confused, surprised, or delighted you?

8. In Chapter Twenty-Five, Sylvie defends the way she cares for people against Kristof's accusation that she is managing them. He says, "From here, it looks like fear." Do you agree that when a person tries to control a situation or another person, it's rooted in fear? If so, fear of what?

9. Kristof struggles with perfectionism, largely born out of his relationship with his father. Karl tells him in Chapter Twenty-Nine, "I hope you have since learned you can stop striving to earn a place you've already been given. You're already a beloved child of God. You can't perform your way into or out of His family." In what areas do you struggle with feeling like you need to perform? What do you think would lessen that pressure for you?

10. Throughout the story, Sylvie works to find a balance between holding on and letting go of

Rose. In your own life, when have you been challenged either to hold on (to a dream, hope, goal, or person) or to let go? How did you manage to do it?

About the Author

Jocelyn Green inspires faith and courage as the award-winning and best-selling author of numerous fiction and nonfiction books, including *The Mark of the King*, *Wedded to War*, and *The 5 Love Languages Military Edition*, which she coauthored with best-selling author Dr. Gary Chapman. Her books have garnered starred reviews from *Booklist* and *Publishers Weekly*, and have been honored with the Christy Award, the gold medal from the Military Writers Society of America, and the Golden Scroll Award from the Advanced Writers & Speakers Association. She graduated from Taylor University in Upland, Indiana, and lives with her husband, Rob, and their two children in Cedar Falls, Iowa. She loves tea, pie, hydrangeas, Yo-Yo Ma, the color red, *The Great British Baking Show*, and reading on her patio. Visit her online at www.jocelyngreen.com.

Books are produced in the United States using U.S.-based materials

Books are printed using a revolutionary new process called THINKtech™ that lowers energy usage by 70% and increases overall quality

Books are durable and flexible because of Smyth-sewing

Paper is sourced using environmentally responsible foresting methods and the paper is acid-free

Center Point Large Print
600 Brooks Road / PO Box 1
Thorndike, ME 04986-0001 USA

(207) 568-3717

US & Canada:
1 800 929-9108
www.centerpointlargeprint.com